Ripped in Two

AJ Kohler

Ripped In Two

Cover Art:
Michelle Crocker

http://mlcdesigns4you.weebly.com/

Photograph provided by:

A.J. Kohler

Publisher's Note:

This is a work of fiction. All names, characters, places, and events are the work of the author's imagination.

Any resemblance to real persons, places, or events is coincidental.

Solstice Publishing - www.solsticepublishing.com

RIPPED IN TWO

a novel

A.J. Kohler

Dedication

Always and all ways, for Cynthia, who has always
believed and never failed to help.

Prologue

Stepping out of the air conditioned house to the covered outside patio was not unlike stepping into an oven, despite the shade. The killer was already sweating some from the heat, not simply the exertion and the sexual gratification as the two sets of gloves were snapped off, one at a time, and outer layers of clothing were removed. The killer checked carefully, though, and no perspiration had escaped those vital outer layers. A slight breeze brought a delightfully cooling evaporation to the sweat-moistened skin and gently ruffled the newly-freed hair.

As always, the outer set of gloves had turned inside-out as they came off. The blood on them made them appear dark purple in the center, grading towards the blue of their edges. The painter's whites were pretty well splattered and in some small spots, even soaked with blood, but other than a few minor stains on the t-shirt, nothing had gone through. The t-shirt would eventually go into the bag with the whites and the gloves for washing with plenty of bleach and, as appropriate, subsequent disposal in some safe location. Booties came off the shoes and were dropped into the bag as well. Despite their blinding appearance, unbloodied painter's whites were actually in some ways superb camouflage, because the wearer became simply one more working person, and who bothers to look at a painter walking along? They were readily available, too.

There was no murder weapon to dispose of this time; the knives that had done the job here were still buried in the bodies. They'd come out of the kitchen in the house, so the police were not going to be able to develop any telltale information out of where and by whom they'd been

5

purchased. There would be no information about the killer coming from them. Thanks to the gloves, there was not one single fingerprint on them to worry about, either.

Satisfied that the crime scene was as free of trace evidence and other clues as it could possibly be, or at least as close to that level of cleanliness as could be managed, the killer picked up the black plastic garbage bag with the stripped-off outer clothes and slipped quietly out through the gate in the back fence. Finding the quickest route through the desert out to the road was easy, since it had already been scoped out, the final exit from the scene as meticulously planned as every other step in the process.

The killer checked quickly for possible traffic and, finding none, started along the barely visible path across the hard-packed soil threading between cactus and scrub trees until reaching the roadway. At that point the killer became simply one more civic minded trash picker, calmly scouring the side of the road for a distance before reaching the car that had waited patiently.

Once in it with the air conditioning going full blast, it was the work of moments to strip off the slightly bloodied t-shirt, use it to scrub at a couple of bloody spots on the skin underneath and replace it with a clean one. The used one went into the bag with everything else, which included several pieces of roadside trash, both above and below the whites and other items.

The killer looked at the face reflected in the rear view mirror and gave a small contented sigh. One or two small spots of blood, unnoticeable from more than ten feet away, that readily yielded to a spit-moistened fingertip. Another unfaithful pair down, and nobody in the police department or the sheriff's department apparently even knew yet that there was a serial killer on the loose in the city. Of course, not taking souvenirs from the crime scenes, leaving no signature, and following no repetitive pattern helped, but the longer they failed to notice, the more that could be accomplished.

The killer, very naturally, found immeasurable personal satisfaction in the effort, but recognition by others for what was being done was not important. If anything, anonymity was more valuable than recognition, because it meant less official notice, hence less potential interference. With some imagination, some continued attention to detail, who knew how long the luck might hold? Even when they did figure it out, they'd be hard pressed to find out who was actually committing all of these murders. That was a certainty. The car pulled away from the side of the road, bounced onto the pavement and drove off towards the center of town.

****

The cafeteria-style restaurant was more than a bit crowded, but Reesa paid no attention. What little attention she spared from her novel, the paperback she held braced open one-handed with the deftness of long practice, was devoted to making sure her fork didn't miss the food on her plate. She was startled when a man's voice interrupted her. "Excuse me, but do you mind if I share your table? The place seems awfully crowded at the moment." She looked up to see a man who appeared to be, like her, in his late twenties. Clean clothes, dark blond hair (almost in need of a haircut), a nice if undistinguished face (long oval, blue-gray eyes, high forehead, clean shaven, chin strong but not dominant, average cheekbones, no lips worth mentioning, but that was a common failing among men – she couldn't help taking down the description to herself), and he looked to be a little bit taller than she was. Probably about six feet or so. Decent musculature but not overdone, as far as she could tell in his slightly overlarge t-shirt and tan jeans, probably about 170 pounds or thereabouts. Not a serious bodybuilder, then, but apparently fairly fit. Someone who probably paid a reasonable amount of attention to his physical condition. Good looking, overall. Might be interesting were she in the market for a partner – which she wasn't. He was holding his tray and smiling pleasantly as he waited for her answer.

She glanced around, uncertain how much annoyance she should feel at being interrupted. Hers wasn't the only table with an open seat, but the others all appeared to have either couples or families at them. If there were any others with single women, honesty compelled her to admit that she was probably still the most attractive choice he had in terms of both age and appearance. Reesa avoided being vain, but she could at least be honest about what she saw in the mirror each morning. She shrugged. "Sure. I won't be here much longer anyway." She gestured to the chair opposite.

She'd just gotten back into the plot of her book when he broke her train of thought again. "I'm Jeff," he said, as he set his plate on the table.

"How nice for you," she responded, just a bit more tartly than she'd intended. Then she felt a bit awkward about her manner. "I'm sorry," she said as she put in her bookmark. One last bite from her plate and she really was finished. Picking up her small purse, she gave him a half-smile. "I'm Reesa." Then she stood up. Tall, slender, rather attractive to his eyes, with slightly wavy dark brown, close to black hair hanging down almost to her shoulders, he began to smile. Then his smile faded just a bit when her embroidered denim vest flipped open as she turned and he noticed the pistol and badge on her belt. *That usually cools them down*, she thought as she walked away from the table. Her attention on where she was headed, she didn't notice him still watching as she left, a thoughtful look on his face.

His smile didn't return when he looked across the restaurant to see another table, this one with two women and a man, all of about the same age, engaged in animated discussion. The very striking platinum blonde, the one facing him and holding court, caught his eye and smiled, nodding at him. He nodded in response but didn't return the smile. Hers got just a little bit broader when she noticed that. He bent to pay attention to his lunch and did his best to shut her out of his awareness, but no matter what he did, he couldn't shake the memories of their times together. His memories of her body against his, his memories of ….

Angrily he shut down the reminiscences. They weren't all pleasant memories. Truth to tell, some of them were *very* unpleasant, and precious few of them were actually pleasant from his current viewpoint. He left more of his meal than he'd intended and departed abruptly.

****

This would probably be the last time they had to meet in someone's living room. The last time they'd be *able* to. The group was beginning to grow with a life of its own; it was already to the point that this large living room was uncomfortably crowded and only the very earliest attendees could possibly have found seats. There wasn't even enough floor space for people to sit there, regardless of how far back Bob and Mary Jones had pushed the furniture, and every chair and the sofa all had people perched precariously on the arms as well as jammed into the seats. Even the smallest chair had two people in it, the woman sitting on the man's lap.

No matter. Based on experience, everybody would want to be on their feet sooner or later anyway. Henry made his way from the kitchen on a circuitous route through the crowd of people, pausing at virtually every couple he passed to greet them by name, clapping the men on the shoulder or arm, gripping the women's hands, thanking them for coming and making sure that they were doing well as a couple. One of his talents was a real facility for remembering people, their names and faces, and he used it well.

The few couples along his way that he didn't already know he made sure to introduce himself to and at least get their names. He tried hard to get more than that, but some people were too private for him, even here. There were more such new couples than there had been; the group was beginning to grow by word of mouth without Henry having to go pull people in himself. On the far side of the room, he stepped up on the hearth for its eight inches or so of elevation and waited until the majority of people were watching him. It didn't take very long, and when they were, conversations faded to a background murmur. When he cleared his throat, even those few still talking fell silent.

"Friends, thank you – all of you – for coming." He took a deep breath. The curtain was going up, and it was time to give the people what they had come for. Here came his invariable opening line. "It's time for faith! Not just faith in the Lord, but the faith you keep with your partner! It's time for your commitment, it's time for your vows! WE

ARE THE AVOWED." He fell silent. A pin dropping would have made a noticeable sound. Then he asked, quietly, "Who are we?"

The group answered. "The Avowed."

Louder. "Who are we?"

"The Avowed."

"Let the whole world hear who we are!"

And dutifully they all shouted at the top of their lungs, "THE AVOWED!"

God, but it felt good to have found a niche. His blessings upon his benefactor, the wonderful heaven-sent person who had found him in the gutter and showed him a way out, a place to go with his life. A way to get back into the mold that he'd fit into so well way back when. Henry tucked that thought away as he launched into the meat of his service. The services were utterly predictable, even repetitive. The prayers were generic and non-denominational, and the few songs were all based on shamelessly appropriated tunes from popular music of decades earlier.

Beyond that, the service was mostly a paean to the virtues of being faithful to one's spouse or partner – Henry didn't attempt to judge either legal recognition or sexual orientation, there was no money in doing so – and fulfilling the vows one had made or implied in joining with that spouse or partner. It was a simplistic theme, and Henry understood that, but it was one that resonated with some people, *enough* people, and that was really what mattered.

When Henry called on anyone in the group to testify, at least one couple could usually be depended on to be willing to get up and talk about past infidelities and how they had found renewed vigor and joy in their relationship by cleaving again to each other (once he had even had a pair of former swingers come forward, and boy, had *that* testimony been riveting), and as always, just in case, he had two shill couples planted in the group. Well, not really shills. Both were really couples, were really adherents to the group and its tenets, and they had actually been unfaithful to each other in the past, so what they had to say was honest, but they knew ahead of time what was coming and were at least primed to speak up if nobody else did.

Henry's gatherings were always interesting, and he worked hard to keep them that way. Just as he had worked hard to gather the people for them in the beginning. All it took was hearing a couple exchanging harsh words in public, or giving each other 'that look,' or even just pointedly avoiding looking at each other.

Henry's other real talent was being able to talk to people like that. Get involved with them, reassure them of the validity of their feelings, promote keeping their relationship going, and offer them the chance to become involved with the group to help them along.

Occasionally Henry had to resort to agility in order to keep from having his lights punched out, but rarely. He could come up with a great line of patter entirely off the cuff, and it was rare that he couldn't either convince people to join or at least to simply blow him off without making a federal case out of it.

And what a group it was becoming! How engaging the services were by now! It kept people coming, it kept new people joining, and most importantly it kept them filling up the collection baskets. Next week he'd find a hall instead of crowding into somebody's living room. Just not too big a place. Not yet. In the meantime, he'd be about

God's work. Everything he did now was God's work, and there was a lot of it to be done. Not just in these meetings, either.

But it sure felt fulfilling to see the collection baskets filled up after the service was done and the people had left. Put on a good show, get their money, give them something in return, leave them wanting more, and everybody was happy. And because it was a religious service, at least after a fashion, and he wasn't trying to sell them anything or promise them anything, nobody was going to say boo to him about it. Nothing wrong with that, either.

* * * *

Bob and Mary Jones stood in the kitchen of the borrowed house and just listened. When the group reached the point of shouting out "THE AVOWED," they slipped out of the kitchen and took their places at the back of the crowd. They exchanged a silent glance when they realized how crowded the room was, but nobody had noticed their entrance.

Just as colorless and unnoticeable as their names suggested, they were retiring people by nature, and it had taken some persuasion on Henry's part to get them to agree to come to these meetings to help out. Of course, persuasion was really Henry's stock in trade. Now, having assisted Henry as he'd rearranged the furniture for the meeting, they stood in the back of the room, holding the collection baskets. When the time came, they'd make their way through the crowd, sliding between knots of people to present the baskets to as many people present as possible, and then standing on either side of the front door, making sure that those few they hadn't been able to approach with their baskets previously couldn't escape without at least having to walk past them.

Afterwards, nobody who'd been there would have been able to describe either Bob or Mary. Somehow, they not only didn't stand out, they were almost impossible to notice. Your eyes just somehow slid right over them, and without some sort of conscious effort, they made no impression on either the retina or the brain. That was fine with both of them; they had no interest in being noticed.

Quite the opposite, in fact, and their usual mode of dress, in drab earth tones of no particular color or pattern, contributed mightily to that lack of impression. Henry was delighted that they faded into the background so readily, too. If nothing else, it helped him stand out that much better, and after all, these services were really all about him, weren't they?

Not that he was in any way denigrating the couple. He had come out of a homeless shelter, freshly washed and wearing clean clothes (almost new) for the first time in ages – longer than he could actually remember, although that was more a matter of alcoholic fog rather than the actual passage of time. He'd been walking along when he encountered them outside a grocery store, radiating fierce anger with each other, and made the snap decision to try putting his newly-conceived plan into action. It paid off. Some time, of course, was spent countering the anger both tried to turn on him to drive him away, but again, Henry was good at that. By the time he was done talking, they'd not only made up with each other, they'd invited him to come live in their little guest apartment. And they helped him run his services.

They *believed*. And they brought friends.

Chapter 1

Detective Reesa Malloy stepped out of the car and simply looked at the outside of the house and its surroundings for a few minutes. One more tan stucco house in a sparsely populated neighborhood of such southwestern style, mostly flat-roofed homes, there was nothing to make this one stand out. Unless, that is, you considered the uniforms, the patrol cars, the crime scene investigators' van, the morgue van, the crime scene tape circling the yard, and now the detectives.

Chuck Palmer, Reesa's partner, used to her ways by now, just waited patiently. She'd go in shortly, after she'd gotten a sense of the setting, the neighborhood, the surroundings. She always preferred to look at the crime scene from the outside in. There was no way to hurry her, but, even young as she was, her closure rate was the envy of the division. For all that he was several years older than she, he was still the junior man in the division, so he was more than willing to let her do things her way.

Occasionally he learned something just from tagging along behind her, and even when he didn't, it was rarely dull (besides, she was easy on the eyes – not that he'd ever tell anybody else that, especially not his wife Pat. But you can't get someone for thinking, can you?). He spent the time looking around for himself, trying to see what sort of appreciation for the neighborhood she was getting while he waited.

She looked at the surrounding houses, though not all that closely, merely trying to get a feel for the area. Apparently a rather large property, most of it left natural with innumerable prickly pear and cholla cactus. There were also a few little clumps of the low-growing hedgehog cactus, the one that bloomed first in the early spring in a riot of either electric red or fuchsia, a couple of good sized barrel cactus, one majestic saguaro with several arms that had to have been here long before the house was built, several mesquites and palo verdes scattered about and the inevitable clumps of grass.

A small lizard darted across the driveway in front of her, ignoring her in its frantic heat-driven search for prey. A chipmunk twitched its tail from its vantage point next to the shelter of a prickly pear off to her right. As soon as she moved, it would turn and flee into the safety of the cactus patch.

Neither of them noticed the scruffily dressed man two houses down, crouched in the shadow beside the house, watching her. Slowly he pulled a small monocular from his pocket and held it to his eye. He watched her until she lifted the crime scene tape over her head and walked into the front door of the house.

Then he stood, turned, and, keeping to the shadows as much as possible, made his way around the house and slipped away, working hard to avoid the barbed spines of the cholla and prickly pear that littered the landscape as he carefully made his way cross-country until he was out of sight of the house. At that point he paused to pull a multi-tool from the pouch on his belt, unfold the pliers, and carefully pick a couple of cholla spines and one complete cholla joint from his jeans before going the rest of the way.

His car was parked a half-mile beyond, but the twelve-year old Honda was a weathered buff color that faded into invisibility in the desert at any distance over a hundred yards or so. He made sure that it ran like a top, but he deliberately paid very little attention to the outside, wanting it to be the sort of car that normally went unnoticed, just the way he tried to be himself when he was working. At least in this dry climate, body rust wasn't likely to be much of an issue, and the inevitable weathering made the car dull, drab, and all but unnoticeable.

Reesa stood just inside the front door for almost a minute, letting her eyes adjust to the dimmer light. Tucson houses tend to minimize the amount of light they allow in during the heat of the day, especially from the south or west, given how brutal the summer sun can be in the desert.

The room was simply decorated, mostly in a southwestern theme. There were some average to less-than-average examples of Pueblo Indian pottery (inevitably, one or two would have 'Made in China' or elsewhere on the bottom) scattered about on tables interspersed with leather and wood chairs and a sofa facing a good sized but older projection TV. The medical examiner was busy with one body, a man's, that lay in a large pool of blood soaking into an Indian-patterned rug, and a crime scene tech was walking the grid around the room. Reesa looked at him as he approached her. "Getting anything?"

He shook his head. "Smudges, blank footprints and shit like that. Nothing that I can see so far that's likely to offer me any usable evidence. A whopping three hairs, only one with a root bulb, and while I'll run it, my best bet from the color and length is that it's probably hers." He nodded towards the female victim, who lay on bare tile. "No sign of any skin impressions anywhere, no drops of anything except what should by all rights be the victims' blood, no prints other than what you'd expect from them and precious few of those, nothing of any value. Honestly, it looks like the room was just cleaned by someone I'd love to have cleaning my place, at least if this isn't the price." He nodded towards the victims again. "Whoever did this was either luckier than hell or else knew exactly what he was doing. Either way, he left us diddly for trace." He moved off, still looking.

Reesa turned to one of the officers watching the work in progress. Indicating the second body, the woman's, she asked, "Hey, Romero, has the ME worked that one yet?" The body's hands were bagged, just as were the man's, to retain any trace evidence in the skin folds or under the fingernails, but that was the only sign that anyone had done anything to it yet.

"I don't think so. Her purse is there, on the table." He gestured at one of the occasional tables dotting the room. "Wife's out on the patio with Wilson, calming down. She's the one who phoned it in, and she was having hysterics when we got here."

Reesa's eyes darted to the windows at the back of the house. A couple of figures outside were dimly visible in silhouette through the heavily-tinted glass. "So who's this? The girlfriend?"

The officer just shook his head. "Don't know. She's dead, I know that much."

The ghost of a smile flitted across her face. "Yeah, I can see that. Quit bucking for detective, Romero. You're not ready yet." He just chuckled in response. Reesa remembered her own days in uniform. Coming to the crime scenes and coming up with suspects in a couple of high profile cases before the detectives assigned to the cases – one homicide in particular, up in Country Club, where the detectives had focused on the wife when Reesa found it obvious that the traces of makeup left by the killer were utterly unsuited to the wife's coloration (but fit his mistress to a T) – had spurred her rapid advance to detective status.

Not that most of the women on the force couldn't have done that analysis just as quickly, but she had already taken the civil service exam for detective, she was in the right place at the right time, and given the opportunity, Reesa had made the most of it. After that, she merely spent her time making sure she lived up to her billing, especially the billing she kept in her own mind.

Reesa picked up the purse and looked inside for the woman's wallet. Finding it, she set the purse back down as she flipped it open and her partner readied his notebook. "Sarah Johnson, age 24, five-six, 126, blonde and blue, lives in what's probably a fifth-floor apartment between downtown and the university." She spelled out the address for him. "No pictures, no sign of any family to speak of."

Reaching down to feel through the paper bag covering the victim's left hand, she added, "And no wedding ring as far as I can tell. Tentatively single." Sarah's body lay on its back, with a kitchen knife protruding from her chest wall below her left breast. There were no other obvious wounds.

Like the man's body, hers was in a pool of blood, although a much smaller one. Her puddle had largely clotted on the sand-colored tile floor. Setting the wallet down by the purse for Chuck to bag, she walked over by the man's body just as the ME stood up. "Talk to me, Doc."

The ME shook his head slowly as he handed over the wallet from the body. "Hi, Reesa. What we've got here, as you can see, is a male Caucasian, at a rough estimate in his early thirties. TOD about three hours ago, give or take a couple of minutes. Say between 10:30 and 11 this morning. Cause of death, well, I quit counting the stab wounds at 25, and there are a whole bunch beyond that. From what I can tell before doing the autopsy, they all seem likely to match the knife that was still stuck in him when I got here. Something like half of them would have been fatal all by themselves. That's not counting cutting off his genitals." Those, and the pieces of fabric that had been cut away to give access to them, lay between his legs, almost a foot from where they'd originally been attached.

Reesa winced to herself, although she let almost none of it show. "That must have hurt."

"Probably did. He hadn't finished dying when that was done to him. Then the killer just stuck the knife into him one last time before leaving."

"Somebody was definitely unhappy with him about something." She turned to her partner, who had yet to utter a word. "So, Chuck, what do you think? Do we like the wife for this?"

He shrugged. "Spouse is often the one when there's a girlfriend involved. On the other hand, she's out there with hysterics."

Reesa arched an eyebrow at him. He was just about her height but stocky enough to give the impression of being noticeably shorter. "And she's having hysterics ... why? Chuck, if the hysterics are real, she may not be the one. *May* not be. On the other hand, sometimes people get hysterical after doing in their victims. But regardless of whether they're real or faked, she's still suspect number one at this point. We need to talk to her at length and check out any alibi she may have before we decide she's not good for it, hey?" He looked a bit sheepish as she went on. "And while we're at it, just how do we know this one was his girlfriend? Aren't you jumping to a couple of conclusions here? For all we know at this point, she was here collecting for dog rescue or some such."

"Sorry."

"Not that it seems like the sort of neighborhood you'd do that in, and if you did, you probably wouldn't do it in the middle of the morning. But let's take it one step at a time here. So far, assuming he's who we believe he is, they're simply two people of opposite sex killed in the residence of one of them. If they were involved with each other, we need some sort of proof before we presume it."

Chuck looked just slightly abashed and shrugged his shoulders. "I calls 'em as I sees 'em."

Reesa smiled patiently at him. "Just don't call them before we know. Until then, it's just a suspicion. Or a possibility. And yes, in this case it's certainly a reasonable possibility. We just don't *know* yet."

She flipped open the man's wallet as she was talking. Nathan Bridgton, address the same as the house she was standing in, basic description matching the deceased. Driver's license picture confirmed it was him, as much as it could before his identity was confirmed more positively with fingerprints, if they were on file anywhere, or dental records. She scanned the remainder of the wallet's contents. The usual mix of credit cards, accumulated business and frequent-buyer cards. He was due a free coffee at Krakatoa, East of Java (a decent coffee shop, in her opinion; she went there herself from time to time). Nothing special. She handed the wallet to Chuck for him to bag and headed for the back door to talk to the wife.

A bit later, when she and Chuck led the wife out to their car to transport her downtown for a more formal interrogation, she found a news crew already setting up outside. Channel 12 news, according to the colorful paint job on the side of the brilliant white van, and that almost certainly meant their star outside crime reporter, Lynne Fox. *The very noticeable, even striking, allegedly blonde Lynne Fox*, Reesa thought. *Shit.*

When Reesa saw Ms. Fox herself step out of the van, microphone in hand, she merely nodded to herself. As Reesa and Chuck helped the newly-minted widow into the car, she heard the reporter's voice behind her calling, "Detective! Detective Malloy!" She ignored it as she walked around to drive back to the main police station downtown, thinking several more uncomplimentary things about the reporter. There'd be someone senior to her on scene soon enough who would make public statements and spare her the trouble, as well as the temptation, to say something to Fox, either something about the case in violation of department policy, which she'd wind up regretting, or something indicating her opinion of Lynne Fox, which was not only also against department policy, it was something she'd *definitely* wind up regretting (although it would sure feel good for the moment).

She did note to herself that however they did it, Lynne Fox and Channel 12 news were always the first ones on the scene. Somebody had to be paying close attention indeed to their police scanner, because they always beat the other channels there by at least five and usually as much as fifteen minutes. The ratings race was a bitch. Of course, so was Lynne Fox, in Reesa's opinion. At least the reporters for the other channels weren't as obnoxious. The guy who usually covered such cases for Channel 5 was actually downright cute, to Reesa's eyes. Unfortunately, he also came across to her as gay. Oh, well. She wasn't in the market for anyone anyway. And no matter which way he swung, she could always look.

****

The tan house was older, in a northwest Tucson neighborhood that assured privacy with its high walls and abundant overgrown vegetation. The walls around the back yard were, in fact, high enough to conceal all but the tops of the Catalina mountains to the north and the Tucson mountains to the west. Even then, unless you were quite tall, to see them you had to be standing under the patio roof, back by the house.

The privacy had been one of her primary considerations when the house was purchased; Reesa wasn't concerned with the view. In fact, Reesa realized, it was the sort of neighborhood where, were she conducting an investigation, she could go to the house next door and tell the homeowner she had some questions about his neighbors. His response in turn could well be, "I've got neighbors???"

Reesa smiled at the thought as she unlocked the door. John Gorham, her neighbor to the east, was a friendly old bear of a man who cooked outside most of the year and always sent either his wife or his youngest son (the one with the painfully obvious crush on her that she never encouraged, but never failed to treat most carefully) over to invite Reesa to join them at least once every other week.

He'd lived there for something like twenty years when Reesa bought the house and made sure she knew it (as well as, with a sly but endearing smile, how little he'd paid for his place).

There was undoubtedly a neighbor on the other side, since there'd been a moving van at the house a couple of years ago, but they had yet to introduce themselves. She stepped inside and allowed herself one long sigh after the door was again locked behind her and the alarm system was set. This was her private sanctuary, the one place she allowed herself to *be* herself, unguarded and undefended except by the alarm.

Other than her parents, on their infrequent visits, and the cleaning lady every other week, nobody else ever came here. Hardly anybody even knew where it was.

She set her purse down on the credenza in the dining room and began her evening ritual. Vest laid over one chair back. Flashlight into the charger, phone plugged into its charger, handcuffs off the belt, holster unsnapped from her belt, the big Glock Model 22 pistol drawn and cleared, magazine and the lone .40 caliber chamber round laid all together in a well-established pattern, ready to be reassembled in the morning. Magazine pouch with spare magazine unclipped from the opposite side of her belt and set close to the pistol.

Then she put her left foot up on the closest chair of the Scandinavian patterned dining room set, right where the wear mark on the teak showed she'd been doing for years (thanks to her mother's periodically switching the chairs around whenever she came to visit, five of the six chairs displayed the same mark), hoisted the leg of her slacks and unstrapped the ankle holster. After briefly rubbing the spot on her leg where the holster had rested, she drew and cleared the little Kahr PM40 backup pistol she carried in it and laid it and its holster alongside the Glock, also with magazine and chamber round arranged just *so*.

Finally she unbuttoned her blouse and hung it from the back of another chair long enough to let her remove her body armor, which she hung over the back of the adjacent chair as she picked up her blouse to put back on.

Feeling lighter and cooler, she headed for the kitchen and the inevitable drink. Just one. Hanging up the vest could wait, and after the crime scene she'd gone to, tonight was definitely going to be a night when she would want a second drink. Her rigid control, though, would hold her to the one drink she always rationed herself. Just like with the way she arranged her guns and ammunition on the credenza, some things had to be kept just *so*. But it was certainly a treat to be able to work normal hours instead of having to keep after an investigation until all hours and then still have to come in at her usual time the next morning.

Sitting in her well broken-in Eames chair, she debated turning on the TV, but the early local news had just ended, and the prime time choices these days were mostly either inane comedies, idiotic cop shows, or idiotic lawyer shows, none of which interested her. All of which she studiously avoided, in fact.

There were a few – *very* few – comparatively good cop shows, but even with most of them she wound up annoyed at the detectives as they went about their business, and she'd proven to her satisfaction many years before that no matter how she spoke or even yelled, the people on the screen couldn't hear her. So she usually didn't watch those, either, except for one reasonably realistic SWAT drama out of Canada which wasn't on tonight.

The news would eventually come on, and at least those were real cops, real incidents. Often people she knew. Idly she scrolled through the movie and documentary channels, but still found nothing to hold her interest. As the screen returned to black, she rolled the partially full glass across her forehead, enjoying the cold moisture on her skin. Low humidity meant it would be dry in minutes, but for that brief time, the cold felt *so* good.

It took perhaps twenty minutes before she finished the last of her drink, dumped her remaining ice noisily in the sink and opened the freezer to consider supper. Maybe tomorrow she'd buy another toy for the stash in her private room. Or maybe not; perhaps a set of Harry Potter books might be better this time. She'd gotten a set last year and they had been very well-received by the Marines, come their Christmas toy drive.

Closing the freezer, she walked down the hall to that spare bedroom, which she unlocked with one of the two keys she wore on a chain around her neck. The room was empty except for a half-dozen or so good-sized boxes, all unopened toys.

There was one frame on the wall, a copy of a sonogram. Written on the mat, in carefully-done but clearly amateurish calligraphy, was the legend "Noli Me Tangere," Latin for 'Touch Me Not.' *No, I'll never touch you, will I, baby? But you still touch me each and every day, don't you? Just you and me, since your daddy wouldn't even stick around to take responsibility for his own dick.* Reesa closed her eyes for just a moment. Boy or girl – she had never found out which flavor – her child would have been nine this year.

The psychological pain of the miscarriage she had suffered in college had diminished over the years, but it had never quite disappeared. She appeased it, and her irrational (she admitted it to herself) sense of guilt, with the toys and such she bought from time to time. Every December, she delivered the whole year's pile to the Marines' Toys for Tots drive. They were invariably delighted, although the check she delivered (approximately the remainder of one Family share's dividend) along with the toys certainly never hurt that response. Then she started over, the toys, when they were age-specific, bought for a child just a year older than before.

She let the memory and its associated pain take her over for more than a minute before closing and relocking the door and returning to the freezer. Mentally she tucked the pain down and gently covered it over. That was her allotment for the day. Some days it was before supper, some days after, but she'd never skip it. She'd also never ever let that pain show, not to another living soul. In fact, other than her mother, with whom she was still very close, nobody even knew.

After supper, she shelved the book she'd finished over her meal and debated what to read next. Her library was mostly science fiction and history, some historical fiction, and a number of professional books. None of those last were on her list of possibles right now; she wanted recreation, not education.

She finally settled on an old classic science-fiction book, one of her favorites, and carried it to the bedroom. She changed into her robe before going back to the living room to read until it was time for the evening news. As she read, she nibbled her dessert – one Reese's Peanut Butter

Cup. Her private joke, just to herself, was that they were really '*Reesa's* Peanut Butter Cups.' She allowed herself two of the treats per week, and here it was Tuesday and she was just having her first. Nibbling slowly at it, she made it last for almost twenty minutes. The memory, when it was all gone, was good for at least another ten.

****

The killer took a few minutes to treasure the memory of a job well done. The terrified look on the woman's face, well, that was perhaps a bit unfortunate, at least for her, but she'd gotten the easy way out. Been *given* the easy way out. The knife had gone in just *so*, a quarter twist to help her bleed, and then let it go so she would fall with it still in her. The man … he'd tried to bluster his way out at first, but the killer took advantage of his shock when the woman had been stabbed, and by the time he'd been stabbed three or four times, he wasn't fighting any longer.

The most delicious moment, the incredible sexual release …. After almost two full minutes of savoring the memory, the killer carefully packed all of the memories away in a mental file. There would be plenty of time to dwell on those memories again later. Now there was more … legitimate work to be done. Plenty of time later to do more of God's work. And there was just so *much* of it to do.

****

Jeff folded his long legs into position as he sat down in one of the chairs in front of Amy's desk. "This is not the way I like losing cases," he said. "Not to mention how hard it is on the subjects, even if the clients themselves come out of it okay."

28

Amy shook her head in sympathy. "No, it's not nice. And this is … what? The second one to go like this?"

Jeff nodded. "Yeah. That one up in the foothills three months ago was the first for me. But you remember that detective I mentioned the other day? The one I encountered at lunch? I saw her arrive at the house today while I was still watching. I've got a sneaking suspicion that she's working homicide. Seems kind of young for it, if she is." Now he stretched his legs out in front of him, crossing his ankles.

Amy regarded him as his friend, not simply his boss, for a moment. "You thinking of getting to know her?"

Jeff shrugged. "Couldn't hurt, I figure. She's easy on the eyes, as a cop she's connected in ways I'm not, and what the hell, it gets lonely sitting in that little house all alone. And trust me, there's no way in *hell* I want to repeat the *last* relationship I had." He snorted. "Maybe this would be different."

Amy shook her head. "I know exactly what it's like being alone in that place. I lived there a lot longer than you have yet, remember. If you want my advice, get a dog. Or two. It's safer, at least judging by your last relationship. Remember, I tried to warn you about her, and you wouldn't listen. Too much thinking with the wrong head, if 'thinking' is the right word to use for that. Oh, by the way, I'll be going to Golondrino for a long weekend again. It's board meeting time."

Jeff shrugged again. "When the Family board meets, I guess the head of the Family kind of has to be there. I'll hold down the fort while you're gone. Are all of you going? And just by the way, didn't you have Alec there in that house with you? Most of the time, anyway?"

Amy nodded. "Without me, there *is* no meeting. But yes, we're all going, as usual. We'll be back late Monday, and I'll be back in here on Tuesday, barring the unforeseen. And in response to your other question, no, he didn't sleep there, not until we were married. After Becky and I moved out of here, I spent my nights alone there until then. Several years' worth."

"Okay, I'll concede the point. Would you mind locking up? I think I'll head out now. Oh, and say hi to Dad for me, would you?"

"Sure. See you when we're back." Jeff walked out the back door and across the alley to the little house on Helen Street.

Once inside the house, Jeff pulled a bottle of beer out of the fridge. Popping the top, he carried it out into the living room, sprawled on the couch, and turned on the TV. Watching some stupid game show, or whatever else he could find, would at least help pass the time until hunger drove him to the fridge to see what leftover was on the menu for dinner. Unless he just skipped it again tonight.

****

Henry Blodden sat on the well-worn and badly sprung sofa in his little apartment, hardly more than an efficiency, behind the garage of the Joneses' house. He was eating a frozen dinner, still almost too hot from the microwave, but his attention was focused on the early evening local news on his TV. Mostly he watched Channel 12 for the news, but tonight he had wound up on Channel 5, and the broadcast was halfway to the weather before he realized his error. At that point, he figured he might as well leave it.

30

The crime scene reporter, a reasonably good looking young man (if you went in for such things – Henry didn't), made a decent report on the Bridgton house murders, but Henry wasn't concerned. It was far more important to look *forward* to God's work, not back on what had already happened. He had more work to do, and starting tomorrow he was going to spend much of the day out looking for the next target of his attention. It might take him more than simply tomorrow to find the right target, but he was supremely confident that he would, almost certainly by the end of the week, locate another appropriate target.

He definitely had to get started, though. Doing God's work just felt so *good*, and how could God possibly not allow him to find the next recipient of his attentions when God so obviously wanted His work done? For that matter, how could it possibly not be God's work when it just felt so *good*? Assuming there really *was* a God, that is. Like *that* mattered, either.

* * * *

In the house proper, Bob and Mary Jones went about their normal evening ritual. It was so well-established between them by now that their conversation even in this was minimal, and by the time the late evening news came on, they were both lying in bed, watching the Channel 8 broadcast. When the weather forecast was done, Bob slid a hand up under Mary's nightgown, along her thigh. No words were necessary. Nor were any used when Mary reached down, took Bob's wrist and gently but firmly lifted his hand off her leg and put it back on his side of the bed.

After pulling her nightgown back down, she got up on one elbow to kiss him goodnight. She turned off the light on her nightstand and, without waiting to see if he was

31

going to turn off his own or read for a while, rolled over and was asleep within minutes, or so Bob presumed from her soft, regular breathing. It was another twenty minutes before he put up his book and turned off his own light.

****

Lynne Fox was still at the studio. Unless she had to be live at a crime scene, she normally tried to be home by the time the 10 pm news came on. Tonight, however, she had some details she had to get taken care of before she could leave. Nothing she wanted to entrust to her staff, but also nothing earthshaking. Just some things that she wanted to do herself. *Needed* to do herself.

While she worked, she mused over where she could have to go tomorrow. The news editor, who might as well be God in the news section of the station (if you didn't believe that, just ask him), would undoubtedly have some really nasty sort of assignment for her. That was fine. No matter how difficult, how distasteful, how downright shitty the assignment she got, she always delivered, always produced excellent quality work, and she was known for that.

Sometimes, with a bit of sarcasm, because of whom the assignment came from, she even thought of it as God's work. It was that sort of dependability, though, (along with her looks) that had gotten her as far as she was already, and that dependability along with a bit of luck – which she fully intended to either cultivate or create – would take her all the way to the top in the news business, a national anchor slot.

Where she clearly deserved to be. Just ask her.

Chapter 2

London, in the reign of Richard III (1483 - 1485)

James ducked, trying to avoid the stinking water thrown up by the rumbling carriage wheels. He was less than completely successful. The driver just laughed as James stood there, dripping. "Ye'd best watch out for yer betters, boy!" he yelled as the carriage disappeared down the street.

James took a deep breath. Anger would not help. The nobility didn't care if the inhabitants of this poor part of London were angry with them, any more than a cat cared if the mice were angry with it. When they chose to run their carriages through the slums, whether for fun or sport, or just because it was the quickest way to get where they were going, the inhabitants made way. It was just how things were. The privileged elite were merely a fact of life, to be borne and endured.

James was not interested in enduring. He burned to be rid of them – not necessarily to do away with them, but to be free of them. To be able to go his own way, without having to bend the knee and knuckle the forehead. Or even just stand for the soaking. For all that he was as yet only about twelve (he did not know for certain), James sought to be his own man, and, burning equally within him, he wanted his children, if he ever had any, to be able to stand straight and bow to no man.

It is one thing to have a dream. It is quite another to pursue it in such a manner that one might actually realize that dream. James knew what he wanted. How to get it … that he was at a loss to describe.

He was walking down the roadway, trying to avoid the piles of horse droppings and puddles of slops in the street while staying far enough away from the buildings to avoid the new contributions to those puddles from the inhabitants of the upper floors, when he noticed a commotion up ahead of him. A boy, smaller than he, was racing down the street towards him, holding a purse in his hand.

Behind him, chasing and losing ground steadily, was a man James had seen frequenting the streets in the area, a man of some apparent means. Making a quick decision, James reached out as the boy passed him and grabbed him around the waist. Lifting the boy off the ground, he ignored the cries of "Gerroff me!" and "Lemme go!" as he extracted the purse from the boy's fingers. This provoked a further torrent of verbal abuse which made even less impression on James.

He dropped the boy and boxed his ear with his free hand. "Get on wi' ye," he told the boy. "And find an honest way to make your pence." The lad ran off, promising all sorts of dire consequences for James, who simply stood there waiting for the man coming in pursuit of his money. James extended the purse as the man reached him. "I believe this is yours, sir."

The man stopped and simply looked at James for what seemed much more time than it actually could have been. "You're a cheeky one, boy." He reached out and took the purse. "But I thank you. Most boys would have taken the purse and run in another direction."

"Aye, sir, I suppose they would. I'm not most boys." James was calm.

"You have a way about you."

"Sir?"

"You were holding my purse. I could have claimed that you were the thief and had you tossed in gaol."

"Aye, sir, that you could, if the watch were here and would listen. I took a chance."

The man bounced the purse on his hand for a few moments. The coins inside clinked quietly, and the sound was one of the sweetest things James could imagine. "But you were honest, and the least I can do to repay you is to be honest in turn, I suppose. Again, I thank you." He opened the purse and pulled out a silver groat. James's eyes grew big. "This is a serious reward, boy. I believe in encouraging honesty and true dealing, and I am willing to pay fairly for it. Do you believe you have earned this?"

James could not believe his good fortune – but he also knew that he might have more of a chance here than at any other time in his life. The nation was in some turmoil, as Richard III, the former Duke of Gloucester, sat on the throne to the disgust of those of the populace who cared, but James was unconcerned with such matters of state. His world was far more narrow, merely the mean streets in which he tried to survive. He stared at the coin, more money in one coin than he had ever held before, and took a deep breath. His mind raced. "Sir, whether or not I have earned it is for you, not me, to say. You know what I did, and you will never know if I did it from honesty or simply from the belief that you were too close for me to flee from.

But if you would, there is a reward I would crave more that is in your power to give and would cost you less."

The man's eyebrows lifted. The boy had cheek indeed, but it might be worth it to see what he wanted. "And just what would that reward be, lad?"

Another deep breath. "I would work for you, sir. I would work for you so that you could teach me how to … how to be rich as you are."

Now the man smiled. "You think I'm rich, lad?"

"You offer me a groat for simply being honest, sir. If that is not rich, then I would learn what rich truly is."

The man threw his head back and laughed heartily. "Cheeky indeed, boy! Cheeky indeed. And yes, honest. Do you work hard?"

"Sir, I shall work as hard as I know how. My mother, may she rest in peace, worked near every day of my life until she grew too weak to work anymore, and then she died of the wasting disease. I would rather not end the same way, but I can work as hard as she did and harder. I can work as long as she did and longer. And I *will*, if I've the chance. I want to earn my own money and … earn my way out of this." He waved his arm to indicate his surroundings.

Now the man was intrigued. "And just how much do you believe your work would be worth to me?"

James looked at his feet for a moment, but ignored the cold water he could feel inside his worn shoes. It would finish draining out through the holes soon enough anyway. Then he looked back at the man and met his gaze squarely. "I believe my work will be more than enough to earn a place to sleep and food for my belly, sir. As for pay beyond that, just as with the reward, you are a better judge than I of the worth of what I would do. But I would learn from you, sir."

"Yes, I believe you would, lad. I believe you would." The man rubbed his chin. "Here's what I'll offer you, boy. Your honesty and your earnestness impress me, and I'm not an easy man to impress. So this is my offer, which you may accept or turn down, but I warn you, I won't offer it again. You must choose now. I shall provide you with a place to sleep, food and drink, and even a … new set of clothes." He wrinkled his nose. "You do as I tell you. It will not always be easy, and you will not always understand why I tell you to do something. I will only assure you that it will not affront your honesty. After one month, we shall see if you will go on working for me. Does that meet with your approval?"

James could hardly believe his good – no, *great* – fortune. This was not a time to delay or demur; he realized that he must grasp the nettle and do so *right now*. And he *would*. "Aye, sir. I shall be … nay, I *am* your man. For as long as you will have me."

"And have you a name, boy? I cannot continue simply calling you 'lad' or 'boy' with no idea of what your actual name is."

"I am James, sir. I know no other name beyond that."

The man extended his hand. "I am William Escarton, called Will. Welcome, James. Come with me." He motioned back the way he had come and set off down the street. James hurried to follow.

By the time the pair arrived at Escarton's shop, James was dressed in clean, if not quite new, dry clothes. "All right, James, this will be your home for the next month. We shall make up a pallet in the back room for you and you will sleep here. Have you your numbers and letters?"

James was uneasy about his response, but since his honesty had gotten him this far, he presumed it was more important to be truthful. "I cannot count beyond my fingers, sir. I read but a little. My mother would take me to St. Giles from time to time and beg the priest to read to me from the Bible as I followed along, but that is all I know for letters." He met Will's gaze fairly but without defiance. "I would learn more of both, and quickly."

A puppy might have been a better choice, Will thought. *At least it would grow into a guard dog. Ah, well, you got yourself into this, Will, and a deal is a deal. Who knows? The lad might surprise you after all.* "John Wycliffe's Bible is not the text I would have suggested to learn on, but done is done. Very well. Learn more of both you shall, and quickly indeed if you are to stay. You have that month, James. I need someone who can read, write, and count if I am going to have someone to truly help me, and you shall need to learn much of it on your own. I haven't a great deal of spare time to offer in which to teach you. But I shall give you what help I can as you use your free time. I have some few books" – James was astounded; books were still rare and valuable. He knew nobody who actually owned one … well, not until now – "which you may work at reading. Numbers you will pick up as you work if you can, and that I can help you more with."

By the end of the first month, Will was suitably impressed with James's work and effort. He might not yet be completely at home with the printed word, but he had made astonishing progress. By the time James had been with Will for six months, he was reading voraciously anything he could find in any time he could spare and was beginning to provide more help for Will than he would ever have expected. Will's business was primarily the trading of commodities – any commodity that someone needed and someone else had. James proved his worth in finding these deals. He had an uncanny knack for finding out who had something being sought, and Will was well enough known by then that people looking for something sought him out. By the time a year had passed, Will made James a partner. A junior one, to be fair, but one who profited from the trades the two of them made in accordance with the risks and investment.

After the second year, Will could not imagine carrying on his business without James at his right hand. The two of them were sitting in the shop one afternoon when a clamor went up in the street, and both of them came out to hear the news that Henry Tudor had defeated and killed the hated Richard and was now Henry VII, the new king of England. They had nothing but smiles for each other.

James and Will had been together for four years when James broached what was, for him, a delicate subject. "Will, I am … dissatisfied being simply James. I believe I need a surname to be seen as a businessman in my own right."

Will looked at the now strapping young man. "Very true, James. Very true indeed. Of course, many of our customers think you are my son, even though I've never married. In truth, I often feel that way myself. Would you like to take my name? By now I think you would hold it as well as I have, if not better."

"Will, I give you all thanks. I shall treasure it until the end of my days and may God grant that my children and their children's children shall always strive to measure up to the standard you have set."

Will smiled. "I'm sure they will, James. And now that you have a surname of your own choosing, will you marry Catherine? You and she have been keeping company for quite some time now."

James blushed. "I have not wanted to tell you, but we have already arranged to have the banns posted. They will start this Sunday. I would have said sooner, but I … presumed your name."

Will felt his face go somber, but then he considered the history between the two of them and smiled again. "You're forgiven, James. But I was right, way back when. You are indeed a cheeky fellow. Now, we have more business to discuss. The master of the Lady Sarah, a caravel you may have noted in the harbor, has offered us a proposition, and I wished to speak with you about it first. He would have us finance a portion of his cargo for a share of the profits."

Eventually the financing of such voyages, both legitimate and … less legitimate – in other words, pirates – became a substantial, and lucrative, part of their business. When Will finally passed away, James, Catherine, and their four surviving children were at his bedside as though they were in truth his family, and indeed, by that time he had no other.

Soon after the death of his friend, mentor, and partner, James called his oldest son in to give him a task. "Will, I need you to find us some land. Some place where our family, no matter when, can always be home. Not here in England, as I want some place where we can be the lords, if anyone is, although better there be no lords there at all. I may never see it, but it must be some place that we, our family, can own and call ours, bowing to none and no matter what other sovereigns may pass, no matter how many years have gone by. Can I depend on you for this?"

Will was significantly older than James had been when he had first gone to work for William Escarton, and he had been a partner in the family business for the best part of a decade. "Aye, Father. How would you have me do this? Should I try to find a location first on a map, or have you some area in mind?"

James sighed. "I don't know, Will. My idea would be to look somewhere in the Holy Roman Empire. Their hand generally lies loose enough on the land that I doubt the inhabitants even notice in some places. I would rather find new land unclaimed by any, but the only such land I know is across the sea to the west, and by all reports, there are savages there who would not only contest our ownership but not be any more inclined to leave us alone than the lords do here. There may well be someplace in the mountains of the continent, though, that you can obtain from whoever lays claim to it and make it ours. I leave it up to you." He clapped his son on the shoulder. Hopefully this wouldn't be the last time they saw each other.

Shortly after Will departed for his task, James commissioned a book. Just empty pages, more of them than he believed would ever be needed, but pages of the best vellum. A binding of the finest leather. A book to last for centuries. When it was delivered, James left it untouched for some years before he sat down to write in it his thoughts and his dreams for his descendants, to be read by whoever

41

would head his family after him. When he had finished as much as he had to write, he was surprised to see how little of the book he had written in. But then he considered how those who came after him would be able to fill it up, eventually. It was enough.

Every so often, a trader or other traveler new-come to England from the continent would arrive, bearing a missive from Will. Not all that frequently, but often enough to keep James hopeful. And reassure him and Catherine that Will still lived.

One winter's day in 1532, a bedraggled couple appeared at the door to James's shop. They were hunched against the driving snow, dressed for the cold but only barely. As the door closed behind them, James's youngest son, Robert, exclaimed, "Faugh! You've dripped enough snow and water on this floor that I shall have to mop it again! What want you here? We are not a public house for you to find lodging and sup at!"

The man looked at the woman, who threw off her scarf and drew herself up to her full height, which was enough (although also only barely) to look Robert in the eye. "I suggest you keep a civil tongue in your head when you speak to me. You must be Robert, the insolent one. If you are able to do so politely, you may address me as Mary. Otherwise you will refer to me as Mistress Escarton."

The man, meanwhile, had been struggling with a bag, and finally set it down. James had come to see the cause of Robert's raised voice. As the man straightened, James's eyes grew wide. "Will? It is! Will!" He turned. "Catherine! Come quickly! Will is home!"

By James's order, no business was spoken of for the remainder of the day, although that evening James did speak of his dreams of an enduring family, a *Family*, to all of those, his wife, the couple's children and their spouses, that he gathered to welcome Will and his new wife home. The following day, James and Will closeted themselves alone in James's office. "We have a place, Father. I hope it meets with your approval, but honestly, if it does not, then damme, you may go find something better yourself!" James, amused by his son's heated statement, merely gestured for him to continue. "I have found for us a small part of the Free State of the Three Leagues. It is in the mountains, north of Italy and south of the Germanies." He pulled out a map and spread it out on his father's desk. "I have marked it here. I know it is not easy to get to, and it is small indeed, being only about two and a half Roman miles on a side, but nothing larger or more reachable was open to purchase except as subject. This is land where we can be our own free state, accepted by the League as any of their older states."

James beamed at his son. "Well done, my boy. Well done indeed. And does this land have a name?"

Will looked at the floor, seemingly finding something utterly fascinating in the well-worn wood. He mumbled, "I gave it a name. I called it Golondrino."

"And why was that?" His tone was gentle, not challenging.

Will raised his eyes to meet his father's. "When I first rode the land, there was a flock of swallows in the trees. There are names in the local languages for the birds, but the words are … unmusical to my ear. The birds all flew off at our approach, except for one, a male who stayed

43

and sang before flying around us. When I was in Spain, they called such a bird golondrino. I liked the word and thought the bird a bit of an omen, so I named our land accordingly."

"And was your task difficult, Will?"

Will leaned back in his chair. "Father, there were times I barely escaped with my skin. Two times I lost the money you gave me to purchase the land and I had to earn more. Well, once I earned it, and once I recovered it from the thieves who took it from me. I am satisfied to say that they will rob no more. But I remembered what you told me, and I thought about my responsibility. My responsibility to our family, and then later my responsibility, as well, to Mary. I accomplished my task, and I have come back."

James smiled. "Yes, you have, my son. And now I have another task for you. The family grows. You have your wife; your brother Richard has not only a wife but a son. Your sister is being courted by another lad who appears to be a sharp fellow, and if he actually marries her, I believe he could be brought into the business. But I am getting too old to run both the family and the business as they need to be run. I am satisfied that you will bring the same sort of ... effort and devotion to running this family that I think it needs. So I am turning over the family and the business to you."

Will was dumfounded. "But Father, you cannot! I mean, I am not ready! I fear I will destroy the family and the business! I cannot–"

His father silenced him with a gesture. "Yes, Will, you can. And you shall. I have faith in you. This book –" he put his hand on the leatherbound volume – "contains my thoughts for the family, the *Family*, as I told you all last night, and how I want to see it continued into the future, as long as we can. Think of them as instructions." Will's eyes grew huge as he realized the size of the book. "No, not the whole book." James laughed. "Just that small part of it, and it is small indeed, that I have written. As will you and those who come after you. This is for you alone, although I would say that you may show it to Mary if you simply must share it with someone. The book is large, not because I had much to say, but because I intend it to last for many years indeed. And I shall be around for some time yet; I am not crossing that great ocean for a while, God willing."

He stood up. "This is your seat, now, Will. Treat it well. Oh, and Richard has engaged a tutor for his son. I have promised to pay the tutor's bill. I trust you will honor my promise. Education of our descendants, of our *Family*, is one of the best investments we can make in our future. Now, Will, if you will excuse me, your mother and I wish to take a mug of cider together. Should you need me, please come ask. I would rather not have to leave your mother's side for a while. I have spent too much time away from her over the years."

After James had left the room, Will remained seated in the chair he had been in for quite some time before going around behind the desk. Settling cautiously into the chair there, he pulled the book in front of him and opened it. He began reading and, as he did so, laying out in his own mind his plans for the Family. Yes, his father was right. Education was important. Vitally important, so the Family would indeed pay the cost. Whenever one of the Family members needed education, the Family would pay for it.

And if some child chose to go into a different line of work, then Will would see to it that so far as he could, or whoever took his position after him, other Family members would be directed to that person, to help their business. Even if the Family had to pay for the work, whatever it might be, to be done. No, not *if* the Family had to. To ensure that Family dealt with Family as much as possible, the Family *would* pay.

But it would also be important not to let others know of the connections the Family shared. If nothing else, what endangered one could endanger all, and the Family fortunes, as his father had made clear in the book, were of the utmost importance. Just as his father had written, best not to let outsiders know of the Family at all. Shifting the book into a better position, he reached for a quill. Then he thought better of what he was doing and set the quill back down again. It would be wiser to do this after a night's sleep and perhaps a discussion with Mary. He set the book carefully into the lowest drawer of the desk and got up from his seat.

James settled into a well-worn chair, Catherine in an identical chair alongside his. He was content. Will had not only done well in contriving the purchase of this land he had described, but faced with a task so daunting that most would have given up – to have had to recoup the money, not once but twice! – he not only finished, he returned with both the land and a wife. The family was safe in Will's hands. The *Family* was safe and would endure, perhaps for longer than he could even imagine. Content, he closed his eyes.

Chapter 3

The top drawer of the credenza in the dining room held Reesa's elastic belly band. She pulled her t-shirt up to her bra and wrapped the band around her stomach, patting the Velcro into place and taking care to leave no wrinkles in it that might chafe her skin. Then she carefully added her now-reloaded little Kahr to the holster in the band and put her badge, handcuffs, and a spare magazine for the Kahr into the other pockets.

She settled the t-shirt down over it, picked up her keys, and went out to her car. Her morning routine called for a couple of miles around the track at the high school several miles from the house, and while she had gotten out of bed a whole ten minutes earlier than usual, she saw no reason to waste the time. Running was a pleasure for her, even over and above the track trophies from high school and college that she still hadn't unpacked since moving into the house years before.

Somewhat private by nature (or so she thought of herself, at least when she could manage to be), the separateness, the solitude of running, suited her personality.

At the track, she carried her two small dumbbells over to the bleachers before her warm-up stretches. Two other early morning runners exchanged nods with her, each just one more familiar stranger's face, as they went by. By the time they came around the same spot again, she was already on the far side of the track. She'd pick up the dumbbells on her next lap.

After her workout was finished, she'd go buy a Daily Star on the way home to read over breakfast, and then back at the house she'd turn on the coffeemaker before heading to the shower. The same thing every day, weather permitting, all routine. Several miles around the track with her accompanying upper-body work left her pretty ripe, but the workout kept her in good shape and a shower was part of her normal morning toilette anyway.

When she was on patrol, word had gotten around midtown rather quickly that 'you don't bother trying to run from the pretty bitch cop, 'cause she'll run your ass into the ground and bust you anyway.' One perp had tensed to run from her down on 12th Street before he did a totally classic double-take. Realizing who he was dealing with, he'd then just stuck his hands out for the cuffs. He was the one who'd passed on that bit of wisdom to her. It still made her smile to herself when she thought of it.

Once at work, checking on the autopsies from the previous day's murders was the first order of business. Reesa held the little black plastic APS film can almost hidden in her left hand as her right forefinger scooped a generous helping of Vicks VapoRub out of it. She smeared it over her upper lip and under her nose, then snapped the can closed before dropping it back into her purse and pulling out a tissue. She wiped her finger with it and crammed it into her purse for later, when she'd use it to wipe off her face.

The sights and sounds of an autopsy never bothered her. The cold of the autopsy room, the sterility of the surroundings, in some fashion actually resonated with something inside of her, and dead bodies were things she could regard with utter disinterest. Visually. It didn't even bother her to watch the ME remove the organs from the body cavity one by one and put them into basins for further processing, although several of the other detectives (particularly those new to homicide) always found reasons to leave the room rather abruptly right about then. Not Reesa. Never Reesa.

Sometimes the smell didn't bother her, either. Other times … For a while, she had tried to correlate her bouts of severe nausea with outside factors. Nothing fit. Not the weather, not whether or not she'd eaten nor what she'd eaten, not even whether or not she was having her period or even just where she was in her cycle. Finally she just gave up trying to figure it out and began using the Vicks all of the time. Enough of that and it was impossible to smell anything else, which worked. She knew she wasn't the only detective who used that little trick, either. It just pissed her off at some level that she needed to.

But maintaining the image, even through the haze of camphor and mentholatum, was the most important thing. And almost all of the detectives who stayed for complete autopsies on a regular basis had done it at one time or another. Hell, it seemed to Reesa that better than half of them *still* used the stuff. Any time there were more than two or three detectives at an autopsy, there was enough mentholatum in the air to clear everyone's sinuses regardless.

Today, she and Chuck had the ME to themselves. Stoically, Chuck watched as the ME counted the stab wounds in the male deceased. The total came to forty-three separate entrance wounds, not counting the slicing off of his genitals. "No hesitation marks there. Looks like a clean slice, and the killer appears to have known exactly what he wanted to do. Just went ahead and did it. But damn! He was seriously pissed with this poor sod about something."

"Was there any particular fatal wound?" Reesa found a certain amount of sympathy for the victim as the subject of the mutilation, but her real issue was the homicide.

The ME chuckled. "No one specific one. There were something like two dozen that would have been fatal, given enough time, and for probably two-thirds of those, we're talking about no more than minutes. I certainly can't say which one actually did him in, if that's what you're asking."

Reesa could hear Chuck swallowing repeatedly, trying to keep his breakfast down. She debated for just a moment whether she should show him some sympathy or just ignore him and let him keep a modicum of dignity before settling on the second course. Returning her attention to the ME, she looked at what was left of the victim. "From your experience, what do you think might have set him off?"

The ME looked away. "So now I'm Quincy? C'mon, Reesa, you know I don't work that way. This is real life, not TV." He smiled. "As for what set him off, I have no idea whatsoever. Maybe it was the wife's brother, father, whatever. Or hers." He jerked his head towards the other table, where the female victim's body lay. "I could speculate about doing such a number on this one and just the one stab wound on the woman, but that's *your* job." He grinned at her. "My job description doesn't extend to the why and wherefore of such things, Reesa. That's why they pay *you* the big bucks."

She returned the grin. "Big bucks my ass. You make more than I do. How about if I just take that as a 'no'? Is there anything else I need to know about these two?"

The ME just shook his head. "No, I don't think so. No signs of pregnancy in the female, no indications of any recent sexual activity, but they were probably interrupted before they got to that stage, since they were still mostly dressed. Other than the stab wounds and such, they were in good health. Of course, I tend not to see them when they're still breathing, so my viewpoint may be a bit biased."

"Occupational hazard, Doc. Thanks a bunch. Okay, we're out of here." Reesa turned and headed for the door without making an issue of it. Chuck had to; he beat her to it. He couldn't wait. Maybe one of these days Reesa would take pity on him and let him know about the Vicks. He *was* her partner, after all.

****

Chuck and Reesa sat at their government-issue steel desks in the homicide bullpen and just looked at each other, sipping their coffee in extended silence. Finally Chuck broke the stillness between them. "So now that we've ruled out the wife in this Bridgton case, based on her alibi and its checking out, just who *do* we like for this one?"

Reesa stopped chewing on her lower lip. "I'm honestly not in a position to say at this point. The wife's got no family close enough to her to be appropriately offended by her husband's affair, and where she had no idea that it was even going on, it's just a tad difficult for me to see how they would have known about it anyway, since none of them live around here. Maybe *especially* since they don't live around here. Even her friends don't seem to be the sort of people who might have done this, and again, since she didn't know about it, they probably didn't either.

Sarah Johnson's only close living relative is her mother, and she's back east.

"Haven't even *found* any serious friends of hers yet, other than a couple of co-workers who also had no idea she was carrying on with Bridgton. Shit, if it hadn't been for those notes from Bridgton we found in her apartment and the calls and text messages on her cellphone, we wouldn't even be as fairly certain as we are that they were actually *having* an affair. Neither one's got any problems at work or in their financials that we can find, and there's nothing else showing on the horizon. Don't know about you, but I'm coming up as empty on suspects as we are on witnesses. Not to mention the utter lack of any usable evidence from the scene. Damn! What about motive?"

Chuck took a moment for some more of his coffee. "Also a good question, and I'm as shy of answers as you are on this one. So since we're just speculating together here, what motive do you think was at work in this case?"

Reesa chewed on her lower lip some more before answering. "Well, on the one hand, motive depends on just who the prime suspect is. But without a specific suspect, I keep coming back to the difference in how they were killed.

"Sarah was stabbed just once, but the killer seems to have known what he was doing there. If he had just slipped the knife in and left it there, she might have been able to survive it, at least long enough to call for help, because the knife blade tends to seal the wound. She probably would, at the least, have been able to live long enough to try to do *something* rather than just dropping and dying where she lay. But instead, the killer gives the knife a partial twist, apparently to ensure that she would bleed out while doing as little other damage as possible. Why? It's a comparatively easy way to kill her. Easy, I mean, as a way for her to die compared to Bridgton, on the other hand, who was stabbed again and again. And again.

"You heard the ME. He was for all intents and purposes dead long before the killer quit stabbing him, even if he hadn't gotten to the point of actually dying quite yet. And let's not forget slicing his genitals off. He was the one who was screwing around on his wife, and given the differences between how they were done in, I have to strongly suspect that either it was something personal against him and she just happened to be inconveniently present, or else that distinction in their activities played a part in how they were killed.

"I almost wish the wife's alibi hadn't checked out. It would've made it so easy to close the case that way, although if it had been her, personally I'd have expected her to do more of a number on the girlfriend. As well. Maybe it was somebody he'd been involved with in the past."

"Another girlfriend?"

"That's certainly a possibility. I know his wife has denied anything like that, but if he hid this one from her, which we know he did, then there's certainly nothing to say he hadn't been doing that for some time with someone else. Perhaps even several someone elses. Of course, there's no sign of it in his cellphone or his emails, so at this point, I guess it's just supposition. But we definitely ought to keep that sort of thing in mind. I just wish we could *get* somewhere. I'd really like to get some traction here."

Chuck finished his coffee and tossed his cup into the wastebasket. "Oh, well, too bad, so sad. Like you've taught me, we have to deal with what is, not what we'd like it to be. You know, it's almost like something the Avowed would love to see done."

Reesa sat up straight. "Who?"

Chuck looked at her, just a bit defensively. "The Avowed. They're this quasi-religious group, I guess you'd call them, pretty new in town. Their leader, Henry Blodden, spends his time in their meetings talking about how great and grand it is to stick to your partner, your spouse, whatever, and to honor, not break, the vows and commitment you've made to him or her. Every meeting they've got some couple or couples who get up and talk about how they used to be unfaithful to each other in the past, but now, thanks to finding Henry and becoming members of the Avowed, they've recommitted to being exclusively with each other and their lives are 'ever so much better than they were before.' Not a bad idea, I'd say, but he seems to be making a lot more of it than I've ever heard about being done before."

Reesa arched an eyebrow at him. "And you know about this how? I mean, have you and Pat been going to their meetings? Either of you been doing something I don't know about? Or *want* to know about?"

Chuck grinned sheepishly. "Well, yeah, we did go once, but it wasn't for anything we did. Pat's sister and brother-in-law have been going, and they dragged us to one of the meetings. It was, well, *interesting*." He paused, leaned back and put his feet up on his desk. "Not anything we need, you understand, but when Eleanor and Jim got up that night to 'testify,' which there means telling in gory detail about the affairs they had been having or involved in before they joined the Avowed, we certainly got an earful.

We decided that it was simply way more information than we wanted and begged off from going back. TMI in general, I mean, not just about Eleanor and Jim. Maybe we're too straight-laced or something. But it's just like a regular religious service, with a collection and everything. It's also growing like wildfire, from what Eleanor's told Pat. They're still after us to go again, but I don't think we ever will, thank God. They're not asking us quite as often now, and I suppose they're starting to get the message."

For at least the hundredth time Reesa thought how nice it would be to have a pretty picture on the sound tile above her desk to give her something more to look at than simply the random field of perforations. She finished her own coffee and tossed her cup. "So you've met this Henry … Blodden, was it? Is he worth looking at, d'you think? Or anyone else in his group?"

Chuck shrugged. "Dunno. He certainly spends a whole lot of time in these meetings promising hellfire and damnation, if not worse, to anyone who breaks their vows to their partner and doesn't repent and return to the straight and narrow. Never heard him threaten such people with a horrible death, but we only went the once, and if it was him or one of his followers who did this, I can't necessarily see him giving himself away like that anyway. On the other hand, given the way he promises them hellfire and damnation, seems to me that promising a violent death for such transgressions wouldn't be much of a change for him to make, even if he didn't have anything to do with these murders himself."

Reesa found this potentially interesting, in a professional sort of way. She let her feet, previously propped on the second drawer of her desk, fall to the floor.

55

"Transgressions, huh? I don't usually catch you using the ten-dollar words." She grinned at him as she shut the drawer with her foot. "Hm. I may have to go listen in on one of his services and try to get my own read on him. Does he get singles, or just couples?"

Chuck was sitting up again and dabbing at a spot of coffee on his tie. "Again, no idea. The one time we went, there were only couples. One couple was gay, but he doesn't care about that. He just says that a vow is a vow, a commitment is a commitment, and you don't need a church service and certainly don't need any approval from 'The Man'" – he put air quotes around that when he said it – "for two people to form a marriage, to form a relationship, a partnership. His underlying principle seems to be that the people's commitment to each other was what really mattered, and it was that commitment that he said needed to be honored and kept."

Reesa was thoughtful. "Hellfire and damnation, huh? It's not a lot to go on, but it's something, I guess. One minuscule bit more than nothing, anyway. How can I get in?"

Chuck smiled, but his tone was serious. "Getting in's easy, but offhand, from my own take on them and from the one time we went, I'd say you're probably going to need a partner with you, or at least want one. Like I said, I never got the impression that it was strictly a 'couples only' thing, but as a single I suspect you'd stand out like a sore thumb. Man or woman, doesn't matter, but you probably need to have *someone* to go with. I mean, I'm assuming you don't want to go in there openly as Detective Malloy."

Reesa grinned at him again. "How right you are. And you've already been with Pat, so you're out."

One of the other detectives wandered into the bullpen, and with a certain amount of trepidation (not to mention stifling some degree of personal revulsion), Reesa called out to him. "Hey, Schuler, want to play my husband?"

Chris Schuler was a tall, blond, sharply-dressed bodybuilder who could have played a surfer boy in any number of situations. Only a couple of years older than Reesa, he was also known in the division as an inveterate skirtchaser, to put it politely. Reesa had other terms for him, considerably less complimentary, that she often thought but never voiced. She also would have picked someone else, *anyone* else, but all of the other five homicide detectives were probably too old to be convincing in the role alongside her. They were also not there at the moment. Unfortunately for her. "For you, darlin', any time. Name the motel."

Reesa snorted. "In your dreams, buddy boy. I've got to get into a religious sort of service and I need someone with me to let me do it without sticking out too much. For various reasons, Chuck's not a possibility. You available?"

He shrugged. "Sure. When and where?" Reesa looked at Chuck, who immediately got busy on his computer, trying to see about the next meeting of the Avowed.

Chapter 4

The unadorned meeting room in the back of the used bookstore was small compared to going to, say, a convention room in a hotel, but Chuck said that from what information he had, and the one meeting he and his wife had gone to, the meetings had always been held in someone's living room before. Perhaps this Henry Blodden was trying to keep the meetings small and intimate. That made a certain amount of sense, in Reesa's opinion, for what little she knew of such things.

She and Chris Schuler walked in, holding hands loosely, and found seats near the back. Reesa shook off Chris's hand as soon as she chose her seat and both of them spent the time before the beginning of the meeting scanning the room, looking for anyone who appeared nervous, suspicious, or even just familiar. They sat not quite touching each other. The one time that Schuler tried to lean against her, she deliberately leaned away and even readjusted her position in the chair, moving herself about two inches farther away from him. Schuler seemed to get the message and straightened up in his own chair again.

Henry Blodden stepped to the front of the room and cleared his throat. Reesa looked at him with unconcealed interest. Her attention would never stand out in a room full of people who all seemed riveted by him, and she decided to take advantage of the opportunity to look him over closely. About five foot ten, he and Reesa could just about look each other in the eye. Light brown hair, thinning badly, not especially attractive, and with a bit of a paunch, he wasn't exactly imposing, but judging from the way he instantly drew everyone's attention, he did seem to possess a fair amount of charisma. Reesa figured it was probably a plus in his line of work. All the charisma in the world wouldn't keep him from being a potential suspect, of course, if the evidence warranted it. Nothing would, in that event.

Behind him, well behind him, stood a couple that Reesa almost missed. Once she noticed them, though, she looked them over carefully as well. They were scanning the crowd and might have been counting heads, but what fascinated Reesa was that she had to work to keep her attention on them. They appeared to have some peripheral functionary role in the meeting, but they were the sort of people that hardly anybody ever noticed. That, Reesa thought, could probably be a real asset at times and in some lines of work, including several in which Reesa had a professional interest.

The one descriptive word that seemed to apply to both of them in virtually all regards was 'medium.' Medium height, medium build, medium brown hair, neither particularly good-looking nor ugly, just ... medium. Not one single thing about them stood out, and even Reesa, observant and trained as she was, would have been hard pressed to describe them in any detail and with any specificity. Then Henry began speaking, and she took her eyes off them and all but forgot them without even considering what she was doing. Charisma indeed.

"Friends, thank you, all of you, for coming. And welcome to those of you who have never been here with us before. Well, who have never been with us before. None of us have been here before, have we?" A titter ran through at least part of the crowd, which Reesa presumed were primarily the ones who were old hands. Henry took a deep

59

breath. "It's time for faith! Not just faith in the Lord, but the faith you keep with your partner! It's time for your commitment, it's time for your vows! WE ARE THE AVOWED." A moment of utter silence. Then, quietly, "Who are we?"

Everyone in the audience, Reesa and Chris included, answered, "The Avowed."

Louder. "Who are we?"

"The Avowed."

"Let the whole world hear who we are!"

And everybody shouted as loud as they could, "THE AVOWED!" She thought that last probably echoed in the farthest reaches of the store outside the meeting room. A slight shiver ran down her spine.

Chris and Reesa exchanged glances. Clearly this guy had *something*. He had managed to sway this crowd into something resembling a near-evangelistic fervor in a matter of minutes, although both of them recognized that the leavening of regulars throughout the room definitely helped bring the newcomers up to speed in a hurry. On the other hand, all of those people had been newcomers themselves at one point, and this group hadn't been going on all *that* long. Clearly he had *something* over and above a good line of patter.

The service proceeded uneventfully, both detectives following along, responding and singing as seemed appropriate at the right times, if only to fit in rather than stand out from the crowd, and, in the process, they were both making their own mental notes about the promised hellfire and damnation.

Other than trying to mirror the people more engaged in the service, Reesa largely tuned out what Henry was saying the rest of the time. She did note with amusement some of the music, which she primarily recognized because her father had insisted on constantly playing what he called 'Classic Easy Listening' while he was working. Songs had been appropriated from the Carpenters, the Captain and Tenille, Olivia Newton-John, and several others that she didn't recognize, or at least couldn't put a name to. Some were sung in unison, to words on sheets of paper passed around, but one woman in the group with an excellent soprano got up to solo on one song and a couple with decent voices harmonized on another.

About forty minutes into the service, Henry announced that it was time for the collection, and out came the baskets. Once again Reesa noticed the unassuming couple as they brought around the collection baskets, and she dropped in a five-dollar bill as the man made his way by the pair. She glared at Chris Schuler until he matched it, but what piqued her interest most was that after the man had gone on to present the basket to the next group of people, she could barely remember whether it had been the man or the woman who had carried the basket they had put their money into.

Next, as it became obvious that the meeting was drawing to a close, Henry asked the entire group to stand. Reesa looked around, but as far as she could tell, everybody, even the ones who were obviously regulars, longtime attendees, seemed a bit puzzled. Once he had them all on their feet, he told them to turn to their partners and embrace them. He told them to recommit to each other, to their partnership, to re-experience the love they had once felt for each other and should be working at feeling still – or again.

As Reesa's arms slid around Chris's neck, his arms encircled her waist and just as she had feared, his hands began to actively caress her back and sides. She could feel them ranging down below the waistband of her panties and up over her bra strap. "Quit messing around, Schuler," Reesa hissed. "This is business, not pleasure."

Chris whispered back, "It could be pleasure, you know. It's just the two of us together, darlin'. Nobody else here from the division." His hands stopped roaming quite as far afield but continued to move around the back of her waist and a bit beyond.

Reesa pulled back, smiled at him and then buried her face in his shoulder. With her mouth almost against his ear, she said very quietly, "I'll put this on a level I know you'll understand, Schuler. Grab my ass and I'll deck you. Touch my tit and you're a dead man." Then she took him by his ears, kissed him and sat back down. They weren't the first couple to break their clinch, although they were earlier than most.

Chris Schuler sat down and leaned back, hands on his own legs. Keeping his voice low, he said, "Loud and clear, Malloy. Loud and clear." He didn't look pleased about it. Reesa didn't worry; she had always been careful not to give him any encouragement. She drew a hard and fast line about not becoming involved with anyone from the Department.

Not that she'd had any involvement with anyone since her college mishap, but according to the rules she had set for herself and that she lived by, everyone in the Department was utterly out of bounds for her. Everybody around her in the Department knew it, too, which, among other things, had always made her relationships with her

62

partners and their wives a lot easier, especially once the wives had the opportunity to meet her for themselves and learned to their satisfaction that she was absolutely dead serious about that boundary. Chris Schuler … well, he'd never been one of her favorite people, even long before this. *And if he'd had the perception that God gave an oyster where the opposite sex was concerned, he'd know it, too,* she thought heatedly.

Of course, there had been that one other incident, too. She'd been on the job for about a year at that point, and she was aware that some of the people in the department were suspicious of her sexuality, given her total lack of response to the advances made towards her. One day at the end of her shift, one of the detectives called to her. "Hey, Malloy. It is Malloy, isn't it?"

"Sure is, Detective. What can I do for you?"

"Call me Sarah. A group of us were going to go for beers after work. Can we get you to come with us?"

Reesa thought for a moment. "Down at Rudy's? Haven't seen you guys there, but . . . sure. I can get a beer with you."

Sarah shook her head. "Not at Rudy's. We go to Posey's, over on 4th Street."

Something about that set off an alarm in Reesa's mind. She'd heard about Posey's from her first partner, her field training officer. He'd been rather explicit about it, although in retrospect Reesa wasn't certain if he was warning her off or simply letting her know where 'such people' hung out – just in case she were one of them. "Uh, Detective" –

"Sarah."

"Sarah. Is this a mixed group?"

Sarah shook her head. "No, just a bunch of women."

Reesa stopped putting her things into her locker and turned to face the detective. After a moment, she spoke. "Sarah, are you hitting on me?"

Sarah looked back at Reesa, a note of caution in her expression. "Not exactly. Not at this point, anyway. More like . . . seeing which way the wind blows."

Reesa turned away, back to her locker. "I'm sorry, Detective. I don't . . . I don't swing that way. I'm not looking for any sort of a relationship, but if I were, I'm into guys, not girls. And nobody from the department. That's completely out." *I want a partner who's watching my back because he's my partner, not watching my ass because he's my lover. Besides, then there's no danger of having someone split on me and leave me in the lurch. Again. Or even just . . . upsetting my life.*

Sarah hesitated for a moment. Reesa would have missed it if she had been less alert. "Oh, well. No offense, I hope? We noticed that you weren't taking advances from any of the guys and we thought it might be worth a try. Better luck next time, eh?"

Reesa looked at her. "No offense taken, Sarah. I'm just not interested." She then turned back to her locker as the detective left.

****

The next morning, Reesa was already at her desk, transcribing and rewriting her notes from the previous evening, occasionally expanding on some points, and nursing her first cup of coffee when Chuck came in. As usual, he had a Starbucks cup for her as well as his own, and he seemed a tad puzzled about what to do with it when he saw that she already had one. She reached out for it anyway, thanked him, and set it just behind the one she was working on as he took his seat. When he realized that she was going to continue typing and wasn't going to open the conversation, he said, "So what did you think of Henry Blodden and his group?"

Saving her file, Reesa took her time finishing her first cup before replying. "They're … interesting. Don't really know what I think of him personally. We didn't exactly stick around to make his acquaintance afterwards; Schuler and I were having some … issues we needed to resolve." Chuck nodded. He could certainly figure out what she wasn't quite saying. Schuler's proclivities were no more secret in the division than Reesa's rules were. He'd heard a couple of the detectives musing about what would happen when the immovable object, i.e. Reesa, was approached by the (in his own opinion, at least) irresistible force, i.e. Chris Schuler.

Chuck could clearly envision what had probably happened, and he knew who he'd have bet on in that matchup. He'd have bet that way even if she hadn't been his partner. "And you're right that as a group, they'd probably be right in line with the sort of murders we've got, although that's a long way from saying one of them did it or even that we should be seriously looking at any of them as suspects or just as persons of interest at this point. I do think they're worth keeping an eye on at least from time to time unless and until we can develop an actual suspect, but I'm also definitely not going back there with Schuler."

"Well, if you're asking me, I'd say we can give it a couple of weeks and take a look at going again then. Perhaps Pat and I could go back, or maybe there's someone else who'd, ah, suit you better. Maybe someone from Ag Assault" – Chuck hooked a thumb across the room to where the aggravated assault squad had its bullpen – "or somewhere else in the Department."

He sounded sympathetic. He probably really was, she thought. For all that he was actually a very good detective and, at some level, quite tough, Chuck Palmer usually came across publicly as a very nice, pleasant fellow, quiet and concerned. He could project sympathy very well indeed and did a marvelous job of getting people to talk to him. On the occasions in interrogations when the two of them decided it was appropriate to play good cop, bad cop, he invariably went for the good cop role. Despite her comparative youth, Reesa was equally good at being the bad cop; it worked out well for them. When she thought about it, Reesa had to admit that her people skills weren't as good as his. Not a serious problem, as her job performance was outstanding. But she was at least aware of her deficiency in that area. She just worked at making use of it.

"That works. Say, did you notice if Henry had anyone helping him with the meeting? Like another couple, real hard to pin down in your mind, that kind of fade into the woodwork?"

Chuck frowned. "No, I don't remember anyone like that." A pause. "Oh, that's the sort of thing you mean, isn't it? People you hardly notice?"

"That's right. Who took the collection the time you and Pat went?"

A long pause. "Now that you mention it, I think there was … a man? No, it was a woman who brought the basket by us. I just … I can't recall what she looked like."

Reesa smiled. "Bingo. Trust me, it's just as hard to remember the guy with her. Probably her husband, since both of them were wearing matching rings, and of course, they're there in the first place. But those are the people I'm talking about. You just … don't see them. Not unless you're looking for them, and even then, the slightest distraction and you sort of forget they're there." She paused for more coffee. "And now, let's see if there's anything else on our plates that we can close in the meantime. It'd be nice to thin the pile a bit. Boosting our case closure numbers couldn't hurt, either."

****

The killer whistled softly and tunelessly while working. This current project, although inventive, wasn't the most difficult of mechanical contrivances to make. It all had to be done just so, though, and the final step of adding the pressurized tanks to the assembly carried its own dangers. That particular operation was done outside, in an especially private corner of the killer's patio, just in case. Thankfully there was a slight breeze as well. Wouldn't do to fall afoul of one's own device, after all. But even if this device couldn't be actually watched in operation, just knowing how the victims would succumb once it was activated had its own appeal, because it wouldn't be pleasant for them. Not at *all*. The killer smiled. Some people will get just what they deserve. And there'll be plenty of opportunities for other killings, ones done face to face, in the future. Depend on it.

****

Weekends were just *so* nice as a break from the day-to-day work routine. Reesa knelt in front of the spot where the new cactus was going to go, jabbing at the

67

compacted soil with her trowel to loosen it without digging a hole hugely larger than necessary. Every couple of minutes, she'd sit back on her heels and wipe the sweat off her forehead. The kerchief around her hair kept it out of her face, but only a sweatband would do anything serious about the perspiration, and she disliked wearing them except when she was running. Even then, she only wore one in the dead of summer, like it was getting to be now. The hole was almost big enough when she was forced to sit back, take off one glove, bend over, and wipe her face with the bottom of her t-shirt. Long practice, and a quick check using the trowel blade as a gauge, told her that although the hole was wide enough, it still needed to be made a bit deeper before she could try to slip the cactus out of its pot and then tip it into the hole.

Jeff sat on a bench under a remuda at the Desert Museum, savoring the partial shade it offered, and just held his sketch pad for several minutes. He usually found someplace out in the middle of Tucson Mountain Park, or sometimes Saguaro National Park, and sketched the cactus, the lizards, the insects, on rare occasion a snake or a family of javelina (both from a respectful distance) – whatever he found. Sometimes he never even opened his pad and just spent his time watching whatever had caught his interest.

Today, though, he'd felt like coming here instead. Amy had originally brought him here when he was first considering coming to Tucson, and like her, he'd fallen in love with the museum – more of a zoo, actually – and with the Sonoran desert. Today, he'd strolled around the grounds until he found a likely spot to sit, see some interesting things and perhaps even find something worthy of sketching. Normally he avoided sketching people.

Family members, largely as a result of Family secrecy, tended to be somewhat asocial by nature, and he was no different in that regard. He usually preferred not paying that much attention to people, other than as clients or subjects of his investigations, and choosing them as objects to be drawn was normally utterly out of the question for him. Today, however, there was a young lady, probably a volunteer, he figured, kneeling about fifty feet ahead of him, working on planting a cactus. She had dark shoulder-length hair, much like that of the detective he'd encountered, he thought, held back from her face with a kerchief, and she periodically sat back on her heels to wipe the sweat off her face. Something about her position when she was kneeling caught Jeff's eye, and he quickly sketched her into the picture on the pad in front of him.

A few quick strokes of his pencil across the paper to establish the positions of the cactus and other major plants in the background, the mountains beyond, and then he worked fast to capture the shape, the pose of the young lady, the light and shadow playing on her. He could fill in the background, the plants and shading later. By the time she tipped the cactus into the hole, scraped the dirt in around it, and stood up, he had enough of her on the paper to fill in the remainder from his mind's eye. He didn't leave the bench for an hour, and when he did, he had what he recognized was one of the best sketches he'd ever done in his pad. It was one that he thought he might even frame and hang in his living room. It'd be nice to put a bit of a personal touch on the house.

Reesa tipped the cactus into the hole and scraped dirt back around it, relieved to be just about finished with the chore. Bach's, the cactus nursery several miles north on

Thornydale, had called her a couple of days ago to tell her
of some new varieties of hybrid *Trichocereus* cactus they'd
gotten in, and while her backyard already had something
around three dozen of the bunching columnar cactus, both
species and hybrids, she was always willing (usually eager,
but today wasn't one of those times) to find room for a new
one, and Bach's generally had the biggest selection in
Tucson, although she visited the other primary growers
from time to time, just to be sure she wasn't missing
anything.

      The hybrids were especially spectacular plants, with
blooms that could be seven inches or so across, and
particularly in the late spring and early summer, might have
six or eight flowers or even more on a plant open at once.
Some days her backyard was a complete riot of color from
cactus blooms in varying shades and combinations of
white, yellow, pink, orange, and red. The real treat was
when it happened on a weekend and she could sit outside in
the morning with her coffee and newspaper, enjoying the
view whenever she looked up and never have to worry
about leaving for work. Well, almost never; homicides
happened on weekends, too.

      Pity that cactus flowers tended to only last one day,
but trikes usually continued to bloom from March or April
into October, so there were normally more flowers on their
way when one group was fading. She leaned on the dirt
around the cactus and carefully scraped and leveled the
garden gravel back around the new plant where she'd been
working before standing up and roughly leveling the gravel
behind her with her feet, where her toes had made holes.
Walking over to her patio, she took off her gloves before
she stripped the kerchief off her head and used it to wipe

her face one last time. A cold can of fizzy water from the little fridge under the counter and she sat back in her lounger to enjoy the garden.

Setting up a garden of plants that bite and stick gets painful at times in the process, but for someone who loves cactus and loves the desert, once the garden is going, it can be an incredible treat. Reesa considered it well worth the effort in the long run, no matter how much pain it cost at the time to set up. Maybe tonight she'd have a glass of wine while she sat in the hot tub outside and could enjoy it some more.

Chapter 5

Jeff pulled his head out from under the hood of his older Honda. What he thought of as his 'good car,' a year-old high-end, fully tricked-out Honda Accord, went to the dealer for service so Jeff could avoid potential warranty issues, although he changed the oil himself a couple of times between visits. But the old beige Honda that he drove for work, the one that faded into the background, both literally and figuratively, had been out of warranty for years, and Jeff preferred to do his own service on it now whenever he could. Of course, it helped that it had no real computerization such as the 'good car' did.

He'd owned the old one since it came off the showroom floor more than a dozen years, 166,000 miles and well over fifty oil changes before. Even when it had gone to the dealer for the same reason, he'd always been careful to check their work and still do some of his own. Right now he was trying to eliminate a dirty sparkplug. Had to be the next one; he'd already replaced three and there was only one more to go. If it wasn't, then there was a different problem he'd have to chase down.

Unfortunately, he couldn't spend the time to inspect the old one properly at the moment. Luckily he'd gapped all of the new ones beforehand. He wouldn't put up with the car running even just a tad rough, so he spun the last one out and started the new one in its place without even looking seriously at the old one, although the cursory glance he gave it suggested that it was, indeed, the problem plug.

Not important now, it could wait, as could trying to figure out why that cylinder was causing a problem, if it was in fact the cylinder and not simply an inherently bad plug. Fingers to get the new plug going in first, turning it gently to make sure it wasn't cross-threaded, then tighten with the wrench quickly. He had to go to work for the afternoon. There was another surveillance to do, and while he'd pretty well gotten a handle on the times he had to do it, when those times came, he had to be in place or else he'd lose it completely. He wiped his hands on a rag, set the plug itself on the toolbox shelf for later, stuck the sparkplug socket on the magnetic strip, dropped the ratchet and extension into their spots in the toolbox drawer, slid it shut and closed the garage as he headed for the house. A quick wash in the kitchen sink and he'd be on his way.

* * * *

Sitting at her vanity, Barbara Morales took special pains with her appearance. Hair just so, add a bit more blush to the cheekbones, another pat of powder to the nose, just to be sure it wouldn't glisten. Perhaps she could put on some more lipstick … no, that would be a waste. She understood, on a visceral level, that Paul was far more interested in having sex with her than with how good she looked. But she knew that she looked pretty good, when she looked better she felt better about herself, and she believed that it showed. Besides, she just *liked* looking good for him. And to be completely honest, she enjoyed sex with him just about as much as he did with her.

When Paul came into the house from the garage, where he'd parked his car safe from prying eyes (it helped that he drove the same model in the same color as her husband), into the kitchen, she was waiting. A bottle of wine was open on the kitchen counter; a pair of stemmed wineglasses waited expectantly nearby. Out in the living room, music played softly in the background. As his arms opened for her, she came to him eagerly. They were entirely safe; her husband was out of town on a business trip and wouldn't be back for several more days. His car sat safely in long-term parking at the airport.

Out on the street, Jeff sat in his car. He'd gotten some decent photographs of Paul's arrival, clear enough to show the identity of the driver of the car as it pulled into the driveway, and clearly showing the license plate as the garage door was just beginning to close. Now he was simply waiting for the opportunity to get some shots through the picture window into the living room, and maybe, if he was lucky, through the bedroom window as well. As he glanced into the rearview mirror, he felt a surge of annoyance as he saw a TPD cruiser pull in behind him.

Setting his camera down on the passenger seat, he worked his wallet out of his hip pocket. He had it in his hand, already open, when the cop came up to the window. "Excuse me, sir, but could I ask you to step out of the car, please?" *Shit!*

As Jeff stood up, he tried to offer his driver's and PI licenses. The cop ignored him. "Turn around, please, and put your hands on the roof of the car."

"Officer, I need to tell you that I'm carrying a concealed weapon."

"That's just fine. Keep your hands on top of the car, feet back and spread them, please." Polite as he was, he was clearly not going to be diverted by anything as minor as a couple of pieces of paper, Jeff thought.

The cop hooked a foot around Jeff's right foot to pull it back even farther and move it more to the side. A quick, business-like patdown, nothing really extensive, told the cop where Jeff's weapon was and that it was probably the only gun on him. No real mystery by then, of course, since the position the cop had put him into had printed it against his shirt for all the world to notice. "Let's go back to my car, shall we? I'm sure you don't want to have this conversation out here in the street. And please keep your hands where I can see them. Then we don't have to have any mistakes, which I'm sure we'd both regret."

Jeff sighed silently. This was obviously not going to be his day.

Inside, Barbara was down to her panties while Paul had yet to remove his pants, although they showed a distinct bit of tenting from his growing excitement. Barbara took his hand and pulled him up off the couch and towards the bedroom, unintentionally offering any watcher outside her picture window a marvelous shot of her wobbling bare breasts while being followed by, actually pulling, someone clearly not her husband. It was the sort of photo opportunity that would not only have made Jeff's day, it would have gotten him high praise from the attorney who had hired him for this particular case. Unfortunately for him, sitting in the police cruiser, he wasn't in position to get the shot and nobody noticed it.

Several minutes later, out in the police car, Jeff was still being somewhat politely but distinctly chewed out by the cop. Some neighbor had complained about him, it seemed, or so the cop told him, and even if he wasn't doing anything improper, he needed to move along. Not spend so much time sitting by the curbside here.

Jeff would have bet dollars to doughnuts (no irony intended there!) that the cop lived in the neighborhood himself and might well have been the 'neighbor' in question, but he wisely said nothing of the sort. "If I thought you were breaking the law, any law, I'd run you in, understand? I'm not the sort of guy who'd bust a taillight just so I'd have some reason to write you up. It's not my style and we don't work that way in this department. But I'm going to have my eyes out for you, and I'm going to be watching this neighborhood. I don't want to see you skulking around here again, got it?"

Oh, yeah, Jeff got it. He mumbled his assent. The cop wasn't going to let him get away with that. "I said I don't want to see you here again, do you hear me?" Now his voice had a bit of an edge to it. Jeff agreed in no uncertain terms before it acquired more of an edge. Even when someone was insisting on being a prick, Jeff, on Amy's advice, did everything possible to maintain at least a decent working relationship with cops. Maybe especially then. He'd also learned much the same sort of thing from his uncle when he was younger. It made life easier all around.

Usually.

Inside the house, oblivious to any faint, strange odors in the air, Barbara felt a bit dizzy as she laid down on the bed. The air conditioning was running, but she initially chalked the dizziness up to the excitement of actually being able to spend a serious amount of time with Paul for a change as she wriggled out of her lavender panties and dropped them over the side of the bed. Paul braced himself against the bed, struggling against a similar dizziness as he unbuckled his belt and shucked his pants and underpants at the same time. He was now showing a serious degree of excitement as he sprang into view.

By the time the two were completely undressed and ready to move on to more intimate activity, Barbara begged off. "I don't feel well, Paul. I don't think we should … I can't. I don't feel well *at all*. And I …."

Paul was no longer showing any excitement, either, because by that point he, too, was not only dizzy but his efforts to get off the bed were themselves strangely feeble. Barbara rolled off the bed, trying to get to the bathroom before her nausea progressed to actual vomiting, but now unable to stand, she fell to the floor. She tried to crawl to the bathroom, hoping to at least reach a tile floor before the increasingly urgent need to empty her stomach took over, but found that she could not even support her own weight on her hands and knees. Paul tried to stand at the foot of the bed, but was no more able to stand upright by now than she, and he collapsed where he was. Overcome by their nausea, they were both unable to move as they spilled their lunches over the bedroom carpet. Cramps tied their guts into knots and, as they lay on the floor, twitching in pools of their own vomit, uncontrollable diarrhea provided the final insult for both of them. Death came well before nightfall, but they were long beyond caring at that point.

****

The basic scene was familiar to Reesa, but having a number of people in hazmat suits milling around the yard and gesturing at her and Chuck to stay a safe distance away from the house was definitely a new one for her. According to the reports they had gotten, the first person on the scene had been the homeowner, when he arrived back in town from a week-long business trip.

The smell in the house – not just the poisonous vapor, barely noticeable by then, but also the smells from

77

the vomit and diarrhea and from three days of decomposition, which taken together were more than sufficiently noticeable, downright overwhelming, in fact – drove him back out of the house almost as quickly as he'd gone in. That, according to the hazmat people, had probably saved his life. Reesa saw what she figured was probably him sitting on the back bumper of the ambulance, holding an oxygen mask to his face. She imagined she could get some small whiff of the odors inside the house all the way out here in the yard, and what she smelled, or at least thought she smelled, was unpleasant indeed, to say the least.

While she was standing there, still getting her initial feel for the neighborhood, one of the crime scene techs came out of the house holding some sort of device at arm's length. He carried it across the gravel yard and set it down safely away from the rest of the people before taking off the hood of his environmental suit. As Reesa walked towards him, he motioned her to one side. "Stay upwind of it. It's discharged, but it may still have some toxicity remaining."

"What is it?"

The tech smiled. "This bad boy is our culprit. Well, the mechanism, anyway. It's really quite ingenious. It was inside the heating system, in the fan housing." He knelt down so he could reach it. "This part is a timer." He pointed. "When it goes off, it arms the system and drops this lever onto the fan. It used to have a hook at the end, but that was designed to break off, because it was just the trigger to set this off." He pointed to a different part. "When the fan starts, just before the hook at the end of the arm breaks off, the pull on the arm opens these containers and charges the air in the fan housing with the contents of the containers, aerosolized, which is then dispersed all through the house by the main system fan. Nothing horribly difficult to make, just really ingenious as all hell."

Reesa squatted down for a closer look, staying carefully upwind of the device. *Ingenious, huh? I suppose that's one way of looking at it. I could think of some other ways of putting it.* She shivered slightly. "So what was in the containers?"

"Doc says the victims both died of some kind of organophosphate poisoning. Could have been nerve agent, could have been any of a bunch of insecticides. There's really not a lot of difference, from what he tells me. I mean, for all I know at this point, these could be a couple of bug bombs with their labels removed." Reesa looked up. Others in hazmat suits were wheeling a pair of gurneys out of the house. The body bags on them had their zippers taped.

The next suit hood to come off revealed the ME, perspiring heavily. "Oh, hi, Reesa. You got this one too?"

She nodded but said nothing. He went on. "Judging from what I can see, they pretty clearly died from some sort of organophosphate poisoning. I can't be more certain of exactly which compound at this point, especially not after three days of decomp in that house, but trace analysis may be able to tell us. Or maybe not, by now. Luckily that's not my problem, so I can lay everything onto you and your people with a clear conscience." He grinned at her. "You don't want to go in there, by the way. Not until the house gets a clean bill of health, and that won't be for quite a while. It might never be cleaned up enough. There was so much of this around … the stuff was *everywhere* in the house, and the other smells … let's just say you really,

79

really don't want to go in there, and I wouldn't be too surprised if the house has to be razed instead of being cleaned."

Reesa watched the body bags being put into the morgue van. Her expression made no secret of her unhappiness. "So tell me how they died. I'm sure it wasn't nice."

The ME shook his head as he worked his way out of the sweltering suit. "Good call. The scene tells you most of it, and the guys got some good pictures of it all. Plenty good, I expect, because nobody wants to have to go back in *there* again. Like I said, I'm not sure they'll *ever* get this place cleaned up enough, it's that bad. The vics would have been a bit dizzy at first. Probably a faint, strange odor in the air, although they may have been too, ah, *preoccupied* to notice, since they were both nude in the bedroom when we found them. What was left of them, anyway.

"Then, after what was probably a fairly brief amount of time, they got weaker. By the time they really got nauseous, they couldn't walk any more. As I read the scene, they tried to stumble, to crawl, even, to the bathroom, both of them, but they couldn't make it. They collapsed onto the floor as they were vomiting and then had some severe diarrhea to top it all off. They were likely cramping to beat the band in the process, and from the positions of their bodies, I think they were having seizures, too, but neither of those really mattered by the time they reached that stage, and death didn't come fast enough.

"At that point, I'm not sure that it *could* have come fast enough for them, if they were still aware of what was going on. I really hope they weren't, because they probably hung on in that sort of state for as much as an hour, lying in their filth, maybe even a bit more. We kind of had to shovel them into the body bags. Decomposition was proceeding quite well, as these things go."

God Almighty, Reesa thought. *Just when I thought I'd seen the worst of it.* Momentarily she clenched her jaw as a sympathetic twinge of nausea struck her. "We got any ID?"

"We're bringing his wallet out. Honestly, he's so far gone I can't even be sure when I compare him to the picture on his license. We'll have to get his dental records to be certain. The woman lives here, at least I think so, and her body's not in much better shape. You've probably already seen her husband over there." He gestured at the man by the ambulance. "Keep an eye on him while you're talking to him, would you? I doubt he was in there long enough to have any real problems, but you never know. If he gets dizzy or nauseous, and those are the real signs we'd be watching for, we can give him something." He flapped his shirt; it had gotten almost soaked with sweat from his time inside the hazmat suit.

"The stench in there was really bad, even through the suit. It had to have hit him like a sledgehammer. But leaving as fast as I'm sure he did almost certainly saved his life." Another tech came out just then and handed Reesa an evidence bag with the wallet and the other contents of the man's pockets inside. Another bag held the woman's purse. Chuck, standing silently behind her and just listening the whole time, took the bags from her.

Two blocks away, through the open driver's side window, Jeff kept his small binoculars trained on the police presence around the house he'd been watching just a few short days before. When he finally saw Reesa's tall, slim form, he set the binoculars down on the seat beside him and slowly drove off.

Reesa looked around the neighborhood one last time before getting back into the nondescript Dodge she and Chuck had pulled from the motor pool for the day. The usual time they would have spent at a crime scene had been quite attenuated by their inability to go inside and actually view the scene first hand, and it was pretty likely that the husband's alibi would pan out. Reesa and Chuck had thought about taking him downtown for more extensive questioning, but just like with Caroline Bridgton, they were pretty sure it was going to be a waste of effort. Besides, Chuck had checked on his alibi while Reesa was questioning him, and he'd definitely been in Cincinnati both on the day of the murders and for several days before as well as a couple of days after.

The crime scene tech, on examining the murder device, had said that he saw no way to set it for more than twelve hours in advance, so Enrique Morales ("Please, call me Henry") seemed highly unlikely to become a suspect at this point. Of course, that could change if they could find any sort of connection between him and whoever had put the device in place, but he didn't need to be told that. They had his particulars, and they could find him if they needed to in the future.

It was no surprise to her when the white van came into view, rounding the corner from Broadway, two blocks down. She didn't have to be close enough to the truck to know what it had painted on its side: KOPN Channel 12 News, Up Close and Personal. *Oh, how lovely. Lynne Fox in the flesh. Hey, honey, go on into the house and see the actual murder scene for yourself!* Now *there* was a lovely thought. Reesa pulled out and drove off, heartily glad to be away from the woman she regarded as the most obnoxious news person in the entire city. Maybe even the most obnoxious person, period.

"You really don't like her, do you? Care to tell me why?" Chuck's question was conversational, but Reesa was startled. Had she spoken her thoughts out loud? Or could he just read her that well? She doubted that she'd actually voiced what she was thinking, but then, her opinion of Lynne Fox wasn't exactly a deep, dark secret, either. Oh, well. Given a choice, she'd rather have voiced her thoughts than have him able to read her like that. Like she actually had that choice.

"Not one bit. On the record or off?"

Chuck cocked his head at her. "Both, I guess."

Reesa took a deep breath, let it out slowly as she drove. "Well, on the record, I think she's a nasty bitch who's just a complete fake, from her allegedly platinum blonde hair to her presumably pedicured feet. Off the record, well, she knows damn good and well that we can't talk about the cases we go to. We can't talk about open cases, we can't talk about ongoing investigations, and somebody who *is* authorized to speak to her will be on the scene before long, someone who will tell her whatever he's allowed to. She asks us anyway. So far, so good. That's her job. But the rest of the guys, she just asks briefly, anonymously, and lets it go. It's just, 'Detective, can you tell us anything?' and when they say no, or shake their heads, that's the end of it.

"Me, she calls by name. She asks, and asks, and asks. Then, when her reports come on, if I'm on the case, she makes sure to point out that 'the detective in charge of

83

the case wouldn't tell her anything' and show my picture
on the screen. Never yours, or Paul's, or Benny's. Not
Ruben's or even Schuler's, and at some level, *he'd*
probably be delighted to give her anything at all on the off
chance she'd take him back to the van and let him get into
her pants. It doesn't even matter whether I'm lead or not, if
I'm at the case and she sees me. That's all it takes for her to
report me as the detective in charge, and I'm the one who
won't say diddly to her. So no, I've got no use for her at
all."

  Chuck looked thoughtful, if a bit taken aback by the
heat of Reesa's response. "And if we're actually dealing
with a serial killer on these cases, then by naming you and
putting your picture out there all the time, I expect she's
painting a target on you as well. That probably doesn't sit
too well with you, either."

  "Yep. I don't worry a lot about that, because to
some degree it comes with the territory, but *if* we are, then
yes, she is. That's not exactly going to put her in any better
light as far as I'm concerned. But just as I've told you
before, let's lay off the serial murderer speculation until
we've got enough of a pattern to see, okay?"

  He was quiet for a good two miles before he spoke
again. This time he voiced what was on both their minds.
"Jesus. Three days old before we even hear about it. This
one's cold. I bet we never close it."

  Reesa snorted. "Won't be the first one we couldn't.
On the other hand, the MO is definitely different. I'd go so
far as to say unique, at least in my experience. If we can
ever get a bust out of it, or even a good suspect, that'll
likely be the reason. You're right about the trail being kind
of cold, though. Damn!" Murder cases are generally critical

in the first twenty-four hours. By then, there should be at least a fair idea of who the killer is likely to have been. If there's no suspicion of a particular person after three days, the chances of finding the killer get quite slim. When the case isn't even reported for three days, well ….

But they still had to go question Paul Genematas's wife. There might be nothing there, and the ID on the body wasn't even completely solid yet, but she was, at this point, the closest thing they had to a viable suspect. If they had one at all.

The receptionist at the bank where she worked seemed quite concerned when they badged her and asked for Colleen Genematas. "Is this about her husband?"

Reesa glanced at Chuck, who simply responded, "We just need to speak with her. Can you call her, please?"

Being told that two police detectives were there to talk to her didn't exactly make Colleen's day, but she seemed all business as she arrived at the receptionist's desk. Not one brown hair out of place, her back ramrod-straight and her suit all but unwrinkled. Reesa wondered if she was as pale as she was from concern over having two detectives ask for her, or was it simply her natural coloring? She introduced herself and suggested that they go back to her office. Reesa asked if it was enclosed, and assured that it wasn't simply a cubicle, the three of them went. As soon as the door was closed, before either Chuck or Reesa could sit down, Colleen turned to them and, her face streaked with tears, simply said, "This is about Paul, isn't it? Damn it!" She stifled a sob.

"Mrs. Genematas, what do you know about your husband's whereabouts for the past several days?" Reesa kept her voice low.

Colleen looked somewhat shocked. "I filed a missing person report on him the day before yesterday. Isn't this what you're here about?"

Reesa tried again. "Do you have any idea where he's been?"

Now Colleen blanched. "He's dead, isn't he? I knew he'd never leave Bobby." She hung her head and let the tears flow. Finally she reached for a tissue and dabbed at her cheeks. Another one for her nose. "Even if he were going to leave me, he'd never leave our son. They're far too close. That's what I couldn't understand when he didn't come home. Where is he? What's happened?"

Reesa took her by the elbow. "Mrs. Genematas, perhaps you'd better sit down." She guided Colleen to her chair behind the desk.

Sitting heavily, Colleen just hung her head as the tears resumed. After a minute or so, she began to shake with sobs. She fought to regain control. "I knew it. He's dead. It's the only explanation." She looked up, her eyes shifting jerkily from one detective to the other. "How? Where is he? Can I see him?"

Chuck responded. "Not right at the moment, Mrs. Genematas. You may not want to anyway, but at the moment the medical examiner hasn't released the body." Reesa glanced sharply at him. This was a bit too much to reveal at this point in the questioning. She took over.

"Mrs. Genematas, was there anybody else in your husband's life? Did he have any outside friends or acquaintances who might have intended him harm?"

Colleen blew her nose again as she collected herself. "It was another woman, wasn't it? I've had my suspicions for almost a year, now, but, well, I have to admit that my own interest hasn't been what it used to be. I'm not going to say I'm happy about it, but it doesn't exactly come as a complete surprise, either. Paul's always been a … a vigorous man, I suppose I'd say. Did she kill him? Who is she?"

Reesa relaxed slightly. Colleen Genematas might be a superb actress, but Reesa's finely tuned senses read her as upset and taken by surprise, even if not without her suspicions at that point. "We're not at liberty to say at this point, Mrs. Genematas, but I can tell you that she did not kill him. She … is deceased, as well." It took another fifteen minutes to establish Colleen's alibi for the time period in which the murder device had to have been set at the house, after which they promised to let her know when the body was released and left. Of course, they'd also let her know, a lot less pleasantly, if her alibi failed to check out. They again politely declined to tell her how her husband had died. Or how his lover had died, either.

After pulling out of the parking lot and turning north on Wilmot, heading for Speedway, Reesa suddenly banged her hands on the steering wheel in frustration. "Dammit! I can put together a couple of apparently unrelated pieces of evidence, come up with a viable suspect, tail him, tie the trace from the scene to him, watch him, haul him in for questioning, sweat him, and almost every time wind up with enough to convict him, or at least move the process along in that direction far enough to turn it over to the county attorney and let him worry about it. But what in the *hell* do I do when there is absolutely nothing, not one goddam *thing*, at the scene that I can use to even *start* with, and not one viable suspect outside of it?"

Chuck looked at her. "Is that a real question for me to respond to, or are you just expressing your frustration? I mean, it's just look for the patterns, ask the questions, and follow up on the answers, right?"

"Since we can't follow evidence that isn't there, yeah. But that's mostly just my frustration talking, I guess. I mean, it's not simply what these cases are doing to our closure numbers. One case, like the Bridgton one, with no usable trace from the scene, I can see. Sometimes the perp gets lucky. But now we've got a second one just like it, right on top of it. With another lucky perp. Or a damn slick one. They pay us to *solve* these cases, not to just go to the scene, stand around, and look like we know we're doing. And as for the by-the-book detective theory, you have to know what questions to ask and, even more important, you need to know who to ask them of. We are, just like before, fresh out of people to ask them of here. I am one unhappy camper, let me tell you."

Chuck shrugged. "Me, too." The pair sat in silence for several more blocks before Chuck tried to reopen conversation again. "So what's your favorite book?"

Ah, yes, the partnership dance, Reesa thought. *About time he got around to it again.* She could do it in her sleep by now. On the one hand, you had to be able to let your partner inside at least some of your defenses, get to know the *real* you. The two of you were partners, after all, and you had to be able to depend on each other. You had to be able to trust your partner and believe that your partner would watch your back just as you would be watching his.

Reesa had never cared for getting a reputation as a difficult partner or a prickly one, although she suspected that at least some detectives who had never worked with her probably thought of her that way. Besides Schuler, that is, and honestly, she didn't give the proverbial rat's ass what *he* thought of her. At the same time, she was bound and determined to keep her innermost self alone and private, so she'd had to learn shortly after getting into the Academy how to dance this particular dance in her own way, to let someone in so far and no farther, without making it obvious that she was drawing limits. By now, she could do it in her sleep.

She glanced over at him. "You read science fiction?" He shook his head. "Then it wouldn't even mean anything to you, I bet. What's your favorite movie?" Toss the ball back into his lap and let him run with it for a while. Chuck was a nice enough guy, but it was so much easier for Reesa to get someone else to dance the dance than to do it herself. And if they started the music, they usually didn't even notice that they wound up doing most of the dancing when they were with her. That suited Reesa very well indeed.

Chuck's discussion of movies took them down Speedway almost to Fourth Street, and the only ones Reesa had time to talk about from her own favorites were the *Harry Potter* films, which she loved as a way to escape the trials and tribulations of real life. God, how wonderful it would be to be able to wave a magic wand, utter some nonsensical quasi-Latin phrase, and make things happen the way she wanted! Chuck was more into blood and gore films – war films, not crime films. That was just fine with her.

No matter what, there was just no way in hell she'd ever tell him – or anyone else, either – about her copy of *The Princess Bride*. She rarely watched it anymore, but schmaltzy and cheesy as it was, she still loved it as much as she had when she was a teenager. Just secretly, now; if the guys in the Department ever found out, she'd never live it down. Come to think of it, watching it again might be a nice diversion for tonight. She shelved that thought for later.

****

It had certainly taken long enough for the murders to get reported, but as the report on the killings came on the local news as the lead story at 10 that night, the killer relived the high, the intensely *sexual* high, of the killing. Not, perhaps, *quite* as intense as when the killing was done in person, right there with the victims, but keeping the methods constantly changing kept the police busy chasing their tails in a different direction each time instead of looking for one single killer. Maybe the next time could be another one done face to face. Now *there* was a delicious thought. A shudder ran through the killer's body, some from the killing just now being reported, days after the fact, some from the memories of previous murders and some from the tantalizing thought of the next one. Done by hand. Done face-to-face. Done close enough to *touch* the victims. To see them, to *watch* them, actually *look them in the eyes* as they died. Ooooh, how enticing is that?

Definitely God's work. Hey, everybody, the handwriting is on the wall. 'Don't go screwing around.' It's not my problem if you don't know how to read. Or don't care to.

****

Reesa paused at the door to the autopsy room. Two three-day-old bodies, well advanced in decomposition, were going to be worse than usual. *Lots* worse. She reached behind her to stop Chuck. "Here." She pulled her film can out of her purse again. "Smear a bunch of this under your nose."

"Hm?" He opened the can. "So *that's* what I've been smelling in there." He dug his finger into the can before snapping the lid back on and handing it back.

She tucked the can back in her purse. "A fresh body is one thing. Three days of decomp is going to be pretty bad. But you ought to know about the Vicks anyway. It helps, at least if the smell is what gives you trouble." She handed him a tissue.

"Thanks. I'll be sure to get my own next time."

The bodies were definitely in bad shape. Tissues were sagging and the faces were approaching unrecognizability. Even through the camphor and mentholatum, the odor was noticeable. Just not overpowering. How the ME could handle it, Reesa had no idea. He looked up. "Hey, guys. Here for the fun?"

"Doc, you have the oddest idea of fun." He just shrugged.

"Just like I said at the scene yesterday, in my opinion, these two pretty clearly died of organophosphate poisoning. It's not a nice way to go, to say the least. Do I need to run over the progression again, or do you remember it well enough from yesterday?"

Reesa looked at her partner, who just shook his head. "No, I don't think we need a recap. Is there anything else about the way they died that we need to know about? Anything out of the ordinary?"

The ME snorted. "Personally, I'd call being killed with bug spray out of the ordinary, but what do I know?"

Reesa raised one eyebrow. "Bug spray?"

"Yes, bug spray. A lot of insecticides are organophosphates, just like military nerve agents. Getting military stuff isn't all that easy, but bug spray is as close as the nearest hardware store or garden supply. Check the warning labels on one of these house bombs sometime. They're bad news to be around." Reesa just shook her head. "Blowing it throughout the house like that, well, it's not something I approve of, naturally, but it's kind of inventive."

Reesa made a face. "Like I said, Doc, you have the oddest idea of fun."

****

Reesa was once again reading while she ate. It was a bad habit, she knew, but she chalked it up to living alone and insisting on eating at least some of her lunches alone. This particular book she had in a long-treasured autographed hardback at the house, but she'd picked up a used copy in paperback from Bookman's for its portability and price. Chuck would generally have been happy to join her for lunch, she knew, but this was the one chance for solitude she had during her workday, and she liked to keep it to herself. Besides, today he was meeting his wife Pat for lunch, the same way he did every Tuesday, and three's a crowd. She had just lowered her eyes to her plate, trying to make sure she actually got her fork into her food, when a man stepped up to the table.

"Reesa? May I join you again?" At some level, she was quite surprised to see him once more. Usually men who tried to hit on her gently went elsewhere once they saw she was a cop. Those who weren't gentle about it she cut dead – figuratively, of course. There was no reason to make more work for herself. She ransacked the recesses of her memory for his name.

"Jeff, isn't it? Sure, have a seat. I'm afraid I'm almost done, though, just like the last time." She waved her fork at the chair opposite hers. He smiled at her as he set his tray down.

"You seem a bit surprised to see me again."

"Well, yeah, to be honest. I know you saw the gun and badge the last time we were here. Most men go away when they find out I'm a cop. Or else they worry about me carrying a gun."

Jeff looked at her for a moment before slowly pulling the spare magazine for his own pistol out of its pouch on his belt, under his shirt on his left side, and laying it gently on the table between them. Reesa just looked at it. "Armed women don't bother me. The senior investigator in my office is a woman, and she's always armed."

As he picked up the magazine to put it away again, Reesa asked, "Senior investigator?"

"Amy Trevethen. She's been there for years, I'm comparatively new." He put the magazine back and pulled a business card out from his shirt pocket to offer her. "Jeff Escarton. I work for A.M. Youngston and Associates."

Reesa took it silently. Being Family herself, she recognized the name. Both names, in fact. Outsiders wouldn't think twice about either name, but anyone who was Family would instantly recognize them. Those two names together fairly screamed 'Family.' Actually, either one alone was a pretty good giveaway, for that matter. That gave her more information about him than he could possibly have realized, but none of it really mattered in terms of what she might have to do with him. Just more data for her mental file. And none of it showed in her expression. "I see. So neither of those will drive you off."

That made Jeff smile again, but only slightly. "Is that what you want to do? Drive me off?"

She shrugged. "I'm not looking for any sort of a relationship. If you just want to sit at the same table over lunch from time to time, I guess that's no problem." She reached her hand across the table. "Reesa Malloy. TPD Homicide."

As he took it gently but firmly, he replied, "Ah. The big leagues." Her handshake told him some things about her as well, although nothing as revealing, or hard to find out (for outsiders, anyway). Her grip was dry, as firm as his, and definitely serious. He figured she was probably not one to rely on her sex or her looks to get her places. That was fine with him, although admittedly he approved of both her sex and her looks. She was also clearly no slouch in the muscle department, either. She didn't try to grind his hand, and that was equally fine, although he could hold his own with most such grinders. Her grip was definitely firm enough to make a significant impression on him, however.

"I guess so, if you want to look at it that way."

"Compared to what I do? Absolutely. I'm known for tracking down and getting the goods on cheating spouses, not killers. But, ah, can a guy call you occasionally to … sit at the same table over lunch from time to time? Somewhere a bit nicer, perhaps? My treat."

Reesa leaned forward and lowered her voice. "I said I'm not looking for any sort of a relationship. I don't need a boyfriend, I'm not looking for a friend, and I don't even own a dog. Now, that said, if you want to go to lunch from time to time, and you can leave it on that level and let me pay for it half the time or go Dutch, then fine. If not, then yes, I am trying to drive you off."

Jeff was still smiling, slightly. Not quite enough to annoy her, she thought, but it wouldn't take much at this point. After a minute or so, he nodded. "Deal. Casual … acquaintances, alternating or going Dutch. Nothing more."

Now why would he agree to that? she wondered. He didn't read as gay, and did read to her finely-tuned senses as interested in her. Just not quite enough for her to decide to stop him in his tracks. Not quite. Oh, well, maybe he's a Boy Scout. She'd see. If he wasn't, well, she could handle men like that. Quickly. Not in a way they enjoyed, either. She'd had plenty of practice. She only rarely had to resort to some of the holds she'd been taught in the Academy; they usually got the message well before she had to reach that point. Usually.

"Into the old sci-fi, I see," he said, gesturing at her book. "I met the author once. He's actually my boss's father. Nice fellow, not at all what you'd probably expect."

Never would guessed that he was Family, either, but with a name like Youngston, I suppose I shouldn't be too surprised. There don't seem to be many of them running around, like that matters. Reesa shrugged again. "He doesn't seem to be writing any more, so I honestly have no idea what to expect of him in any event. I've got another copy of this at home, but it's a hardback copy that I got him to autograph at a convention when I was a teenager. I've had it for years, so I don't bring it out to places like this." She stacked her plates and stood up. "I really do have to get back to work, though."

Jeff stood politely. "No problem. Do you have a card, or do I just call Homicide and ask for you?"

95

Reesa ducked her head to dig into her purse as well as to hide her slight flush. She really didn't want a relationship. No complications, that was her motto. But sometimes the loneliness got to her, just a bit, and this was one of those vulnerable moments. Pulling out one of her cards, she handed it to him. "Can't always tell from one day to the next when I'll have time, but go ahead and call. Just expect that it may have to be a last-minute thing, and if we've got something arranged, I may have to cancel the same way."

He carefully found a spot for it in his wallet. "No problem. I'll give you a try later this week. Oh, I almost forgot. I've got a couple of things for you." Reesa stiffened; that could be trouble. Process servers had been known to start like that, and if that was what he was doing, this acquaintance was going to come to an abrupt end, Family or not. Jeff looked at her and noticed the reaction. "Oh, heavens, I'm sorry. It's nothing to worry you. I've just got some timelines on the Bridgton/Johnson and the Genematas/Morales cases that I thought you might find helpful. Nothing really valuable, I expect, but some minor info you probably don't have." He handed over a couple of folded sheets of notepaper.

Reesa took them, unfolded them and looked at the upper one. It showed, with details, the time that Nathan Bridgton had arrived back home, when Sarah Johnston had arrived at the house, when the wife had arrived several hours later, when her screams had first been heard, and when the first police unit had arrived. The second sheet was much the same for the other case, at least up until the point that the cop had run him off. She just looked at Jeff and arched her eyebrow.

He shrugged. "Like I said, nothing really valuable, but I had the information from my own surveillance and wanted to pass it along. Saw you arrive at the Bridgton house and then saw you at the Morales house, so I figured you were working both cases."

"You saw me arrive? Where the hell were you?"

Now he smiled, disarmingly. Just pleasantly, not triumphantly. "On the Bridgton case, I was in the shadows beside a house about two doors down. I stayed there until you finished your … survey of the neighborhood, I guess you'd call it, and walked under the crime scene tape. The Morales house, when the police finally came to the scene and then you arrived, I was in my car down a couple of blocks. I'm decent at what I do."

Reesa refolded the papers and jammed them into her purse. "Well, thank you for these. I'll make sure they get into the case files and note you as a witness."

Now Jeff seemed a bit disconcerted. "I didn't see anything that has anything to do with the killings, you know. I'm just a witness to some of the peripheral events."

"Yeah, I know. But I'll put your name in anyway. On that basis. I have to." Jeff just shrugged. Reesa's feelings weren't so clear to her.

She took her confusion out into the parking lot. Dammit, he seemed to be a nice enough fellow, polite, respectful, and not at all put off by her being armed. Or a cop. Which, for someone who wasn't a cop himself, was unusual in her experience. But she really *didn't* want a relationship. Did she? He was willing to do things on her terms, and he seemed to have some understanding of the sorts of things she did. So just why was being around him bothering her at some visceral level? Could it have anything to do with being distant cousins? Probably not, as she thought about it. Family relationships could get *awfully* distant. Usually were, in fact. Most people had no idea who their fourth or fifth cousins were, and with the Family, she and he could easily be tenth cousins or even more distant. Oh, well, that didn't really matter.

Chapter 6

Reesa waited to do anything more about it until she got home around supper time. She debated with herself, but finally decided to do a bit of investigation on her own behalf for a change. Something that didn't involve a homicide or even a crime, for a most pleasant change. She smiled as she picked up the phone and dialed.

"Business office." A nice, clear connection, to the point that it was hard to remember she was actually speaking with someone halfway around the world who was working in what was, there, the wee hours of the morning. At least they were available around the clock.

"This is Family member Reesa Malloy in Tucson, Arizona, USA. I'm looking for a private investigator."

"I'll need your Family ID number, please. If you don't know it, it's on your medical card and your passport."

Reesa dug through her wallet. "Hmm. Driver's license. Commission card. Gym card. Medical card—"

"That's it."

"No, sorry. That's the one from work." She dug a bit more. "Okay, here it is." She pulled the card out of her wallet and rattled off the number.

"Just a moment, please." The person on the other end was back quickly. "We show one private investigation firm in your area, A.M. Youngston and Associates on East Speedway. You may contact either Amy Trevethen or Jeffrey Escarton." A phone number was given, and it matched the office number on Jeff's business card.

Reesa thought about that for a couple of seconds. "Is this A.M. Youngston the same as the Family CEO?"

Now the voice on the other end of the phone seemed to be choosing her words carefully. "Yes, it is. However, you are warned that A.M. Youngston does not see anyone in person and does not take or return phone calls. You will get a response with letters or emails. Other than that, you are instructed to deal with Ms. Trevethen or Mr. Escarton only."

"Do you have any other information about CEO Youngston?"

"There is no other public information available on CEO Youngston." Now *that* was damned interesting. *A.M. Youngston. A.M. ... Y. Amy. Amy? As in, say ... Amy Trevethen?* Reesa decided to try to figure that one out with a different tack. Jeff had said that the author of the book she had been reading was his boss's father, after all, and if she really was A.M. Youngston, then she was clearly his boss. Among other things.

"How about authors? I also need to talk to an author, well, I'd *like* to talk to one, anyway, about a manuscript I've written. I think I may need some help getting it into saleable form."

A momentary pause. "That's quite a change, from investigator to author. What kind of author do you need? We have two who are listed as mystery writers, three non-fiction and one romance."

Romance? Reesa shuddered involuntarily. "Actually, the manuscript is science fiction. Are there any authors in that area?"

The voice on the other end took several seconds before responding. "We do have one science fiction author, but he is listed as retired."

In for a penny, in for a pound. "Well, could I try him anyway? I figure he ought to know more about the field than a romance writer."

The voice on the phone chuckled. "Yes, you're probably right about that. Well, no promises, but the author is Colin Youngston, in Denver, Colorado. I'm not showing any phone number and I'm not allowed to give out residence addresses."

Bingo. Now Reesa smiled. "Oh, that's all right. I'll see if I can locate a phone number for him from here. Thank you very much." Once she knew the city, she could take it from there herself.

It only took her moments to locate his phone number on the internet. An unlisted number would only have taken her a couple more minutes to find. A deep voice answered on the third ring. "Hello?"

"Hello, Mr. Youngston? This is Detective Malloy with the Tucson Police Department. I've got a question or two for you about your daughter." If her suspicions were right, this would be all she'd need. If not, well, "sorry, wrong information" worked.

His voice became agitated. "Is Amy all right? What's wrong?"

Reesa's smile got just a bit broader. *Amy Trevethen, 'the senior investigator,' my ass*, she thought. *Talk about transparent disguises.* "Oh, no, she's fine. I'm just trying to check out some information on her … on an application she filed. She identified you as her father, and I'm simply trying to verify all of her information."

He sounded relieved. "Oh, Lord. You had me worried for a moment there." He covered the mouthpiece of the phone, but poorly, and Reesa could hear him faintly as he said to someone else, "It's Tucson PD about Amy. But she's fine, it's just routine." He came back on the phone. "Yes, I'm her father. Is there anything else I can do for you?"

"Oh, no, sir. We're good. I've got the information I needed, and now I'm satisfied that it's correct. Thank you very much, and I'm sorry to have disturbed you."

"Think nothing of it, Detective. Glad to have helped. Good night."

She hesitated before picking up the phone again. This time she had to consult the back of her medical card for the phone number. "Genealogy office. May I have your ID number, please?" Reesa read it off the card again to the accompaniment of computer keys clicking on the other end of the phone. "What may we do for you … Miss Malloy?"

Reesa hesitated. *Was this a smart move? Well, why not?* "I'm looking for my relationship to Family member Jeffrey Escarton of Tucson, Arizona."

"Do you have his ID number?"

"No, I don't. The business office just gave me his name."

"I see. Wait just a moment, please." A pause while she heard a keyboard clacking. "The closest relationship is twelfth cousin, once removed. Would you like the entire list? There are four relationships between the two of you, that's merely the most recent."

Four relationships? She could be here all night thinking about that. "No, thank you. That's good enough for now." *Twelfth cousin? That's hardly related at all. Regardless of whatever 'once removed' means.*

****

A witness interview was something Jeff would just as soon skip, but he didn't appear to have the option. At least the detective was willing to come to his office rather than making him come down to Homicide. Probably because he was such a peripheral witness, he figured. She, on the other hand, wanted to see the Family CEO for herself while remaining, or at least trying to remain, fairly anonymous.

She arrived right on time, and he met her at the front door just as the clock in what had originally been the living room of the little house on east Speedway chimed the hour. As he led her down the hallway to his office, he stopped momentarily to introduce her to Amy. Reesa murmured the appropriate responses, but her eyes never quit moving around the office, taking in all of the details. It didn't escape her notice that Amy was inspecting her just as intensely. Had her father told her about Reesa's call? No ready way to find that out, but she decided to assume that he had.

Some coffee for each of them, then to his smaller office where Reesa allowed Jeff to take the chair behind the desk. Jeff viewed it as an edge, while Reesa recognized it for what it was, an effort to establish a certain amount of dominance in the interview, or at least resist any attempt she might make to take the upper hand. That was fine with her; this was nothing crucial. All she really had were some questions about the timelines he'd given her and what he'd been doing when he observed the occurrences he'd noted. Dominance wouldn't matter. Certainly not now, anyway. She could always haul out the whips and chains later, if she needed to. That thought provoked a small smile inside, where (as usual) she didn't allow it to show.

The initial questions, the ones intended to develop some degree of rapport between the questioner and the witness, went very well. Reesa learned quite a bit about Jeff and his history (giving up almost nothing of her own), and neither of them found the other difficult to talk to. Reesa asked one or two questions that could have related to the Family, and Jeff sidestepped the matter very easily – so much so, in fact, that if Reesa hadn't known about the Family and about Jeff's being Family, she never would have noticed the evasion.

Since they had nothing to do with what he'd seen, of course, she could go on anyway. Just with some mental notes that, under the circumstances, she'd never put down on paper anywhere. His timelines really were almost all he had of import to the cases; his accompanying notes already showed the makes, models, and license numbers of the cars as well as how the various people had been dressed. In the final analysis, there was hardly anything that Reesa's skilled questioning could add to what he'd already given her.

****

Bob and Mary Jones set up the chairs for the service with quick, quiet efficiency. For them, it was to some degree just a repetition of their regular job, where they worked hospitality for one of the larger Tucson resorts, and setting up chairs, tables, and such for meetings was something they could do almost without thinking. If nothing else, it was a lot easier than rearranging living-room furniture had been, and for a pleasant change from their day jobs, there were no tables to be covered in sparkling white tablecloths that each had to be carefully pinned in place just *so*. By the time they were finished,

though, some of the people were already arriving for the
meeting. They hurried to get back to the front of the room,
where they could take their places behind Henry. Then
Mary remembered that he wanted them in the back of the
room in the future and, catching her husband's eye, jerked
her head in that direction. Where, among other things, they
could be certain to stick their collection baskets under the
nose of anyone who left early.

Once again Henry would open his service with the
same litany. Having found a niche that worked, he figured,
it was worth sticking with. As the old saying goes, if it ain't
broke, don't fix it. Along with the Joneses, he'd arrived at
the store more than half an hour before the meeting was to
start, and the first order of business for him was to hang the
brand-new gold-on-royal-purple 'Avowed' banner on the
front wall, behind where he would be standing. Personally
Bob thought it a bit garish, but Henry was far too proud of
it for Bob to say anything negative to him about it.

Then, as Bob and Mary set up the chairs, Henry,
with the help of the two couples he'd primed for testifying
if he didn't have anyone get up on their own, arranged the
various paraphernalia where he could get at the items he'd
need during the service and where Bob and Mary could get
to whatever they might have forgotten that they needed.

Then he waited until almost all of the people, the
congregation, had arrived. After greeting those present and
welcoming those who were new, he started right in. "It's
time for faith! Not just faith in the Lord, but the faith you
keep with your partner! It's time for your commitment, it's
time for your vows! WE ARE THE AVOWED." A
moment of utter silence.

At the end of the litany, once again the entire congregation shouted it out loud: "THE AVOWED!" The building didn't shake, quite. It was time to be about the Lord's work. And there was plenty of it to do, too. Henry could be busy for quite some time to come. In fact, he probably would be. Almost certainly would be. For the rest of his life, even. But first, there was a congregation to be preached to and taught – or reinforced – in their fidelity. Thank God for the faithful (in both meanings), the *generous* faithful … and thank God for the unfaithful as well. Both groups kept him in business, one way or the other. *All* of his business. He had God's work to do, in this as in all things. And he was always about God's work in everything he did.

So to speak.

****

Lynne Fox sat at her desk and stared at her computer screen. She had a whole series of notes on the murders she'd gone out to report on. Four of these couples murders, so far. Eight dead bodies. She started a new file, listing the similarities between the killings. There was a definite pattern there, and she was angry with herself for failing to see it before now. In fact, it was almost glaringly obvious, once she tried looking at the murders more analytically as a group. But it gave her something to work with here, and she probably had some time yet. No hurry at all. She could, however, begin to lay out what she'd need, sketch out the outline of what she wanted to say. Decide how to suddenly spring it on the city. See what Those-Who-Must-Be-Obeyed would want from her before they'd allow her to take this special report on the air.

And hopefully not just one. With any luck (and more than a little bit of good management), there could be an entire series of these reports. She'd have to be sure that they were the best, most captivating reports she could possibly turn out (which shouldn't be all that hard; she knew her viewership figures and she knew how to do her job very well indeed), and that meant that the first one, the one that would establish the format and initially capture the viewers, had to be absolutely perfect. Even if it was a bit too early yet for the reports to begin, it wasn't too early to begin drawing up the initial draft of the proposed report. There would be more murders in the pattern, of that she was quite certain. And getting a Peabody award for this project … was that too much to hope? God, how lovely would *that* be? And how much of a boost towards a national slot would it mean?

Lynne began typing her outline. By the time she'd gotten just the bare-bones outline down in a format that she found reasonably satisfactory, it was almost 6:30 in the evening. Save the file, there'd be plenty of time to work on it again later. Right now it was time for supper. Time to savor the lifestyle she'd earned, and try (unsuccessfully as always) to block out the memories of all of the hardscrabble times she'd had after her parents had broken up (had they really? She'd never had the urge to go back and check on them) with one final unbelievable screaming match after another of her father's many affairs. That was the point at which she had run out of the house with nothing but the clothes on her back and the money in her wallet, to make her own way on the streets and never go back, a fourteen-year-old girl who luckily could (and often did) pass for eighteen or nineteen. A girl who would do

107

whatever was necessary, *whatever*, to make her own way to the top. And did. And would continue to. No matter what. Bet on it.

Chapter 7

Marjory Bergstrom approached the house with a certain amount of trepidation. Always before, she and Ron had had their trysts in motels, hotels, and other rent-a-rooms around town. This was the first time he'd had her to his house, because this time his wife was off helping her sister after the birth of her niece in Denver. They had at least a night to be together, perhaps more. It was going to be quite exciting, once she got past the issue of Ron's wife in her own mind. And she had to admit that honestly, if that had been all that much of a hurdle for her, she probably wouldn't have been carrying on with him in the first place.

The house itself was nothing special. Light beige stucco that looked as though it had originally been truly white, a brick-outlined archway over the front walk where it went through the low wall surrounding the entryway courtyard, and, like so many Tucson houses, only one story high. A pitched red tile roof and natural, i.e. desert, landscaping. Marjory had driven by it before, of course, if only because she had to see where Ron lived. But there was nothing, other than Ron himself, to make it stand out in her mind from the other houses around it in the older neighborhood north of Fort Lowell Road.

Ron Harris was trying to set a more sedate pace between the two of them today than he had in the past. The two of them tended to have some rather energetic sex when they finally got down to business, but he seemed to have, or at least be able to counterfeit, some appropriate degree of empathy for the nerves he probably figured Marjory would undoubtedly feel, at least at first, about being in his home, in the place where another woman normally held sway. He

109

met her at the door with a glass of wine for her, and gently led her to the couch. As they sat, he suggested that since they had plenty of time, they could just relax there and enjoy each other's company for a while rather than rush into anything. Marjory found his concern reassuring and caring. So much so, in fact, that when he finally reached for her and began to slowly unbutton her blouse, she let him do so without protest. In return, after he had undone the third button, she began to unbutton his shirt as well and then proceeded to twine her fingers through the hair on his chest.

When a strange figure walked into the room, though, both of them jumped to their feet. "Who the hell are you and what are you doing in my house?" Ron was indignant.

The figure was dressed in almost blindingly white clothes, with a white cap and blue gloves. Marjory's heart sank. This did not feel good *at all*.

Then Ron squinted at the newcomer. "Don't I know you? I'm sure I've seen your face before. Aren't you ..." The killer lifted a large pistol, and a bullet to the stomach stopped his question before he could finish. Marjory's eyes widened as he doubled over in pain, or perhaps shock, but she stood as though rooted to the spot by the unexpected assault. The next bullet impacted just above the bridge of her nose and the back of her skull erupted in a fan spray of blood, bone fragments, and brain matter. Her wineglass dropped from nerveless fingers as her body collapsed into a heap on the floor, her blood mixing with the wine that spilled from the remains of her shattered glass.

A second bullet hit Ron, this one in the groin. He, too, fell to the floor, now writhing in pain that had finally gotten through to his brain. Another shot shattered his right shoulder, the next his left knee. Two more directly into his genitals, then another pair into his heart. His face was left undamaged as the killer made some adjustments to the crime scene before walking out the back door to the patio.

A black plastic garbage bag awaited the gloves, painter's whites, booties and pistol there. Within minutes, there was merely another civic-minded citizen walking along the next road to the north, picking up some trash along the roadside for a couple of blocks and bagging it conscientiously along the way before eventually climbing back into a waiting car and driving off. Nothing noteworthy at all. Nothing to cause any onlooker to pay any attention to what was going on.

****

The house was in a more crowded neighborhood than the last couple of houses Reesa had been called to. In that neighborhood, of course, that meant only that there were houses every hundred yards or so along the street, not that they were crowded together like the houses even closer in to downtown Tucson. The vegetation was also a bit younger than some of the more established neighborhoods, such as where Reesa herself lived. While that meant that any watcher would have had a fairly clear line of sight in most directions from eye height, the sight lines in the area were still blocked from about chest level down to the ground with cholla, prickly pear, yucca, mesquite and other native vegetation. Reesa looked around carefully, but she saw no sign of Jeff or any other watcher. She also realized that if he were crouching somewhere out there in the scrub and cactus to the north, or peering around any number of houses she could see, he could easily be invisible to her.

Not really her problem. Or her concern at the immediate moment.

The house itself was a bit less … territorial was the word that occurred to her. Her house had low ceilings, thick exterior walls and was generally built along lines that would have been at least passingly familiar to the people who'd lived here in adobe houses when Tucson was so young that Indian raids were not only a recent memory but at times still a present danger. This house was probably built in the mid to late 1960's and had a somewhat more airy and open feel to it.

Inside the house, the basics of the scene were still the same familiar ones. The medical examiner was working on one body, the other body was waiting with hands already bagged, a crime scene tech was walking the grid around the room, but this time there were several cartridge cases on the floor, each one flagged with its little yellow evidence marker. Another tech was picking them up and bagging them. He looked up at her as she came in, and she said, "So let me guess. These aren't going to help us any."

He chuckled. "Reesa, after I get these back to the lab, I can tell you whether they all came from the same gun. I can tell you, at least in broad terms, what the class characteristics are and from that, what the gun is or at least could be that they were shot in. Not necessarily the specific model, but I can definitely narrow it a long way down. I can do much the same with the bullets that we get out of the bodies and surroundings." He hooked a thumb over at the victims. "But without a gun to compare them to, I probably can't say for sure which particular model of gun fired them, much less tie the bullets and cases together, and if there's no record of that specific gun in any of the databases, I won't have one single idea who may have fired the shots, even just from the standpoint of which unsub from which other unsolved crime did these two in. You know that."

Reesa grinned at him. "Hey, John, can you blame me for wanting you to pull the magic rabbit out of your hat? I mean, I can dream, can't I? And uh, 'unsub'? You've been watching too much TV." John just snorted in response.

"Look, Reesa, you really don't *want* me to give you more than that. Let's say the bullets could come from gun A, B, or C. The cases could come from C, D, or E. I tell you all of this, and you're going to be looking for gun C. But the shooter could have gone to the range and picked up a bunch of brass some Fed, or one of the security guys from one of the major corporations around here, left behind – they get their ammo for free, and every reloader is picking up what they've shot – so while the shooter who fired these cases used A, and the killer in this case used gun E, you're not looking for either one. Way too many variables.

Then, just to add one or two more possible wrinkles, let's say that these bullets are .40 caliber, just like the cases. If these cases didn't come from the killer's gun, then he might have been using a 10mm, and there's no way to tell that from a .40 with what we have here or even with the bullets we pull out of the bodies, because both rounds use exactly the same bullets. Hell, I suppose he *could* have loaded the bullets into .38-40 cases or even an old .401 Powermag and shot them with a revolver or two, then left us this brass to throw us even farther off."

Reesa just shook her head. "You're right, John. Way too many variables and, at this point, too much information as well. Tell me what you can when you've got something definite, okay? However little it may be?" Walking by the woman's body, dutifully trailed by Chuck, Reesa could readily observe that she had been felled by a single shot. The spatter pattern of blood, brain matter, and bone fragments behind her strongly suggested that she'd been shot standing and dropped where she was shot.

Not so the man near her. Reesa could see at least half a dozen impacts without looking too hard, and smears on the floor indicated that he'd moved at least some during the time he was being shot, although shattered tiles visible underneath him showed that at least some of the shots were delivered while he was down and probably pretty much right where his body was lying. The ME's off-the-cuff account told her much the same sort of information.

Very much like the way Bridgton and Johnson were killed, she thought. *What do you bet she's not married? And the shots directly into his crotch are very much like cutting his genitals off, aren't they?* She carefully guarded the grimness she felt. Bending down, she felt the woman's left hand through the paper bag. No, she didn't seem to have any sort of wedding ring on, any more than Sarah Johnson had. *That's probably significant, but what does it mean? What does it tell me that I can use? If anything? Does it mean these murders are connected to those? And most important, does it tell me anything about who did this? I want something to at least point me in the right direction. Anything.*

At least this time the spouse hadn't been the one to call in the homicides. A neighbor had heard the noise of the shots, muffled though it was by the insulation of both houses, gotten suspicious, and eventually come over to look

114

in the picture window. Hard as it could be to see inside Tucson houses with the sun behind her, she had managed to see the bodies lying there. *Thank God for busybodies.* If nothing else, the wife could be spared the worst of it. She, poor woman, would merely have to cope with the aftermath. Assuming, of course, that she hadn't been the perpetrator. According to the neighbor, so the responding officer's report said, the wife was out of town. That would have to be checked out.

As Reesa walked from the house past their car, so she and Chuck could go check out the residence of the neighbor who had called it in, she saw the inevitable Channel 12 news van (It now had a banner reading 'First On The Scene!' painted under the channel and network symbols on the side, above 'Up Close and Personal!') outside with the equally-inevitable Lynne Fox setting up for a report. *Bitch.* Chuck broke the silence that hung between them. "You know, back before I became a cop, I used to be disappointed by how hard it was for the reporters to get the cops actually on the cases to talk to them. Now I'm one of the cops, and I can't begin to tell you how grateful I am that the department won't even *let* us talk to them."

Reesa grinned at him in response. "Got that right. And especially *her*. You're the lucky fellow here. She isn't even going to *try* to talk to you while I'm here."

He went on, switching topics. "What puzzles me about these murders is that there's no sign of any sort of arrangement of the bodies and no sign of any sexual activity. Other than on the part of the victims, that is, although they've not been killed while they're going at it. And it sort of feels to me like there ought to be something

115

sexual from the killer. Or maybe some sort of signature. You know, serial killer sort of stuff."

He had a point, Reesa thought. "Well, yeah, *if* we're dealing with a serial killer, anyway. Now if we found semen or other body fluids from the killer at the scene, we'd have some good evidence to point to who he is if he's in CODIS, or at least confirm an ID once we have a suspect. And, assuming these killings are connected, which I'm not ready to at this point, given the varying ways these people are being killed, then there are several, possibly even plenty of bodies he couldn't arrange anyway. Maybe it's just not his thing. Their thing. Whoever's thing. But one way or another, whoever did this couple clearly gets off by offing people. He just may not be getting off … like that. Whether he's responsible for our other murders or not."

And still no sign of Jeff. Maybe this wasn't one of his cases. Maybe he hadn't gotten here yet. Or maybe he was here, just not somewhere where she could see him. *Or maybe I don't really care,* she thought.

****

The killer took some extra time to savor the memory of a job *very* well done. There was always that much more satisfaction from doing it face to face, and the sexual release from such an experience, well, it just had to be felt to be believed. Taking a partner, *any* partner, to bed, no matter how good (some past ones, one in particular – a momentary flash of anger there – had been *very* good indeed), paled in comparison. There was just *nothing* to compare to it. As a way to get off, it was utterly beyond description. And then when you came down from the high,

116

even just the memory was almost good enough to set it off again. *Thank you, God!*

Changing methods constantly meant that inevitably some killings had to be done from a distance. There are, after all, only so many ways of killing someone, two someones, actually, in person and being in a position to watch them die. Especially when it's necessary to avoid duplication. When the opportunity arises, though, then doing it that way is just so *delicious*. Maybe the next time could be another one done face to face. Ooooh, two in a row? That was something to think seriously about. What a way to be about God's work.

****

Bob Jones pulled out another trolley of chairs to set up for the meeting. There was something about these meetings, both the setting up and taking down, and about the meetings themselves, that he found so much more satisfying than doing the same sort of work during the day at his regular job. Mary seemed to be of the same mind. He and Mary had found themselves, their true calling, he felt, in being with Henry Blodden and the Avowed. Being his first adherents, in fact, ever since they took him in to live in the little guest apartment behind their garage.

He and Mary still went to work each day at Desert Saguaro Lodge, but not until he and Mary had encountered Henry had they been so moved by anything that they would willingly somewhat curtail the extra income they earned by painting houses, for Bob, and cleaning them, for Mary. Nor did Bob have as much time any more to go to the library or to sit in Bookman's when he could, sometimes for hours on end, reading murder mysteries and playing them out in his mind. Now, he and Mary had God's work to do. And there was always going to be plenty of God's work. After all, if God wanted there to be an end to this, His work, He was perfectly capable of stopping people from sinning, wasn't He? So as long as there continued to be sinners in the world (and there always would be, of course) ....

Of course, there would also always be people who needed painting done, or houses cleaned, too. Wasn't cleanliness next to godliness? That probably meant, he thought, that everything he did, everything Mary did, was, in some manner, God's work, didn't it? And both he and Mary had more jobs coming up soon.

Bob and Mary were both aware, at some level, of how comparatively invisible they were. For them, it was a job skill, honed over the years of bringing refreshments into occupied meeting rooms, fixing the inevitable accidents and near-disasters, and generally doing whatever needed doing while fading into the background and making themselves as unnoticed, and unnoticeable, as possible during whatever was happening in the meeting rooms. They had learned how to do that very well indeed. It was something they did exceptionally well, and it was a serious help in what they did. In *everything* they did.

****

As usual, Henry opened his service with what had now become his standard lines. He greeted the congregation, welcomed the newcomers, and began his spiel. "It's time for faith!"

And once again the entire congregation – for that truly was how he was now looking at them (when he didn't see them as sheep to be fleeced, of course) – shouted the last line out loud: "THE AVOWED!" Tonight he gave them just a bit more than usual. Not only did he preach hellfire and damnation for those who strayed, but for the first time, he explicitly spoke of them coming to no good. Even possibly coming to a violent end, if the transgression merited it. Henry seemed to be quite convinced of it, in fact, as he got into the swing of things, and since he was ad-libbing at that point, he got *quite* a ways into it. One of his talents was delivering a good line of patter on the fly, and he made full use of it.

By the time he was done, the whole congregation was filled with righteous anger towards those who strayed. It could even be described as righteous fury without exaggerating. Well, not *too* much, anyway. Henry was pleased, very pleased indeed. Raising this sort of emotion, this sort of commitment to one's partner, this sort of rage towards the unfaithful – how could this be anything *but* God's work?

And these people were so easy to sway, so easy to channel and direct. So easy to lead, so easy to *drive*. Henry felt *good*. It was almost … sexual, as he thought about it. Not as good as bedding a partner, or even … but there were definite sexual overtones to this, too. That was worth thinking about. Of course, if they knew of his own extra-curricular activities, they wouldn't be so pleased with him, would they? But they'd never find out. He'd make very sure of that. After all, it was God's work, too, wasn't it? And since it was God's work, since God so obviously wanted him to do it, God would help him keep it all secret, wouldn't He? God? Henry snorted to himself.

****

Lynne Fox sat back and read the document on her computer screen. Her proposed special report was really beginning to take shape, and from what she had down already, it was going to be a real bombshell. Normally with a special report of this nature, she'd have her staff do much of the preparation, much of the initial stages of setting up a report like this. Well, not 'like this.' There *was* no special report 'like this.' This one was *her* baby, through and through. For several reasons. And the name she'd picked for the perpetrator ... that was definitely going to make viewers sit up and take notice.

Might help get it picked up nationally as well, which certainly wouldn't hurt her possibilities of landing that national anchor slot she wanted. Craved. That she *deserved*. Overall, the report looked to her like it had just about everything it needed to really catch fire with the viewers. A little bit more polish, then just one more pair of murders and she could finish it, submit it to the station management.

Once they gave her their preliminary approval – *of course they would!* – Lynne could begin getting the graphics ready that she'd need to actually tape the report. That was work that she could put her staff on to doing. Make her life easier. This would be just the first report of a series, she reminded herself. Like she didn't know that already. Lynne couldn't be certain, off the top of her head. Would management submit it for a Peabody? Would she have to ask them to do it? Or if they didn't, or wouldn't, could she submit it herself?

Chapter 8

A quiet tone announced the arrival of an email on Reesa's computer. When she pulled it up, she motioned Chuck over to her side of the desks. "We got a thumbprint off one of the shell cases from the Harris house. Look at this." She gestured towards the screen.

"Huh. Not only in the system, but Border Patrol." The face of a young lady in a green uniform stared out of the screen at them. Her name was Gabriela Marquez. "I'll see where she is today." He circled back around to his own desk and reached for the phone. It only took the one call to locate her, but Chuck had another wrinkle. "They said they want one of their own Internal Affairs people present when we speak to her."

Reesa arched her eyebrow. "I don't see why. Whatever's going on, it's got nothing to do with her job. On the other hand, of course, one phone call from them to whoever's running the show at the checkpoint and we'd never get to see her without him, I suppose. You did tell them not to call ahead and warn her we were coming?" Chuck simply nodded.

Driving south on I-19, they discussed how they wanted to approach her. "I think we need to keep in mind that the crime scene was bare of all usable trace except the brass," Reesa said. "Frankly, I find it just a bit difficult to accept that anyone who can clean up a scene that well afterwards would be so sloppy as to leave a clearly thumb-printed piece of brass, with their *own* thumbprint, right out there in the middle of the floor. It's just a bit too pat, you know what I mean?"

Chuck was nodding. "But we can't forget that sometimes it's just that sort of slip-up that lets us nail a suspect."

"Very true. I'm just suggesting that we start slowly and not make any presumptions. Let's try her on the photo of Harris first."

"I'm glad we were able to find that photo of Marjorie Bergstrom. Thought we might need a good one."

Reesa chuckled. "I'm glad we did, too, because you're right, we might need it. And getting shot right between the eyes somehow tends to spoil the portrait." Chuck snorted.

There was no crossover at the checkpoint that loomed over the northbound lanes north of Tubac, near Agua Linda, so they had to go down to the next exit to turn around. Reesa looked around as they crossed over the freeway. "I never get down here. You?" Chuck shook his head.

They went through the checkpoint in the right-hand lane, flashing their badges at the Border Patrol officer waiting to ask their citizenship status. They pulled off the road by the trailer just north of the checkpoint shelter. Again holding up their badges as they got out, an officer walked up. "I'm Supervisor Plainton, and I'm in charge here," he said. "What can we do for–" he squinted at the badge Reesa was holding – "Tucson's finest?"

Chuck smiled but made no response. Reesa simply said, "We need to speak with one of your officers, a Gabriela Marquez."

He paused for a moment. "Can you tell me why?"

Reesa kept her face still. "Her name came up in an investigation we're conducting. That's all we can say at this moment."

The supervisor looked thoughtful. "I got a call from the main office telling me you'd be here to speak to one of my officers and that they were sending someone from OIA to sit in. He's – there he is now."

Another car pulled in and the Internal Affairs officer, in the same green uniform as everybody else except the detectives, walked up, his hand extended. "Steve Archuleta. I understand you need to speak with one of our people." He, Plainton, and Reesa conferred for about two minutes as she filled him in on the circumstances of the situation. She asked him not to interrupt their questioning unless it was vital, and he agreed. "I've got to warn you, though, she's likely to be really unhappy about having me here. Now I know you had no choice, but if she is, let me take care of her on that angle, okay?"

Finally he nodded to Plainton, who looked around, then motioned one nearby officer over to him. "Hartsman, go relieve Marquez," he said. "She's working the far lane. Send her over here." The officer trotted off, dodging the cars as they started up again after satisfying the officers questioning the drivers. Shortly Marquez walked up, drinking from a bottle of water. "Gabriela, these detectives say they need to speak to you." He turned to Reesa. "Any particular place? We don't really have any place you could use inside the trailer, and anyway, our air conditioning's on the fritz today. Would that table work?" He motioned at one of the picnic tables under the shade shelter adjoining the trailer to the south.

Chuck was nodding. Reesa introduced the two of them and Archuleta, who garnered a concerned look from Marquez. Then Reesa simply said, "That table will be fine. Officer Marquez?" She gestured for the officer to precede them, and Archuleta simply tagged along, saying nothing. Marquez looked at Reesa, apparently hoping for some clue in her expression as to what was happening, but Reesa kept her carefully-schooled neutral expression in place as they walked over. Archuleta offered nothing either when she looked at him again. Reesa took a seat next to Marquez on the bench, while Chuck and the OIA officer sat across from them. They let her sit in silence at first.

"So what's this about? Am I some sort of suspect in something? Or since you've brought OIA in, am I supposed to have done something wrong? When OIA shows up, it usually means that the shit's about to hit the fan, and I seem to be the only target here." Her voice was getting steadily louder.

Steve Archuleta leaned forward. "Officer Marquez, my being here wasn't their idea, and they had no say in the matter. There's also no investigation being carried out on you by OIA. I'm here to protect the Patrol's interests, nothing more, and if nothing comes of this, then I leave and there's no file on you at my office. In the event that this goes down any other way, you'll be protected."

This seemed to settle her down somewhat, although by no means completely. She turned to Reesa. "I assume you're not here just to pass the time of day." Marquez still seemed just a bit put out, possibly by having her work day interrupted, or maybe just defensive. *Can't be helped,* Reesa thought. *That's the breaks of the game.*

Chuck began. "No, you're not a suspect at this time. Your name just came up in an investigation we're conducting, and we wanted to be sure we touched all the bases."

Reesa slid a picture of Ron Harris from the folder she was carrying and pushed it over in front of Gabriela. "Do you know this man?"

Marquez looked at the picture with some evident curiosity, but no other emotion, before looking up at Reesa and then Chuck. "Doesn't look like he's in very good shape, does he?" When neither detective responded, she went back to the picture. "Nope, never saw him before. If he's dead, do I presume that's the subject of your investigation? How'd my name come up?"

Reesa didn't answer. Instead she pulled another picture from her file, this one the shot of Marjory Bergstrom that the detectives had gotten from her home. "How about this woman?"

Marquez took the picture in her hands to see it better. After several minutes, she said, "This one looks healthier than the other, huh? Is this your suspect? Or is this another dead one?" She set the picture down on top of the one of Ron Harris. From what Reesa could see, Officer Marquez seemed utterly disinterested in both of them. Perhaps she really didn't know them.

Chuck leaned forward. "Where were you this past Tuesday afternoon, say between noon and four pm?"

Marquez's eyes narrowed. "So I *am* a suspect? Aren't you supposed to be … no, you're not arresting me, so you're not certain yet. Well, I was right here. Got plenty of witnesses, too. At least three-quarters of the guys here now and hundreds of motorists. I got here early in the morning and didn't leave until after five. So if that's when this happened, you can just cross me off your list, okay?"

Chuck sat up straighter. Reesa said, "These two were killed together Tuesday, in the early afternoon, in Tucson. Your fingerprint turned up on a shell casing at the murder scene."

Marquez's eyes got wide. "My fingerprint? I never saw either of these two before and I wasn't anywhere near Tucson then. Besides, I guarantee you, if I caught my man screwing some other woman, I wouldn't shoot him!" Her voice was getting quite strident. "He'd choke to death, because I'd cut off his dick and stuff it down his throat!" Reesa and Chuck exchanged glances.

Reesa put her calm, concerned face on. "Do you know a Nathan Bridgton?" Marquez shook her head. "How about Sarah Johnson?" Again the head shake. She didn't appear to either of the detectives to be dissembling; she seemed genuinely unaware of both names. Chuck wasn't as good at concealing his emotions as Reesa; his puzzlement was evident, at least to anyone who knew him. Marquez wasn't looking at him, though, as her attention was squarely on Reesa by now.

"More victims? Was this last Tuesday, too? Should I be getting a lawyer?" She glanced at Archuleta, but he remained as silent and detached as he'd been all along.

Reesa shook her head. "No, I don't think so. Not at this time. But can you give me any reason why your fingerprint should show up at a crime scene when you weren't anywhere near the place?"

Marquez shrugged. "On a piece of brass? Got no idea. We go to the range, we practice, we shoot. We leave the brass lying around, or we sweep it up, toss it in a bucket and walk away. That's the last we see of it. I got no idea where it goes from there."

Again Reesa and Chuck exchanged glances. This time, though, Reesa stood up. "Thank you, Officer Marquez, for your time. I believe we're done here, at least for now. You can go back to work."

Marquez stood up as well and stepped back across the bench of the picnic table. "Go back to work? Just like that? You come in here, wondering if I'm a murder suspect, bring along someone from Internal Affairs, ask me a bunch of questions and now I'm just supposed to go back to work?"

Reesa looked her in the eyes, the expression on her face hardening just a bit. "Yes, Officer, just like that. At least at this time, we're accepting what you've told us, and that takes you off the list of possible suspects. If anything changes, we'll get back with you. In the meantime, you can go back to work. Just like that."

Marquez flounced off – Reesa couldn't find any better word to describe it. The set of her shoulders suggested that she was furious, but neither Reesa nor Chuck cared very much. How the fingerprint had gotten onto the brass was still an unanswered question, but if Marquez had been here, with a dozen or so good witnesses (uniformed witnesses were always good on the stand) when the murders were committed, it was going to take a lot more than an errant fingerprint to make anything stick, even if there were something there. Slide her name way down the list.

For now.

Archuleta looked at Reesa. "Get up on the wrong side of the bed this morning, detective?"

127

Reesa looked at him. "Huh?"

"Let's simply say that I thought your people skills weren't at their best just then. I was wondering if this was your usual method, or is there something more going on? You dismissed her kind of cavalierly after pulling her off work and questioning her about a murder, two murders – or was it four? – that she might have been involved in. Especially with someone from OIA sitting in as well. I'm sure you must realize how upsetting all of that's going to be to most people."

Reesa shook her head. "Actually, I knew it at the time. I was just about to apologize when she blew up, and then .... I'm just ... we're a bit frustrated, okay? These cases seem to consist entirely of dead ends or no information whatsoever, and we're tired of being taken for a ride by our killers, which has been happening all too often lately. I also didn't get a lot of sleep last night. Not that that's any excuse, but that's how it is."

Chuck covered a yawn. "Sorry, I didn't either."

Archuleta appeared a bit mollified. "I guess I'll go see if I can placate her a bit. If you don't mind, that is. No reason for the two of you to stick around for that, and at least she's not angry with me. I don't think so, anyway."

Chuck and Reesa thanked him before heading back to their car.

Chapter 9

Reesa stepped into the cool darkness of the house and waited for her eyes to adjust. As she took a step towards the bodies, a crime scene tech hollered, "Stop!" When Reesa turned towards him to see if she was the problem, he said, "You're just about to walk through an impression and ruin it. It's probably not going to give us much of anything worth mentioning, but I've got to get it anyway." He crouched down and gestured. "I believe it's a butt imprint with shoeprints, such as they are, in front. Let me get it up first."

Fascinated, Reesa watched as the tech dusted the impression, photographed it, and then picked it up with tape lifts. He had to use four of the biggest size lifts to get the entire impression, laying each one down in order, carefully, to cover the entire area. When he straightened up with the last one, she said, "So tell me what you got here."

"Well, near as I can make out, the killer was sitting here cross-legged. No, scratch that. *Somebody* was sitting here cross-legged, and I'd say in just about the same time frame as the murders. Draw your own conclusions about who it was. Personally, I'm betting that it was the killer. But what do I know? I mean, that's *your* job, not mine. I just gather the evidence." He grinned. Reesa looked at the bodies. Sitting there, the killer would have been in position to simply watch the pair, to look them in the eyes, as they died. "After a while, the killer drew his feet most of the way together. Probably at that point he brought his knees up and wrapped his arms around them, but I can't tell that from simply the impression on the floor. It's just the directionality of the foot impressions that suggests they were out farther and on their sides before they were pulled in, plus my own interpretation of what I'd be doing if I pulled my own feet in like that. So it's not absolutely certain, just how I read the impression. Tile doesn't take great impressions."

Reesa clapped him on the shoulder. "Don't feel bad about it. That's more usable trace than we've gotten out of any previous crime scene like this – hell, out of all of them put together. Well, trace, anyway. We don't know how usable it's going to be. Anything more to get from it?"

The tech looked at his tape lifts. "I may be able to give you something on the cloth the killer was wearing, but from the looks of this, it'll be little more than an educated guess."

"Whatever you can get, huh? Even an educated guess is better than nothing, and nothing is exactly what we've had so far." She stepped over to the bodies themselves. The ME was just setting up and hadn't yet disturbed the bodies' bindings. Chuck hung back just a bit, trying to get the bigger picture.

Both bodies had duct tape over their mouths and around their wrists. They lay on their stomachs, next to each other, with their feet drawn up behind. The man had apparently knocked against the coffee table in his struggles, but the wedding vase on it (*wasn't* that *just too stereotypical for words? Or maybe too ironic!*) had just bounced on the Indian rug beneath it and now lay on its side by one leg of the table. The victims' heads were up, sort of, although they were sagging against the restraints now. Each body had its feet pulled up behind it, and ropes led from the feet of each body to the throat of the other. From the looks of the ropes and the angles of the lower

130

legs, it was apparent that only by holding the legs up as high as possible could tension be kept off the other person's neck. After giving the restraints a fair amount of consideration, she said to the doctor, "If I understand this one correctly, then as one gets tired and lets his or her feet go back a bit, it chokes the partner. Then when that partner loses consciousness, *his* feet go back and that chokes the first one."

The ME nodded. "That's how it appears to me as well."

Reesa looked back towards where the tech had found the impression. "And all the while the killer is sitting right there on the floor in front of them, apparently quite comfortable, watching them fight their muscles, trying not to kill the one they were carrying on with. Then whichever one was weaker killed the other first, after which …. This is one truly sick puppy we're dealing with here."

The ME was nodding. "Sure looks that way to me, too. You aren't just figuring this out now, though, are you, Reesa? I thought you were better than that." He grinned.

Reesa grinned back. "Gee, thanks, Doc. No, I've known it for some time. But this" – she gestured at where the killer had been sitting – "really takes the cake. Of course, I guess if you're getting something out of the killing, then watching them up close and personal as they die has to be the icing. Or maybe it's having them kill each other. Or both. But something seems to have been awfully enticing for this killer."

"I guess it was."

Chuck stepped up with two wallets in his hand. "Got their IDs here. Jonathon McGuire and Robin Gutierrez. It's her house. He lives up in the foothills. Her husband's out on the back patio with Romero. And he looks a bit familiar to me. I just can't place where I've seen him. McGuire, I mean. I haven't seen the husband yet."

Reesa peered at the body in question. "I've seen him before, too. Wait a minute." She stood still while her mind worked furiously. "Got it! He's one of the Avowed. He was there the time that Schuler and I went. He almost got up to testify, looked around, and then apparently thought better of it, so he sat back down. Wife's this short redhead. She seemed sort of reluctant to, ah, share her experiences. That might be why he didn't say anything."

"Yeah, now I remember. They were right up front the time that Pat and I went. He's got a voice that really carries, at least in the living room we met in then. Well, he did. She kinda faded into the woodwork, I thought, although not as well as that couple that helps Henry."

Reesa said nothing in response. Did the Avowed keep any sort of membership records, she wondered? If nothing else, she and Chuck could get their own photo records of people leaving some of the services. Not a lot of evidence, but then these cases hadn't offered much evidence of any kind at all, so far. That's assuming they were all connected, which Reesa still hadn't fully concluded yet. Well, no, there hadn't been much evidence whether they were connected or not.

And of course, she and Chuck had to go pay a visit to Mrs. McGuire when they were done with Raul Gutierrez and left here, too. Given this connection, though, maybe it was time to begin paying closer attention to the Avowed. It certainly couldn't hurt, and if nothing else, it made it look like they were doing something instead of sitting on their hands. She just had to find someone to go back to the meetings with. Someone other than Schuler. *Anyone* other than Schuler.

****

"Let the whole world hear who we are!"

And as always, the entire congregation shouted it out loud: "THE AVOWED!" Normally, at this point, Henry launched into his service. This time would be different. Very different. He didn't begin speaking immediately. Instead he stood in front of them, his eyes roaming over their faces, settling only momentarily on a few specific individuals about whom he had … reservations. And on a few he found particularly … interesting.

Finally he began to speak. "I've spoken before about what awaits those who stray, what awaits those who violate the oaths they've sworn to their partners, to their *sacred* partners. Brothers and sisters, now you can see for yourselves what happens to those who leave the path of faithfulness to their partners. Now you can see for yourselves what it means to come to no good. Now you can see for yourselves what it means to die a horrible death!" He stood stock-still, using nothing more than his voice and his gaze to hold them. He did it well, and he knew it. Tonight he put everything he had into it. Brief as it would be, and it would be, it was going to be a night for them all to remember. He'd make sure of that.

"Some of you remember Jon and Peggy McGuire. Peggy can't be with us tonight, because she is bereft. Her husband, her partner, her *sacred* partner, Jon McGuire, broke his oath to her." Now he thundered: "He violated his oath to her!"

Henry's voice then dropped until the congregation had to strain to hear it. Not a sound disturbed the silence in

133

the room other than his voice. "Tonight Jon McGuire twists and burns in hellfire, damned for all eternity, because he broke his vows. Not three days ago, Jon McGuire was murdered along with the woman with whom he was breaking his vows. With whom he was carrying on. A most terrible murder, because he and she were strangled in their own weakness."

His voice returned to a normal level. "Brothers and sisters, let this be a warning to you. I warned you of the hellfire and damnation that await those who stray, and I've told you that such people will come to no good." He thundered the next line. "Here is the proof!" Snatching up the Daily Star, he waved it in front of the congregation, already folded so that the article on the murder was uppermost. The headline on the article read, *Local Businessman and Lover Murdered During Tryst*. The only sound in the room was the faint noise from foot traffic in the store outside.

Finally Henry let his arm fall. After a minute, he raised his arm again and jabbed the paper at the congregation. "Don't let this happen to you!" Setting the paper down, he then turned and walked away from the front of the room. It took several minutes before people realized that the service for tonight was over with no more than that brief exhortation, and began to stand up to leave. The mood in the room was particularly somber. As they passed the collection baskets that Bob and Mary were holding, on their way to the door, most people stopped to drop in some money. Henry later found that the collection had surpassed all previous records. And not one of the people who'd been there could have said, an hour later, whether the baskets were sitting on tables or being held by someone.

****

The killer savored a number of memories. Some were good, some were not so good. But the discovery had been made and repeatedly reinforced that killing was a lot like sex. When it was good, it was great. It was … utterly indescribable. When it was bad, well, it was still pretty good. And the ones where the killer was able to *watch* the victims die, look them in the eyes as their lives ebbed and their eyes dimmed until the light of life finally winked out, those were absolutely the best. Like this last one. The killer shuddered slightly, very pleased. In more ways than one. This was definitely God's work. This was *right*. And it just felt so *damn* good.

****

Lynne Fox waited while the printer hummed its way through her proposal for the special report she'd drawn up. She'd put lots of hours into it. Not just her own, but by now her small staff had put a couple of dozen, no, make that several dozen hours into research, legwork, and (after the report was largely finished, of course) generally batting the concept around with her, helping her fine-tune it. The structure and work, though, were all hers. *All* hers. She was going to get all of the credit, and dammit, she was going to *earn* that credit and deserve *every bit* of it. Now it was time for the payoff.

Read through it once more, make sure every point is touched on, the wording is the best she can manage, the copy is clean and complete. Make another copy and then give a quick run-through to the accompanying PowerPoint presentation to make sure that it, too, is clean, complete and free of any goofs. If there were any, somebody on her staff was going to pay dearly for it. Then take the whole package to the news director.

Pitch the concept directly to him with both the hard copy and the PowerPoint. Then, if he's anything less than completely onboard, convince him that it will get viewers. Lynne was utterly certain that it would get viewers like nothing else (naturally she would be), and then (of course) it would in turn lead to an ongoing series of reports that the entire city would hang on. Probably even beyond the city. Phoenix and the rest of the state for sure. Maybe the region, even (possibly) the whole nation.

Reports, of course, that Lynne Fox herself would do, each and every one of them. Her staff could help even more, at that point, but *her* name and *her* face would be on them. Her name and her face would be all *over* them. She can *do* this.

She, Lynne Fox, is going to be a household name all over Tucson, if not beyond. No, definitely beyond. The Phoenix network affiliate would probably, almost certainly pick up the reports, and that means most of Arizona would see her in action. Then maybe she'll become a weekday anchor. Maybe she can even get out of this little backwoods excuse for a city and get into a *real* market. Or even a *national* gig.

All it really takes is one good break, right? And God breaks those who don't make the breaks for themselves, right? By now, this was a story she knew by heart. All she needed was a chance to tell it to the viewers, and she'd make sure she got that. Maybe she could even pry a statement out of that close-mouthed bitch, Detective Malloy. God knew she'd keep trying. Didn't this Malloy broad know *anything* about how women have to stick together? Just a little help would be nice. One little bit of information, one comment on the cases. If not, well, she was plenty photogenic enough to make a nice backdrop to the comments about the refusal of the detectives to comment on the cases. What the hell, even if it wasn't one of her cases, that image would work. Nobody else would know or care anyway, and it'd teach her not to blow off the press. It'd teach her not to blow off Lynne Fox.

Chapter 10

Jeff looked around to see how much of a buffer zone they had in the restaurant. It was later than the usual lunchtime; nobody else was seated at the immediately neighboring tables, and nobody at all seemed to be paying attention to them. He was still cautious, though, and kept his voice low. Appearances could be deceiving. "You know, I have to wonder if they're all connected."

Reesa cocked her head. "If what are all connected?"

"These couples murders. You've got – what, three or four cases of them now?"

Reesa hesitated. She didn't like talking about her work to outsiders, but she had to admit that she was pretty consistently drawing a blank here. Maybe two heads were better than one, and perhaps, just perhaps, an outsider – this outsider, anyway – might come up with something that she and Chuck had been unable to see or find so far. It wasn't like he didn't have some connection to at least a few of the cases, anyway. "Four. The stabbings at the Bridgton residence, the gassing at the Morales residence, the gunshot victims at the Harris residence and the strangulations at the Gutierrez residence. And you didn't show up at the Gutierrez place until later, when Chuck and I were just leaving."

Jeff shook his head. "It was a new case and I hadn't had the opportunity to pick her up and establish her routine at that point. It was just dumb luck that I was able to get there at all. The Harris case I hadn't even known about until I saw it on the news." He was persistent, though, and returned to the original topic. "You still don't think these cases are all connected."

Reesa looked at him, approaching being annoyed but fighting her automatic reaction. He might wind up giving her something to work with, and she figured that having been involved in three of the cases perhaps gave him a certain right to talk to her about them. "Well, the honest truth is that I don't know one way or the other. I'm trained to see patterns, you know, but in these, I don't think there's a clear pattern. There's no signature, no repetition, no … there's plenty to suggest to me that they are, but I don't see the sort of structure that would convince me. And so far, at least, there aren't any of the sorts of clues that usually signal us that we're dealing with a serial killer. Chuck thinks they may be related, but he admits that it's just a hunch for him, so I've been kind of holding him back until he can come up with something more concrete."

"Not the first serial killer to do that sort of thing. Remember Peter Kürten."

Reesa frowned. "Who's he?"

"More like who *was* he. The Vampire of Düsseldorf, the Monster of Düsseldorf, the Düsseldorf Ripper and several other terms. Killed a whole bunch of people in 1929 over the course of about ten months, if I recall correctly. But he killed them all in different ways, too, and the German police took quite some time to realize that the murders were all being done by the same killer."

"And that leaves us with the idea of one killer who leaves us no pattern at all. How are we supposed to figure out who he is? Especially when he leaves us no usable trace evidence at the crime scenes, either?" Her expression betrayed her frustration with the cases. Her fingers trembled with frustration, too, but she stilled them as soon as she noticed the movement. Jeff didn't miss it.

139

"I could suggest that keeping you from finding him is probably at least a part of his intention," he responded dryly, "but I expect you already know that. Anyway, as far as a pattern goes, let me see if I can lay it out the way I see it. First, in every case, one or both of the victims were being unfaithful, and in the Bridgton and – what was the other one? Harris? – the Harris cases, the unfaithful partner was, ah, rather more brutally, or at least spectacularly, murdered than the single one. When both partners were being unfaithful, they've both been killed in similar fashions. Oh, and add in as another part of it that whoever is doing this is, as you noted, very consistently leaving diddly in the way of forensic evidence. That's a pattern right there, isn't it?"

Now Reesa was starting to be a bit more interested. Jeff had just put his finger on something that had been nibbling at the back of her mind but that she hadn't been able to bring to the fore and articulate. In trying to look at them as connected, Chuck had, so far, been operating more on feeling than on anything he could spell out. "So what are you suggesting? That some ... some moralist with alopecia is out there killing people who are cheating on their spouses?"

"Alopecia?"

"That medical condition that leaves you with no hair. I mean, that may not be what's really going on with this killer, but one way or another, I'd normally expect to find enough trace left at the scene to at least suggest if not conclusively establish who the killer is. Or at the very least show me enough about the perpetrator that I can tell it's the same one, case after case. What's so goddam frustrating about these cases is that in each of them, there isn't one

140

goddam *thing* in the way of trace evidence left at the scene that's worth a damn, either for identifying the perpetrator or even just showing that it's the same one each time." Her voice, although still quiet, was heated with emotion.

"Ah." Jeff was nodding. "I see what you're getting at. I probably wouldn't describe the killer exactly that way, but when you boil it all down, then yeah, I suppose that's pretty much exactly what I'm saying. That's your pattern, right there, including making sure the crime scene is as clean as possible afterwards. God! It'd make a great title for a Perry Mason book, you know? *The Case of the Killer House Cleaner*. If he's using different methods of killing his victims each time, then it's going to be harder to spot. But it's still a pattern, and I think you ought to try looking at it like that, that they are all one series of related killings. And ..." – he leaned forward towards her, but only a bit – "what about out in the county? Up in the foothills, say, or even farther out, like in Pinal County? We really don't have any idea just how far afield this person is ranging, if it *is* just one killer doing all of these. I've had one of my own cases up in the foothills go blooey on me in much this same way, about three months before the Bridgton case. For all we know so far, this killer could be operating as far north as Casa Grande or even all the way to Phoenix and beyond."

Reesa chewed on her lower lip as she toyed with her flatware. He did have a point. She'd only looked at killings in Tucson proper, so far, because her department's jurisdiction didn't go much north of River Road. But any killer in the area could also be hitting targets outside of the city, since much of greater Tucson was outside of the city proper, and the Catalina foothills, Marana, Oro Valley, and points even farther north offered a lot of additional area in which a serial killer (if that's what they were dealing with here) could be out hunting.

There was also Green Valley to the south, although the average age of the residents there might offer the killer fewer targets of opportunity. Or maybe older residents made for a hotbed of infidelity. When her mind got to that point, Reesa didn't know and at least right now, at this stage in her life, she decided that she didn't really want to. But she'd check it anyway, just in case. "Let me get Chuck on it. I'll talk to him as soon as I'm back at the station."

Marana, Oro Valley, Green Valley, and the other cities in the area were dry holes, but the Pima County Sheriff had two cases from up in the foothills that fit the basic description. Copies of the county files came in a couple of days later. One case – from the date, that had to be the one Jeff had mentioned – was a bludgeoning. The man, unmarried, took one sharp blow to the back of the head. The woman had been beaten to a pulp. Face crushed beyond recognition, clavicles shattered, ribs not just cracked but repeatedly struck and broken in multiple places, even in one case completely shattered – someone had really gone to town on her. The ME, in his report, suggested from the impacts that a baseball bat had been the weapon, but there hadn't been anything left at the scene.

Faint trace in the impact sites suggested it had been an aluminum bat, so it would have been comparatively easy to clean as well, in addition to being one of several thousand such bats in Tucson. *Hell,* Reesa thought, *hose it off and leave it at a park by the ball diamond. It'd be gone within the hour and* nobody'd *ever find it again.*

142

The other case was a bit more … inventive. Not to mention a bit less easy to reconstruct. The couple had been bound together, nude, with duct tape, on the bed. They had probably been unconscious at the time, because one of each of their hands had been bound to opposite sides of the headboard and one of each of their feet to opposite legs of the bedframe. There was no sign (such as there was at all) that either had tried to resist being secured like that. Then some accelerant, specifically gasoline (the report said it was standard grade Valero gasoline but couldn't identify the exact station it had come from), had been poured over and around them while on the bed, saturating the mattress and the surrounding carpet, before being torched. Eventually the whole house had gone up, but the couple had been beyond caring by then. Both of them were married to other people.

****

"This is Lynne Fox, KOPN 12 News, first on the scene, up close and personal, with a special report on a series of homicides that have been committed recently around the Old Pueblo. Over the past six months, there have been not one, not two, but at least *six* couples murdered in and around Tucson, and in every case they have not been a married couple. Or, to be more precise, at least one of the victims in each couple has been married, but not to the person they were involved with and with whom they were killed. We've prepared a graphic for you …" – angrily Reesa stabbed the power button on her remote to turn off the television. The hint of a smile on Fox's face as she made her report was just too much for Reesa to take, and besides, dammit, she and Chuck had just put the full list together themselves two days ago. Now here this bleached blonde bimbo was already spreading it all around the airwaves, which was inevitably going to gin up some real panic in the city.

It sure wasn't going to make Reesa's own job any easier. She also ought to be watching the report, since the four of them that had happened within city limits were all her cases. Gritting her teeth, she turned the set back on. "This has been Lynne Fox, KOPN 12 News, first on the scene, up close and personal, with a special report on the Tucson Ripper. Now back to you in the studio, Mike." *Bitch*, Reesa thought. *Christ Almighty*. She and Jeff had just begun seriously chewing over the possibility that all of these killings were related and here this broad is telling the entire city that they are. *Not two days after we've gotten the county files, too. The Tucson Ripper, my ass. Melodramatic horseshit.* Her phone rang.

"Malloy .... Yes, sergeant. I know about it .... No, I, ah, I didn't see all of it .... Yes, I'll pick it up off their website and watch all of it before tomorrow." She swiveled the phone away from her mouth and ground her teeth, just for a moment. "No, I don't know how she caught on. I've just begun looking at the killings that way myself, and to be completely honest, while I'm leaning that way more than I was, I'm still not entirely convinced yet .... Yes, sergeant. I'll see what we can do .... Yes, sergeant."

She held the phone away from her ear while the sergeant continued to talk; he was loud enough that she didn't miss any of what he was saying. Finally he ran down. "Yes, sergeant. I understand that shit rolls downhill. Hey, you can always assign someone else to the next one in the door, with our blessings. Thank you, sergeant .... We'll knuckle down .... Yes, we're working on it .... Tomorrow, then. Good night, sergeant." *Shit does indeed roll downhill,* she thought. *When he gets his ass chewed, he finds someone lower than he is on the totem pole and chews* their *ass. Tonight was simply my turn.*

Then another thought intruded. Had Jeff been the leak to Fox? He had been the one to suggest she try looking at county cases, and he'd also been the one to not only suggest that they were all related but to actually articulate a pattern in all of the killings that tied them all together. A very convenient pattern, at least as far as Lynne Fox and her Tucson Ripper report was concerned, since she'd obviously tied them together herself, at least for the purposes of her report. That meant that she'd pretty certainly identified the same points as Jeff had. Kind of had to, since they were the only points all of the killings had in common.

But Jeff was Family. That meant he knew how to keep secrets, as she'd confirmed in her interview with him. Could she find out if he were the one who'd talked?

The next morning, she and Chuck put their heads together. First things first. "If we're dealing with a serial killer, then we've got a pattern we can draw up, such as it is, and based on it, we ought to be able to at least sketch out a bit of a profile. So let's try to look at this as though they really are all part of one pattern, one serial killer at work doing all of them. What's he like?"

Chuck leaned back in his chair and looked up at the ceiling. "Well, he's clearly an organized killer, so he's likely to be quite intelligent, charismatic, and fairly well-educated. That's what the book says, isn't it?"

Reesa grinned at him. "Very good. He's controlling the crime scene and leaving – so far, at least – no usable evidence that we've found whatsoever. He's left us some minor trace, like at the Harris residence, but when he has, it's been useless. Hell, in that case we can't even prove conclusively that it's connected to the crime at all. For all we know at this point, it could have been planted just to send us off on a wild goose chase. If Marquez is dealing straight with us, it was, and at least for a while, it did.

We expect he's targeting people who are strangers to him, but we're not seeing any suggestion that he himself has got any direct sexual involvement with the victims. Not that we're ignoring that sexual involvement between the victims is one of the common threads running through all of these murders, perhaps the most important one, but he's not waiting to get them actually in the act. Is he returning to the crime scenes? Where are those pictures from the Bridgton crime scene?" She rummaged through the files in front of her to find the pictures that had been taken of the spectators. "Okay, here are those." She flipped through them. "Shit! There's nobody there! I mean, sure, we got a couple of looky-loos, but no crowds. Too sparse a neighborhood. Let's try the Morales one." She picked out another folder. "Okay, we got a bit of a crowd here. And of course, the media's always there. You got the county files?"

Chuck pulled out the pictures from the county cases. Just like the Bridgton case, there were no crowds and precious few spectators at all. It took the pair less than twenty minutes to conclude that no unknown spectators were readily visible and common to any two scenes, much less more than that. "So much for that idea. We've started a profile that, at this point, includes at least twenty percent of

146

the men in Tucson, maybe more. What's next?" Reesa was chewing on her lower lip and didn't answer immediately.

"Well, that profile does include Henry Blodden, doesn't it? I know we've got nothing specific to tie him or any of his people to any of these cases, other than the Maguires being among the Avowed, but since we're kind of casting a real wide net here, he ought to be in it. And he does seem to have quite a bit of charisma. On the other hand, if we quit worrying about the charisma, which is common according to the book but hardly inevitable, then that couple that helps him set the place up and take the collection seem to do a marvelous job of fading into the woodwork, which would probably be a major point in their favor if we wanted to look at either or both of them as the guilty parties. Shit. Just *looking* at them is hard enough for me to do. And the way they work the services, I'd bet that they'd be organized as hell and quite able to control a crime scene if they chose. There've been serial killers who aren't charismatically enhanced, haven't there?"

Just then Jesus Almirez, the lieutenant in charge of the Crimes Against Persons division, came into the bullpen. Albert Cotton, the homicide sergeant, close on his heels, whistled sharply before calling, "Can we get everybody's attention here, please?" Reesa looked around. All six of the other homicide detectives were present, and she was a bit surprised to realize that half of them had come in without her noticing while she and Chuck had been wrapped up in their discussion of the cases. Most of the aggravated assault detectives, on the other side of the aisle, stopped what they were doing to listen as well.

Lieutenant Almirez was brief and to the point. "Gentlemen – *lady* and gentlemen." He cocked his head towards Reesa by way of brief apology. "We have a new priority. These cases, the so-called Tucson Ripper cases, for those of you who didn't see Lynne Fox's special report last night, are now top of the list. *Our* list. Detectives Malloy and Palmer will continue to be lead on the cases they've already gotten, but if we can, we're going to try to spread out the responsibility for any new ones that arrive. Sergeant Cotton, here, will assign different teams to new murders insofar as he's able to when they come in, if we recognize them in time and have anyone available.

Detective Malloy, Detective Palmer" – he looked directly at Reesa – "this isn't to be in any way critical either of the two of you or of your performance on the murders we've had so far. We, the administration, just feel that it may be helpful and certainly can't hurt to get more pairs of eyes on these cases, and we want to nail this perp, or these perps, if these aren't in fact all one series of cases from a single killer, before we have any more dead bodies on our hands. If we can't do that, we absolutely want to find him. *Now*. We want to drag his ass in here, off the streets, toss him into a holding cell, and put an end to this killing spree. So wrap up whatever else you're working on, people, hot or cold, give Detectives Malloy and Palmer any help they can use with the cases we've got already, and we'll all jump on any new cases that come in. Let's get this son of a bitch and get him fast. Any questions?" When nobody responded, the lieutenant turned on his heel and walked out.

Sergeant Cotton looked around as everyone continued to sit where they were. "Okay, people. You've got your marching orders. Let's get cracking." With that, he headed for his office and shut the door behind him.

Reesa was less than comfortable being the center of attention, but she also realized that it had been largely luck of the draw. Had any other team drawn the first group of cases, she'd be one of the onlookers, wondering just what she and Chuck could offer them at this point. For that matter, she really had no idea what any of the rest of them could do for her, either. Finally she shrugged. "We're kind of shy on usable evidence at the moment, guys, and we're fresh out of viable suspects. Or we've got way too many, take your pick. But Chuck and I'll put together what we've got and we'll copy all of you on it later this morning. Then you can see what we're up against and let us know if you've got anything to offer." That seemed to satisfy everyone, and gradually the bullpen returned to normal.

Chuck came around to sit in the chair next to Reesa's desk. "One other question." He looked around; nobody else was close enough to overhear. "How does he find his targets? Is Tucson such a hotbed of infidelity? The couples we've seen so far appear to have been carrying on with each other for some time, but is that a factor? How does he find whoever he's going to target next?"

Reesa leaned back and put her feet up on the drawer again, her elbow on the desktop. "I've been trying to figure that out for some time. Just like everything else in this case, or these cases, I've got no idea at all. Have we tried finding any common factors between their lives?"

Chuck shook his head. "Not seriously. I mean, we've taken a cursory look at a few things, but we haven't really scoured their lives."

"Well, then, we've got something to do with our time, don't we? Assuming, of course, that these killings really are all related. Some part of my mind keeps coming back to that issue, maybe because I don't want to believe we've really got a serial killer on our hands. Of course, if they're not, then how each of the killers is finding the targets just became a complete crapshoot."

****

Henry parked his car at the far end of the lot. A faded eight-year-old Kia didn't exactly attract attention, but the less he was noticed, the better he felt about it. And of course, the car had been cheap, which was, at the time, the most important point in its favor. He looked up at the building in front of him. He much preferred homes, if only for their greater privacy. But when you're doing God's own work, you do it when and where God wants you to do it. If God wanted you to take off your clothes and dance naked along Congress Street during the lunch hour, well .... No. Henry was still just a bit body-shy, at least in public. If God wanted him to do that ... he chuckled. Not a chance. If God wanted? That merited a derisive snort. He tucked the wine bottle he was carrying carefully under his left arm and dropped his key ring into his right pocket. Then he straightened up and walked on in as though he belonged there.

****

The hotel suite was better than expected – better, in fact, than they had originally become used to when they began their affair. Hector held the door open as Angela stepped inside. Neither one was a stranger to the room any more. It was an extended-stay hotel, and Hector had held a long-term lease on the suite for the best part of a year, now. There was a real convenience in having a regular place for the two of them to meet, safe from prying eyes, nosy (and talkative) neighbors, and all of the other problems that could arise from doing this at home. Either of their homes. Today, though, the suite seemed cleaner, spiffier, and just somehow ... *brighter* than usual.

Angela's eyes lit up. There was a bottle of wine with two glasses, *very* nice wine indeed, on the coffee table in the suite living room. Hector was really trying to make today special, she thought. Not that wine was out of the ordinary, for the two of them, but a nice French wine! She'd seen bottles like that selling for twenty dollars, thirty dollars, or even more. Then there were the bottles she vaguely noticed in the locked cases or cages at the liquor stores – could this perhaps be one of those? Angela didn't know, but this definitely didn't look like one of the bottles that Trader Joe's put out front with the chalk signs announcing the low price. Or on the bottom shelf with all of the other cheap wines. Some of them were actually fairly good, but cheap was inescapable.

Obviously the management was grateful and trying to show that gratitude with a nice bottle of wine for them, Hector thought. It probably was very nice indeed for them to have a room like this that was paid for long term and only used once or twice a week. The two of them were both down to their underwear before they poured any wine, but then they toasted each other (just a sip right now), set the glasses down on the nightstands and she stepped into his arms. Before Hector joined her on the bed, he topped off the glasses. For afterwards.

By the time they would normally have been starting on a second, more leisurely episode, they felt a bit dizzy. Then abruptly Hector began twitching. A full-blown seizure followed, with his whole body jerking and quivering, but by then Angela's heart was racing to the

151

point that she couldn't have managed to call for help even if her brain had been working well enough to realize that she should have. Both of them were dead within the hour.

* * * *

Sergeant Cotton stuck his head out of the office door. "Malloy! Palmer! In my office." Chuck looked at Reesa, who just shrugged. Looking around, there were no other homicide detectives in at the moment. They didn't exactly jump up, but they didn't drag their feet, either.

"So where are we on these cases?" Cotton glanced at the two of them before returning his primary attention to the papers on his desk. The detectives were used to it.

Chuck and Reesa exchanged glances again. "Well, Sergeant, we really aren't anywhere at the moment. We've got no usable trace on these cases, no witnesses, and we either have no real suspects or else we've got to cast such a wide net that we're including a whole lot of the people in Tucson."

Now Cotton looked up, first at Chuck, then at Reesa. "Nobody at all?"

Chuck took a deep breath. "There is this one—" Reesa cut him off.

"There's a group here in town," she began, "kind of a quasi-religious group, that looks as though it might at least be interesting in relation to these cases. They concentrate on praising partnerships, fidelity and things like that. There's nothing specific about them, but the fellow who runs the meetings promises a lot of hellfire and damnation to people who screw around on their partners, and one of the more recent victims was a … a member of their group. Such as they have any actual membership, I mean."

Now Sergeant Cotton looked directly at them as he leaned back, his chair squeaking plaintively. "You been to any of their meetings?"

Chuck said, "I have," just as Reesa also tried to respond that she'd been to one.

"Together?"

Chuck shook his head. Reesa said, "I tried going with one of the other detectives, but I'm looking for someone else to go back there with."

Something about her expression had given her away. "Went with Schuler, huh?" He smiled momentarily. "You think it might be productive? Worth going again, I mean, and maybe keeping an eye on someone in the group?"

Reesa hesitated. "We really don't know. Personally I think it's a bit of a long shot, to be honest, but it's not like we've got anything else at this point. We're kind of shooting in the dark on these. I couldn't begin to label anyone there a person of interest, but with nothing to point anyone out, I at least wanted to be doing *something*."

"Well, I'm not going to tell you to carry out surveillance on them when there's no real evidence to back up the idea with. If you think it's worth pursuing, then find someone else to go with. Whoever you want, I don't care. But take it slow and careful until you've got something to show for it. In the meantime, another one came in. Looks like it could be another Ripper case. I ought to hand it to somebody else, but you two are the only ones here, so it's yours, too. The residence hotel on the northwest corner of Alvernon and Speedway. You know it?" Reesa and Chuck both nodded. "It's all yours. Go." He handed them the file before he waved them away and went back to the papers on his desk. They both recognized a dismissal.

Okay, so we've got one more case to leave open on our desks, Reesa thought. *Once more we draw the shitty end of the stick. Is this good or bad? Can I get back to you on that?* When she stepped out of the car in the parking lot, she was (at some level) pleased to see that a crowd was beginning to gather. At least she'd have plenty of faces to compare with other crime scenes. Someone behind her spoke. "Reesa? It's nowhere near as much, but I've got a couple of details for you on this one, too." *Damn. Jeff again. For all I know, he could be Lynne Fox's source. Maybe not. How to handle this one?*

She decided to try being cool to him until she had more information on which to base a decision. "Thanks," as she took the notebook page he offered.

As she did so, the crowd parted to let in a news team. "Excuse us! Coming through! Okay, that's good enough. Let's set up right here. Get the connection and the sound levels checked, people, and get it done right *now*, if not five minutes ago, because we're going live with this one as soon as we're set up."

Reesa's eyes went dark as Lynne Fox herself led the news crew up to the crime scene tape. First on the scene, yep. That fit. Up close and personal fit, too, since any closer and they'd be on the other side of the tape and then Reesa could arrest them for interfering with the scene. What a delicious thought *that* was. "Detective Malloy, I hope you'll offer us some commentary on this case after you've had a chance to see it as well as something on the Tucson Ripper in general." Lynne's crisp, businesslike voice tone changed suddenly and significantly. "Hi, Jeff," she said, in a lower, more sensual tone. *Damn, the woman is actually purring.* Reesa would have been bemused by the change if she didn't dislike Fox so much. Jeff nodded but said nothing. Reesa didn't miss the subtle but unmistakable hardening of his expression as Fox returned to the van to get ready for her live shots. She and Jeff moved off a ways.

"Well, she's striking, I'll give her that. I've also got to say–" Jeff cut her off.

"Stop. Turn around, put your back to the truck. She's a fair lip reader, among other things."

Reesa's eyes widened a bit at that, but she did as he suggested. "I was going to say something about her hair color having come out of a bottle, because I'm sure I saw it on a Clairol box last weekend. I'd also lay odds that her carpet and drapes don't match. Beyond her being thoroughly obnoxious and generally objectionable, that is."

Jeff took his time about responding, being careful to keep his own back to the news team as well. "I could say meow, I suppose, but you're not wrong. She actually is a blonde, although the near-white shade you see is a lot lighter than her natural color. I guess that's the carpet and drapes you're talking about. Her natural color is much like Amy's, although while I'll call Amy dirty blonde, since that's the term she uses herself, on Lynne I'd have to call it dishwater blonde, with a certain amount of … relish. I wouldn't dare use that term with Amy, she hates it, but I really don't give a shit what Lynne thinks of it. Lynne is also controlling, very possessive, and gets a real hair up her ass about her man having anything at all to do with other women."

Reesa looked at him, one eyebrow arched. That was a series of comments that she thought strongly suggested that he and Lynne had something more than a mere acquaintance, which in turn made her more than a bit skeptical. Or maybe just suspicious, particularly given the feelings she and Fox had for each other. Well, she knew how she felt. She could probably imagine how Fox felt about being blown off or ignored. Of course, 'something more than a mere acquaintance' would certainly explain the purring. "And just how do you know all of this? Especially about the hair color?"

Jeff colored slightly. "She and I … used to have a bit of a relationship. I called it off after several months, because I couldn't handle her shit any more. Make that *wouldn't* put up with it. She's also got quite a mean streak, if that matters."

Reesa said nothing at first, simply chewing on her lower lip. *If he's telling me the truth, then he's probably not her source. Or he's lying to me, but he definitely doesn't read as anything but seriously upset with her and trying to be less involved than even just knowing her. Hmm.* "I take it you don't have much to do with her any more?"

"Try nothing. *Less* than nothing, by preference, but she's been turning up at the same homicides you and I both have, which kind of limits me. It's also kind of inevitable, given her job. She's good at what she does, I'll give her that much. Reluctantly. But nothing more than that, not one damn thing." The heat in his voice was evident, the way he growled the last sentence even more so.

"Who were you tracking here?"

"Hector Apsoulas. His wife has suspected the affair for some time, but when she decided to do something about it, she needed proof. That's where I came in." He spoke just a tad louder than he usually did, to be heard over the traffic on Speedway behind them, although not enough to carry to any interested parties trying to overhear. "He's got a long-term lease on a suite here, and it only gets used twice a week, tops." Just about then the ME arrived, and Reesa apologized to Jeff for having to leave him out in the parking lot to deal with Lynne himself.

He just smiled. "Trust me, I can be elsewhere. Will be, since there doesn't seem to be anything to keep me here any longer. She's got to stick around. Just keep me posted, okay?" She gathered Chuck up by eye, jerked her head towards the building, and the two of them headed on inside. By the time they got around to interrogating the spouses, they'd had to put off their dinners for several hours. When murders happen in the middle of the day, though, spouses tend to have alibis that hold up. And they have to be checked out anyway, no matter how long it takes or how late it runs. *Shit!*

****

The killer lay in bed awake, not thinking at all about God's work at the moment but simply staring towards the ceiling in the dark and actually seeing in the mind's eye what had to have been the scene in the room where Hector and Angela had died. Thinking how simple it had been to place the bottle and glasses in the room, how effective the poison would have been, and how the couple had succumbed. Had they died before they managed to … or afterwards? Probably not during. Hardly mattered, though, really, did it? Dead is dead, and nasty deaths from poison can be *very* satisfying, even if one doesn't get to actually *watch* the victims die. Not exactly satisfying for the victims, of course, but they shouldn't have been screwing around. They brought it on themselves, after all. They made

157

a conscious choice to stray. And taking them out felt so *good*. The killer's body trembled briefly. The killer was definitely doing God's work – this was an utter certainty as the killer's mind returned to earth.

****

"Who are we?"

"THE AVOWED!"

Henry took a deep breath. "Brothers and sisters, I believe you've all seen the news about the couple that just perished this week, poisoned in their love nest while they were engaged in breaking their vows to their partners. Engaged in unholy congress with each other!" He let his gaze roam over the entire congregation for two whole minutes while the room stayed still and quiet. A poorly-muffled cough from near the back, the only sound in the room, echoed off the walls, and Henry began speaking again. "At least this time neither of the guilty parties – I'm speaking of the lovers, the victims here, not the killer – were any of ours. That doesn't make what they were doing one bit better, you understand. Not one bit."

He hung his head. Cheap theatrics could work wonders, he knew, in pulling a congregation along to where you wanted them, so long as they were used sparingly. Then he raised his head and looked directly at the congregation again. "And while what the killer is doing is wrong – never forget that, it's *wrong* – still, the killer, whoever he may be, is, in his way, doing God's own work. He is exacting His own punishment on those who break that very special relationship, that little bit of God, that exists between partners who have sworn, whether formally or informally, to each other. To be *true* to each other! God's own handiwork, God's own *self*! So while we

158

condemn the killings, while we condemn the killer for doing wrong, let us keep in the back of our minds that the real guilty parties are those people who stray from the path of righteousness and faith with their partners. If they had held to their partners, the way we all know we should, then they would never have fallen afoul of this killer. And where this killer is only taking out those violators and not harming any innocent people, that killer is, indeed, at some level, our brother and doing God's work!"

As Henry himself was doing God's own work, both in these meetings and ... elsewhere, he reminded himself.

The Joneses, unnoticed as always, stood at the back of the room, scanning the congregation. When the time came, they'd carry the collection baskets to the front and work their way to the back of the room, so that people could see them coming (the baskets, not the Joneses). They could also see other people putting their money into the basket before it got to them, which as Henry had taught them, tended to improve the take. Just as standing at the doorway afterwards caught those few who might have been missed in the initial collection. Or, through peer pressure, those who might just not have seen fit to drop something in the basket when it first came around to them. Even the occasional soul who felt that they should have given more and decide to do so before it's too late. Everybody deserved a second chance, at least for something as small as donating money. Not that it was exactly a small thing to Henry, of course.

****

"This is Lynne Fox, KOPN 12 News, first on the scene, up close and personal, with another special report on the series of homicides that have been committed recently in and around the Old Pueblo. For those of you who missed our live report right from the scene earlier today, there's been yet one more couple murdered in Tucson just this week. Let me recap the previous murders for you before we get the details of this latest one."

Reesa gritted her teeth. She didn't know which was worse – having to sit through the reports by this bitch or hearing her repeatedly twit the entire Tucson Police Department (and the Pima County Sheriff's Department as well, she reminded herself) for their ongoing failure to bring the series of homicides to a screeching halt and apprehend the murderer. Or murderers; Lynne Fox's opinion (*bitch!*) was hardly the last word in whether or not these were one ongoing series of murders or just a whole bunch of coincidental murders that simply happened to have some features in common.

Just as in the previous report, Fox didn't give any details that the police had held back. There was nothing to suggest that she had a pipeline either into the Department or to the actual murderer, which Reesa thought was a great pity. Even knowing how impossible it would be to do, to get away with, the mere thought of getting Lynne Fox into an interrogation room and sweating her was just so … enticing. It'd never happen, of course, but she could dream, couldn't she? She and Chuck could play bad cop, bad cop for a change. Do him some good to be the heavy for a while.

Judging from the way he'd talked about these special reports, he didn't have a lot more use for this bleached blonde bimbo by now than Reesa herself did. And damn, but she would just *love* to come over all energetic in questioning Lynne Fox. Especially since (as usual) whenever Fox got around to mentioning the way that none of the detectives would talk about the cases, Reesa's picture got flashed on the screen. Every single time, including this one. Damn cameraman didn't even get her good side most of the time. *Bitch!* And just how unfortunate was it that bright lights and rubber hoses were now so out of fashion?

Later, lying in bed, Reesa punched and squeezed and nudged her body pillow until it was comfortable. She was, she had to admit, increasingly troubled by the number of cases mounting up on her desk that she didn't look like she would ever be able to close. They certainly weren't going to do her numbers any good, but fundamentally she was much more bothered by her inability to even develop a single suspect for any one of the cases. She understood that if you closed the cases, your numbers were good. If you didn't, they weren't. Chasing numbers was the wrong way to go about things. Chasing suspects was the way to succeed. Finally fatigue took over, and she just wrapped herself around the body pillow even tighter and drifted off.

Chapter 11

Bob Jones busied himself with the preparations for his painting job. A small pickup with a ladder rack, almost exclusively used for his outside work, that held a paint-spattered aluminum stepladder and a similarly-decorated extension ladder that he wouldn't need on this job. Several five-gallon buckets of properly colored paint, rollers, roller screens, paint trays, various-sized brushes, blue tape, drop cloths, and all of the little paraphernalia that painters kept handy. He'd put the whites on over his street clothes last thing, just before he got into the truck.

After getting his own truck ready, he helped Mary. Two large buckets filled with cleaning supplies, and he had to refill her spray bottle of orange cleaner. He personally felt that Simple Green did as good or even a better job, but Mary insisted that some of the people she cleaned for hated the smell of it but never complained, or not as much, anyway, about their kitchens smelling like an explosion in a citrus grove. *Whatever works*, he thought. The vacuum cleaner went in, leaning drunkenly across the back seat, then two brooms and two mops – just in case there's a problem with one (although as he often thought, *what's to go wrong with a broom or mop?* But Mary insisted). Swapping out is so much quicker (*wouldn't a spare vacuum make more sense?*).

Finally Mary came out of the house and locked the door. Like Bob would soon be, she was dressed in painter's whites. Bob had convinced her that it made a good impression on people, to come to clean all in white, and of course, when you had to rub a recalcitrant spot with your arm, it looked a lot better if the cloth that was actually

162

doing the rubbing was brilliant white. In a word, it just looked more *professional*. No matter *what* you were doing.

****

Jeff slid behind a Palo Verde tree, careful to avoid the devilishly long thorns, and squatted down cautiously. He'd give the couple in the house he was watching some time to get down to business before he tried getting closer, hoping for a good shot through the window. After checking his camera carefully, he paid more attention to what was coming through his phone and over his earbud. Some endearments, some conversation, but hardly the sounds of two people in a hurry to get on with sex. They sounded, Jeff thought, more like a couple comfortable with each other and aware that there was plenty of time.

He would rather have had a bug in the room; it was difficult at times to hear Betty Petrovik through the tap on Henry Wellman's cellphone. But beggars and all that, he thought to himself. Half a loaf is better than nothing. Besides, tapping into his cellphone was a lot safer than committing a burglary in order to get bugs put in place, and then there was the rebroadcast hub to install. Afterwards, of course, the bugs and hub had to be retrieved, so as to minimize the traces left, which meant yet another burglary. Way too risky. Cellphones were lots quicker and easier, besides leaving far less evidence of what he'd been doing. Finally what he could make out of Betty's voice made it sound as though they were going to get down to what they'd really gotten together for.

"Come on, honey, let's move this into the bedroom." A long pause. "Oh, look. Richie's taken over the bed. You know he sleeps there at night? C'mon, Richie, come to mama. It's time to get off the bed."

"He's not moving."

"Oh, I know that, Henry. I'm not blind. Richie! C'mon, boy!" Her voice was a bit fainter. She seemed to have stepped farther away from the phone that was probably on Henry's belt. "He's not waking up."

"Oh, let's not disturb him. You know, we could use the couch in the living room. Been a long time since we've been so … impulsive. Let the poor dog sleep."

"Well …"

"What harm can there be? And he's obviously comfortable."

"I don't know. It's almost like he was drugged."

"Oh, don't be silly. Who'd want to drug Richie? He's such a sweetie. And besides, who's been to the house to do it? Here, come on."

On the one hand, Jeff preferred to have video with his soundtrack. But even this was more than he usually had. He could imagine the two of them making their way back along the hallway to the living room, and he lifted his camera, braced himself, and trained it on the window. *Next time, dammit, bring the tripod.* Yes, there they were. Henry sat on the couch and pulled Betty down onto his lap. Jeff adjusted the polarizing filter to make sure he had as much glare reduction as possible. She wasn't fighting Henry. Quite the contrary, she was busy undoing his shirt buttons just as he was undoing her blouse.

Jeff had two or three good shots and they weren't quite fully undressed when there was the sound of a sudden explosion over the cellphone link, and through the other window, Jeff saw the bedroom erupt in flame. His jaw sagged. Of all the things that could have happened, this was *way* off his list of possibilities. After giving in to sheer

164

astonishment for what felt like a whole two minutes, he buckled back down to work. Whatever happened to Henry, Betty, and Richie, he had a job to do. Nobody was going to pay him to sit out here in the desert, catching flies with his mouth, he reminded himself. 'Call me a horn toad and feed me *flies* for breakfast' worked as an expression of astonishment (one of his college girlfriends had been very fond of it), but it definitely wasn't a culinary suggestion. Anyway, breakfast was hours ago. That memory provoked a small smile as he bent back to his viewfinder.

Henry leapt up. "What the hell?" Betty fell off his lap and hit the floor but was too upset to even notice. She jumped up and, in no more than her panties, she started to race toward the bedroom, only to be blocked by the smoke and dust roiling down the hallway. Jeff did get a decent shot of her passing in front of Henry, if either one was recognizable in the finished photo and the dust in the air didn't make it all too indistinct anyway.

"Richie!" From what Jeff could see through his telephoto lens, there was never going to be an answer to that call. Perhaps something in the closet could have survived, but from the type and amount of debris that had flown out of the shattered window, the bomb had been placed either in or under the bed and had been more than plenty big enough to have taken care of anyone in the room. Poor Richie was a goner. Jeff figured that his own work here was probably done, at least for the day and likely completely. He quickly took a few additional, less important shots before packing up and leaving as unobtrusively as he had arrived. Listening to the cellphone tap as he walked off, it sounded as though Henry's ardor had cooled rather abruptly. No real surprise; Jeff figured he couldn't have kept his own mind on such things with an explosion like that in his own bedroom. Of course, his house was distinctly smaller. But Henry was now muttering about being lucky not to have been in bed at the time and maybe if he were smart, he wouldn't take such chances again.

Smart move, buddy. Pity you didn't come to that decision a long time ago. Of course, that's the sort of thing that keeps me in business. He heard Henry holler a cursory goodbye to Betty as he let the door slam behind him. No way to tell what Betty was doing, but not a lot of need, either. Her scream as she finally saw the inside of the bedroom was loud enough for Jeff to hear first-hand, and Henry was too far away by then for his cellphone to pick anything up anyway. Jeff pulled out his own cellphone and turned off the reception of the tap. The least he could do was call 911 as he left. Speed things up just a bit, maybe.

****

Two days later, Jeff decided to take advantage of some free time. He headed for the police station downtown, hoping to catch Reesa at her desk. If she were there, she'd probably appreciate a break from paperwork. She'd already expressed (in a roundabout way) her lack of enthusiasm for the amount of it required by her job, but that seemed to be a curse common to a lot of jobs. Jeff's was little better. You do what you have to.

When he arrived, she was in. He sat cautiously in the chair by Reesa's desk. "There's another one to add to your collection. The explosion in the Petrovik house, two days ago."

Reesa looked at him, puzzled. "Who was killed in that one? I don't recall it."

166

"No reason you would, I expect. The house is up northwest, between Silverbell and I-10, way out in Sector 1 of West Division. The only one killed in the explosion was Richie, a Golden Retriever who was something like eight years old. He was sleeping on the bed, and Betty Petrovik decided not to disturb him. Henry Wellman thought that was a good idea, so the two of them went back out into the living room and were just, ah, beginning to get down to business, shall we say, when the bomb under the bed went off. The local people from Operations West have the case, and they don't seem to know what to do or where to go with it. The Feds came in and looked at it, but they didn't have any more ideas than TPD, other than reconstructing the bomb. Very simple, ordinary dynamite, if a bit more than was needed, fairly easy-to-obtain parts, basic timer circuit."

"A dog." Reesa didn't sound pleased.

Jeff looked back at her with a hint of defiance. "Yes, a dog. Not the point. The dog was sleeping unusually soundly; Betty tried to call him off the bed and he didn't stir. He just slept on, as though he'd been drugged. She even commented on it at the time. And feeding him some drugged hamburger, say, if you think about it, wouldn't have been a bad way of making friends with him, keeping him quiet and occupied while planting the bomb under the bed. If he'd been sleeping somewhere else, Henry and Betty would have been on the bed, ah, having at it until they, well, until the bomb went off. Definitely not the way they would have ... let's just say that it would have been an outcome they hadn't planned. As it is, I think that little episode has probably terminated their affair equally well, if a bit less publicly. At least when he left her house, Henry was muttering that he'd never go back there as long as he lived, and I got the impression that he seemed to have the idea at some level that going back there could be related to how much longer he lived. He was quite shook up."

Reesa sat back and took all that in, then fixed Jeff with a piercing look. "And you know all this how?" The air hung silent and charged between them for several minutes.

Finally Jeff responded slowly. "I suppose the answer to that depends on what you plan to do with it."

Now it was Reesa's turn. She chewed on her lower lip for almost a minute before replying. "Just so I know how much … credence to give what you're telling me. Personally. I'm not going to notice it otherwise. Or make any … explicit notes about it, either."

Jeff's nostrils flared. Reesa exercised her patience. Finally, "I was listening in on his cellphone. I heard everything that happened around him, everything they said. Off the record, of course."

"Oh, of course." Reesa snorted. "That sort of thing could get you into real trouble, you know."

Jeff grinned. "What sort of thing? I never did anything, never said anything. And in less than a week, even his phone won't show anything."

A rueful smile. "Riiiiight. Okay, back to the issue. A dog. Jeez."

"It may have been a mistake, but it certainly fits the pattern." He held up a hand to keep her from responding. "Such as the pattern is, I mean."

"But bombers don't … I mean, this perp has never … no, back up. If we assume for the sake of argument that these murders are all being done by one person, then he's never used a bomb elsewhere. So how do we know it's him?"

Now Jeff raised an eyebrow to her. "And just what method of doing in his victims *has* he used before? That's why, you said, you had so much difficulty coming up with a pattern, because each killing is entirely different, except for the pattern of the choice of victims. Oh, and let's not forget the absence of any usable forensic evidence at the Petrovik house, too, and that, I'd have to say, is definitely pattern material as well, at least in my comparatively untutored opinion. Is that the hurdle you can't quite get over? Well, this is another case that would have been on the list if only Richie had gotten off the bed or gone to sleep somewhere else in the first place, because both Betty and Henry are married to other people.

"And if Richie was given some doped hamburger, like I said, maybe just a bit too much, it's only natural that he would have kept right on sleeping no matter what Betty had to say to him. Okay, maybe this isn't one of them. BATF figures the bomber is inexperienced with explosives, because of the overkill factor. They said that the bomber used at least half again, perhaps twice as much dynamite as would minimally have done the job, and still generously more than what an experienced bomb maker would have used for the job, allowing for some degree of insurance for the bomb, just to make sure it would do what it was supposed to. It's also the only case, so far, that I know of that fits what little pattern there is and where the killer hasn't managed to do in his victims. But it definitely wasn't for lack of trying on his part, and if he had, it would fit the pattern like a glove. Oh, and for what little it may be worth, the locals don't know about Henry Wellman. Their report

169

simply shows the incident as a bombing in the Petrovik house, reason as unknown as the perpetrator. I didn't see any need to tell them anything more when they questioned me."

"They questioned you?"

Jeff shrugged. "I called it in to 911 as I was leaving. I presume they found me that way, because I got a call asking me who I was and would I mind coming in to answer some questions. There was a certain impression given that a refusal wouldn't be the best idea I could have. I told them I was driving through the neighborhood when the bomb went off."

Reesa sat silently for several minutes, trying to see how it fit. Finally she had to agree. "Yeah, I guess you're right. Well, maybe. Close enough to be worth keeping in mind, anyway." She found the file on the department computer and added it to her list. "But if anyone else sees this, I could get laughed out of the division and find myself back on uniform patrol again. A dog. Jesus."

Jeff just shrugged. Then, with a small smile, "Do I have to make some sort of amends here? I can certainly offer you dinner. Home cooked, fancier than lunch, my place."

Reesa hesitated. "Just dinner? It's clear that if I come, I'm not going to be on the menu?" *Goddamn it, why am I talking like a teenager going out on a first date? Maybe because the last time you had a sexual relationship with anyone, you* were *a teenager. You're an adult now. Grow* up, *Reesa! You can at least* talk *like a mature woman, even if you're not going to go to bed with him.*

Jeff nodded. "Just dinner. A cocktail, maybe some wine with dinner, pleasant company. *Very* pleasant

170

company, at least as far as I'm concerned. Nothing more."
Reesa smiled at the compliment.

****

Fresh out of the shower, Reesa looked at the pastel pink bag lying on her bed with what could charitably be called mixed feelings. Pulling the lingerie out, she unfolded the first tissue paper packet. Three layers of tissue. Pale pink, pale lavender, pale blue. Then she simply looked at the delicate, lacy, and ridiculously expensive pale coral silk bra it had contained. Next to it she put the similarly frilly (delicate, lacy, and ridiculously expensive) matching silk panties. She'd gone into the store to buy pink, but the saleslady convinced her that pink was just *so* yesterday and that the coral would suit her coloring far better.

I guess times have changed from white, pink, blue, and black. Coral indeed! Although it is a pretty color. But this is preposterous. You told him sex wasn't going to happen tonight and he agreed. Now you're going to dress up in underwear that looks like you want him to screw your eyes out, and he'll probably never even see it. Do you even know what you want? Besides getting laid, that is. God, but you're fucked up.

Yeah, all these years is way *too long to go without, and he's definitely the best choice you've seen since you got to Tucson. Maybe even before that. He's Family, he presumably knows how to be discreet even if only because he's Family, he's a distant cousin of yours because he's Family, you could talk to him about the Family if you wanted to because he's Family, he's not in the Department ... you could do worse. He's almost certainly loads better than dickhead was back in college, right? We won't even mention Chris Schuler, now, will we?*

171

*And Jeff would do it if you let him, you know it. He
wants you, in spades. That you've read, loud and clear.
Long before you told him there wasn't going to be any
tonight. So far, though, he's taken exactly the right tack
with you. Interest you can't ignore, but so delicate an
approach ... shit! The ones who come on too strong are just
so much simpler to deal with. Blow them off, so to speak,
not the way they're hoping for, make them go away – with
a come-along if necessary – and you're done.*

*So what do I do if he tries anyway? Do I give in?
Probably. Let's be honest. Make that* certainly. *If I knew for
sure I weren't going to, I'd just wear my usual underwear
and not worry about it. Save myself the hand washing, if
nothing else. And if we do, then what? Do I let things move
to the next level? Do I hold him at arm's length and not
quite trust him anymore? Such as I trust him now, of
course. Or do I cut him adrift and shut things down
completely? And how upset do I get if he continues to be a
Boy Scout and doesn't even try? Especially after telling
him that's what I demanded? Shit!*

*And of course, notice what's happened with that
relationship you said you weren't looking for. Maybe you
weren't looking for one, but it seems to have snuck up on
you and bitten you on the ass anyway. Even if he's simply
just a friend at this point, he's definitely gotten inside your
defenses by now, hasn't he? He'd leave a real empty spot in
your life if he disappeared now. And what does that tell
you? I mean, if the two of you did, and you then tried to cut
him off completely, you'd feel it, bad, now, wouldn't you?
And holding him at arm's length and not trusting him
wouldn't be a lot better in that regard, either, would it?
He's just about as close to you as Chuck is, except that you*

172

and Chuck have an absolute understanding that it's not sexual and won't ever be sexual. You and Jeff ... don't quite fit that mold. You don't have that boundary to rely on.

Screw it. So to speak. Let's just see what happens. And hope for the best, whatever that may be. The only problem would be what to do if I wake up in his bed with him tomorrow morning, and if nothing else, I can let that issue wait until I actually do. If I do. With any luck, I'll wake up alone in my own bed. And I think that's better. Don't I?

****

Jeff held the door open and gestured for Reesa to walk inside. "Welcome to my humble abode." He smiled to indicate that he saw the humor.

Reesa looked around. "Kind of small." And it was, but some of the furnishings were utter top-drawer, even if they didn't exactly coordinate. Others ... weren't. It was almost as though the initial decoration had been done inexpensively by one person and then someone with a far bigger checkbook had come in to add some accessories and generally put their own somewhat confused imprint on the place. Reesa wondered which one was Jeff.

He shrugged. "Yeah, it is. But it actually belongs to my boss, and I was ... asked to live here. Basically told to, in fact. That gives me some ... tax advantages. I also know that Amy and Alec, her husband, lived here from the time they were married until they built their new place. They even had Becky, Amy's best friend, living here with them for much of that time, and if it's small for me, it had to have been ungodly cramped for the three of them."

Reesa smiled to herself. Jeff was working hard to maintain the distinction between 'his boss' (the unseen

173

A.M. Youngston, of course) and Amy, the 'senior investigator.' Of course, since he had no idea that she was Family, he clearly had no idea that she had any understanding or concern that Amy actually *was* his boss, much less what else she was. Someday, maybe, she'd let him know. In the meantime, she could keep up the fiction, too. She looked around. *Three adults in this place? How sardine had that been?* "If you'd come to the kitchen for a moment, I've got to check on our dessert."

Reesa cocked her head. "You're really doing this up, aren't you? I mean, dinner is one thing, but homemade dessert, too? If you've done it all yourself, you've really pulled out all the stops." On the way through the living room, she noticed a very nice framed pencil sketch. She paused on her way past to look at it closely. There was a kneeling woman digging in the ground, a cactus waiting to be planted. Reesa thought it almost could have been a sketch of her working in her garden, except that her backyard certainly didn't have huge cactus beyond and a view that stretched on forever. Pity. She wondered who the model had been. "Hey, Jeff? Who's the artist on this one?" The table in the dining room was set, candles waiting for a flame and wineglasses at the ready.

In the kitchen, Jeff gestured her towards a chair before he cracked the oven door and looked inside. "The sketch is one of mine. I found this … volunteer, I guess she was, at the Desert Museum one day and it just sort of took off from there. As for dinner, well, I figure anything worth doing is worth overdoing. And I don't get a lot of chances to show off my cooking these days."

He closed the oven carefully, then looked at the small pan on a back burner of the stovetop and stirred the contents. He took a pair of oven mitts and carefully shook the paella pan. "Actually, Alec, Amy's husband, taught me how to make paella. Dessert, well, I've done a fair amount of baking since I was a teenager." The small pan smelled both lovely and fattening, Reesa thought. Ignoring the chair for the moment, she leaned over the stovetop to smell it more closely, catching some of Jeff's scent at the same time. *If I've got a problem, just feed me chocolate until it goes away.* She'd run a couple of extra laps around the track in the morning as penance. As she stepped back, Jeff pulled the bundt pan out of the oven and set it on a potholder on the counter.

Reesa's eyes widened as the combined odors of chocolate and peanut butter caressed her nose. Could he know of her weakness for peanut butter cups? Impossible, but there it was anyway. She got her face back under control before he turned around. Maybe more than a couple of laps. "You are a man of many talents, aren't you?"

Jeff just smiled. "Wine, beer, or Scotch? I'm afraid I don't have much other liquor, but Scotch is about all of the hard liquor I drink."

Figuring she was better off staying out of the cook's way, Reesa finally sat in one of the chairs at the kitchen table. "Scotch, I think, would be fine. Water and one ice cube, please." She watched Jeff debate about a bottle from a selection of three or four in the cupboard. Finally he pulled out two bottles and offered her the choice of 12-year Macallan or 15-year single barrel Balvenie. She gestured at the Balvenie. Good taste, she thought.

After fixing Reesa's drink along with his own, Jeff leaned over the paella pan on the stovetop and sniffed. Then he took a spoon and dug cautiously, delicately, in the pan before turning his attention to the bundt pan now sitting on the counter. He carefully turned out the cake onto a rack before again stirring the glaze still in its pan on the stove. Then he picked up his drink and leaned back against the counter, where he could watch Reesa.

She finally broke the silence. "You'd really like to take this to a girlfriend-boyfriend sort of relationship, wouldn't you?" *Would I? And is there a more adult way to phrase that?*

Can I get back to you about that? Both of those?

Jeff gave a rueful smile. "Hm. Give me a moment to respond, would you? I'd like to … phrase my reply to that most carefully." Reesa watched his eyes closely. His actual answer was clear to her; it had been for quite some time. But what he said, how he said whatever he was going to say, and how it came out, was definitely going to be interesting. "I'm trying to say this as carefully as I can. I've heard what you have to say on the subject. Let me just put it that … when, or if, you change your mind about having, um, that sort of relationship with someone, I'd like to be … around. Good enough?"

Now the hot potato was in her hands. She was acutely aware of the sleekness against her most intimate areas of the silk underwear she had on, just as she was all too aware of why she'd worn it. Not that the mixed emotions there were resolved; she was simply all too aware of all of them. And dammit, it wasn't even remotely fair to be critical of him for doing (not doing!) what she'd demanded that he do. Or not do, however you looked at it. Even if at some level she hoped he'd try her anyway. But it also wouldn't be fair to him to encourage that when she didn't even know how she'd react to him the next morning if he did. Didn't even know how she'd react to *herself* if that happened. "Okay. I suppose I can accept that. How long do you expect to wait?" She added a smile to let him know it wasn't a challenge. Not completely, anyway.

He shrugged. "Until we're done, I guess. If we're not going to, ah, take this to another level, well, no. Let me rephrase that. When the relationship changes, if it does, and eventually I figure it'll kind of have to, it's pretty much got to be either going to that level or calling it quits. I figure that we'll know which way we're going when the time comes. Until then, I don't feel any need to hurry anything. Well, not much, anyway." He grinned, and she returned the expression with a great deal more certainty on her face than inside her head.

****

Dammit, she thought as she turned her Toyota Avalon onto Oracle northbound, heading back to her own house. *He was a perfect gentleman, and that's exactly what I told him I wanted. So why do I feel so ... dissatisfied? Dammit! Well, hell. Better a Boy Scout than an aggressively oversexed shit like Chris Schuler, right? And winding up dissatisfied because nothing happened is a lot better than lying in his bed afterwards, or the following morning, or both, wondering what to do about him next. In other words, still dissatisfied, but having taken that step that I couldn't undo. This way, at least, I can just let things keep going the way they are. That works, I guess. For now.*

****

The explosion and Richie's death had finally been reported on the evening news. The killer was unhappy, to say the least. *Goddam people should have just kicked the dog off the bed and gotten on with their fucking right there.*

Too much sedative. Way too much sedative. Mustn't make that sort of mistake again. Probably most people with dogs would leave the dog there if they couldn't wake the fuzzy bastard. Sexual pressure mounted. The killer missed the release, the sheer overwhelming *pleasure* of a kill made well, even at a distance. Another one had to be done, and soon. This one would be another face-to-face killing. It *had* to be. The craving for the sexual release, the *need* for that sort of release, ensured that. There'd be no chances of such an untoward result this next time, that was certain.

****

Henry Blodden walked to the front of the congregation and spent two or three minutes just scanning the assembled people. Truly they were becoming a congregation in all senses of the word, he realized. And he was finally completely back into the preacher mold he'd been in before his wife had all but destroyed his career, his *life*, along with his marriage. He sent a quick blessing to his benefactor, the incredible person who, with nothing more than some coffee, plenty of coffee, to be honest, and a ready ear, had lifted him out of the gutter and then, with a few carefully-phrased suggestions, set him on this path. Not that he'd told that (blessed!) person of his real take on religion and such. Appearances had to be kept up, at least in that regard, at all costs. Even if there was no dignity left. But in any event, *this* was his proper life's work. *This* was what he was meant to do. Not just these gatherings, but all of … *this*. His current life. He enjoyed his current life. He was about God's work. Every day, in every way, in everything he did. *Everything.* Including ….

With a little bit of luck, and a certain amount of management, tonight's take would be even bigger than before. Looking toward the back of the room, his eyes sought out the Joneses, standing unobtrusively (did they have any other way to stand?) in the back of the room, collection baskets waiting in their capable hands. One thing he'd managed to teach them fairly early on was to make sure that nobody left without passing by a basket, even if that meant that it had to be held by the door during much of the service to catch any early departures. And now there was enough built up that he could salt each basket before the Joneses passed it around with several five-dollar bills, a couple of tens, and a twenty.

So much better than running scams that wound up with the police hunting for him. Henry felt satisfied, very satisfied indeed, and smiled broadly inside, although he continued to control his outward facial expression and kept his features in a carefully neutral appearance. He straightened his stance, just fractionally, and began. "Friends, thank you for coming, and welcome to those of you who have never been here with us before. It's time for faith! Not just faith in the Lord, but the faith you keep with your partner! It's time for your commitment, it's time for your vows! WE ARE THE AVOWED."

Chapter 12

Aurelia Quiñones was working hard to conceal her excitement. She'd been uncertain how to respond when Freddie Gardner had initially come on to her. She was a satisfied married woman, after all. Well, maybe not all *that* satisfied, but definitely married. No, she reminded herself. Not any more. Not since the divorce, no matter how much she wanted to deny it. No matter how much she *did* deny it. The single life didn't really suit her, but that was reality now. Freddie wore a ring, so he was clearly married. But he was persistent, and he kept explaining to her – in mostly oblique, roundabout ways – what she was missing, and how her ex would never have to know. Of course not. She lived her own life nowadays, and her ex didn't control what she did. Or know about it, either. Freddy also claimed his wife was fine with it, but men, after all, you know ....

Today was going to be the day. Freddie had his house all to himself, his wife was out of town for the day, and they were going to meet there. She hardly bothered to think about being with Freddie in his wife's home. She was far too busy thinking about just being with Freddie. That bulge in his pants ... could it possibly be for real? I mean ... really? She'd never been with anyone like that, and if he really knew how to use it .... And he was just such a *nice* man. To think that he'd be interested in *her* of all people. The divorce had been especially hard on her self-esteem. Her heart sped up as she pulled into the garage that he'd left open for her. A row of well-established mesquite trees on the far side of the driveway screened any cars in the garage from prying eyes. Even the oppressive heat in the garage couldn't dampen her rising enthusiasm.

Such a nice, caring man! A chilled bottle of white wine, covered with small beads of moisture, better wine than she usually drank (that wasn't hard to do, she thought; almost any bottle was better than the boxes of wine she normally bought, especially now), actual stemmed glasses, and even one red rose awaited her arrival. Freddie wanted the two of them to take their time. Get to know each other even better first. That was fine with Aurelia. They could sit on the couch, sip their wine, and even talk a bit. Settle her nerves. After a while, feeling a bit emboldened by the wine and his presence, his proximity, and what she'd already decided to do with him, she reached out her hand. *Oh, my God, that bulge really is all him!* While part of her recoiled from his sheer size, another part of her was absolutely thrilled. Her husband had definitely had nothing to compare with that! Freddie simply smiled.

They were both naked on the bed and Freddie's size was about to be almost painfully evident to Aurelia when someone else stepped into the room. Aurelia's eyes grew wide as she let go of Freddie. His penis suddenly went limp and shrank, relatively speaking.

"Who … who are you? What are you doing here?"

Freddie was a bit slower on the uptake, but angrier when he spoke. "Yeah, who are you? What do you want? This is my house, and you're trespassing!" The stranger just smiled and approached the bed. Suddenly a pair of handcuffs seemed to materialize in the stranger's hand, so suddenly that it was almost as if it had been magic, and it was quickly snapped onto Aurelia's wrist. Freddie tried to roll over to get off the bed, but the stranger produced a stun gun and pressed it against his leg as it was triggered. His body convulsed, and, tossing the stun gun aside, the stranger grabbed his wrist and quickly snapped the other cuff onto it, linking them together. As Freddy regained control of his body, all he could say was, "What …."

The stranger reached under the foot of the bed and drew out a piece of rope already tied into a loop. Another pair of handcuffs fastened one of Freddie's ankles to the rope, and circling quickly around the foot of the bed, the stranger repeated the action with Aurelia's ankle and pulled the rope taut, tying their feet to the bed. A fourth set of cuffs secured Freddie's other hand to the headboard. The two of them were now utterly trapped on the bed, nude to the stranger's eyes. Aurelia was embarrassed and could feel herself blushing furiously, but Freddie just seemed to be angry by now and growing angrier by the moment.

The stranger then left the room. Freddie and Aurelia looked at each other, puzzled. The stranger came back in moments, carrying a large cloth sack. The contents of the sack seemed to move, and a dry rustle sounded faintly from inside it. Aurelia's heart sank. Some part of her had always known that this whole episode was going to be something she should not have done, and it looked like that was going to be even truer than she could ever have imagined. For just a moment, she thought of her husband. Had being married to him really been so bad?

Had she ever had quite this sinking feeling?

The stranger then upended the sack on the bed between them. A number of large and unhappy rattlesnakes fell out, and both Freddie and Aurelia tried to scramble away from the snakes, which began an agitated seething movement between them as the air filled with the sound of their unhappy buzzing. The handcuffs kept the two people together while the rope and Freddie's wrist being cuffed to the headboard kept them on the bed, and when one drew back an arm, the other's arm came with it. The result was a thrashing that increasingly upset the snakes yet produced no net movement away from them. The first bite was to Freddie's wrist, and he yelled as two fangs sank into his flesh like a pair of red-hot needles. He jerked, pulling Aurelia's arm forward, and the second bite was to her forearm. She screamed and began to cry. The stranger just stood in the doorway, eyes gleaming above a fearsome, almost feral smile as the snakes thrashed and continued to strike any time the pair on the bed moved. They moved a lot, at least at first.

The fifth bite Freddie took was to his neck, and the fangs sank deep into flesh. One pierced the left carotid artery and discharged a lethal load of venom directly into the artery, from where it spread throughout his brain. The snake, a Mojave rattlesnake, carries a high percentage of neurotoxin in its venom, and almost immediately Freddie showed difficulty breathing as parts of his brain stopped functioning properly. Others would fail in short order. Aurelia tried desperately to hold still as the largest snake, a Western Diamondback, made an angry, agitated coil in front of her face. The snake's tongue vibrated up, then flipped down in a terrifying rhythm. The upper body of the snake trembled with its agitation and its tail kept up a furious buzz. As Freddie's arm moved, Aurelia's arm moved with it, and as the movement broke her concentration, she jerked her head back from the snake. This was enough to make the snake, already more than ready, strike towards her head, but as she drew it back, the snake's strike went slightly off-target. Both fangs delivered a large dose of hemotoxic venom directly into her right jugular vein, and from there the slug of venom traveled directly to her heart, destroying blood cells all along the way. From her heart, the venom spread throughout her circulatory system, destroying ever more of her vital blood cells.

The pair's struggles grew fainter and diminished to nothing within less than thirty minutes from the first appearance of the snakes on the bed. The stranger watched it all from the doorway, unmoving save for the occasional tremor, and expressionless beyond the gleaming eyes and horrible smile. When satisfied that both were dead, the stranger picked up the stun gun and the empty sack before leaving the house by the back door. As the bodies on the bed relaxed in death, the snakes finally began to calm down and their rattles fell silent one by one.

Outside the back door, the painter's whites – unstained, this time – went into the inevitable black plastic garbage bag along with the cap, booties, and gloves. The killer was absolutely enthralled with this one. Not only was there the incredible, indescribable delight in watching both of them get just what they deserved, dying in absolute terror and pain, *looking them in the eyes* as they died, but the whites could even be used again, because there was not a drop of blood or other bodily fluid, other than perspiration, anywhere on them. Even a forensic specialist probably couldn't tie what was in the bag to this job. *Does anyone test snake DNA? Probably not*, the killer thought, and nothing else would even begin to establish the killer's presence in that house. *Oh, look, there's a piece of roadside trash to pick up and drop into the sack.* And there's the waiting car, just ahead on the side of the road.

****

Bob pulled into the driveway before pushing the button to open the garage door. Mary's car was already there, parked on the left. He pulled in beside it. From the passenger seat beside him, he took the plastic bag that held his used whites to carry them inside for washing. He'd take care of the painting stuff later, when the sun wasn't beating down quite so strongly. When he stepped into the house, through the laundry room, he found Mary's set of whites already sitting on top of the washer. After carefully checking all of the pockets, mostly for the blue nitrile gloves he and Mary both wore to keep their hands clean while working, he put both sets into the machine and started the wash.

****

Henry sat in the laundromat, waiting for his washer to finish. Once it did, of course, he'd have to sit even more, waiting for the dryer. But such was the price of his extra-curricular activities. He kept his head down, since he really preferred to go unseen outside of the services. Especially here, washing a set of painter's whites he'd borrowed from Bob's stack for his ... excursion today. Now, as he always did, he had to wash any possible bodily fluids or other soiling out of them, make sure they were once again sparkling white, and return them to the stack, folded just as they had been before.

Bob would, Henry felt certain, tell Henry to go ahead and borrow them if he needed them. But that would mean revealing why he needed them, where he went in them, and what he did. That would definitely not be a good idea. As for anyone recognizing him, of course, precious few of his congregants ever came into a place like this, and even fewer would be caught dead (*there's a chuckle!*) in this part of town. There weren't even any English language magazines among the various magazines and loose pages strewn about the tables. The ones here looked like they'd been rejected from some Mexican doctor's office waiting room for being too old. No matter. Henry had brought a book to read, a used murder mystery involving a detective and a con man who was the actual murderer. *The author needs to improve his research*, Henry thought as he started Chapter 12.

****

Chuck was not happy. "You know, when Lieutenant Almirez said they'd assign other people to the cases that came in, I figured that meant we'd get a break from these shit cases. Then we wind up with the Apsoulas case, and now this one too. I tell you, there's a plot behind all of this."

Reesa laughed, although without much mirth. "Chuck, eventually you're going to learn, if you haven't already, that there are plenty of sticks to go around, and each and every one has a shitty end waiting just for you to grab or be handed. This is simply the breaks of the game. One way or another, it's our case. If we didn't have this one, we'd have some other case that we'd probably dislike equally as much. Suck it up, partner."

There was quite a crowd by the time that Reesa and Chuck arrived at the Gardner house. The morgue van she expected, just as she did uniformed officers. A fire truck was a bit unusual in her experience when there was no apparent fire, and animal control was definitely new, especially in the absence of any barking dogs. Everybody she could see was milling around outside and nobody was making any effort to enter the house.

Stepping up behind one of the uniformed officers, she tried to find out why. "So why are we all standing around out here?"

He turned around. "Rattlers. Apparently there's a bunch of 'em in the house, and we're waiting for animal control to give us the all-clear." Reesa just shook her head. No matter how she felt about snakes, no goddam rattlesnake was going to keep her from doing her job. If nothing else, she compared a possible rattlesnake to Sergeant Cotton. And to Lieutenant Almirez. The snake lost. Both times.

She looked at Chuck, who hesitated for a moment before saying, "I'll see what I can get from the people out here."

Chicken, she thought with a smile to herself, but simply said, "I'll check out the scene inside." As she reached the front step, an animal control officer came out of the door holding a cloth sack well clear of her body. "Let me have some room. I think we've got all of them," she said. "Six good-sized ones. Four Western Diamondbacks and two Mojaves." Looking at Reesa, she added, "Detective, if you want to go in, let me put this bunch in the truck and I'll take you in. Just in case there's another one we haven't found yet." She was about two inches shorter than Reesa, but at the moment, Reesa was quite happy to look up to her.

As she was led into the hallway, the officer cautioned her. "If you hear a snake, freeze, and holler if I'm not right with you. I'll come find him and grab him. Otherwise, I think I got all of them, except for the one-eyed trouser snake in the bedroom. Just don't keep moving forward if somebody starts buzzing at you."

187

Reesa nodded, a puzzled look on her face. "One-eyed trouser snake?"

The officer cocked an eyebrow at Reesa. "You've never heard it called that?"

"Oh, sure I have. I'm just surprised to hear it here." The officer grinned. "Oh, just you wait. You'll see what I'm talking about." *Stick to business,* Reesa thought. *You know how out of your depth you get whenever you try talking about sex and your own personal life. Think we ought to do something about that? Shelve that thought for later. Stick with business. It's safer.*

A few feet further down, as Reesa passed the open door to a bedroom, there was an angry dry *Bzzzzzzz!!* from just inside the doorway. Suddenly Reesa found herself jammed back against the animal control officer, pinning her against a wall while Reesa crouched, her big Glock pistol drawn and pointing towards the doorway where she could no longer see the snake after moving back. Heart racing and hyperventilating. Some of it fear, some of it simply atavistic reaction. All of it utterly involuntary.

"Um, detective? Excuse me, detective?" Gradually Reesa's alarmed response lessened and her body relaxed fractionally. Finally, when she thought the detective wasn't quite so on edge, the officer tapped her on the shoulder. "Detective, if you'll let me by, I can grab the snake." She lifted her Pilstrom tongs. "I really don't think you want to shoot him in the middle of your crime scene. Besides, it's sure to be noisy if you do, and a lot of the people outside will probably get pretty upset."

Reesa turned cautiously to look at her and finally allowed herself to straighten up and smile. "Gee, I don't know why you'd think that. I should think they'd be delighted as hell not to have to deal with one more of these damn … things." She gestured towards the offending reptile. The animal control officer grinned back at her as she edged by the detective in the hallway.

When Reesa was finally able to enter the bedroom, she found the ME already working the woman's body. She surveyed the scene and, upon really looking at the man, murmured, "Oh, my God. Schultz is dead." *So that's what she was talking about. Ah, ah. Stick to business. Or make jokes. Either one is safe. If you don't go any further.*

The ME looked up sharply. "Don't you dare! I've already had to threaten to do an autopsy on my assistant before he's dead just to keep him from telling me that joke, and I'd already heard it, separately, from two of the firemen *and* the animal control officer. I don't need it from you, too. And trust me, I've no intention of taking his … *equipment* home to show my wife." Reesa just grinned at him.

"Anyway, white male, white female, both look to be in their late twenties or early thirties. TOD about two hours ago, give or take. As you can see, they were cuffed together and restrained on the bed. It looks like the snakes were then dumped in between them and their struggles trying to get away upset the snakes even more, which caused them to get bitten multiple times. One of the snakes was actually coiled up between the bodies when I first got here. Snakebite is generally nowhere near as dangerous as most people think, but multiple bites in the head and neck are bad news no matter how you look at it. There's also a small pair of burn marks on the man's leg that makes me think he might have gotten hit with a stun gun or the like. I've got to tell you, this kind of a crime scene is a first for me, but I'm happy to let you collect the murder weapons here."

"Oh, animal control's already done that, thank God. I'll let them check for any serial numbers or other identifying markings." The ME just chuckled in response. "D'you know who called this one in?"

The ME shook his head. "I'm not sure. It may have been the wife; I seem to recall hearing somebody point her out to me and saying something about that. But I wasn't all that concerned about it at the time, and then when I saw the first snake, I figured I had lots more important things to think about. More immediate, too."

When she finally left the house, Reesa was not surprised to see Lynne Fox and her Channel 12 news crew setting up, nor was she really surprised to see Jeff waiting for her. The Channel 5 team was just arriving, and Channel 8 couldn't be far behind. On the one hand, Lynne Fox's designation of the Tucson Ripper was rapidly catching on throughout the city, and all of the channels were not only using the term, they were giving the cases more air time and, presumably, more personal attention than the run-of-the-mill murder now. On the other hand, the rattlesnakes made this particular set of murders truly unusual and, at least in Reesa's experience, one of a kind. Well, two of a kind. Not that she wasn't thankful about that.

Reesa was shaking her head as she walked up to Jeff. "Another one of your cases?"

Jeff shook his own head. "Not this one. I happened to be driving around and saw the Channel 12 van barreling along, so I figured I'd follow it and see where they were going. Wound up here. Saw Chuck and figured you were probably inside."

Reesa went on. "This is one for the record books, I think. I've heard of some people trying to use a rattlesnake as a murder weapon, but that usually means putting it in a mailbox or something like that. It doesn't work, either. This is the first time, at least among any of the cases I know about, that anyone's done something like that successfully." She gave a bit of a shudder. "I may have nightmares over this one. Jeez! What those poor people had to go through."

She was too absorbed in her own thoughts, her memories of the bedroom and what the victims had to have endured, to notice the look of calm concern in Jeff's expression. "Is there anything I can do to help?"

"No, I don't think so. It's just .... I don't especially like snakes. And this ...." She looked around. "I heard that the wife called it in. Where is she?"

Jeff shrugged. "If that was her, well, that's a good question. There was a car heading out of the driveway rather quickly as I drove up, and one of the uniforms was trying to stop it. Let's see." He scanned the people in the area. "That one." He pointed. As Reesa started off in that direction, he called, "We still on for lunch tomorrow?"

Reesa waved. "As far as I know. Check with me then. See you."

Well, at least he'd been smart enough to find out where she was going, Reesa thought after she'd spoken with the officer Jeff had pointed out. She and Chuck could head on out and see her at her sister's immediately. As she and Chuck were going to their car, Lynne Fox called out to her. "Detective Malloy! Can we get some comment from you on this case? Or a comment on the Ripper?" As usual, Reesa ignored her.

****

"Yes? May I help you?" The woman at the door blocked it with her body, preventing Reesa and Chuck from seeing into the house.

They flashed their badges, and Reesa carefully set her foot into the doorway so the door couldn't close. "Mrs. Gardner? I'm Detective Malloy, and this is my partner, Detective Palmer. We need to ask you some questions about ... your husband."

The woman got a distinctly sour look on her face. "That son of a bitch. I'm not his wife, she's my sister. She's not up to talking to anyone right now." She tried to close the door.

Reesa's foot blocked that effort. "And your name, ma'am?"

"I'm Martha Barstow. We can't do this right now. Meggan's too upset." She kept trying to close the door, without effect beyond a certain amount of discomfort to Reesa's foot.

Chuck pushed against the door. "Ma'am, we're sorry to insist, but we really need to speak with her right now. We'll be as brief as we can be, but it's really important." He pushed just a little bit harder, and the woman gave ground a bit. "Ma'am, you can really help us here. You can help your sister here."

Reesa took over. "Mrs. Barstow, we'd really rather just speak with her here. We could take her downtown, and we will if we have to, but we'd really rather just do this quietly, here in your home, than have to make a major production of it. Which would you rather? Honestly? Which do you think would be easier on her?"

192

The woman's reluctance was plain on her face, but the alternative of having her sister taken downtown for more formal interrogation seemed to tilt the balance enough. Of course, if it turned out that there was a need, Meggan Gardner would be going downtown anyway, and both of them were capable of figuring that out, given time. On the other hand, if there was nothing there, then this could indeed be short and sweet. Well, maybe not sweet, given the circumstances, but comparatively short, anyway.

Meggan was sitting on the couch, a box of Kleenex on the coffee table in front of her. Several wadded-up tissues were scattered around the box, but she appeared to be done with her tears for the moment. Chuck and Reesa introduced themselves and showed her their credentials.

Reesa took the lead. "Ma'am, we're truly sorry for your loss." She paused, but got no response. "We don't like to bother you at this time, but we need to ask you some questions about your husband." Mrs. Gardner nodded but said nothing. "Were you the one who found the bodies?"

Meggan shredded the tissue in her hand. "Not really. I walked in and found a rattlesnake in the hall, so I backed out and called the fire department. I guess they actually found the bodies. Somebody came out and told me that Freddie was dead, and they wouldn't let me in to see him. I ... I ... that's when I left." The tears began to flow again, although she ignored them.

Chuck reached out with a new tissue, which Meggan took from him. He retrieved the remains of the used one from her hand and put it with the others on the table as she blotted her face. Reesa went on. "Mrs. Gardner, can you tell us where you were today?"

Meggan dabbed at the corners of her eyes before starting to twist and shred the new tissue. "I was at work most of the day. Freddie told me he didn't want me home before three, so I took my time about getting home." Chuck and Reesa exchanged glances.

"Where do you work?" Meggan gave her the particulars, and then Reesa asked, "Not home before three?"

"He had some woman coming over. Look, he'd ... he was into sex. I mean, he was *really* into sex." A few more tears made their way down her face, but she ignored them. "He got us involved with swingers groups, nude beaches ... he had this tremendous ... *thing*, and he was so proud of it. Had to keep showing it off, had to keep using it."

Behind her, Reesa could hear Martha muttering "bastard," but ignored her.

Meggan kept on. "I didn't really enjoy sex all that much any longer, but Freddie reveled in it. The Schlong, he called it."

Reesa leaned forward. "You're talking about his penis."

Martha broke in. "Of *course* she's talking about his penis! His dick, his cock, his schlong! Jesus, you couldn't escape the damn thing! Go for a swim in the pool? He wouldn't wear a suit, even if he was the only one nude. Or if he did, the goddam thing'd be sticking out one leg of it and he'd be sure to call your attention to it if he thought you hadn't happened to notice it, like there was any danger of *that* ever happening! Want to go sit in the hot tub? He'd be the last one in so he could dangle it in front of everyone's face! He was a pig! Meggie, he *shamed* you!"

Her sister turned to her, her face a picture of utter pain. "Marty, *stop*! He's *gone*, I've *lost* him. I don't have *anyone* any more. Isn't that *enough* for you? *Please!*"

Chuck stood up and walked over to Martha. "Mrs. Barstow, please. We have to do this with your sister. I know it's upsetting, but it's necessary." His voice grew quieter as he led her out of the room.

Reesa handed Meggan another tissue. "You were saying? About your husband's penis?"

"Oh, yes. He had this tremendous one and ... and he loved to use it. He had to do it, all the time. First thing in the morning, last thing at night ... sometimes we couldn't even get into the house. He'd want to do it right there in the garage. Anywhere, any time. We finally reached ... an accommodation, I guess you'd call it. He could ... could have anyone he wanted, and I'd let him use the house. Not say anything. At least he wasn't going to some cheesy motel. He'd let me know, and I'd stay away. Just so long as he didn't bring some disease home, I didn't really mind. Not all that much, anyway. It kept him ... busy. Occupied. Happy."

She started to laugh, bitterly, but it turned into a crying jag. She twisted the tissue until it came apart in her hands. She looked at the pieces before dropping them on the coffee table, and Reesa had another one ready for her. She looked up at Reesa. "I'm not some poor abused thing, you know. When Freddie and I first met, we both wanted it. A *lot*. I loved him. Oh, I know that Martha came to despise him, but I always loved him. He was a caring, gentle man from the very beginning. I always thought that after we were married, as my ... my desire cooled a bit, that his would, too. When it didn't, I tried to do more, tried to keep him happy. After a while, I just couldn't. For a time there, I didn't even dare pick up anything I dropped on the floor. I had to ask him to pick it up for me. Sounds funny, doesn't it? Trust me, when it's that predictable, it stops being amusing.

"But he just couldn't help himself. He was never rough about it, just so incredibly persistent. And huge, of course, but he was always so careful about that, because he really didn't want to hurt me. Or anyone else. Rough stuff never interested him. Then when it was more obvious that I was losing interest, he thought that swinging might help. We tried that for a while, until I finally said I was done with that. No matter what we tried, I just wasn't interested the way he was.

"Nude beaches, well, they weren't so bad. I mean, everybody's naked, and I'm hardly one of the beautiful people, so nobody really noticed me. He got noticed a lot, but he loved it. That's really why he wanted to go. And I always thought he'd be a great father, as gentle and sweet as he was. That was before we found we couldn't have any kids of our own, but we were looking into adopting. And God help me, I still love him!" The tears began flowing once more and Reesa changed Meggan's tissue again.

"This may be a difficult question, Mrs. Gardner, but was there anybody who would have been interested in harming him? Some angry husband, perhaps, or somebody else upset about his ... activities?"

Meggan thought about that for over a minute. "I really don't think so. Most of the women he ... they were women he knew from the swingers' groups, or single women, that sort of thing. And he really tried to be considerate of that, as far as I knew. I guess ... I guess if someone were that upset, it'd be someone I didn't know about. I didn't get into the specifics with him. You understand."

Reesa found herself nodding, although Meggan Gardner had described a lifestyle she doubted she'd ever quite understand, in fact. "One other thing, Mrs. Gardner. Are you familiar with a group here in Tucson calling themselves the Avowed?"

Meggan looked up through her tears. "Who?"

"The Avowed. They're sort of a quasi-religious group. They hold meetings one evening a week, as far as we know. I'm just asking if you've heard of them."

Meggan shook her head. "No, never. The Avowed? That's a funny sort of name. What do they preach?"

Reesa shook her own head. "Nothing that you and your husband would have been interested in, I'm sure. It's not important. I'm just trying to touch all of the bases here. Mrs. Gardner, thank you for speaking with us. If you think of anything, please call me." She handed Meggan her card. "Anything at all. I believe we're done here for now, though. Let me collect my partner and we'll be out of your hair. Again, thank you for speaking with me and I'm … we're both deeply sorry for your loss." Meggan just waved her current tissue without looking up.

On the way downtown, it was several blocks before either detective was interested in talking. Finally Reesa asked, "So what did you get out of the sister?"

Chuck snorted. "Well, as you heard, she detested her brother-in-law, but I don't think she'd have done anything to hurt her sister. She told me several times how shameful she thought his antics were and how disgusting she found him personally, but her concern always came

197

back to her sister, and much as she hates to admit it, and she does, she knows her sister loved him dearly. They're twins, by the way. She also said that she'd been home with her son when Meggan came knocking on her door. Well, just knocked once, opened it, and ran in crying, apparently, all in one motion. Martha sent her son next door as soon as she found out what had happened. I walked her over to retrieve him, and he's, well, he struck me as a bit slow. I let him play with my cuffs for a couple of minutes, and when he gave them to his mother, she couldn't figure out how to work them. That seemed to me to be real, not an act, for what it's worth. She said that she and her son were out shopping this morning, and if that checks out, then her alibi's good, too."

"So we've struck out again. Shit!" Reesa slapped the steering wheel with her right hand to emphasize her words.

Chuck shrugged. "Well, there's still Raul Quiñones to check out."

Her voice was still a bit acid. "Sure, there is. But if you aren't seeing a pattern here already ... no, I know you are. You've been saying so longer than I have. Anyway, if this is another one of the Ripper's cases, and it looks like it is, then I'll bet that he's been just as much in the dark as most of the other spouses we've talked to so far. Probably even more so, since from what he told us on the phone, they're divorced now. That's assuming he even cares, although you're right, we do need to check him out. Hell, Meggan Gardner probably would have been in the dark if she hadn't been a willing accomplice. Well, acquiescent, anyway. Didn't you get the impression that she'd rather ... no, you weren't there. She knew about her husband's ...

extra-curricular activities, I guess I'd call them, and she said she was okay with them, as these things go. My impression was more that she tolerated them for the sake of his happiness, a bit of peace in the house, and to keep from having to put out for him constantly. But she didn't seem to be so much upset as resigned to what he was doing, so no matter how you look at it, it doesn't look like she's a decent suspect here either. Shit!"

Chuck looked thoughtful. "There's one thing here that doesn't fit, you know." Reesa gave him a brief sideways glance as she drove and gestured with one hand for him to go on. "Aurelia Quiñones is recently divorced. She should have gotten an easy way out, at least judging by the Ripper's other cases. Not that I can see how you do that with a bunch of rattlers, but as a single, she wasn't running around on anyone."

"Hmm. Now that you mention it … that hadn't even occurred to me. But if the Ripper is one real single killer, then this sure feels like one of his. Everything else fits, and I'm *damned* glad to know that the son of a bitch isn't infallible, because it's a mistake like that that's probably going to give us a lead to the son of a bitch. But you're right. I don't see how you could tell the snakes to bite her one real good one early on and take their sweet time with Freddy. He also probably would have been bitten elsewhere if the killer could have managed that."

Chuck smiled. "So that wouldn't have been just swelling, huh?"

"Oh, shut up."

****

As usual, Reesa was at her desk the next morning when Chuck came in. After the obligatory coffee, she asked, "Did we get serial numbers on those handcuffs?" She was sorting through her notes from the crime scene and interrogation of the wife. Thoughts of the rattlesnakes and what the victims had to have gone through in their last moments kept running through her head – most unpleasantly. She hadn't slept well the night before, either, thanks to too many dreams about rattlesnakes and being unable to escape them.

Chuck looked through his own notes. "Most of them didn't have any. Cheap imported crap, every one. Probably picked them up at a swap meet, gun show, or the like. We could check out Tanque Verde Swap Meet ..."

Reesa grimaced. "Oh, I expect we will at some point. I just have some trouble imagining anyone who can clean up after himself like this killer can being so sloppy as to buy a quantity of cuffs in our own back yard all at once and make himself unnecessarily visible. Don't you?" Chuck nodded. "And you said 'most of them' didn't have numbers. What did?"

Chuck got an odd look on his face. 'The pair on their wrists had a serial number. It's an old pair of Peerless cuffs. The problem is that when I ran the number, it turns out that those cuffs were originally sold to a cop in LA."

"A cop in LA? So what's the problem with that?"

"Well, I said they were old cuffs. The *problem* is that he bought those cuffs in '62, retired in '84 and died in '97. There's no record of the cuffs themselves one way or the other after his purchase of them."

"Damn."

"Yep."

"Any identifying markings or serial numbers on the murder weapons?"

"The murder … You're kidding." Chuck looked a bit indignant.

Reesa grinned at him. "Yeah, I am. But I sure loved the look on your face when you figured out what I was asking. Anyway, so once again we're up against a dead end. Shit!"

****

"This is Lynne Fox, KOPN 12 News, first on the scene, up close and personal, with another special report in our series on the homicides of couples that have been committed recently around the Old Pueblo. We had still another couple murdered in Tucson this past week in a most *unusual* fashion. Let me recap the previous murders for you before we get into the details of this latest one, and believe me, this one is going to send chills up your spine. It sure did mine." Alone in her sanctuary, Reesa let out a loud sigh. Some days it felt like *everybody* was riding her ass. Lieutenant Almirez, Sergeant Cotton, and even Lynne Fox, who just had to keep reminding everybody in the entire city that these murders were going on all around town and beyond, and neither the Tucson Police nor the Pima County Sheriff's deputies were having any success in finding out who was doing them.

Over and above, of course, making sure that everyone in Tucson knew that she, the one and only Detective Reesa Malloy, wouldn't say anything to Fox and her audience about the murders or the Tucson Ripper. Both with her words and with a shot of Reesa leaving the crime scene, apparently just to create the impression that everybody would know *lots* more about all of the crimes, if only Reesa, and *only* Reesa, would tell her viewers something. *Anything.* For what Fox showed on the screen,

Reesa might as well be the only homicide detective in the entire city. Shit, Jeff had been closer to some of them, almost close enough to catch the killer (but still only *almost*) than she had. Than anyone on the force had. And he was probably the only one, other than her partner, who wasn't riding her ass. *Whoops. Maybe that wasn't the best thing to be thinking about right now.*

When Fox got into the general details of the snakes and what happened with them, Reesa couldn't stop a shudder. Never especially fond of snakes – the mere idea of being trapped like that, thrashing, with more than a half a dozen good-sized rattlers 'up close and personal,' to use one of KOPN's signature phrases, would be almost enough to give her nightmares. No, more than 'almost.' She'd already had one and didn't really have to be reminded of the details yet again.

Reesa figured it was a safe bet that this pair of homicides was going to get even more attention than most, although she still had some lingering reservations in her own mind about whether they were all connected the way Lynne Fox was presenting them. *Of course,* she reminded herself, *when Lieutenant Almirez and Sergeant Cotton are convinced of it, my little old opinion doesn't really count for much, does it?* And such of her reservations as she still had left were fading anyway.

****

"THE AVOWED!" The congregation thundered the final response to the opening litany, and Henry was quite sure that at least some of the Desert Saguaro Lodge staff had heard them quite clearly. This was the first time they'd met in such a large venue, but with the Joneses' help, he'd been careful to get their smallest room of the ones available along the hallway and at a cut rate to boot. There would be plenty of time to move into larger ones as his congregation continued to grow, and by now, he was certain that it would. Who knew? Maybe he'd even have to start a second group. That would mean two nights a week, which would cut into some of his extra-curricular activities, but it would also mean that much more in the collection baskets and he could keep the individual meetings that much smaller. Got to keep one's priorities straight, after all.

He took his usual deep breath before beginning to address them. "Brothers and sisters, welcome. Welcome to all of you, each and every one, whether you've been with us before or not. I'm sure you've all heard about the latest couple that were just murdered this past week, killed by the same serpents that seduced Adam and Eve from the path of righteousness, the path of faithfulness" – no reason not to bend the story a little bit in his favor – "in the Garden of Eden. Let's think about the irony of this!"

Reesa and Jeff sat near the back of the room, watching the people and listening, barely, to Henry's speech. His words brought back her feelings when she'd stepped into the Gardner house, determined to make it seem to anybody watching as though she were utterly unconcerned about encountering a rattlesnake, while the mere possibility scared her silly inside, safely hidden where her iron control would make certain that she'd never admit it to anyone else. Well, anyone other than the animal control officer, that is.

Jeff didn't seem uneasy about being here, but Reesa admitted that she had some concern herself. If Henry had seen her with Schuler at the meeting some weeks before, would he feel that she had violated her 'oath' to him by coming here with Jeff instead? *An 'oath' to Chris Schuler?* *God save me, please. Like I'd like to be shackled to that satyr for even five minutes. Hell, five seconds. With a crop of angry rattlers between us, even. But will that cause a problem? What the hey, done's done. Just have to talk our way out of it if there is any trouble*, she thought. Near the end, when it came time to embrace your partner, Reesa was more tense than she had been with Schuler. Of course, while he'd turned out to have widely roaming hands, she had at least expected it from him. She had no idea at all what to expect from Jeff.

As it turned out, when the time came, he kept his hands still behind her, respectfully, she thought, on her waist and back. She couldn't have asked for more (or would that be less?), and surprisingly when she actually thought about it, she found herself relaxing into him, letting her body mold itself to his. Comforted by the feel of his hands on her back, the feel of his body against hers. Unusually for her, feeling safe. And very comfortable indeed.

When they finally broke from one another with a soft but superficial kiss and sat down, they were among the last half-dozen or so couples to do so. Reesa filed that observation away for future consideration. She found it a bit puzzling at some level (not to mention a bit disturbing, but less so than she would have expected). She told herself she could mull it over before she fell asleep later. Safely alone.

Departing was more leisurely than the last time Reesa had come. Just like before, she could have been among the earliest of the congregation to leave, but she felt no need to rush, other than to escape the group, and Jeff remained in his seat, relaxed and watching the other people as they left. She arched her eyebrow at him in a question, and he merely murmured, "No reason to hurry. If we're supposed to be observing, like you said, then let's take as much time as we can without looking like we're trying." He had a point, and she firmly sat on her discomfort (with the service, not with him!) as she leaned back in her chair to watch as well.

By the time they finally got to the door, at least three-quarters of the people had left. Henry's hand had to be a bit sore by now, but he gave no hint of it in his expression. Reesa took it firmly. "This is truly a marvelous group you've gotten together here, Reverend."

Henry just shook his head with a tired smile. "No reverend, young lady. Just Henry. We're all brothers and sisters together here. There'll be no ranking for us in Heaven, and I'll accept none here." He cocked his head. "I do believe I've seen you among us before," he said. "Weren't you here … well, not here, but with us before, oh, about six weeks ago or so?" Henry had an incredible memory for people, for names and faces. It had stood him in good stead in this business for the entire time he'd been preaching. Not just now, with the Avowed, but even earlier, back when he was at least looking like a respectable minister. He used it shamelessly, just as he had (for that matter) even before he ever found the religious angle to work.

Reesa's smile was dazzling as she tried to throw him off-track. "You have a marvelous memory, Henry. Yes, I was. But I had to leave quickly that night and couldn't stay around to tell you what an incredible impression you made on me."

Now Henry's eyes seemed to bore right into her head. "And you weren't with this gentleman, either. You were with another man. A little taller, perhaps, and a bit more … tanned." *Oops.*

Jeff spoke up quickly. "We're new as a couple, Henry. We both recently separated, very appropriately, from the partners we'd had before and only got together about three weeks back. So we're new to each other, but we're … trying to forge a good relationship together. We thought these meetings might help us. I'm Ray Fields, and this is—"

Reesa stuck her hand out to take Henry's as soon as Jeff let it go and picked up her end of the conversation before he could invent a name for her. "I'm Molly. Molly Carpenter. And yes, Ray's right. We're just in the beginning of our relationship, and I had thought when I was here before that your words were so important, so moving" – *Quit gushing, girl!* – "that I just had to come back, had to bring the two of us here. We're hoping that this relationship works out for us so much better than the ones we just got out of."

Henry smiled. "Just remember to deal honestly with each other, to honor your vows and whatever commitment you make to each other, and I'm sure the two of you will have a long and happy future together. Now, if you'll excuse me, please. I'll be looking for you again next week." Dismissing them with that smile and another brief handshake, he turned to the next couple behind them.

Once safely in Jeff's car, Reesa let out a breath she wasn't aware she'd been all but holding. "God! I never expected him to remember me! Thank you for helping to talk us through it, Jeff. But 'Ray Fields?' Where did that come from?" *Like I can't figure it out.*

Jeff shrugged. "Older cousin of mine from way back. Haven't seen him in twenty years or more, since I was a young kid, but it was a name I figured I'd remember if I needed to use it again, and he probably won't mind me using it in the meantime."

I'm sure he would *remember it. Raymond Escarton Fields? How could he possibly forget it? So the last Family CEO was his cousin, huh? And one close enough to know personally? Not that the entire Family isn't all cousins at some point and to some degree, but he's definitely Family, like I had any doubts about it before,* Reesa thought. *I mean, close cousin to one Family CEO and now working for his successor?*

Jeff went on. "You know, though, the thing about Henry is that he doesn't really seem all that three-dimensional to me. He's more like a … a polyester-clad preacher from Central Casting who's going to go back into his box now until the same time next week. Or maybe a life-size cardboard cutout of a preacher. Even an inflatable doll, if that doesn't bring up any unwanted side images. What does he do in his down time? Where does he live? Where does he go? Does he do any of the other things you expect a preacher, a minister, to do?

"I mean, this whole thing seems kind of flat. Two-dimensional. There's no suggestion that he does anything, pardon the expression, ministerial in between meetings or that he's even completely thought out what he talks about. Most important, and related to that, what drives him?

"Frankly, this looks kind of, no, a *lot* like a con game, when I get to looking at it more critically. Not that fidelity doesn't have a lot to recommend it, and I'd never say that at least some of the people aren't getting something out of it that matters to them, but it all seems sort of … superficial. Except for the services themselves, there's just nothing there. And I trust you noted the overflowing collection baskets? Did you notice that they weren't empty when they first came out?"

Reesa let her lower lip go. "I think I see your point. Neither Henry nor his operation exactly presents as a complete, well-rounded genuine sort of religious-type operation. That 'deal honestly and honor your vows' sounds like the same sort of pap he gives out during the meetings, just recycled enough to sound, well, not exactly fresh, but sufficiently different to slide by most people. I'd probably stick with the two-dimensional characterization, but that's just me. And yeah, the blow-up doll image does call up some … unfortunate connotations." She grinned, although it was hard to make out in the darkened car beyond the gleam of her teeth.

"Henry does have some of the con man feel to me, too, now that you mention it. That said, what to do about Henry is the real question for me. Putting him under surveillance on nothing more than the sort of vague suspicion we've got so far is probably going to raise some serious questions in the Department, and I've already been told that the sergeant won't tell me to unless I come up with at least *something* first. If I did it anyway, I suspect I'd be getting into some serious potential First Amendment issues here, at least as far as they're concerned, and either I find something on him that I can show to justify some actual suspicion and damn fast, or somebody'll likely come down on me like a ton of bricks.

"I'll see what I can find, but I don't think I can just start tailing him on nothing more than the zip we have so far except that he seems more like a con man than a real preacher. I mean, if he is a con man, and this is his scam, then I'd even question whether he's breaking any laws here. He's certainly not breaking any that I can think of, because he's making no promises, no offers. All he's doing is preaching fidelity and love and then asking for contributions. Given that, even if it is a scam, it's crafty as hell and probably completely legal as far as I know." Jeff simply nodded, looking thoughtful, as he started the car. "Let's not forget that couple that carries the collection baskets around, too. The mediums. Who are they, and where do they fit into this?"

Jeff's expression, under the streetlights they passed, looked a bit puzzled. "The mediums?"

Reesa chuckled. "My term for them. Think about them, if you noticed them well enough. Medium height, medium brown hair, on both of them. Medium looks – not too good, not too bad – medium *everything*. Not one single thing about them stands out. They're the epitome of unnoticeability." Jeff mumbled something that Reesa figured indicated understanding.

"One other thing," Jeff added as he drove. "Like I said, what drives Henry? Assuming for the moment that he really is some sort of preacher, then why did he become a preacher in the first place? There are lots of reasons why people do, I know. Some are seeking something, some feel a real calling for the position, some want the authority and respect, and some just figure it's an easy way to make a living, although those last usually find that doing it anywhere even close to well takes a hell of a lot more work than they'd expected beforehand. I don't know about you, but for all of his charm and charisma, and *that's* undeniable, Henry certainly doesn't give me any genuine confidence that he's really in it because he believes that God told him to do it, or because he feels he's got something to offer people. My own feeling is that while what he's saying resonates with the people there, which is why he's being successful, he himself is in it for what they've got to offer him. Money, I mean, along with possibly a bit of ego boo."

"Ego boo?" Reesa looked a bit puzzled.

"Strokes. Psychological reinforcement. Ministers looking for it can get quite a bit, if they try. Really good ones don't."

"You seem to know a lot about that sort of thing."

"My mom's younger brother was a cop. Then one day he decided that God was calling him to be a minister and he went and did it. Never looked back. Neat man. I loved him a lot and I really looked up to him. Always willing to talk to me, both while he was on the force and after he left it, and along the way he told me in great detail about becoming a minister. Not the mechanics, so much, but about how he 'got the call' and what it had meant to him.

"He also loved shooting, even after he turned his collar around, and he kept it up. He taught me to shoot, too. He said that God had suggested to him that he shouldn't hunt any more, but there was no problem with shooting, just with killing, and of course, if push came to shove and he had to shoot in defense of someone, well, defending others was right in line with all of the things he'd been doing while 'serving and protecting' and that ministers

210

served and protected, too. He even gave me the backup gun he'd carried when he was on the force, the same gun I'm carrying now."

Reesa was thoughtful. "You know, I never really looked at Henry like that. It definitely puts a new spin on him. Don't know how we're going to do it, but we probably ought to look a bit more closely at him. You're right about that. I think I'll try to get his fingerprints next week."

Chapter 13

They sat at opposite ends of the couch in Reesa's living room, a cold bottle of white wine, glistening with beads of moisture, sitting on its coaster on the coffee table between them. "I've got to say, Mother, it's really wonderful having you here alone. Nothing against Dad, but not only can't you and I talk the way we used to with him here, but I always have this feeling that some part of him still looks at me like I'm a virginal 12-year old in a white pinafore."

Her mother took a sip of her wine. "Of course he does, Reesa. It's the most natural thing in the world. No father wants to see his little girl as all grown up, and I had much the same sort of problem with your grandfather. I also suspect that seeing his daughter as a police officer, as a detective, is even harder, at least for Rafe. But you're right, it is lovely to be able to talk together like this again."

"There's nobody else I can even begin to talk to this way."

"And I am very happy that you'll do it with me, although I wish you had a really close friend that you could do it with, more frequently, at least on an as-needed basis. Someone closer to your own age."

Reesa chose to ignore that last. "So tell me again why you're here and why you're alone this time."

"Just as I told you over the phone, dear, I'm speaking at a judicial conference in San Diego on Thursday. Your father couldn't come because he's got an *en banc* hearing coming up in the Third Circuit. I'm also delighted that you'd take time out of your busy schedule to get me to and from the airport."

Reesa waved off the compliment, then sat silent for a moment. "I thought you said Dad was giving up going to court when you were named to the Supreme Court."

Her mother chuckled. "Your father give up court work? The way he loves to litigate? Not a snowball's chance in hell. He just limits his appearances now to Federal court, where he can't wind up in front of me." She paused. When Reesa didn't say anything, she continued. "Let's move this into the kitchen. You may be fine, but my body's still on Pennsylvania time. I'm three hours off, and I'm starving. I'd like to get going on supper."

Reesa stood up. "Fine. Put me to work. The salad was your idea, so you're in the driver's seat. Tell me what to do." She smiled. "Make me feel like I'm fourteen again."

Her mother grinned back at her. "Haven't I always been in the driver's seat in the kitchen? At least I don't burn water."

Reesa stuck her nose in the air. "Neither do I. I have much too much sense than to put myself in a position to do anything of the sort. I don't even remember the last time I turned my stove on." The two of them shared a laugh over that.

While her mother was engaged in slicing, dicing, and otherwise making a salad out of the ingredients they'd stopped to buy on the way home from the airport, she continued their discussion. "So tell me, Reesa. How's work going these days?"

"Well, it's not easy, you know. Being the rough, tough detective when you're a woman. Especially in Homicide. I'm always primed to overhear someone saying, 'Yeah, we've got seven dicks in Homicide. Then there's Malloy.' Or some other equally stupid, insulting, sexist,

213

and *patronizing* shit comment like that. I've always got to stay on top, always be the best. Make sure that everyone knows I'm just as tough and ready to go in first as any of them. More so. I think they already do, but I'm definitely going to keep it that way as long as I'm with the department.

"Actually, outside of hearing things like that in my head, and that's the only place I do hear them, I'm utterly thrilled to be the only homicide dickless." She finished with the cucumber she'd been peeling, cut off the ends, and passed it to her mother.

Her mother smiled. "You get so passionate, Reesa. Does anyone actually say such things? And such crude language." A large heirloom tomato fell prey to her deftly wielded knife and was quickly reduced to small pieces which she scooped up and added to the bowl.

Reesa snorted softly. "Say such things about me? In this day and age? I don't think they'd *dare*. Certainly not where anyone else might hear it. But *I* hear it inside, and that's where it ultimately matters. That's what I have to live with, *do* live with, all day, every day. That's what makes me stay tough. And yes, it's crude. Mother, I'm a cop. We use crude language. But it's a great job, and I love it."

"So I see. Here, chop the greens. No, don't use that knife, use the big one. Remember, Reesa, you can always talk to me if it gets to be too much. Or even just if you want to. On to other matters. I asked you this in the car, and you politely deflected the question. Are you seeing anyone?"

"I did not *deflect* it. I said no before I changed the subject."

"Oh, come on, Reesa. I've known you all your life, and I know when your 'no' means 'no.' I also recognize perfectly well when it simply means that you want to avoid discussing something, especially when you immediately change the subject. I call that deflecting. Talk to me, dear. It's just the two of us." Her mother opened the refrigerator. "Where's the dressing? Oh, there it is. Done with the greens yet? And do you want the rest of the turkey for another tossed salad, or should I start adding mayo to it now?"

"The greens are in the bowl, and I'll have to save it for another tossed salad, or maybe a sandwich. There'll be plenty of stuff left over, I'm sure, and I tossed my mayo when it started to look patriotic. You know, red, white, and blue. *Inside* the jar." Her mother waited patiently, and finally Reesa sighed. "Well, there is this guy ..."

"So you are seeing someone. Have you slept with him?"

"*Mother!*" Reesa's knife clattered onto the cutting board.

The Honorable J. Franklin Malloy, associate justice of the Supreme Court of the Commonwealth of Pennsylvania, just shrugged as she finished assembling the salad. "I'm simply asking, Reesa. You're certainly old enough by now to have a sex life of your own without my judging you over it. I also haven't forgotten that ... what did we agree to call it? That *episode* of yours in college, and no, your father still doesn't know about it. Not from me, anyway. But your wellbeing concerns me quite a bit, and I know you've been alone for a number of years, to the point that I'm becoming seriously concerned.

"It looks to me as though you hole up here, with your books, your garden, and your TV, and avoid any sort of social life or other involvement, which is ... worrisome to me. I thought that you seemed to be much happier at some deeper level when you were in that relationship, at least before it ended so … poorly. The honest truth is that I want to see you happy like that again.

"I also presume you're still assuaging your feelings over that episode by stashing away toys in that back bedroom you keep locked up and then giving them to the Marines every year the way you used to. Quite unnecessary, but harmless, as we've agreed before. So I ask. I'm sorry if it bothers you, but I'm just being your mother. I love you and I'm concerned for you." She pulled Reesa to her and held her daughter close for a moment, then let her go.

Reesa made a moue as she went for the flatware. "Well, I don't completely avoid having a social life. I go out with the guys for a beer after work periodically. But I'm pretty much a loner, you know. And no, I haven't slept with Jeff. It's … not that sort of a relationship. Not that I believe he wouldn't want to, and he's not gay. I certainly don't think so, anyway. He definitely doesn't read to me as gay. But he's being quite the Boy Scout and not making any unrequested advances. Yet. We just go to lunch together from time to time."

Her mother took another sip from her wineglass before putting it on the table and taking her seat. "Reesa, you're not a loner. Remember, I've known you since you were born. I was actually there at the time." She grinned at her daughter, who grinned back. "If you were really a loner, you wouldn't have been half so attached to Frank and Grace. You also wouldn't have fallen so hard for him back in college or been so upset when he ran off. Admit that much, at least. You may want to be alone, but you're no loner." Reesa stuck out her tongue at her mother, who appeared unconcerned. She took some more of her wine. "So tell me about this fellow. How did you meet him?"

"In a restaurant over lunch. He asked to sit with me because there weren't any other seats available, and then he did the same thing again about two weeks later."

"And he knew about you?"

"That I'm a cop?" Her mother nodded. "Yeah, well, he certainly knew the second time. He'd seen the badge and gun the first time. But he's a PI and carries, too, so he wasn't concerned. Oh, and get this. He's Family."

Her mother stiffened slightly and paused, her fork in mid-air. "You told him about yourself?"

Reesa shook her head. "Oh, no. Not a chance. But his name is Jeff Escarton, and if that name weren't enough of a dead giveaway all by itself, believe it or not, he actually works for A.M. Youngston." She picked out a piece of turkey, then put it back down in favor of a piece of tomato.

Her mother considered that for a moment. "Just like the Family CEO. And eat your turkey, too. You need the protein."

Reesa chuckled. "Yes, Mother. Thank you ever so much for making me feel fourteen again, just like I requested. And she *is* the Family CEO. I checked."

Her mother arched an eyebrow. "She? The current CEO's a woman?"

"After he gave me his business card, my curiosity kicked in, so I came home and called the Family business office. Asked about a private investigator here in Tucson, and the woman on the other end gave me A.M. Youngston and Associates. Told me to deal with either Amy Trevethen

217

or Jeff Escarton, and that A.M. Youngston wouldn't take or return phone calls. Yes, she said, this is the A.M. Youngston who's the CEO, and that's all she'd tell me there. Now I thought that was strange to begin with, especially considering that the CEO's initials spelled out the name 'Amy,' but Jeff had already mentioned Amy as the 'senior investigator.' So I did a quick inquiry elsewhere and found out that she is, in fact, A.M. Youngston herself. I don't know if 'A.M.' stands for Amy something, and if so, for what. For all I know, she may have taken the nickname just from her initials, but I can't tell either way, because all of her old licenses simply read A.M. Youngston, but that's her, all right. Also, when you go into the building – it's a renovated house – she's got the only other office. The big one; Jeff's is quite a bit smaller. So yeah, I'd definitely say that's her."

"A quick inquiry elsewhere? What does that mean?"

Reesa swallowed and smiled. "The second time Jeff came to my table over lunch, I was rereading *The Star Where I'm Headed*. You remember."

Her mother thought for a moment. "Not that god-awful science fiction convention with all of those people in costumes. I'm certainly glad that you never got into such things to that degree."

Reesa's smile got just a bit broader and she chuckled again, deep in her throat. "Why, Mother! Where's your sense of fun?"

With a look of clearly feigned superiority, her mother responded, "I had it surgically removed when I was first named to the bench." She managed to keep a straight face for whole minute longer before they shared another laugh together.

"Oh, pooh! Find it again, because I think you've been getting much too stuffy since you became a judge. Anyway, yes, that's the one. Mother, *The Star Where I'm Headed, Second Star on the Left,* and *Vac Suit Repairs Made Easy* were my absolute favorite books back then. They're still high on my list, but I just *had* to get them autographed when I heard the author was coming to town. That's why I made you take me to the convention. Anyway, Jeff told me that Colin Youngston was his *boss's* father. So I got his general location from the Family business office, found his phone number, and I called him. I identified myself as a TPD detective and said I was calling about his daughter. His first response was to ask if Amy was all right. So yeah, that's her. Oh, and do you know that there's a romance author in the Family?"

Now it was her mother's turn to smile. "Oh, yes, I do indeed. In fact, if you ever come back home, you'll find a whole set of her books in the library, each one personally autographed to your father and me. I'm sure she'd give some to you as well, if you asked. The author's name, well, her pen name, is Regina Harding. I'm sure you don't read her books, so you'd never notice how many of her over-tanned and improbably muscled heros are named Franklin or Rafael. She also uses Janis quite often for her more sultry heroines, and had at least one character named Reesa, two Mirandas, and a Merissa, as I recall. Not that I read them, but I've flipped through enough of them to see all that. That's your Aunt Gina."

Reesa's eyes grew wide. "*Aunt Gina?* You're kidding me!"

"Not a bit. Regina Harding Corliss."

Reesa looked thoughtful. "You know, I don't believe I ever knew her middle name. But she can keep Merissa."

"Perhaps you never did know it. But I do wish you'd get over your reaction to the name Merissa. It's been years. Anyway, Gina thinks it's an absolute hoot that she can sit at her computer for several hours at a time, a few weeks a year, turn out a couple of hack-written books – that's her description, by the way, not mine – that will sell very nicely, while I have to go off to work in an office every day, five days a week, and then bring work home evenings and weekends. Naming her characters that way, well, that's after me and your father. And you, too."

Reesa just shook her head. "To think that your cousin, your college roommate …. Oh, God. That's just *priceless*." She started to chuckle and only with some effort kept from breaking out laughing.

Her mother stood up and Reesa began stacking dishes. "Anyway, back to A.M. Youngston and this Jeff Escarton. Do you think she knows about you?"

Reesa nodded. "Oh, I figure it's likely. I expect her father told her about my call, and the only reason I'd have been concerned about that relationship would be if I were Family myself, right? Besides, I had to identify myself to the business office."

"Well, yes. You're probably right. But from what you're saying, then, apparently she hasn't told this Jeff Escarton about you, even though he's Family, too. What's he like? And are you going to tell him about yourself? Dessert?"

Reesa shrugged. "Possibly. Telling him about me, I mean, assuming she doesn't tell him first. Dessert, yes. Make that probably telling him, if the right time ever comes. He's willing to hang around – said he wants to, in fact – until our relationship changes, whichever way it goes then. Admits when I press him that he wants more but won't push me to get it, at least as long as I tell him I don't want him to. He's being very much the super gentleman with me, which is ... nice. Refreshing, even. And it's something I can handle without, well, abreacting. So we'll see.

"He's right about one thing. The relationship is bound to change, one way or another. If nothing else, I want to resolve it somehow. But I'm still a bit uneasy. Make that a lot uneasy. Just less so than I'd be if he tried to push me, because if he did, I'd know what to do about it. Or maybe that makes me more uneasy. Hell, I don't know. Anyway, at this point, I have to admit, if I broke it off, damn it, I'd *miss* him. As for what he's like beyond that, well, he's tall, fairly well-built, nice looking, and very ..." She shrugged. "Respectful, I guess I'd say. He's got nice taste in restaurants and ... well, I find I enjoy being with him."

"Ah, Reesa. It sounds like you've found ... a friend. Or are at least in the process of developing one. That's great. I think it's fantastic, in fact. You need a friend. So the two of you just have lunch together? And what dessert goes with the rest of this wine?"

"Well, he did have me over for dinner at his place one evening. Cooked the whole meal himself, every bit. Even dessert, and he's a very good cook, at least with what he made. I warned him ahead of time that I wasn't going to sleep with him, and he didn't so much as try me, damn it. I even had on silk underwear, just in case." Reesa got out two of her peanut butter cups and handed her mother one.

Her mother chuckled as they headed back into the living room. "Definitely conflicted. Pay him back." Reesa's eyes widened. "No, I'm not saying you should sleep with him. Do as you see fit in that regard, I trust your judgment. But have him to dinner here." She looked again at her peanut butter cup. "With white wine? Barbaric."

"Barbaric, my ass. Peanut butter cups go with anything. But have him to dinner here? How? I can't cook like that! You know how I cook! I open cans or heat frozen! When I bother at all!"

"Reesa, order in a pizza. You can even have it catered if you want to. I would go so far as to offer to pay for it if you would like me to. But return the invitation. Even if the relationship doesn't turn out to go anywhere farther, you should give him something back, and you should do it here. Dinner isn't a lot. And … perhaps it will go somewhere." She paused to finish her candy. "You're right. They do go with white wine. Amazing."

"Don't push me, mother. I'll think about it."

"As I said, I'm not pushing you to sleep with him, Reesa. I'm trying to help you have a friend. At least based on the ones I know, Family members tend to be so private and guarded that serious friendships are rare, except with a spouse or with other Family members. Since he is one, whether he knows about you or not, even if you were to let something slip, it wouldn't matter. He sounds to me as though he would be good for you."

"Mother." Her voice took on a bit of an edge.

"As a friend, dear. Simply as a friend. Whatever else he might become would be up to you, whenever you feel it would be appropriate. If ever." Her mother looked around the room. "I don't see anything of Frank and Grace here. I kind of thought that I would."

Reesa got a somber expression. "I didn't keep a lot of their things. It was … awfully painful when I had to clean out the house."

"I'm sure it was. After all, with you spending almost all of your after-school afternoons there, they were almost as much your parents as Rafe and I were. We were very lucky to have them living next door to us."

A slight smile. "Well, if I couldn't be safe with a cop and his wife, where could I be? And they said a couple of times that I was the daughter they never had. Remember when Uncle Frank took me to the shooting range? The first time?"

Her mother shook her head. "Your father and I were most upset. Especially when you came home and announced that you were going to be a detective just like he was. But you were very good to them, too. Very attentive, especially towards the end."

"They deserved it."

"Yes, they did."

"And now I am a detective, just like he was, and I love it."

"Didn't he leave you some guns? Surely you kept those."

Reesa nodded towards the coffee table. "Guns, handcuffs, and at least some of the shields and badges from his family. All of them now, actually, since I finally managed to get reproductions of the ones he didn't have, although doing that was a major production. You wouldn't believe the hoops you have to go through to get a really good badge, even if it's one that's no longer in use. But I eventually did, and they're all in there. Want to see? I've got the key."

"Thank you, Reesa, but no. You know I don't particularly like guns. I put up with them, because it's your job, but I really haven't the interest or appreciation. I'm just sure that Frank would be flattered to know about your treasuring them."

"There's a picture, too. In the bedroom. Right alongside the picture of you and Dad with me, I've got that picture of them with me, too." She paused. "God, I miss them."

Her mother took Reesa's hand. "I'm sure you do, Reesa. They were very special people and they were absolutely wonderful to you. Even before they left you everything. They loved you, there's simply no other way to say it."

Reesa shrugged. "They didn't have anyone else to leave it to."

Her mother squeezed Reesa's hand and shook it once sharply. "Don't. Don't you *dare*. They did that because they loved you and because you loved them, too, not because they didn't have anyone else. They *wanted* to do it for you."

****

Jeff sat in his car and perspired. The desert camouflage t-shirt he had on wasn't too bad, but on Amy's advice he always wore jeans. He had confirmed that it was a good idea, because they were a lot safer than shorts would have been when he had to hike through the desert, where the plants bit and the animals could bite worse, but they were hot this time of year. Not quite as hot, perhaps, in the sand and khaki colors he typically wore while working as regular blue ones would be, but they were by no stretch of the imagination cool. Oh, well, it was what it was, he could live with it. He'd lived in Tucson long enough to learn that he didn't have a lot of options during the summer months. And his reaction to winter temperatures these days strongly suggested that he'd become as acclimated to the weather as he was going to. God knows that he never used to be upset when the temperatures got near freezing.

He'd already gotten enough pictures of the errant wife welcoming her lover at the door, as well as the lover arriving. Getting any pictures of them together inside the house was going to be a lot tougher. Given a choice, he'd much rather be working a job in the city proper, where lines of sight tended to be tighter and more on a level than up here in the Catalina foothills. Not that he really ever had a choice, unless he wanted to turn down a job, and he was just a bit too hungry, professionally, to do that without a lot better reason. There was a knoll not too far away from the house that ought to give him some sort of line-of-sight into the windows, both in the living room and what he figured was likely the bedroom. Working his way up to it would require that he park the car and hike, but if he started now, he'd probably be in position in thirty to forty minutes. Hopefully they'd still be at it. Hell of a waste of time and effort if they'd finished by then, but those are the breaks of the game.

Inside the house, thanks to air conditioning, the temperature was a lot cooler. The temperature between Martha Tennenholz and George Hocksley was warmer than the rest of the room, of course. There was plenty of moisture between them, and some of it was perspiration, too, not that they cared. Suddenly, though, Martha pitched forward onto George, and he could probably be forgiven for thinking it was just some sort of sudden change in her motions ... for a moment.

Then a face framed by white swam into his view just before his eyes were covered with something dark that stuck to his skin. He tried to remove it, but Martha was in the way of his arms reaching for the tape. Then something tightened around his wrists behind her. It felt narrow and hard, but he had no idea what it was because he couldn't see it. Then more of the same sorts of thing were tightened around their arms where hers lay along his, with a sound each time that resembled, faintly, a zipper. Then their legs were similarly fastened. Tied together, they struggled for another position. Sex was now the last thing on their minds, and anyway, he'd shrunk to limpness just about the time his wrists were immobilized.

The last actions were when he heard that sound again, first as another tie was tightened around Martha's neck, and then one last one around his. The killer simply stood back and waited patiently as the couple struggled against their bonds. They struggled to breathe and both turned red before Martha's face went purple and she ceased struggling. This seemed to intensify George's attempts to free himself, or even draw a breath against the constriction of the zip tie. It was only another minute or so before he, too, turned purple and then became still.

The opening of their sphincters as they died added a distinctly different and unpleasant aroma to the musky scent that they had originally generated, but the killer's

226

eyes remained bright and the eager smile remained as a quick check showed that no trace evidence had been left. A faint tremor shook the killer's body. Carefully gathering up every single one of the remaining zip ties, the killer left the house through the back door before removing the covering clothes and gloves on the back patio and fading away unseen. *Shouldn't put tape on the eyes next time. That ... had been a mistake.* Watching the eyes as the victims realized their fate and then succumbed to it made it all even more ... delicious. But this one had worked well enough, as these things go. It would do. It would have to.

Up on the knoll, Jeff arranged himself cross-legged on the ground and set up his tripod at minimum extension in front of him. Wiggling the tripod both made sure it was securely set and lowered it just that fraction of an inch that he needed. He slid the plate under the lens into the clamp on top of the ballhead, tightened the clamp, and loosened the ball itself. He adjusted the friction before turning the lens to its maximum magnification. Not enough.

Tightening the ball again, he took a tele-extender from his bag and put it between the lens and camera body, then had to adjust the camera's position once more to look inside the house. The dimmer image didn't help, but at least he now had plenty of magnification. He was actually slightly higher than the windows of the house, so he was able to look downwards into them. Or at least he would have been, if not for the reflections off the windows. He dug in his bag for a polarizing filter and fitted it into the filter slot in the lens, then adjusted the angle until the window reflections disappeared. Nothing in the bedroom. Was that the right room? How about the living room?

Oh, *shit!* They were there, all right, but that was a position never mentioned in the *Kama Sutra* or any other sex book Jeff had ever perused in his younger days. They weren't moving, and they didn't have a healthy look to them. In fact, they looked ... Jeff cranked the magnification up to its highest. Judging by the protruding tongues and discolored faces, they were definitely dead. Damn! Maybe, just maybe, if he'd been in position sooner ...

He cut that thought off unfinished. Saving lives wasn't really his business. Not that he wouldn't do it if the opportunity arose, but that wasn't really what he was there for. Well, at least there'd be no problem closing in now, although he figured he was probably better off staying outside of where the crime scene line would probably be drawn. Less to explain, if nothing else. Packing up his gear, he headed back to his car. Once again he thought, *This is* not *the way I like closing cases.*

It only took him another forty-five minutes or so to find and reach a closer vantage point, one he wouldn't have dared use to see people who might look out the window and notice him. No such problem now, unless his previous assessment of the situation had been completely wrong. He'd take that chance. The view through his little monocular confirmed what he'd seen from the knoll. Definitely too late, and equally definitely another case gone. *Damn!* He pulled out his cellphone and debated for a minute. Finally he hit speed dial for a number he knew by heart anyway.

"Reesa, it's Jeff. You know any of the people over at the Sheriff's Department?"

"I know a couple well enough. Why?"

"There's been another couples murder, this one up in the foothills. It took me a while to get into position to see them inside, and it looks like the Ripper struck while I was working my way up there. I was on a knoll a ways from the house and a bit higher before I could see them, but they're both dead. It looks like they probably were when I got set up there, although they were fine when I left my initial position. That was at least an hour and a half, close to two hours ago now. I could probably call 911, but I thought you might want to steer it to someone you know and possibly come out here yourself."

"I'll see what I can do. Give me the address."

After hanging up, Jeff headed back through the scrub brush and cactus to his car again. By the time he arrived near the house, the deputies had already set up a perimeter and were keeping the public, including Jeff, outside the tape. Reesa pulled up and parked alongside one of the Sheriff's Department cars. One deputy tried to wave her off as she pulled in, until she flashed her badge at him.

She caught Jeff's eye and nodded, but went over to one of the other Pima County deputies and identified herself first. Jeff couldn't hear what was said, but at least some of the motions were obvious. He seemed to be gesturing her to go on into the house as he lifted the crime scene tape for her to duck under, but she came over to Jeff first. "Bob Brice, the deputy I know, is inside, and I'm going to go talk to him. I'll come see you afterwards. Can you hang around?"

Jeff shrugged. "Not like I've got a lot to do at the moment, and somebody's probably going to want to take my statement anyway." He didn't look happy. Reesa waved the deputy she'd been talking to over and told him about Jeff before heading into the house.

Inside, the crime scene was generally familiar to Reesa, if she didn't count the number of strange faces. Spotting Detective Brice, Reesa called to him. He turned to face her. "Reesa! Delighted you could make it. Still running for fun?"

She nodded. "Oh, yeah. Every day, in fact. You?"

He laughed. "Mostly from my ex-wives, these days."

Reesa gave him a sharp look. "Ex-wives? Are you and Kathy ...."

Brice shook his head. "Oh, no. We're fine. It's just a joke. And it's why I couldn't ever be involved with you. I have to be able to outrun the women I'm with." A quick grin. "Okay, enough joking. So, any quick impressions for me?"

Ignoring the first, she responded with a quick shake of her head. "Nope. Haven't really looked at it all that carefully yet, but given what I've seen in my own cases, I'd be a bit surprised if you came up with anything helpful no matter how hard you look. I'm just here because a friend of mine found, well, saw the vics shortly after they were killed and suggested I call you directly instead of calling it in to 911 himself."

One of the crime scene techs was down on his hands and knees, looking under the furniture. He paused at the sofa where the victims had obviously been before their struggles moved them to the floor. "Well, well, well. What do we have here?" He reached underneath, carefully, and withdrew a hand with an empty brass cartridge case. "Look at this. .40 Smith and Wesson and, unless I miss my guess, never reloaded. No sizer marks, anyway, and no other signs of having been reused." He carefully bagged it and started to move on.

Reesa went over and touched him on the shoulder. "Excuse me. Were you saying something in English?"

He chuckled. "Sorry. I tend to talk to myself when I work. I'm Bill Turner." He stuck out his hand.

Reesa shook it, the latex gloves both wore hindering their grip just slightly. Neither really noticed. "Reesa Malloy, TPD Homicide."

"TPD? Oho. Here to see how the other half lives?"

"Sort of." With a smile. "But you were saying something about the cartridge case you found."

He pulled out the bag. "Oh, yeah. Look here." He smoothed the evidence bag over the side of the case. "I can't be completely sure without checking this under a microscope, but when you reload a case, you begin by running it into a sizing die to squeeze it back down to factory specs. Even with a carbide die, it usually leaves some scratches along the case that you can normally see with the naked eye. If the die is new and smooth enough that there are no scratches, then the case can look burnished, but it's still possible to tell that it's been resized, at least under the 'scope. Understand me?"

"Um, I think so. What you're saying, then, is that this case looks like it's factory new."

"It's been fired, of course. But just the once, from what I can see with the Mark 1 naked eyeball. It's exactly the sort of thing I find at the range behind every Fed and Raytheon Security type, among others, that I shoot with or around. They get their ammo for free and just leave their brass lying around. I get a lot of my own .40 caliber brass for reloading that way. Pretty much all of it, in fact." That comment about Feds and their ammunition tickled something in Reesa's memory.

"I take it you shoot for fun."

The tech smiled. "Every chance I get." Reesa thanked him and stepped back over by the detective.

"As I was about to ask, who's this friend of yours?" Bob's question seemed honest enough.

"A PI that I know. He was watching one of the vics, tailing him here, and after he came inside, it took Jeff a while to get set up where he could see into the house without being too obvious. Well over a half-hour, from what he told me. By the time he got there, they were already dead. Then he came closer to check again before he called me. Figure not less than two hours, in all, from the last time they were known to be alive."

"You think he's telling you the straight story?"

"You mean do I think he might have done it?" Reesa shook her head. "No, I don't think he's the killer. He's just been in the wrong place at the right time more than once because of his job."

They were both squatting down, examining the bodies more closely. "You too close to look seriously at him?"

Reesa gave that a moment's thought. "Don't think so. It's a judgment call at this point. I mean, I've got a number of these crime scenes, every one with diddly in the way of trace, so even if it is him, I couldn't tie him to any of them. If you've got any ideas in that regard, I'm all ears. Until then, I've just got to go with my gut, and my gut says he's simply upset by losing cases this way. Besides, I can't say that we're *that* friendly." *Well, not at the moment, anyway.*

"So you'd be able to admit it if you had any suspicions about him."

Reesa nodded. "Absolutely."

Bob looked even more closely at the zip tie around Martha's neck. "This stuff should give me a decent partial print."

Reesa snorted. "Knock yourself out. The killer seems to be double-gloving. There's never been so much as a hint of a print at any of my scenes, even as little as you might occasionally get through a single glove. And he does a damn good job of cleaning up after himself, too. I mean, my place should be so clean."

"So you think this is more of the Tucson Ripper's work, huh?"

"If you believe in that shit. Like I said, I've got a bunch of these cases, although this is the first one I've seen where they've been killed while actually having sex, although my snakebite case came close. While I'm willing to accept that they *may* be connected, I've yet to be completely convinced of it, and without some sort of trace at the scenes, I couldn't prove it even if I thought they were. Or deny it if I thought otherwise, for that matter. But step outside. Who's first on the scene from the media? Lynne Fox and her team is outside, setting up for a report, bet on it. I saw the Channel 12 truck coming up the road as I walked inside, and you know that cases like this are her beat these days. We can take our own bets on it if you want, but I'm not going to bet against it, and for damn sure she'll say it is anyway. Good ratings are all that matter to that bitch."

Bob simply smiled. "You don't sound as though you like her."

"She's an arrogant pain in the ass and fake all the way through, from the color on her toenails to her dyed hair and her ..."

Bob stood up. "I get the picture. And I agree with you, for what it's worth." He grinned. "I'd better go talk to this PI of yours. He seems to be the only witness I'm liable to get with any information worth a shit, however little it may be. Introduce me?"

Reesa stood with him. "Sure. You know, it's more of a hunch than anything else, but I'd like to have our lab guy take a look at that cartridge case your man found. One of my cases was a shooting, and there were a bunch of empties left at the scene. Something your man said triggered my memory about what our guy said at that crime scene. Just in case, I'd like to have him compare them. Would you let me take it?"

Bob thought for a moment. "Well, there's been no shooting here, so it's kind of peripheral evidence at best. Sure, why not? I'll log it out to you. But bring it back when you're done with it, y'hear?"

Reesa just grinned at him.

Outside, Jeff was waiting as patiently as he could in the hot Tucson sun, wondering if his sunscreen was really doing him any good. It certainly didn't keep him from sweating, but he hadn't really expected it to. Luckily for him, the Channel 12 news team had set up well away from him. He'd have made sure of it in any event, even if he had to circle around to the opposite side of the perimeter. The Channel 5 team was between him and them, which didn't bother him one bit. Reesa walked over to him, just on the

234

other side of the crime scene tape. "Well, you were right. They're both dead, and it looks like another in the same series, if it is a series." She glanced over her shoulder at Lynne Fox, who was setting up for her report. "I'd sure like to know how she manages to beat the other stations to the scene. Anyway, I've got a bit of evidence I need to run down to our lab. You need anything?"

He looked around. He could see the PCSD detective approaching, and he figured he'd have to give a statement as to what he'd seen. "I think I'm going to be busy for a while. You free for lunch any time in the next couple of days?"

"Probably Wednesday. Let's make it supper, before the meeting. Call me, okay?" Reesa made the introductions before walking off.

As she was walking back to her car, she heard Lynne Fox calling her. "Detective Malloy! Can you tell our viewers why you're here at a county crime scene? Are TPD and Pima County joining forces to work on the Tucson Ripper's cases? Are you setting up a task force? Can you give us any input on the Ripper and the murders he's committed? Detective Malloy!" Reesa ignored her. As usual.

****

"Detective Malloy? Excuse me, Detective?"

Reesa walked towards the door, disarming her alarm with the remote as she went. Who in the hell was at her door? Who even knew where she lived? And who in the *hell* would be here at this hour? She unlocked the door and opened it.

The last thing she would have expected was to have a microphone thrust into her face as Lynne Fox stepped into the doorway. "Excuse me, Detective, but I've been trying for quite some time to get some input from you on the Tucson Ripper, and I've gotten the feeling that you've been avoiding me. This came in to my office, by the way, and I think you'll be interested in it." She held out an envelope with Reesa's name on it. As Reesa took it from her, Fox went on. "I'd like to ask you some questions about that once you've seen it. But in the meantime, this is a very important story, you're the lead detective on most of the cases, all of the ones in the city proper, anyway, and the citizens of the Old Pueblo want to know just what's going on and what they need to worry about."

Reesa wanted to shut the door. Badly. Unfortunately, the reporter's position made that impossible. A microphone wasn't exactly a deadly weapon, was it? And how the hell had Fox found out where she lived? That was one of Reesa's most closely-guarded secrets. "I'm sorry, but I don't give interviews, I don't comment on ongoing investigations, and I especially do not do anything of the sort here in my home and after hours. Please leave." Lynne's blue-gray eyes met Reesa's brown ones, and finally Lynne blinked.

"But Detective, people are *worried*. People in our city are, quite frankly, terrified by what's going on, and they want to know what sort of danger they're in, how close the police are to solving the case and how soon the Ripper is going to be behind bars. As I said, you're the lead detective on most of the cases, so you're the best person Tucsonans can turn to for that information. I have to be able to tell the public what they so desperately want to know. *Need* to know."

Reesa took a half-step forward, closing in on Lynne, deliberately invading her personal space, and the reporter stepped back a small distance almost involuntarily. It gave just enough room for Reesa to shut the door, and she could still hear the reporter trying to ask questions as she relocked the door and reset the alarm. *Bitch!* Okay, tonight, just this once, she'd pour herself a second drink. Anything to let that little incident settle.

First things first. She got a knife from the kitchen and slit open the envelope. It contained a printout of an email.

Dear Ms. Fox:

You appear to be ahead of the police and sheriff in figuring out about me, and since there's no further point in hiding, I thought it might be appropriate to offer my congratulations. Perhaps now my efforts will be seen in the city for what they really are.

My activities will continue. There are plenty of appropriate targets out there, and I have several more potential ones lined up. I'm not going to provide a timeline for you, but rest assured, you shall have plenty of additional opportunities to make more of your special reports. Please do. I enjoy them. It's just too bad, I suppose, that I must remain in the shadows, so to speak.

And thank you for the name. I hadn't really considered how I wanted to be addressed, but I find that I like it.

Until the next time.

The Tucson Ripper

Underneath the signature line was a listing for a YouTube video. Reesa went to her computer and carefully keyed it in, then hit Enter. It only took a few seconds to come up, and as the opening notes of the song rang out, she recognized it instantly.

Just got home from Illinois, lock the front door, oh boy!
Got to sit down, take a rest on the porch.
Imagination sets in, pretty soon I'm singing,
Doo, doo, doo, looking out my back door.

My back door??? Well, on the one hand, since the back door exit was something they'd kept hidden, that certainly made this seem that much more … genuine. On the other hand, how *dare* this bastard make light of what he was doing? This was definitely a night for more alcohol. Reesa topped off her wineglass, and, on a whim, set it on the counter while she went into her bedroom and stripped off her clothes. She'd go out and sit in her hot tub for a while. The belligerent aerial ballet of the hummingbirds always diverted her, and she needed that or something like it tonight.

Once settled in the warm water with her second glass of wine and disappointed by the absence of the little birds, she let her mind drift to see what might come up out of the murk. *Uncle Frank, what do you do when you have a really hard case?*

In her mind, she could hear him reply. *Reesa, it's the really hard cases that make the job so fascinating. You follow the evidence. There's almost always something you can use.*

But what if it's a really, really *hard case? What if there's no evidence at all?*

Reesa, use your training. All of it, not just what they gave you at whatever academy you went to. Everything, right on back to what I teach you here. Everything you've learned in your life. Gather every bit you can find, no matter how inconsequential you may think it is, and lay it out in your mind. See what jumps out at you.

Reesa had been silent at that point for a whole minute – an eternity, at that age. She must have been about eight or nine. Then she had pressed on. *But what if nothing jumps out? What if there's nothing at all?*

Frank Wilton had sighed. Reesa was a darling girl whom he loved as though she were his own daughter, the daughter he and Grace would never have. But when she got onto something like this, she wouldn't let go until she'd worked it to death. A good trait for a detective to have, but it could get a bit trying in a child. As always, he was patient. *Then you listen to your gut. Sometimes your subconscious can put things together that you haven't even recognized as being related and come up with something that will help you. If it does, it'll find some way to let you know. You've got good instincts. Let your subconscious help. And sometimes, Reesa, you just have to accept that you can't solve every single crime you get. We win a lot. We don't win every time.*

She didn't accept that she couldn't win every time. Oh, she knew it happened, and there came a point that she could let go of a case that simply couldn't be cleared. But she fought tooth and nail to solve each and every case she got, no matter what. She didn't even realize it, but she was significantly more tenacious about that than most of the other detectives around her. Finishing her second drink, she stepped out of the tub and reached for her towel. She still needed to head down the hall to her special room for her evening emotional allotment.

****

The next morning at the station, she showed Chuck the email she'd gotten from Lynne Fox. He looked it over and then looked up at her. "What's this website down here?" He pointed to the line under the signature.

Reesa snorted. "*Looking Out My Back Door*, by Credence Clearwater Revival. Think that means anything to us?"

Chuck's eyebrows went up. "You mean like how our killer gets away from the crime scenes?"

"That's exactly what I mean, and that's why I think it's real. *Bastard!*"

"And the son of a bitch enjoys fifty-year old rock music. Who in the hell does that? I mean, is that crazy or what? Are we the elephants or the tambourines?" Reesa shrugged. Chuck tapped the sheet of paper. "And he's going to kill more. Says so right here."

"Yep. It does. So let's get this around to everybody and let them take some of the worry off our backs. But let's let them find out about CCR all by themselves."

Chuck was still looking at the paper. "Can we track this email address? I don't recognize the domain."

Reesa got a sour look on her face. "You're not likely to. It's somewhere in the Middle East, and we're not exactly able to get anything out of them with a warrant. Of course, the way things can bounce around the net nowadays, it could have been sent originally from somewhere down the street, but the only way we could ever figure that out would be to get the original with all of the hidden data on it, and you know our chances of doing that."

Chuck's sour look matched hers. "Yeah. Zip."

Just then the phone rang. "Homicide. Malloy."

"Detective Malloy, this is Lynne Fox." *Oh, just fucking* lovely. *To what do I owe this pleasure?* Reesa wondered. "I was wondering if you'd had a chance to look over that email I left with you yesterday?" Chuck was looking curiously at Reesa.

"Yes, Ms. Fox, I have." Chuck's eyes opened quite wide. *Lynne Fox?* he mouthed. Reesa nodded, her disgust clear on her face but carefully kept out of her voice.

"Do you have any opinion about its authenticity? If you believe it's real, I'd like to include it in my next special report." *Bitch!* Reesa was having some difficulty maintaining her cool. "Of course, if you think it's not really from the killer, than I presume it won't matter whether I mention it or not, will it?"

"Ah, we'd really rather you didn't do that, Ms. Fox. It's, um, well, we're still considering our reaction to it, but … we're leaning towards believing that it's real."

"Oh, you are? Then I'd *really* like to bring it in. And that website reference. It's to an old rock tune. Do you know the significance of that?"

Reesa took several breaths through her nose to keep herself calm. "I'm afraid I'm not at liberty to tell you more than that at this time, Ms. Fox." Several more breaths.

241

"Well, if you expect me to keep this email under wraps, then you've got to give *me* something, Detective. Something to, ah, make it worth my while."

"And what sort of thing would make it worth your while?"

"Well, some sort of ... of exclusive. Something that the other stations wouldn't have access to, at least at the same time."

Reesa rubbed her forehead. Exclusive? Hm. "Exclusive? How about this. When we're ready to make a bust, I'll call you before it goes out. You'll be there on the scene about the time it hits the other stations' scanners. Would that work for you?"

Fox was silent for a moment. "Well, it's less than I'd hoped for ...."

"It's really all I can offer you, at least at this time. But we'd really appreciate your not mentioning the emails on the air. I'm not ... I don't think I can offer you anything else."

"I'd still like to get your comments on the Ripper and the cases, you know."

Reesa's nostrils flared. "And you know that I can't do that. Not and keep my job."

Another moment of silence. Then, just as Reesa was about to ask if Fox was still there, she spoke. "Well, if that's the best you can do, then I guess it'll have to be enough, won't it?" She laughed. "You drive a hard bargain, Detective. Thanks for the input, anyway. See you at the next crime scene!" The line went dead.

As Reesa hung up the phone, Chuck finally gave voice to his reaction. "Oh ... my ... God!" *The* Lynne Fox?"

"The bitch herself. Wanting to know what we think about the emails and bargaining for an advantage to keep them off the air."

"Kind of a worthless bargain for her if we can't find someone to bust."

"Yeah. But I think she knows that, don't you? On the other hand, after her reports, getting a front-row seat if and when we do get one, that ought to make her reputation, don't you think? And until we do, she keeps putting these reports out there spotlighting our supposed incompetence. What's she got to lose?"

****

Henry took a deep breath. *Think of the congregation, think of this meeting. Forget your extra-curricular activities for the time being.* "Brothers and sisters! Welcome! Welcome to all of you who have been here before, and welcome to those of you who are new. As I'm sure you all know by now, we've had yet another in the series of murders by the Tucson Ripper." *Oh, God, not him, too.* Sitting near the back of the room, Reesa and Jeff leaned gently against each other. As Henry got more into his speech, Reesa found her mind beginning to wander even more than usual.

The warmth of Jeff's shoulder and arm was quite comforting, and she'd definitely gotten the idea that she could relax with him in a way she never would have dared with Schuler. Or anyone else. *And once more, so much for that relationship you said you weren't looking for. Hell, any closer and it'd be so much for that boyfriend you said you didn't want, either. You know he'd take that position at the drop of a pair of ... of a hint.* With an effort, she brought her thoughts back around to the business at hand.

243

What did drive Henry? Studying him, she had to agree with Jeff's analysis. He didn't seem to present as anyone with a deep conviction, when she could, with effort, distance herself from his undeniable influence. Henry certainly could call on quite a bit of charisma when he needed to, but when Reesa managed to cut through that, he really did seem like the two-dimensional cardboard cut-out preacher Jeff had described him as resembling. It also didn't escape her notice that 'preacher,' with a small 'p,' was the only term he'd use for himself. She'd heard some of those who came try to call him a minister, but when Henry heard such things, he always corrected them gently, just as he had her when she attempted to call him 'reverend.' He had a warm and intimate manner, but it didn't seem to go all that deep when you looked hard.

Maybe Jeff was right to wonder what he did in his down time. If she couldn't tail him, perhaps Jeff would have some ideas. Or maybe she'd get a hit off his prints and get some data on him that way. She looked around. *Oh, yes, there are the mediums, waiting patiently at the back of the room, holding their collection baskets. I probably need to get their prints at some point, too.* Then she let her attention return to Henry, with some slight musing about her developing relationship with Jeff, and as always, the Joneses slipped out of her awareness without leaving a ripple.

On her lap, the book she'd prepared for Henry's prints sat waiting in its plastic bag. Jeff had been quite fascinated to watch her carefully clean the cover with one of the alcohol wipes she always carried in her purse, paying special attention to the areas where people would have handled the book when they picked it up off the shelf to

look at and even to the inside flaps of the dust jacket. As
the service was drawing to a close, after the embrace (how
good Jeff felt – and how nice it was not to have to worry
about roaming hands!), she pulled the book out of the bag,
careful to handle it with her left hand and only by a corner,
and she jammed the plastic bag into her pocket, patting it as
flat as she could. As they joined the line of congregants
filing out past Henry, she held it by her side, away from
casual contact from others without making what she was
doing look obvious.

    Then they reached Henry, and it was her turn.
"Henry, what a marvelous service, as always. But I wanted
to ask whether you were familiar with this book I found."
She extended her left hand, and he took the book from her
with his left hand. Opening it, he planted his fingers on the
back cover just where she'd expected and cradled the book
in his hand, making good contact with each fingertip. *Shiny
paper takes real good prints,* she thought. After he'd read
the cover flap blurbs, both front and back, he handed it
back.

    She took it, handling it again just by a corner, as
Henry told her that while he wasn't familiar with it, the
book (*The Magic of Relationships*, by Amber Stern)
appeared as though it might have some valuable advice and
he'd have to look further into it when the opportunity arose.
Then he thanked her for bringing it to his attention and
moved on to the next couple behind Jeff and Reesa. Once
out into the parking lot, Reesa worried the bag out of her
pocket and dropped the book into it.

    "Do you need to check that in with the property
clerk, or whatever you call it? I can take you to the station
if I need to."

Reesa gave it a moment's thought. "No, I don't think so. I can take it home with me and get the prints run tomorrow. It's not like they were evidence of anything, so there's no chain of custody to worry about. I just want to run his prints, see if he's who he says he is and whether he's got any kind of a record. So no, just take me to your place and I'll drive on home from there. I've got to hit the firearms lab tomorrow anyway, because it was closed when I got there yesterday, I didn't have the chance to get there today, and prints are just down the hall. That cartridge case did have to go to the property room, but it's already there."

Chapter 14

Reesa walked into the TPD firearms lab Thursday morning early. Forensics was not her greatest interest; she privately felt that good old-fashioned legwork solved a lot more cases than forensics did, although she'd never say so publicly. At the same time, she had to admit that the scientific approach definitely had its place at times and had on more than one occasion tied a suspect to a crime she would have been unable to close otherwise. Her real problem, when she thought more analytically about it, was that she just felt a bit out of place in a sterile laboratory. Give her a nice bloody crime scene and a dead body or two any day. She knew how to treat a crime scene, how to preserve or at least not destroy trace evidence, and she could usually even lift a decent fingerprint when she had to, which, thankfully, was rare. But it really wasn't her interest.

The firearms tech was bent over some sort of apparatus Reesa had seen before but still didn't really understand. Not her job. "Hey, John. Got a minute?"

He looked up, jarred out of his concentration. "Oh, hi, Reesa. For you, anything. Whatcha got?" He smiled.

She set down the bagged book she had in her left hand and held up the evidence bag she'd retrieved from the property room clerk. "There was another couples murder yesterday, this one up in the foothills. SD's handling it. Strangulation case. But this was under the couch at the scene, and I thought maybe you could compare it to the shells from the Harris crime scene."

"Can do. In fact, I think I may still have those here. Or at least some pictures of them." It took him several minutes to locate the pictures, during which Reesa leaned against a lab table and looked around, trying to understand everything she saw. She failed. "Here they are. Let me see that." Taking the bag from her, he opened it carefully and put the case under the microscope. He fiddled with it for a couple of minutes, saying nothing. Then he pulled back and looked carefully at the pictures. "I can't tell you anything for certain without all of the cases to put side by side on the comparison 'scope, but my impression – don't quote me – is that they probably all come from the same gun. Look here." He indicated something on the picture.

"So just what am I supposed to be seeing here?"

He chuckled. "Sorry, I get too wrapped up in what I'm doing. Occupational hazard. This is a close-up shot of one of the cases from that earlier murder scene. Here, on the edge of the case head, this is the mark left by the ejector. See this mark, like a scratch, across it? That's on every one of them, and it comes from a tiny ridge on the ejector itself. Now just so you know, we pay the closest attention not to the case head markings, but to the firing pin imprint on the primer, since that by definition comes from this firing of the cartridge. Here, on the firing pin impression in the primer, there's this slight bulge" – he pointed to the mark he was indicating – "that's the result of a tiny chip out of the nose of the firing pin. Now take a look through the 'scope here." He moved back to let Reesa look through the microscope.

"They look the same. I mean, I see the same markings, on the case head and on the primer both."

"Exactly. I know you know the basics of this already, but this is it in practice. Every gun is different, each one puts its own unique marks on the cartridge case as it operates, and they're like fingerprints. For fresh brass, it's just as good as fingerprints, in fact, although the impressions do change over time. The firing pin impression is made when the gun fires and the firing pin hits the primer, and the ejector mark is made when the case is slammed against the ejector right afterwards, just as the slide comes back and kicks the case out of the gun. Like I said, I'm not going to go out on a limb here and say anything definitive without comparing this case firsthand to those others, all of them, and checking out all of the marks under the comparison microscope, but my first impression, off the record, is that they're probably out of the same gun. We're definitely headed in that direction, okay? That's what I can give you, pretty much *all* I can give you with any sort of certainty, at least, until I can do a better inspection. Need me to?"

Reesa debated with herself momentarily. "If you would. No great hurry, it's not going to get us a bust. But it will at least suggest a connection between the murders. Thanks, John. You're a dear." She picked up the book and turned for the door.

"Oh, one other thing I can tell you. I'm pretty sure that these cases from your murder scene are a red herring." He tapped the pictures.

Reesa turned back towards him. "What do you mean by that?"

"Very simple. The cases almost certainly didn't come from the gun that fired the bullets."

Reesa looked just a tad impatient. "Okay, explain." She was, but she could contain herself. This might be important. Of course, the experience she and Chuck had had with Gabriela Marquez had already made this the most likely possibility anyway, but it never hurt to have it confirmed by the evidence.

John shrugged. "The cases are entirely consistent with Heckler and Koch pistols, including the H&K P2000, just like what the Border Patrol uses and probably at least a bunch of the other Feds around here as well. But the H&K's all have polygonal rifling. That's a smooth rifling, and it's not formed the way the barrel that shot those bullets was. Well, not quite all of them; the very first pistols in that family had land-and-groove rifling, but the rifling they had isn't the same as what's on the bullets from your crime scene anyway. It's possible, I suppose, but I'd have to say it's unlikely as hell that one gun made those rifling impressions as well as these case head impressions. The odds are pretty overwhelming that there were two different guns involved somewhere along the line, unless somebody put an aftermarket barrel in, and that sort of thing is generally done by gun enthusiasts, not criminals."

Reesa was nodding slowly. "So in other words, the cases give us no usable forensic data whatsoever instead of the merely way too little we were hoping for. Gee. Where have I heard that before?"

Now John smiled at her. "Want the worst of it?" Reesa just raised an eyebrow. "There are fragmentary friction ridge impressions on the bevel at the case head on some of them. Nothing usable, because there isn't enough to let us match, even if we could somehow put all the pieces together and get a decent part of a whole fingerprint. It's just enough to tease, and to show that the cases were probably picked up at the range with bare hands. Just very carefully. That's apart from the one clear print, of course, and that was only on one case."

"Shit. You're right, that is the worst." *Although if these cases were picked up at a range, it probably explains where Gabriela Marquez's fingerprint came from*, she thought. Reesa turned to leave.

"So when can I take you to dinner?"

She favored John with a smile. "Next lifetime, my friend. But I definitely owe you one." She was still smiling as she closed the door behind her. He was sweet, but her ironclad rule against involving herself with anyone in TPD covered him, too. And as many years as he and she had played out this dance, it could just be as much a game to him as she treated it. No matter. She wasn't going to change her position, and he knew about it anyway. He kept trying, nicely, and she kept turning him down nicely. All within the rules.

The next stop was just across the hall at the fingerprint lab.

Barbara Mason was watching something develop in a fuming cabinet. Reesa cleared her throat. "Huh? Oh, Reesa. Hi. Got something for me?"

She held out the bagged book. "I need you to print this. I handled the corners" – she indicated the areas – "and the subject handled it around the spine, cover and flaps, inside and out, front and back."

Barbara regarded the book for a moment. "That should be in paper, you know."

Reesa shrugged. "Plastic was what I had."

"And no evidence tag."

"No, this is for ID. It's not from a crime scene. This may be a person of interest in the Tucson Ripper cases, and I'm just trying to find out if he's really who he says he is

251

and if he's got any kind of a record. He's not a suspect at this point, and we'll have plenty more if he becomes one."

"Okay. I'll run the prints through AFIS and email you with the results. Good enough?"

Now Reesa smiled. "Sure. Think you'll have it by tomorrow?"

"The prints I may have later today or else tomorrow, unless something really urgent comes in. I've got some time, at least at the moment. AFIS you'll get whenever I get it. They usually process non-criminal searches pretty quickly, but once I start it, I'm at their mercy."

****

Jeff and Reesa met for lunch early the following week at a little Mexican place in South Tucson. It wasn't easy to find a table away from others – the place was fairly popular – but they worked at it. After the initial pleasantries, once the waitress had left the table, Reesa told Jeff about the email, the fingerprints she was waiting on, and the cartridge case that had been found at the crime scene. "We'll have to see about Henry once I've got a hit on his prints, assuming he's in the system. The cartridge case isn't a lot to go on.

"Actually, it's nothing probative at all, I'd say, since according to our tech, the cases left at the Harris house apparently didn't come from the murder weapon and this is, as far as we can tell at this point, just one more case out of the same lot fired in the same gun. But at least it appears to give us a suggestion that there's an actual connection between two of the murders, a bit more than just the pattern we've seen of the selection of victims. That'd make your patterns hang together that much better, and then I'd say yes, we do seem to be dealing with a serial killer here. And then the email, if it's genuine, confirms that."

Jeff frowned. "How do you suppose the case wound up there?"

"The living room was carpeted. I tend to think it fell out of the killer's clothing, like from a pocket or a pants cuff, something like that, and rolled under the sofa. Might have been kicked there accidentally. But with the carpet, it could have landed silently and gone unnoticed when the killer cleaned up."

"Shit! I still wish I'd gotten a look at the killer when he was in the house. And does anybody wear pants cuffs anymore?"

Reesa laughed. "Not that I've seen, honestly. But if you had seen the killer in action, then what? It'd take time to get a SWAT team out there, probably even longer for PCSD than it would for us, and you know that's what they'd have sent if you'd reported a Ripper murder in progress. Unless they didn't believe you, of course, which is probably the more likely possibility, and in that case you'd have been on your own anyway. As fast as this son of a bitch can vanish, assuming he's ever seen in the first place, it probably wouldn't have accomplished anything anyway. You'd still have been up on that hill, on the wrong side of the house, and for what?"

"Wrong side of the house?"

Reesa nodded. "Unlocked patio door, just like most of the others. The only time we've found all doors locked was at the Morales house, when the back door had one of those spring locks you can lock without a key before you close the door. Every other one, the door to the patio has

253

been left unlocked. And even there, the deadbolt hadn't been locked. Don't repeat that, it's one of the things we're holding back. I probably shouldn't have told you."

Jeff's turn to shrug. "Nobody to tell, except Amy if I'm talking to her about it, and that's just to brainstorm with her from time to time. Trust me, she tells nothing to *anyone* unless she wants to. Anyway, it's not much of a piece, but it is one more. I assume that's how you believe the killer leaves the house."

"Well, yeah, that's what it looks like. It's always out onto a patio, always a shaded area, always as secluded as there is available, and there's always some way off the property from there, a gate and a path or something, out to a road. What sort of camouflage the killer uses, I've no idea. But it's kind of hard not to imagine the killer exiting the house through that back door, collecting whatever he doesn't want to leave behind and just … walking away. That's one of the reasons we think the email is real. At the end was a reference to a YouTube video. CCR's *Looking Out My Back Door.* The son of a bitch."

"And he leaves no trace at the scene. Obviously a CSI fan, or the like."

"Damn TV shows." Jeff chuckled quietly. Reesa's comment was obviously heartfelt. Then Reesa's expression changed, although Jeff couldn't have characterized just what it changed to. "I'd, uh, I'd like to invite you to dinner. Pay you back for that marvelous dinner you cooked for me. Are you free this Saturday?"

Jeff hesitated. She didn't seem eager to offer the invitation, yet something in her manner suggested that it was very important to her. He couldn't quite put his finger on what that was, or why he got that impression, but it almost screamed at him. He listened to that inner voice. "Yes, I am. Your place?"

Reesa hesitated, but gamely nodded as she replied. "Sure. I should warn you, I'm not much of a cook. Don't do it at all, really, but I can order in a pizza or something."

Jeff did his best to look nonthreatening. "You like soup? Or chili?"

"Huh?"

"I can bring a pot of either one over, reheat it on your stove, and go from there. Either one is better reheated than when it's first made anyway, and you can keep the leftovers. No cooking necessary."

"You don't have to …"

Now Jeff smiled warmly. "Really, I'd enjoy it. Tell you the truth, I just made a pot of chili yesterday and put it away to, ah, age for a day or two. No problem to just bring it. How about it?"

"Uh …"

"Please say yes." His tone was more gentle than usual.

Reluctantly. "All right. Yes."

"And you've got a big pot? Something like you cook spaghetti in?"

"Well, yeah, but …"

"Beer or wine? Beer usually goes better with chili, but if you're not a beer drinker …"

"Beer's fine."

"I need the address."

"Oh." Reesa was just a bit flustered. "2925 Tierra Incognita. It's way up northwest, a bit north of Orange Grove, well west of Oracle, almost to Thornydale." *God! Giving an outsider my address and inviting him over. Will wonders never cease? And can I stand it? Will the heavens fall?*

"Not too far from Costco. Good enough, I can find it. Does five o'clock work?"

"Sure." Now she wouldn't meet his eyes, but he was working hard to conceal how he felt anyway and barely noticed. Definitely a major step, equally definitely one she was very uncomfortable with. He needed to tread very delicately. At least he realized it in time. "I need to warn you …"

Jeff put his hand out towards hers, stopped. "I know." He dropped his voice to a near-whisper. "No sex. Just dinner."

It was the right thing to say, obviously. Now she looked him directly in the eye. "Thank you, Jeff."

"No problem." And surprisingly, he found that he meant it. The relationship that seemed to be developing was far more important to him, he found as he looked at it, than simple sex. Or even complicated sex.

****

That evening, once settled with her drink, Reesa picked up her latest book purchase. She'd felt horribly self-conscious shopping the Romance section at Bookman's, but nobody had seemed to notice. Certainly the clerk at the register couldn't have cared less. Looked at rationally, they probably saw way too many books and way too many people buying them over the course of a day to give any thought, much less interest, to who was buying what, but Reesa hadn't been able to quite shake the persistent feeling that everybody in the store knew who and what she was and what she was buying. And they were all snickering at her. She purchased it anyway.

Ripped In Two

The title was *In the Dark of the Day*, and the cover featured a windblown couple who were just too perfect for words. She turned it over, and staring at her out of the picture on the back cover was, indeed, her Aunt Gina. Not a bad picture, Reesa thought. But the blurb! Just the beginning was bad enough.

If there were such a title as Queen of the Bodice Rippers, Regina Harding would definitely be a contender. Her latest continues in the same path as her previous books, with a thrilling combination of steamy sex scenes and personal intrigue that few can match!

Reesa opened the book at random and began to read.

Janis trembled, all but overcome by the hunger within her. She tried to will the lights to dim, but all of the willpower she could muster failed to change their intensity. Not so the intensity of the feeling deep within her, though. As Rafael advanced towards her, she could feel her own arousal grow. He reached out and touched her, caressing her cheek, each contact sending little electric shocks through her body. Slowly he unbuttoned her blouse and let it fall. Suddenly released from her paralysis, she began to grasp at his shirt. Unable to manipulate the buttons, she finally just ripped it open, buttons flying in every direction. As they bounced off the baseboards, he smiled at her, a smoky, sultry smile that promised even more, and soon. Very soon. His fingers unhooked her bra, and as her breasts tumbled free, he swept her into his arms and moved towards the bed. Pressing against her from below, she could feel his erection making its presence unmistakably clear. She huddled against his chest and traced one finger around his nipple.

Reesa looked up from the book. The first problem she had with it, of course, was that she could not even *begin* to imagine the Janis and Rafael she knew, her own parents, in such a situation. Or at least not describing it like that, anyway. *A 'smoky, sultry smile'? Dad? You have* got *to be kidding me! And the rest of it! People obviously buy it*, she thought. *But my God! What a load of ... of crap! And to think that Aunt Gina, my own Aunt Gina ... Mother, perhaps you should have left me in the dark.* She was smiling at that last. She closed the book and stood up. She'd read enough. This book would immediately go into the bag of used books in the laundry room, the bag destined to go back to Bookman's the next time she went. Maybe she'd reread some good old science-fiction. Or possibly something newer. A mystery, even.

****

When Reesa walked into the Homicide bullpen Friday morning, she found Chuck already hard at work at his desk. Piles of pictures covered the surface. He motioned her over to him even before she could get to her own desk opposite his.

"Couldn't sleep, so I came in early and I've been going over the pictures of the looky-loos at all of the crime scenes." Reesa noticed that a number of the pictures had someone circled. The one he was looking at was obviously the last crime scene, the one up in the foothills. "Just got these last ones in from your buddy at PCSD and figured I ought to compare them all." He drew a circle around Jeff's face on the print. "Look at this." He took the top pictures from each stack, and Reesa noticed each one had a face marked similarly. Jeff's. "There's only one face that comes up in the overwhelming majority of the crime scenes. We hadn't really noticed him before because we knew who he was, but he shows up even at most of the scenes before we knew him. It's your boyfriend."

"He's not my *boyfriend*." Reesa's voice was sharp, but she kept the volume down. They weren't alone. "He's just a guy I know."

"Well, whatever. But look here. You know about these" – he set out pictures of the last four crime scenes – "but look at this one." 'This one' was a picture of the street out in front of the Morales home. Chuck had circled a car off in the distance. "That's Escarton's car, and he's sitting in it with a pair of binoculars, watching the crime scene."

Reesa nodded. "He told me he was there, down the street. So far, no surprises."

"But you're the one who taught me about how often the killer shows up in the spectator crowd, and that cross-checking the crowds was one of the better ways to develop suspects in multiple killings."

Reesa started chewing on her lower lip. "Yeah, I did. Did you find anybody else?"

"Of the looky-loos? Not a damn one. Just him. And I think I've got him – I can't be sure, the resolution isn't as good as I need, but I *think* it's him – at the Maguire and Harris houses. If it *is* him, then it's virtually a clean sweep." Reesa considered that for several minutes. Did she need to revise her assessment of him? Was she inviting the actual killer into her home? Was Jeff really coming to have dinner, or did he have some more sinister intention? Her gut reaction about his motivations and her concern over his presence at so many of her crime scenes warred for domination. They were too evenly matched for either one to prevail. Or maybe he was simply giving the killer targeting information. Voluntarily or ... not. It remained to be seen, but only an idiot would fail to follow up on what could be a possible lead, and Reesa was nothing of the sort. Neither was Chuck.

Her internal debate was cut short by an email from the print lab. They'd gotten a hit on Henry's prints, and he did indeed have a record. She called Chuck around to her desk. "Look at this. Our boy Henry's got a sheet. Nothing too serious, just some busts a number of years ago in Ohio for running confidence games, and then he seems to have wised up. Oooh, this is interesting. Let's see. Arresting officer ... now I just need a number for Cincinnati PD." It took a couple of minutes to get in touch with the arresting officer, Lester Forham, who was now a lieutenant in the Cincinnati PD, but when she did, he definitely remembered Henry Blodden.

"So he's out in the desert now, huh? What's he up to these days?" Reesa explained to Lieutenant Forham about the Avowed. "Ah, yes, that's the Henry Blodden we know and love. Detective, I never did figure out when he turned to what he used to refer to as preaching whether I was glad he'd found a legal way to run his game, and I could let him be, or disappointed that I couldn't run him in for it. A couple of the guys went to look in on his services, and they reported that he seemed to have a good line of patter, but we couldn't figure out any decent way to get him to stop or move on without potentially creating a major constitutional issue, assuming that he was actually breaking any laws with what he was doing, and that was far from clear. Then he and his wife got into a major and very public knockdown dragout for some reason and he disappeared. I figured he'd surface again somewhere eventually. I'd offer you any help I could, but it sounds like he's your problem now and there's damn-all we can do for you here. This got anything to do with the Tucson Ripper we're hearing about?"

Reesa snorted. Just how far did the publicity run? "Honestly, Lieutenant, we don't know. I wouldn't want to call him a person of interest at this juncture, but his name did crop up in our investigation on the Ripper. I wanted to know if he had any history, so I ran his prints. At this point, that's all we have."

"I wish you luck, Detective. From what we hear out here, you could use it."

"That we could, sir. Thank you for your time."

"Glad to help. Call me if you need anything else."

She looked at her partner. "Okay, con man to preacher, that transition I can see. Con man *or* preacher to very good and very imaginative serial killer, that I've got a bit more of a problem with." *I'd sure rather it were Henry than Jeff. Do I have a choice? Not really. Deal with what is, not what we wish it would be. Yes, Uncle Frank. I remember.*

Chuck was nodding. "I'm with you on that. It's interesting to know he's got some background, but I'd agree with you. Going from there, either 'there,' to being the Ripper strikes me as kind of improbable. Not that we've got a lot of other people to look at right now, though."

"There's always that couple that works with him."

"If we can ever get any ID on them, you mean."

"Yeah. If. But until we do have something, let's go back to Jeff for a moment. He's shown up on a lot of the Ripper's cases, you're right. But if he's not the Ripper, is he some part of the targeting process?"

Chuck looked sharply at her. "You think he might be feeding information to the Ripper? Or are you just too close to him to be willing to consider him as the killer?"

"Information might not necessarily be going to the Ripper with his knowledge. Yes, I suppose he could be the Ripper himself, but I've spent time with him and dammit, I've got to listen to my own inner voice sometimes, particularly when that's all I have to go on. If he is the Ripper, then he's the most stone-cold liar I've ever encountered and he ought to be in politics. Could I believe it? Give me some evidence and yeah, I probably could. But without it, all I've got to go on is my gut, and no matter how far back from him I step, my gut keeps saying no. It's also possible that he could be finding targets for the Ripper out of his own files. But if there's anything at all going on there, it's also equally possible that the Ripper could have some sort of line into his files that he doesn't know about, as an alternative."

****

"I don't like coincidences." Amy didn't look happy. In fact, she looked as though she were on the verge of anger.

Jeff wouldn't meet her eyes, preferring to look off in the distance – well, across Speedway – out the window.

262

"I don't either, and I'm worried that I've done something here that I shouldn't have. I just have no idea what it could be. The problem I've got is that I've been involved with most of the Ripper's cases, and it's not like we're the only PI office in the city. One or two I could see, just from random chance. But so far, counting the first one up in the foothills, I've had …" He counted for a moment as Amy waited patiently. "Seven of the Ripper's cases. That's seven out of … nine?"

Amy looked away for a moment before correcting him. "Ten, by my count." She looked concerned.

"That's still way too many. Hell, even coincidence only goes so far, and as you like to say, 70% is passing. Frankly, I'm getting seriously worried that the Ripper is getting information off me in some fashion."

Amy opened a drawer and pulled out a disk. "If you are the source of even some of the Ripper's targeting information, it's got to be coming from your computer." She looked at him sharply. "Doesn't it?" There was a bit of an edge to her voice.

He got a worried look on his face. "Hey, you don't think that I …"

She shook her head. "No, I don't. Not knowingly, anyway. But I just wanted to be sure you hadn't been shooting your mouth off where you shouldn't or anything like that."

Jeff's response wasn't quite angry. "Hell, no! I haven't said a word to *anyone*! You know me, I'm a loner unless I'm in some sort of relationship, and right now she's the closest thing I've got to one of those. Shit, other than Reesa, I don't have anyone *to* tell, and if there's anyone whose innocence I'm certain of, it's her."

Amy looked at him over her shoulder as she headed out the door of her office. "Gee, thanks." Her tone was desert-dry.

"No, wait. I didn't mean ..."

Now she smiled. "I know. You also know I couldn't let it go."

"Yeah, I suppose I do. Sorry."

As she headed for his office, she responded, "So let's take a look and see just what sort of problem we're up against. Whatever it is, it's going to stop right now. That, I can promise."

Chapter 15

When Reesa opened the door, she found that Jeff was standing, cooler at his feet, as he waited patiently for her to answer her doorbell. It was a good-sized cooler, too, one he had to carry with both hands. "Didn't know how much beer to bring, or what you like, so I brought plenty," he said as he struggled to get the cooler through the door. She found that she was holding her breath as he stepped through the doorway. *An outsider here? In my house? In my home? What's the world coming to? Even if he's harmless? Worse, if he isn't?* Quietly she exhaled and resumed her normal breathing.

Once all the way inside, he looked around. "Kitchen's through there?" He nodded in the indicated direction. Reesa nodded in response and he headed off through the dining room. As she trailed behind him, she watched to see if he noticed the Glock and its ammunition laid out on the credenza. She couldn't tell for sure if he saw it but figured he probably did. He didn't turn his head as he went by it. The minor weight of the Kahr in her ankle holster was more noticeable than usual. *Dammit, Mother, I invited him here because you wanted me to, and now I may have invited a serial killer into my home, one who would specifically benefit from killing me, too. Satisfied? I swear to God, Mother, if he kills me, I am going to come back and haunt your chambers.*

Once in the kitchen, he began pulling containers out of the cooler. As he stacked them on the counter, he explained. "I usually pack chili in containers like this. Makes it easier to pull from the freezer for a meal. Two meals or more each, actually, for one person, but that's a

265

reasonable amount to defrost at any one time. Anyway, I figured I'd put it all in your pot, let it heat up slowly while we have our first beer, and then we can put the leftovers back into the containers. Hope you've got freezer space. Oh, and I've got two different kinds of beer, too. Don't think we'll be drinking more than this. If nothing else, I've got to drive home." He chuckled as he pulled two six-packs from the cooler. The chilled bottles were already glistening with moisture. "This one" – he hoisted the Spatenbrau – "is really good, but it's German and if you're used to American beer, it may be kind of heavy for you. This other one" – he nudged the six-pack of Fat Tire on the counter next to it – "isn't quite as different from the usual American-style beers, but it's also quite good."

The beer triggered a brief memory. She had been about fourteen and, as had so often happened, that evening she was eating dinner with Frank and Grace next door because her parents were working late. Uncle Frank, now retired from the police force, was having a beer before dinner. Reesa asked him, for probably the hundredth time, what it tasted like. "Okay, Reesa, I'll let you taste a little bit." He raised his voice. "Gracie, bring me another beer!"

From the kitchen came Grace's voice. "No, Frank!"

"Gracie, the girl's got to learn what it tastes like sooner or later."

"Frank, you can't just give her a beer."

"Okay, then, I'll pour some in a glass. Bring me a glass, please."

Grace came into the room carrying a shot glass. Instead of handing it to Frank, she held out her hand for the bottle. "I'll pour it. I know you, you'd top this off. I can be sure she gets a decent taste without any chance of her going home tipsy." Frank wasn't completely happy about that, but finally gave in.

Grace poured about half an ounce into the glass, and Frank looked at it. "More than that." At about the three-quarter ounce mark, Grace stopped and handed the glass to Reesa, who thanked her politely.

After sipping it cautiously, she looked at him. Trying to act more mature than her years as usual, she said, "I think I can see why you like it." She drained the glass. "Thank you for letting me try it, Uncle Frank. Maybe I'll like it better when I'm older, but right now, I think I'll stick with root beer." Frank started to chuckle.

Finally Reesa returned to the present and found her voice. "Let me take those." She put them in the fridge as Jeff noted the extent of empty space in it. *She's probably got plenty of space in the freezer, too*, he thought.

Once the chili was heating as slowly as the stove would allow, Jeff and Reesa took beers and headed back towards the living room. Stopping at the credenza, Jeff looked at her Glock lying there with its magazine and chamber round. *Does he know I've still got my backup on?* Reesa wondered. Then he looked at her. "Do you mind if I add mine while we're here?" Reesa shook her head and watched, tense, as Jeff handed her his beer to hold before pulling a small pistol not quite like anything Reesa was familiar with from a holster at the small of his back. He cleared it and laid it next to hers, right where her Kahr usually lay. As she allowed herself to relax fractionally, he took back his bottle and ushered her the rest of the way to the living room. He didn't seem to have noticed her concern.

Finally Reesa opened the conversation. "I take it that's your uncle's pistol, the one you mentioned?"

Jeff nodded. "That's an original Seventrees ASP. It's pretty much a collector's item these days, there weren't a lot of them made. It started out life as a Smith & Wesson Model 39, then it was cut down on both ends, lightened and generally smoothed all over until it's almost more like a well-worn bar of soap. It's quite accurate at gunfight distances, even if the sights are a tad unusual. I kind of wish it were a bigger caliber, but .40 S&W didn't even exist when they were made, so 9mm is it."

"Well, it does answer one question I'd had. Now I understand why you so rarely lean forward or bend over."

Jeff's eyebrows went up. "You noticed?"

Airily Reesa responded, "Oh, I notice lots of things. It's my job, remember? But I couldn't understand why you wouldn't lean way over towards me in a restaurant when we were trying to keep our conversation quiet – unless we were sitting in a booth. Even then, when you do lean forward in a booth, you either keep your back arched or you turn slightly so your back is toward the wall end of the booth. Sometimes both. Now I understand."

"Quite the detective."

"Like I said, it's my job."

Reesa took a deep breath as quietly as she was able. She could probably relax; if he were the killer, he likely wouldn't have disarmed himself so readily. *Unless, like me, he has another holdout hidden somewhere else,* she reminded herself. Or else he was the killer but he wasn't going to do anything to her tonight. Now that he knew where she lived. He sat on one end of the couch as she took a seat in her Eames chair facing him and swung her right foot onto the ottoman. The left, the one with the pistol in the ankle holster, would stay on the floor.

But being able to ease off on her tension just a bit gave her the chance to address an entirely different topic, something which was not going to be an easy subject to broach, but one she still felt she needed to know. It would also give her more chance to assess him, decide yet again whether he was dangerous. Or in general what she was likely to do with him. "So now that we're both here, tell me why you're willing to be such a Boy Scout with me. I'm more used to men splitting when I make it clear that I won't have sex with them. Assuming they've gotten to that point at all, of course."

Jeff slowly, cautiously, twirled his bottle in his fingers. It took him a while to order his thoughts, but Reesa exercised patience. He seemed to have some problem meeting her eyes as he spoke. "Let's start with the point that explaining means I have to go into ... previous relationship and girlfriend sorts of things. Will that cause a problem?"

Reesa shook her head. "No, I really want to know. It's not like we've got that sort of a relationship right now ourselves, and I *did* ask. I understood what I might be asking for."

Jeff shook his own head sharply as though he were trying to clear his mind. "Okay. I had a relationship that was one of these 'Hi, your name is Jeff? Let's go to bed' sort of relationships. Lots of sex. I mean *lots* of sex, and very fast. So much and so fast that it ... clouded my judgment, let's say, on the rest of the relationship. Including about her. No, make that *especially* about her. So after I got fed up with being the trained seal and called it off, I decided that I could wait. Find the right person to be with and take my time. No need to jump into a new relationship, no need to jump into bed with anyone, no need to rush anything. Let the ... let however things develop determine the speed for a change."

"That was Lynne Fox, right?" Jeff just nodded, a rueful expression on his face. "And am I your 'right person to be with'?" Reesa looked slightly skeptical. Felt more so, even though she realized she and Jeff now had a relationship of some sort whether she'd wanted it or not. Dammit, it was presumptuous as hell of him! Or at least it would have been, if not for .... The obvious question, of course, was where would it go? Along with when would it go there? And, for that matter, should it? Did she want it to? She didn't have answers. Yet. He better not, either.

Now he looked her squarely in the eyes. She noted it and silently gave him a checkmark for it in his response. "Honestly? At this point, I can't say. Don't know. After some of my experiences, I'm not entirely certain how I would know. But I haven't felt any warning signals yet, I've been looking for them a lot more than I would have done before, and, well, I hope this doesn't upset the apple cart, because I'd be really disturbed by that if it happens, but I'd have to say that I think you definitely could be. *Could* be.

"Remember, I'm just talking about the 'right person to be with,' not 'Miss Right' now and forever. We're not school kids any more. But you're definitely head and shoulders above anyone else right now, that's for sure. Hell, there *isn't* anyone else at the moment and I'm not looking, either. So I figure I can let you go at whatever speed you feel you need to and we can take whatever time we both need to figure it out. To be completely honest, it's a refreshing change for me. Like I said at my place, I expect the relationship has to change eventually, and I'd like to be around when it does. If we're not the right people for each other to be with, we ought to know by then. Probably know if we are, too. In the meantime, I think we're getting to be friends, and I figure that's a good start."

"Hoping it gets better. Goes further."

He shrugged. "Right now, sure. But willing to wait and see. Trying to take it as easy as needed. In a nutshell."

Had she invited the killer into her home, her sanctum sanctorum, even if he weren't going to harm her (here, now)? She still didn't think so, but she also still couldn't completely shake her awareness of the possibility. As for being the right person to be with, as he put it ... well, not if he were the killer. That much, at least, was certain. If he wasn't, well, she could wait and see, too. No reason to hurry. No reason at all. He was right about that, and she had plenty of reasons herself to take her time with this, see how it all shook out. Didn't she?

But damn! She was right the last time. She'd said she wasn't looking for a relationship, but here this one had snuck up on her and bitten her on the ass while she *wasn't* looking. And dammit, assuming he *weren't* the killer, if he walked out of her life now, she'd *miss* him. When she could bring herself to really look at him, yes, she did think of him as a friend, even if not as close a friend yet as .... So all of this 'right person' talk ... wasn't as upsetting, or off-putting, as it might have been. *Would* have been. As much as she wanted it to be, at some level.

At some deeper level, she found herself wondering much the same about him. She'd never let it show. Bet on it. She could barely find it herself, even though she now knew it was there, and she found it just a bit discomforting when she did realize it. A relationship would mess up her routine, the settled part of her life. But she also wouldn't have to be alone all the time ....

And of course, now here he was, in her house, her most private sanctuary, and the heavens hadn't fallen, the earth hadn't opened up and swallowed the house, or her, or him, and she was even more comfortable than she would have thought she could ever be with an outsider here. Would wonders never cease? She could almost imagine ... no. She wouldn't go there.

Chapter 16

Chris Schuler came into the bullpen about twenty minutes after Reesa had arrived on Monday morning. "Hey, Malloy, you've got mail!"

Reesa looked up. "What, now my email is on your computer?"

He waved an envelope in the air. "Nope. Real mail, with an envelope and postage and everything." He flapped it a couple more times for emphasis as Reesa stood up and walked towards him. "Oh, and look at this. It's from Channel 12. You making nice with Lynne Fox now?"

Reesa stepped close to him and stuck her hand out, flat, between them. She kept her voice low so nobody else would hear. "The envelope or your guts in my hand, Schuler. *Now.*"

With an inscrutable look, he slapped the envelope into her hand. "Could have been fun, you know." His voice was just as low as hers. She ignored him as she walked back to her desk.

Slitting the envelope open, she extracted one folded sheet of paper. It turned out to be another email, very similar to the previous one. A sticky note on it simply said, 'Another one for you. L.'

The email was much shorter.

Dear Ms. Fox:

Just a quick note to let you know that you'll have fodder for another of your special reports soon. I have finally selected my next targets and planned an even more inventive way of taking care of them. I believe you'll find it most ... interesting.

For obvious reasons I cannot be more specific about either the date or the identity of my targets at this time, but it will not be long in coming.

The Tucson Ripper

Once again, there was a YouTube listing underneath the signature. Reesa checked it against the earlier one, and it was different. She showed the sheet to Chuck. "You think it's genuine?"

Reesa set it down by her computer and started typing in the website. "Dunno at the moment, but let's see what this video is." The opening notes were the same as those from the video on the previous email. "Damn! Now I'll have that goddam song running through my brain all day. I think this son of a bitch is laughing at us and I don't like it. Not one bit!"

Chuck shrugged. "Who would?"

Reesa flared her nostrils. "I'd love to get hold of Fox's computer. Where are these messages really coming from? What's all the information that's buried in them and doesn't show on the printout?" She headed for the copier.

After she'd passed around copies to all of the other detectives, Chuck responded to her earlier comment. "I'd like to, too. But even trying that would get the ACLU and half the lawyers in southern Arizona down on our backs, not to mention everybody above us in the department."

"And we'd be hung out to dry. Yeah, I know. What's more, we'd deserve it. *Shit!*"

Just then the phone rang – the one on Reesa's desk, not her cellphone. "Homicide, Malloy."

"Detective Malloy? This is Amy Trevethen. I've got some information I'd like to share with you privately. Can you come to my office?"

Too aware of Chuck's look from the other desk, Reesa kept her features schooled into her usual expressionless mask. "Certainly. My partner and I ..."

"No. Just you alone. How soon can you make it?"

Reesa looked up at the clock. "I can be there in ... how about twenty minutes?"

"That's fine."

She reached for her purse, and Chuck looked up expectantly. "Just me. I suppose you can come if you really want to, but you'd be sitting out in the car in the heat and I've got no idea how long I'll be."

He looked concerned. "Just you alone? Are you sure?"

Reesa smiled at him. His concern was sweet, as well as good partnership etiquette, but hardly necessary in this instance. "Yes, I'm quite sure. I'll be as safe as ... as if I were with my family." *Now there's a bit of irony there. I will be with my Family, as it were.* "I'll probably catch lunch before I'm back."

Amy met her at the door. "Detective."

"Ms. Trevethen."

Amy ushered her into the big office and shut the door as she gestured for Reesa to take a seat. Before she sat down, Reesa noticed a frame on the wall with some words in it. She went over to look more closely at it. The typeface was quite fancy, but the prayer was not what Reesa might have expected.

*Lord, make me fast and accurate, let my aim
be true and my hand faster than those who
would seek to destroy me. Grant me victory
over my foes and those that wish to do harm
to me and mine. Let not my last thought be
IF I ONLY HAD MY GUN; and Lord if
today is truly the day that you call me home,
LET ME DIE in a pile of empty brass.* -
Gunsite prayer

Amy watched her, a slight smile playing across her
face. "Never heard that one before?"

Reesa shook her head. "Interesting philosophy, but
no, I've never seen it. Does it . . . does it have some special
meaning for you?"

"Well, I try to keep it as a personal philosophy. My
father gave me a pistol course at Gunsite for my high
school graduation present, just before Col. Cooper sold it.
It's in Paulden, north of Prescott. Ever been up there?"

Reesa shook her head as she sat down. "Not to
Gunsite, no. I've heard of it once or twice, but I've never
been. I'm really not what you'd call a shooting enthusiast."

Amy took her own seat behind the desk. "Well, too
bad. It's education, you know. I daresay you could get the
course paid for if you went." She paused momentarily.
"Give me half a moment here." She busied herself at her
keyboard for more than a minute before looking up.
"There. The security system's now completely off in this
office. No sound, no video. We're as private as we can be."

Reesa arched an eyebrow. "Is that really
necessary?"

Amy's expression was solemn. "Yes, I believe it is. A significant portion of this conversation will never have happened, and I think that having no record of it anywhere will make that a lot more ... practical."

A small alarm went off in Reesa's mind. "What part?"

"Oh, I believe you'll know when we get there, *Cousin*. May I call you Reesa? I'm Amy."

So that's the way this is going, Reesa thought. "Sure. You've got the clout to call me whatever you want, I guess. I presume you've told Jeff about me?"

Amy held out a large envelope. "No, I haven't. That's your choice, not mine, and I only found out about you because I've got resources he doesn't have access to. Resources like, among other things, hearing about your calls to the business office and my father. Not that Jeff couldn't probably find it with a hint or two, but lucky guesses aside, the only one who can make that choice is you, just like it's your choice whether or not to tell him about this conversation. He gets no hints about you from me, he has no idea I'm talking to you now, and I don't propose to tell him.

He's up in Phoenix for the day, by the way, so there's no danger of his walking in on us. But forget the clout for the moment. It doesn't work all that well here anyway." They shared a grin. "Let's stay on target here, shall we? This is the fundamental situation that I called you about. Jeff and I were ... concerned about the number of cases he's had that turned out to be Ripper cases. If you're half the detective I think you are, that my contacts in TPD suggest you are, then you've probably considered the same thing. I went over his computer with a fine-tooth comb, and

I found a spyware program on it. I believe it was slipped in with a bogus email, but it happened long enough ago that I can't be sure and can't track it. In here is a disk with a copy of the program on it, and you can have your people check it out if you choose. There's also a written report on what it does, but to summarize it briefly, it sends a coded data packet of Jeff's new files out on the internet. That packet bounces around through a couple of servers in the Middle East before coming to rest in an eastern European location where the data waits until it's called for, and that's why I can't go any further than that with it."

Reesa sat up straight. "We'll have our computer people go over Jeff's computer ..."

Amy's voice was flat. "No, you won't. I won't permit it. Even if there were anything still there for your people to find, I wouldn't, and believe me, there's nothing there now. I took care of that."

Reesa's eyes narrowed. "I can get a warrant."

Amy leaned back in her chair and looked at Reesa for almost a minute. "Yes, I daresay you can. And since we're laying all of our cards on the table here ... we are, right?" Reesa nodded. "Before you can get one, I can make a call to the State Department and by the time you get back with it, this is the official embassy for the Republic of Golondrino and we've got diplomatic immunity here. Jeff and I both personally, as well, for what it's worth." Reesa sat back. She'd never imagined this twist. "Now, I trust, you see what I mean about certain parts of this conversation never happened. There are several reasons why Golondrino has no diplomatic relations with most countries. We can't avoid the ones we share borders with, of course, but that's all. We have some relations with Switzerland and minimal relations with Austria and Italy. That's it. The US has been trying for some time to establish relations with us, and we've pretty consistently turned them down flat. One of the major reasons they want relations, and one of the major reasons that we don't, is that they would then feel that they had a right to demand information from the Bank of Golondrino."

Reesa frowned. "I don't think it would happen that quickly. I mean, people would have to meet, and think about it, and ..."

Amy chuckled. "Oh, trust me, it would happen and just that fast. It's not like we're some little flyspeck of a country with barely two quarters to rub together and both of those headed into some dictator's pocket while he's got his hands out for more. I mean, yes, we are a flyspeck, but not the rest. The US knows very well who we are, and while I believe that they don't know about the Family, they know we have lots of money in the Bank of Golondrino, a certain amount of it belonging to US citizens who happen to be taxpayers and they want to know more about it. *Everything* about it. I've already been approached, both of my immediate predecessors were approached several times each, and I have every confidence, given how badly the US government wants that information, that it would happen exactly that quickly. Especially if that speed were the condition for establishing relations."

Reesa appeared to be a bit shocked. "But why ..."

"A lot of people, like yourself, leave some or all of their Family dividends in the Bank until they ask to have them paid out, and while the bank does report to the IRS, Inland Revenue, the Bundesministerium, and so on, it only reports on what's actually paid out to you in your country of residence. Until you ask for your money to be sent to you, the US doesn't know anything about it and, more importantly to you, can't find out anything about it. Among other things, that means that not only your accumulated dividends, but also your interest on the account comes tax-free as well. I might be able to keep the Bank's records private if we had relations with the US, but I can't be sure. And the US has nothing to offer us that we want in return for relations, so we ignore them and, other than trying to convince us to give them those records anyway, they generally ignore us in return. For what it may be worth, the bank also doesn't say a word about what you draw out in person. If you want to go to Golondrino and take cash out of the bank, you're in a country where you're a citizen and it's nobody else's business, either, as far as they're concerned."

Reesa shook her head. Taxes weren't her issue at the moment. "So you're saying that my trying to go through Jeff's computer is going to … inconvenience a lot of the Family." Reesa looked a bit skeptical. Her job versus the Family? Helluva situation. Damn! Now there were *two* computers that were turning out to be highly important in trying to figure out who the Ripper was, and trying to look at one would cause a major legal flap while the other would make for a serious diplomatic incident. Definitely a helluva situation. In fact, it sucked big time.

Amy was continuing. "And it wouldn't be successful anyway. I think some of them would call it more than an inconvenience, though. The only people who wouldn't feel it are those who draw all of their dividends each year, pay their taxes on it and go their merry way. Anyway, the long and short of it is that no, you or your people can't go through Jeff's computer. Your people also wouldn't get anything beyond what I'm giving you, unless you're taking it to someone like the FBI, and I'm not certain that they could, either. I'm good, to be blunt. And frankly, *cousin*, you don't want to get crosswise with me. I may not have much clout here in Tucson, but where I have some, you'd be surprised at how much I have."

Now the detective sat up straighter again. "What sort of ..." Amy cut her off.

"Understand that I'm really not trying to make your life more difficult. Now, in that regard, and against my better judgment, I've also included in that envelope a partial list of Jeff's clients, specifically those in which there are some allegations or suggestions of infidelity, that have come into the office in the last six months, other than the ones that the Ripper has already taken care of. What you do with that list is up to you, but I strongly suggest that you not mention where it came from, because I'll deny it and you won't be able to prove otherwise."

Reesa shrugged. "Where else could it have come from? I'd kind of had to get it from either you or Jeff."

"You and I both know that's circumstantial at best, and by the time the issue of proof came up, his computer would show another spyware program, this one traceable to TPD, and at that point I'd be quite happy to have your people take his computer apart and find it. Then *somebody* would have some more explaining to do, and nobody would be looking all that hard at the evidence any more. Like I said, I'm good." Amy grinned at Reesa, who merely shook her head.

"Okay, so it didn't come from anyone we can trace. I guess … I guess I can live with that. I can call you a confidential informant, can't I?"

Amy nodded. "Fairly accurate, I'd say."

Reesa went on. "But one of the other things we've had to consider is whether Jeff is the Ripper himself. Just to, as you say, lay all our cards on the table. Have you thought about that?"

Amy sat silently, but she was obviously mulling something over in her mind. "Yes, I have considered it, and no, I don't think Jeff is the killer. I really don't. I've known him longer than you have, and as far as I can tell, he's not that devious. He doesn't give a lot away, true, but what he does you can pretty much rely on. Actually, I'd say that once he shows something of himself to you, he's almost transparent in that regard. That, too, of course, you can do with as you see fit. But getting back to the killer himself, whoever he is, I'm personally offended by the idea that someone would fish in our pond, as it were, and I'm *very* interested in getting that person off the street. Probably as much as you are, although I have some different considerations to keep in mind.

"There. I think that's everything I needed to tell you, but you've probably got some questions for me. Go ahead."

Reesa sat back, chewing on her lower lip for several seconds. "What do you expect me to do with this list?" She tapped the envelope.

Amy shrugged. "Like I said, that's up to you. There's probably three or four names on that list that are new enough to be potential targets for the Ripper, if that's what's going on, but there's certainly nothing to stop him

from going after one of the older ones that's still open
instead. And you've had Ripper cases that don't appear on
this list."

"Like the snakebite one."

"Like the snakebite one, yes. Jeff told me about
that. He was out, actually coming back from another
surveillance, when he saw the news van go barreling
around a corner ahead of him and, being a snoop by nature,
thanks to my training and a certain amount of innate talent,
he decided to follow them to see what was up. He could
never have done that one anyway. Unlike me, he's got a
healthy distrust of snakes and doesn't know which are
which. Doesn't want to find out, either, although he enjoys
watching them from a respectful distance. But no, that's
one that wasn't on his list. I'm merely giving the list to you
because that same information has already gone out to
whoever planted that program. Now it's your baby."

Reesa mused for a moment. "Unlike you. So you
trust snakes."

Amy shrugged. "I know about them in general, I
tend to like them, and I know which is which and how to
act with them."

Now Reesa stared right at Amy's eyes. "So are you
the Ripper?"

Amy laughed. "Ah, jeez! What a question! I
suppose I asked for it, but no, I'm not, either. He may make
some of my clients very happy, but it doesn't do anything
for our income, because then they don't need our services
any more. Besides, I have no concerns whatsoever about
who's sleeping with whom. It really doesn't matter to me at
all, other than making a certain amount of money from it,
and the idea of killing people just because they're not being

faithful to their spouses, outside of my own household, anyway, is simply way too foreign to me. I've also seen that sort of thing happen, just once and way too close for comfort. With my best friend, in fact, although she herself survived it. Another story. Besides, I really like what I do, not just here but for the Family, too. I like it way too much to risk it like that."

Reesa felt that it was time to change the subject. "How much clout *do* you have?"

Amy chuckled. "There, as CEO, pretty much all of it. If I said 'Off with your head,' then if you were there, your head literally would roll. Sorry for the thought, but we just ran Disney's *Alice in Wonderland* for our very precocious daughter over the weekend and it stuck in my mind. Anyway, it would cause quite an uproar in Golondrino. They'd have to find someone to do it, the Board would be appropriately shocked, and they'd probably get a removal motion before the Family if I did that without a really good reason. But that would be after the fact, because I genuinely do have that much power.

"The CEO is very close to an absolute monarch, and pretty much the last one in existence, if we ignore several dictatorships. Certainly it's the only one left I know of that's been around for centuries. There are some limits on my authority, but damn few and they mostly have to do with the board and Family procedures. I probably have the authority to ignore those, too, if I pushed it. The only reason that the CEO's position and its powers have survived unchanged for so long, in my opinion, is that the position isn't hereditary and a CEO has the option to choose a successor from the entire Family."

Reesa shook her head. "That's ... unbelievable. I mean ... Never mind." She paused. "What relationship are you to me?"

"Tenth cousin. Oh, there may be, probably are, in fact, other relation levels beyond that; the Family has had periods of intermarriage, mostly because of Family privacy and the fact that we tend to move in the same social circles, so it's a long way from unusual for two Family members to become involved, often before they find out about each other. Sometimes without *ever* discovering about each other. There are only a very few lines that separated back near the beginning and never crossed paths with the Family again. But I don't worry about such things myself. There's a very nice fellow, slightly crazy in my opinion but functionally so, who runs the Family genealogy office and absolutely loves figuring out such things. Give him a chance and Bernard will talk your ear off as he details how you descended from Will, Richard, Deborah, or Robert Escarton, combinations thereof, lines crossing, re-crossing, and crisscrossing, and far more in that area than you can possibly imagine. Probably more than you want to know. You can also call his office, just like with the business office, give him your Family ID number and find out your relation to any other Family member. Just be prepared to have to make an excuse to get off the phone, because if you've gotten Bernard instead of one of his assistants, you will."

Reesa smiled at that. "I've spoken with the genealogy office, although I guess I got one of the assistants." Then she sat up straighter as something else hit her. "Escarton, you said?"

Amy cocked her head. "Yes, that's right. Oh, you don't know. I tend to forget how little I knew before I got into this position. The Family Founder took the surname Escarton from a friend, as he had none of his own that he knew. Jeff is one of the very few – three, in fact, in his generation – who have an unbroken male line for almost five hundred years now back to James, the Founder, and still carry the name. Not that that means anything in the Family, other than screaming about Family membership to anyone who recognizes the name, as I presume it did to you. Even that really only became widely known because it was my predecessor's middle name and since he put up a front as a stuffed shirt, insisted on using it all the time."

More for Reesa to digest, eventually. But something else occurred to her. "Did anybody get in trouble over my call?"

Amy all but laughed. "Of course not. I listened to the recording, and Fiona did everything perfectly. It wasn't her fault that she was overmatched, and she doesn't know that Colin Youngston is my father, anyway. I've had no reason to publicize it."

Reesa couldn't conceal her surprise. "You actually listened to it?"

Amy nodded. "Any call that discusses me is brought to my attention. You wouldn't believe the calls that come in for me, most of which involve some allegedly red-hot investing opportunity, but anything that seems like it could affect me gets passed on to my office for my own consideration. Margarete, my secretary, goes through them in detail to summarize them for me, and most of them are ignored from there on. Yours, since Jeff had mentioned your name just that afternoon, caught my attention and I listened to the recording."

"And just what does Jeff have in mind for me? He told me about his relationship with Lynne Fox, but I'm a lot more concerned with where he's planning to go than where he's been."

Amy raised her eyebrows. "He told you about that? I'm surprised. That in itself is a lot more than he says to almost anybody. All he's said to me, though, is that he'd like to get to know you better. That plus a ... personal compliment or two."

A bit flustered by that last part, Reesa decided on a less threatening tack. "You said Will, Richard ..."

Amy got a serious expression on her face. "Let me give you the capsule version of Family history. Will, Richard, Deborah, and Robert ..." The conversation lasted long enough that Amy and Reesa went off to have lunch together while Amy told Reesa far more of the Family and its beginnings than Reesa had ever even considered. By the time they were done with lunch, Reesa found that she was more comfortable with the head of the Family than she would ever have imagined being.

****

Once back at her desk, Reesa contemplated the envelope Amy had given her. She was still staring at it when Chuck came back in from lunch. "More trouble? Or the magic answers to all of our questions?"

Her train of thought broken, Reesa shook her head. "Neither. Some more information, some possible targets for the Ripper. That's all."

He sat down and leaned back. "More information? I presume you're going to open the envelope sooner or later, not merely prostrate yourself before it?"

She grinned at him. "Already done that. Opened it, I mean." She lowered her voice – probably needlessly, as nobody else was in the bullpen. "Here's what I've got. There was spyware on Jeff's computer. Don't even think of getting a first-hand look at it, we can't. Take my word for it. I've got a copy of the program, a report on what it does, and a list of possible targets taken from his recent clients. I can't attribute any of this, but I'm welcome to use it myself however I see fit."

Chuck looked thoughtful. "Can we track the spyware?"

"Don't think so. According to the report on it, it sends a data packet out to bounce around several servers before winding up in another, where it sits until it's called for. It's purportedly not possible to trace who calls for it or who has called for it in the past, and all of the servers are in other countries. Not all exactly friendly ones, either. The program came in, I'm told, too long ago to trace the email it was attached to."

Chuck was looking at her intently. "And you got all this where? Escarton's boss?"

Reesa returned his gaze, expressionless. "I believe I'd best not say one way or the other."

"Kinda had to be, didn't it?"

"I'm not saying. Let's just leave it at that, okay? I'm satisfied that it's genuine, and trying to identify the source will probably cause a lot more trouble than it's worth, it'll definitely tie us up in knots, and it won't work anyway. If I have to say anything about it, it came from a CI."

Chuck just snorted. "And you said some possible targets?"

"Oh, yeah," Reesa replied dryly. "I've got a list of his recent clients whose information went out courtesy of the spyware and who have some suggestions of infidelity in their case files. In broad strokes, ones that would be of interest to the Ripper. We can't go staking them all out, I figure, because there are too many, they're too scattered, a couple of them aren't even in the city, and we haven't got any sort of schedule for the Ripper beyond that email that just tells us it's coming soon. We've also got no assurance that the next targets are even on this list. But for whatever it may be worth, we've got these names and addresses."

"To do what with, then?"

She sighed. "Ah. The sixty-four dollar question. It'd obviously be easier if I could get more out of Jeff about them, but since he doesn't know we've got the info to begin with, that's out. I guess we start looking at them, try to figure out how their own houses stack up in terms of what the Ripper seems to like, and then try to figure out how the lover's places stack up, too. Then maybe we'll have an idea who, if anybody, to stake out. Got any better ideas?"

"And we have to figure out who the lover is along the way, right?"

Now Reesa grinned. "Hey, if it was easy, they wouldn't need us, now, would they?"

****

Jeff and Reesa arrived early for the evening's meeting. Quite early, in fact, before the room was completely set up. They stood around as unobtrusively as they could, but after about fifteen minutes, their patience was rewarded when a cart was pushed into the room

289

bearing several trays of glasses and coffee mugs. Reesa was initially disappointed when the person pushing the cart turned out to be a stranger, but as he began setting out the coffee cups, Bob and Mary Jones came over to lend a hand. She smiled to herself.

Mary was setting out the water glasses while Bob and the stranger set out and stacked the coffee cups. Reesa made a careful note of which cups Bob placed on the table.

As they walked off, Reesa turned to Jeff. "Give me your car keys."

"I could help."

She shook her head. "No, you stay here. That makes it look more like I went to the bathroom, or back to the car to get something I forgot." Jeff dropped the keyring into her outstretched hand. Reesa stepped quickly into the room, picked a couple of napkins off the stack and shook out two of them. With a quick glance to see if anyone was watching, she draped a napkin over the coffee cup she'd chosen and, through the napkin, picked it up by the handle. She took a step to her left and quickly took a water glass, holding it by the stem with the second napkin over her fingers. Once outside in the corridor, she jerked her head over towards the dark end of the corridor.

"Here," she said, handing him the cup. "Just take the handle and use the napkin." She quickly wrapped the glass in a third napkin before fishing a plastic bag from her purse. She dropped the glass into it before taking the cup back from Jeff, swathing it more completely in the napkin already guarding it and carefully set it into the bag as well. "Be right back."

It took just over five minutes for her to come back, walking from the direction of the bathroom and drying her

290

hands with a paper towel. Jeff smiled warmly, but she wasn't looking at him, instead scanning the people beginning to arrive. "Anybody notice me?"

"Not that I could see. Most of them only arrived after you'd gone out the door anyway. Got them safe?"

"Quite safe, although it may be a while before the pocket behind the passenger seat gets back to normal. It's a bit stretched."

Jeff waved his hand. "No problem. I'm just as interested as you are in getting something out of this."

****

Henry busied himself cleaning up the meeting room along with the Joneses, helping them gather all of the Avowed's paraphernalia together, before counting the evening's take. *This preaching business is really starting to become lucrative,* he thought. *Even after paying for the meeting room. And the police leave me alone, which is a distinct improvement. I've even got enough extra to ... well, to be even more about God's work. Keep on branching out. I've got another visit to make soon.* He separated out the seed money for Bob and Mary next week, for them to put into the baskets before they passed them around. Then they fit everything into the boxes it had come in, packed just so, where it would stay until next week. In between meetings, they all had plenty of other things, each his or her own, to occupy their time. Plenty of ways to keep themselves busy. And happy. Plenty of God's work to do.

****

Reesa and Jeff were sitting at an outside table at a restaurant on east Speedway, trying to keep their conversation as private as they could. A couple sat at a nearby table with their dogs, but despite the misters that kept up a constant losing battle with the late summer heat, most of the diners, quite reasonably, preferred the air-conditioned interior tables. It gave the two more privacy, which suited them. Jeff was speaking, working at keeping his voice low. Still not leaning forward much. "I can tell you a bit more about … our mutual friend. I know where he lives, now, if you want to call it living, since he's apparently in a little apartment behind the garage of the mediums' house. Kind of a guest apartment sort of place. Their name is Jones, by the way. Bob and Mary Jones. Doesn't that just fit? My problem is that he still spends a good deal of his time away from there, and with the other jobs I've got, I haven't been able to pick him up yet anywhere else or even follow him to wherever he's going. I–" Reesa's cellphone rang.

She raised her hand to stop him. "Malloy."

"Reesa? Paul Bennett. Benny and I just caught one of the Ripper's cases, and we'd like you to come take a look at it. I think you'll find this one … different."

Her eyebrows went up. "Different how? So far, they've *all* been different. What's this one, scorpions?"

Paul chuckled. "Nothing quite so exotic. It's just something we think you probably ought to see. Consider it an experience. Or maybe just amusing. It's definitely a new one for us. Can you come?"

Reesa thought for a minute. "I'm having lunch with a PI friend of mine. How soon do you need me there?"

"Pretty much ASAP. Is this friend the one who's been involved with these cases? Bring him along if you want. We won't tell. Oh, I've already called Chuck, and he's on his way."

"Give me the address. We'll be right there." Jeff gave her a questioning look, and as soon as she hung up, she simply said, "There's been another one, and thank God, Chuck and I didn't pull it for a change. Paul Bennett wants me to come see it. You're invited, too, if you want to come. Just remember not to touch anything." Jeff just shrugged as they both stood. He took one last bite of his sandwich before heading away from the table.

The crime scene was a large house not far from the Arizona Inn and the University, in one of the older nice sections of town just off the east side of Campbell. Definitely a high-rent zone, to Jeff's eye, with high walls overgrown with Cape honeysuckle, pyracantha, bougainvillea, and jasmine surrounding small but well-manicured yards and with lots of privacy, even if the large houses were on fairly small lots and close together, at least compared to houses in the foothills or out in less-cramped places like Rita Ranch.

He managed to park on the opposite side of the house from the Channel 12 news van, but as he and Reesa walked around to the front door, even through the hedge surrounding the house and separating the driveway from the front entrance, he could hear Lynne Fox berating her people. He stopped and wordlessly gestured to Reesa to listen. "Goddamn it! No, you moron! Not here! Set the monitor up there! Where I can see it and where it's not washed out by the fucking sunlight! Lupe! I need more powder for my nose! Where's my IFB? Lupe! *Where's my Goddamn earpiece?* Have you got the connection yet? Well, call the station! Fucking incompetents!" Reesa looked shocked, but Jeff just gestured her to wait. "Oops, that's too much, isn't it?" A pause and a sigh, loud enough for Jeff and Reesa to hear. "Okay, guys, figure out where and get your sitters. Friday night?"

Jeff could hear the photographer mutter, "McMahon's."

Lupe responded, "Nope. Not this time. Hacienda del Sol. Morons is bad enough, but 'fucking incompetents' is definitely Hacienda material."

Lynne could be heard sighing some more. "Okay, Hacienda it is, then. Lupe, have we got the connection? *Please?* Okay, everybody, we're just about on the air." Another pause.

Then Lupe's voice saying softly, "We're on in three, two, one –" Jeff could imagine her finger elevated, then pointing at Lynne instead of saying 'zero.'

"This is Lynne Fox, KOPN 12 News, first on the scene, up close and personal, live on location with a special report at the house just east of University Hospital where we have yet another pair of murders by the Tucson Ripper."

With some shock still evident in her expression, Reesa just looked at Jeff as they resumed heading for the doorway. His voice was low. "She's horribly abusive to her people. They don't like her, they don't trust her, and yet they're fanatically loyal to her. I think it's mostly self-preservation on their part. She understands at some level that they could screw her up badly, so whenever she figures she's gone too far in what she screams at them, she makes up for it by taking them and their spouses or partners all out to a fancy dinner, and then she's nicer to them for a while. A *short* while. This time, I'd expect her to be back to normal come Monday or Tuesday at the latest. She's lavish with gifts and bonuses for them on their birthdays and

Christmas, out of her own pocket, so they stay with her and take it, but there isn't a one of them that would hate to see someone stick a knife into her back. There also isn't a one of them who wouldn't rush to tell her who did it, if she survived it, because if she did, she'd have anyone who knew and *didn't* tell her for lunch, preferably barbecued. A most nasty person, overall. If she weren't so good at what she does, she'd be out on her ear."

Reesa shook her head. "That's crazy. I mean, it's utterly screwy. But I knew there had to be more to dislike than what I already knew. And you had a relationship with her?"

Jeff snorted. "Only until I started thinking with my big head. Or thinking, period." Reesa chuckled at that. He looked around as they entered the house. "Hm. Never had any cases in this neighborhood." Reesa glanced at him, but he was still looking around. It seemed to be genuine.

Once inside the house, after greeting her partner, Reesa introduced Jeff to Paul Bennett and his partner, Guillermo 'Benny' Benavidez. Paul was a short, dapper man dressed in a summerweight suit that still showed its creases. Benny was more reminiscent of a bear dressed in jeans and a shirt. The actual crime scene was in a room of the house that had been set up (with some major, and expensive, fitness equipment, Jeff and Reesa both noted) as a private gym, and from what Jeff could see, the victim had been a serious bodybuilder. The man, that is. The woman looked more like she'd been a runway model.

Both of those descriptions were before their murders, of course. Jeff was working hard at keeping his lunch down, but it was clear to him that even Reesa found this one disturbing at some level. Both bodies had their arms duct-taped to barbell bars – the woman to a curl bar – and then had had weight plates piled on their chests. The woman had, so far as Jeff could see, a fifty-pounder, two twenty-fives, and a number of smaller plates all stacked on her chest. The man had three fifty-pounders on his chest, two more twenty-fives and a couple of medium-large dumbbells stacked precariously on top. They had probably been dead for a while, because both bodies had been compressed by the weights until their chests were obviously quite sunken. Flattened, even. Paul finally broke the silence. "You have to admit that this killer is one inventive son of a bitch."

Benny chuckled. "These people are just depressed."

Reesa shot him a sharp look. "Bad taste, Benny. You shouldn't joke about such weighty matters." Then she grinned. Using his pinky, he chalked up a point for her. Turning to Jeff, she didn't see the shock she expected, which she felt was a point in his favor as well. "Homicide humor. You've got to get used to it."

He shrugged. "Not really unexpected. My uncle warned me about cop humor years ago."

"And this scene is just as bare of usable trace as you'd expect." Paul signaled the ME and the uniforms to go ahead, remove the weights, and begin processing them and the bodies. "Possibly we can get a print or two off the tape, but even there, I'm not awfully hopeful. I'd say it's another Ripper case, sure as hell."

Reesa had a sour look on her face. "*If* there's a pattern and *if* there's a Ripper, you mean."

"You don't believe it?"

She hesitated. "I'll concede that there may be. And absence of evidence is not evidence of absence. Let's just say that I'm not completely convinced, not yet. Or maybe I just dig in my heels when I feel like I'm being steamrollered by everybody from Lieutenant Almirez and Sergeant Cotton down to Lynne Fox. I mean, Jesus! They're all different! We've got stabbings, fire, blunt-force trauma, rattlesnakes, strangulation, explosives–" Paul shot her a sharp look.

"Explosives? Which case was that? I've been kind of expecting it for some time, but I haven't seen anything like that come through yet."

Jeff spoke up before Reesa could open her mouth. "It was a failed attempt at a house way up northwest, in West Division. The bomb was placed under the bed, but the homeowner's dog had been doped up, I suspect by the killer when the bomb was being put in there, and the couple decided to let him go on sleeping on the bed. They were both in the living room when the bomb went off. BATF has been, shall we say, quite vexed at their inability to recover any usable trace from the bomb parts, but you know the Feds. They wouldn't dream of asking you guys in homicide about it, and since nobody died in the explosion but the dog, well ..."

Paul and Benny exchanged glances, and Paul then looked at Reesa, but she wouldn't meet his eyes, or just maybe hadn't noticed his glance. He then turned to Jeff. "And you think that's another Ripper case?"

Jeff looked back defiantly. "Personally, I'd bet money on it. I was outside the house when it went up. Every bit of it, outside of the lack of victims, fits what passes for a pattern in the Ripper's cases to a 'T,' and what was the last time you heard of a bomber leaving nothing in the way of usable trace? Even, or maybe especially, by the time BATF got done going over the pieces of the bomb with their customary fine-tooth comb?"

Paul looked at Reesa again. "He's got enough experience with the Ripper's cases?"

"Oh, yeah. He's been involved to at least some extent with, what … six of them?" Jeff held up some fingers. "Seven of them. Since three of the murders, two of the ones he's been involved with, are county cases, that's right up there with the number Chuck and I've been working."

"Okay, then. I'll take it as another one." *Good of you,* Jeff thought. He didn't let it show. Reesa's thoughts were in the same vein, and she didn't let them show, either. Paul looked at Jeff sideways. "You're not the Ripper yourself, are you?" He was grinning.

Jeff just snorted.

When the pair walked out of the house through a different door than they'd come in by, they found that Lynne Fox and her news team had set up in the driveway they wound up exiting by. As they tried unsuccessfully to skirt the area she'd commandeered, she noticed them. "Hi, Jeff." *A definite purr in her voice, the bitch,* Reesa thought. The photographer caught Jeff's eye and nodded to him.

Then she reverted to her on-air style. "Detective Malloy, is this one of your cases? Can you confirm that this is another of the Tucson Ripper's murders? Can you offer us any comment on the cases? Can you give our viewers anything at all?" As she stuck out her microphone, Reesa looked at Jeff. His expression was just as much ill-disguised distaste as she imagined hers was. With a short, sharp shake of her head, she just walked off without making any reply. She'd be on tonight's broadcast, sure as

God made little green apples. Illustrating how the detectives on the case wouldn't say anything to the press, as usual. And saying anything would not only get her in major trouble in the Department, it wouldn't change her appearing in the report one bit. Just as obviously, whatever she and Lynne Fox had agreed on over the emails hadn't changed anything else, either.

Chapter 17

When they got into Jeff's car, Reesa stopped him from driving off immediately. After a few moments' thought, she said, "Take me around to the other crime scenes, please. In order. Well, can you spare the time? I suppose I ought to ask first."

Jeff smiled. "I thought you'd never ask."

"Oh, bullshit. Let's just go to the first one." Reesa smiled back as she gave him the first address, while he pulled away from the curb.

The first one was the fire case in the foothills. Jeff hadn't seen the house before, so he pulled up out front. It was still a burnt-out skeleton, with some stubs of cinderblock walls remaining to give the structure of the house some suggestion of how it had looked before the fire, but what little wood remained was utterly charred. The cactus closest to the house were, just like the house, burned-out skeletons. Reesa looked it over carefully before stepping out of the car. "Wait here. I want to look around back."

"Wait, hell. I'm coming with you." Together they walked around to the patio behind the remains of the house. Reesa looked at where the door had been, the remains of the patio, then around the yard, until she found the path that led out to the road. *Doo, doo, doo, looking out my back door.* Jeff was already there, scanning the roadway. "If I were trying to park and look inconspicuous, I'd probably park down there." He gestured off to the east. "Find a place maybe two hundred yards down or so, depending on what I'm using for camouflage, pull the car off to the side of the road and leave it."

Reesa looked in the indicated direction. "Had it been early morning, I'd disagree. I don't think I'd want to come in with a low sun at my back. But anytime around mid-morning or later, yeah. That's probably where I'd go as well. Farther from the more heavily-traveled road, fewer people to notice me. And if I remember the report, TOD was somewhere in the middle of the day, so that fits. You *sure* you're not the Ripper?" She chuckled. "Okay, let's go to the next one."

By the time they reached the fourth crime scene, the Morales house, Jeff thought he had pretty well figured out Reesa's plan. It looked to him as though she was trying to scope out all of the crime scenes from the viewpoint of the killer and figure out where the killer had likely hidden his vehicle, which meant where he had approached from and where he had returned to. Jeff figured she was trying to put an additional part of the pattern together in her mind and see if she could build more similarities in how the killer had acted. Some more data to confirm the serial-killer hypothesis. Or contest it.

"Now initially I was right here, trying to set up for photos through the living room window there. I'd just gotten the camera set up when a police cruiser pulled up behind me, and the cop rousted me out. He claimed that one of the neighbors had complained about me and demanded that I move on." He glanced in his rear-view mirror. "That very cruiser and cop, in fact." He hooked his thumb over his shoulder.

"Let me handle this, okay? Just sit tight and don't say anything."

"Nothing?"

"Not one single word."

301

The officer came up to Jeff's door and tapped on the glass. Jeff rolled down the window. "Mr. Escarton, isn't it? I thought I made it plain to you the last time I found you here that I didn't want you sitting here."

Reesa leaned over. "Officer—"

"Just sit back, please, miss. This isn't any of your affair. Now, Mr. Escarton, I want you to step out of the car—" Reesa opened her door and stood up. "Miss, I told you to sit back down in the—" Reesa flipped her vest back to reveal the badge on her belt.

"That's *Detective* Malloy to you, Officer ..." she squinted to see his nametag. "Decker. This is a *homicide* investigation, Officer Decker. This investigator is assisting me in trying to find the Tucson Ripper. Now if you'd like, I suppose you could come down to headquarters with me and explain to Lieutenant Almirez just why you feel it's necessary to roust a citizen who is not breaking any laws when he's helping us try to find the Ripper.

"Perhaps in the process you'd also like to explain to Lieutenant Almirez why you feel you have the power and authority to interfere in *my* investigation. Perhaps you could at the same time explain to Lieutenant Almirez why you felt it was necessary and appropriate for you to stop this man from finding the Ripper when he's been closer to the Ripper several times than we have been so far *at all*.

"And finally, Officer, perhaps you'd care to explain to your division captain – that's Captain Burleson, isn't it?" Officer Decker nodded, looking more than a bit stricken. "Perhaps you'd like to explain to Captain Burleson just how you managed to interfere in the Ripper investigation when it's now the entire Department's number-one priority." Reesa paused. "Think you'd enjoy being on foot patrol in the Barrio, Officer Decker?" He shook his head, looking rather pale. "I didn't think so. It's not the nicest assignment to have. Trust me, I've done it. Now I suggest you return to your unit and find some legitimate way to justify your paycheck while I've still got the chance and at least some of the inclination to forget all of this. Think you can do that?"

"Yes, ma'am. I'll do that. Thank you, ma'am." His expression suggested that his feelings were rather different from his words, but Reesa didn't care. No matter what he thought of her, she was senior to him and was going to stay that way.

As Officer Decker pulled his car around Jeff's and sped off, Reesa got back in and refastened her seatbelt. Jeff looked at her with ill-disguised admiration. "That was actually most enjoyable from this vantage point. Thank you."

She waved off his thanks. "I didn't do it for your amusement, although you're welcome to it. He deserved it. He had no business interfering with you the way he did, and while I expect the Ripper was probably long gone by the time you got here, given the whole poison-gas scenario, if this had been a couple of the other cases, you might have been instrumental in helping us catch the Ripper right here." Then she looked down at her seatbelt. "That was stupid. We've still got this place to check out." She popped her seatbelt and opened the car door again.

As she and Jeff walked across the street toward the house, he simply said, "Thank you anyway."

****

Chuck was waiting for her in the bullpen the next morning. "We got the results on those fingerprints you took in the other day."

Reesa arched her eyebrow. "Well? Don't keep me in suspense."

Chuck pulled up the email. "Two sets of prints, one on the cup, the other on the glass. The prints on the cup aren't in the system, so there's no idea who that is."

"That was the man. Their name is purportedly Jones, by the way. Bob and Mary Jones." Chuck looked up at her, his own eyebrows raised in a question. "Jeff found them. Henry lives in their guest apartment, behind their garage. The names kind of fit, don't they?"

He turned back to his computer screen. "If that was the woman whose prints were on the glass, then she's had a whale of a name change. Those prints are in the system, all right. They belong to a girl named Ekaterina Boskorova, from some place I never heard of in New Jersey. MapQuest says it's a suburb of Newark. A string of arrests from age eighteen to about twenty-two, then she dropped out of sight for more than ten years, until now. Did some minor time for assault, appears to have been some girl gang sort of thing. But here's the part you're really going to like. She was arrested in her father's murder."

Reesa leaned over to look at the mug shot. "Let's see. Darken the hair a bit, put on a few pounds, add about ten or fifteen years, and yeah, that might be Mary Jones. Probably is, if the prints match." She straightened up. "But dammit, it still smells. Why would someone go straight for ten years or more and then suddenly start out on serial killing? Assault to murder, that I can see. It's an easier progression to get my head around than con man to killer.

Murder to murder is even easier. But it doesn't make any sense! Let me see the report on her father's murder."

She pulled up a summary. "Hm. Police called to their apartment multiple times, domestic disturbances. Father having multiple affairs, father beating up his wife. Then he moves out but apparently comes back with some regularity to beat on her some more. Finally ... oh, this is interesting. Somebody put a knife into him a whole bunch of times and then cut off his genitals. Arrested, mother and daughter."

She read a bit farther in silence. "So the only thing that got the daughter off was that the mother insisted that she had done it all, the daughter said nothing and the DA couldn't prove the kid had had anything to do with it. Rather than try to prove they'd been acting in concert or have them pointing fingers at each other, the DA let the girl off on a plea deal where the mother admitted the killing, went to trial just on the battered wife defense, and then the jury bought the defense. Oh, lovely."

"The way he was killed sure sounds familiar."

"Doesn't it, though? Nathan Bridgton all over again. Okay, then, Mary Jones, or whatever her real name is now, just popped up to the top of our list."

Chuck was leaning back, his feet propped up on a desk drawer as they had been when she walked in. "What about the husband? He's not even in the system, so we've got no idea who he really is, what he's capable of, or what he's been doing."

"Shit, for all of the evidence we've gotten out of the crime scenes, the man in the moon could be coming down to do these murders, given what we can prove." She went to her own chair, but began pacing instead of sitting down.

Finally Ruben Esquivel looked up from his own desk as she passed it for the third time. "Hey, Malloy!" Reesa stopped to look at him. "Either siddown or take it outside, eh? Some of us are trying to work here."

"Sorry, Ruben." She sat heavily in her chair. "It makes no sense," she repeated. "But I think it's time we put in some hours surveilling her."

****

Sitting in the nondescript Dodge, Chuck and Reesa perspired freely in the heat and prayed for overcast. Unfortunately, the monsoon was sparse this year and their prayers went unanswered. A block away, they could see 'Mary Jones' getting into her car, dressed in whites, to go clean somebody's house. Reesa turned the key, and as the engine roared to life Chuck turned up the air conditioning. As Reesa closed the windows, he stopped and just stared out of the windshield. "Who's that?" A dull buff-colored Honda was pulling out behind her from a parking spot halfway to the Jones's driveway.

"Oh, shit. That's Jeff." Reesa pulled out her cellphone and called him as she pulled away from the curb. "Jeff, it's Reesa."

"Hey. What's up?"

"You might have told me you were going to be tailing Mary Jones."

"Huh? How did you … oh, is that you? In the Dodge behind me?"

"Yes, it is. Both of us." Reesa spun the wheel as they took a corner. "So just how long have you been following her?"

"This is my third day. It shouldn't be so bad as yesterday, she starts at the Lodge at one today. Yesterday

306

must have been her day off, because she cleaned three places. You ready for this? One of them was the Gardner place."

"The Gardner place?"

"As in Freddie and Meggan Gardner."

Reesa swung the phone away from her mouth. "She cleans the Gardner house." Chuck's eyebrows went up, but he said nothing. She rotated it back down. "Anything else?"

Jeff paused before answering. Finally, just as Reesa was about to ask if he'd heard her, he said, "This is starting to look a bit familiar." The procession was heading into one of the pricier neighborhoods in the Foothills. "If she turns into the second driveway, I'll … " Mary's car disappeared into the indicated drive. "Oh, shit. You're not going to believe this." Jeff drove on by and pulled over about a block away.

Reesa was puzzled. "Not going to believe what?"

Jeff's voice was pitched lower than usual. "That's Fox's place. She cleans Lynne Fox's house, too."

Reesa pulled in behind him. "Oh, shit." She hung up as Jeff walked back to the car she and Chuck were in.

Reesa rolled down the window as Jeff walked up. "If you want to take over from here, I've got some other things I can do. I've been on her for three days now, and it might help if my car wasn't behind her for a while. Judging from her last couple of days, how long she usually takes to clean a house as well as how big this one is and how it's furnished, she probably won't do anything from here except head home to change and then to the Lodge."

Chuck looked at Jeff. "You know what Fox's house is like inside?"

Reesa waved him into silence. After a moment's thought, she replied, "Sure, we'll take her from here. What about her husband? We should probably keep an eye on him, too."

Jeff consulted his phone's screen. "Actually, he seems to be at Bookman's on Speedway," he said. "That's where his car is, anyway. Maybe he's having coffee at Beyond Bread instead." Reesa and Chuck exchanged glances, then Reesa looked back at Jeff, her eyebrow raised in question. Jeff shrugged. "Electronic tracker. I put it on his car at the Lodge two days ago."

"And Henry?"

Jeff touched a few spots on the phone screen. "He's out in Marana today. Saw him drive out earlier, well before Mary left, and his car's up at an apartment complex there. Has been for over an hour now."

Reesa looked at Chuck. "The wonders of modern technology." She turned back to Jeff. "We'll take her from here, then, and keep an eye on her tomorrow morning, too. Meet at your place before the meeting tomorrow?"

"Sure. Same time?"

"For supper first? Yeah. See you then."

****

When the two of them were settled in the restaurant with their plates full of salad, Reesa looked around before speaking. "I told you that Henry has a record back in Ohio. Well, I got the results on the mediums' prints. This is what I didn't want to tell you out in the street yesterday."

Jeff leaned forward cautiously. "Bob and Mary Jones."

Reesa chuckled. "That's one part of it. We've got no idea about him, he's not even in the system, if that means anything. But she definitely is, and her name isn't Mary Jones. Or at least that isn't the name she grew up with." Jeff raised his eyebrows and cocked his head. "Her name is, or at least was, Ekaterina Boskorova, and she's from a suburb of Newark. Got quite a record back there, too."

Jeff's expression showed serious interest. "I'm all ears."

"She's got a history of assault and such, for starters. It looks like mostly gang stuff, and she did some minor time for it. It also starts pretty abruptly when she turned eighteen, which makes me expect that she's got a sealed juvie record, too, if it matters. Then – are you ready for this? – she was involved in her father's murder. Her father apparently had numerous affairs and got into regular loud, noisy fights with her mother. Eventually he moved out, but even afterwards he kept coming back to his favorite punching bag. Finally he came back one time too often, and wound up being killed just about the same way Nathan Bridgton was killed, *including* getting his genitals cut off. She and her mother were arrested for it, and her mother insisted that she had done it all by herself. The weapon was one of their kitchen knives, also just like in the Bridgton case, but because it was, nobody could get anything from the fact that her and her mother's prints were both on it. When her mother kept insisting that she and she alone had killed the old man, while our girl said zip, the prosecutor took a plea deal on that and let the mother go to trial just on the defense. The jury bought her story of battered wife syndrome, and so both of them walked."

"And she cleans houses, too," Jeff mused.

"And she cleans houses. Yeah."

"Lynne's place was always very clean." He was silent for several seconds. "So does this make her a suspect?"

Reesa chewed on her lower lip for several seconds. "Not a suspect at this point, although I'd definitely call her a person of interest. Let's just say that a lot of pieces are falling into place, but we still can't connect that part of the puzzle to the rest of it yet. If we can do that, then she'll definitely be a suspect."

Jeff watched the play of expressions on Reesa's face. She was, by now, far less guarded with him than even she was aware of. "And you like her for it."

"Personally? Oh, you bet. I'm a bit surprised to be looking at a woman, I admit. Female serial killers are what, one out of six or so? Seven? But I'm a lot less concerned with her plumbing than I am with whether she's the one committing all these murders and being able to put a stop to them."

****

There was another envelope from Channel 12 waiting on Reesa's desk when they got back to the station. No stamp this time; it had apparently been hand-delivered. Reesa took her time getting some coffee before sitting down and picking it up. She waved it at her partner. "Care to bet that this won't do us any more good than the previous ones?" He just shook his head.

Dear Ms. Fox:

I saw your recent report on my last pair of killings, and I was impressed. You certainly do an excellent job with your live reports. It's unfortunate that Detective Malloy isn't more cooperative, isn't it?

I have just about settled on my next targets. There are just SO MANY potential targets in this area, it gets a bit difficult to choose sometimes. But I believe I have identified the next recipients of my attentions. Just as before, of course, I cannot give you any more information than that right now, but I feel quite certain that you will do your customary excellent job of reporting on the victims, after the fact, as it were.

Until then.

The Tucson Ripper

Yet another YouTube video was under the signature. For a moment, Reesa wondered what was the noise she was hearing, before she realized that it was the grinding of her own teeth and stopped. This time, she nailed the pause button in the playback after three notes.

Chuck flipped the paper onto her desk. "I see you rated a personal mention this time. Still think it comes with the territory?"

Reesa was breathing noisily through her nose, but stopped and looked over at him. "Huh?"

"The target on your back. You know, the one that Fox has painted on you with her mentions of you in each of her reports, and now this in the email. Worried?"

"At this point, I'm so *pissed* at Fox and the Ripper both that I'm ready to chew nails and spit bullets. At least if the sonuvabitch came after me, I'd know who to shoot. Worried? Hell, no! I'd love to have him come after me. I've got a whole magazine full of ammunition with his name, whatever it is, on each and every one. And I'm *dying* to get him in my sights."

"Try not to let it come to that, okay? I'd hate to have to finish being broken in by someone else, like someone who is most likely to be ah, *between partners*."

Reesa's eyes flicked over to Schuler's desk. There was only one detective in the squad who had trouble keeping a partner. She grinned at him. "I'll do my best."

****

"Friends, thank you – all of you – for coming." Henry took a deep breath before giving his standard opening line. "It's time for faith! Not just faith in the Lord, but the faith you keep with your partner! It's time for your commitment, it's time for your vows! WE ARE THE AVOWED."

Jeff and Reesa spoke and hollered the expected responses right along with the rest of them, although they both looked at it more as additional camouflage, simply blending in with the crowd. Most of their attention in these services was on the other people and singing the songs, blending in with the crowd. The biggest reason they found any real enjoyment in the meetings, the biggest reason they kept coming, was that both Jeff and Reesa treasured the 'embrace your partner' moment (although neither would ever willingly reveal that to the other).

Try as they might, there wasn't anyone in the congregation that they could tag as more likely than any other to be the Ripper, and while serial killers could certainly blend into crowds, there were way too many

312

people in the Avowed to keep individual tabs on. None of them showed up in more than one of the crime scene photos that they could find. Even then, only three out of all of the faces had been familiar, each had only shown once, and no two at the same location.

There was Henry, of course, and the Joneses (or Boskorova and her husband, whatever his real name might be), but even there, it was at this point just an unfounded suspicion, with nothing more than some circumstantial evidence to support it. While Boskorova's past certainly gave rise to some suspicions, the problem was that once she had left New Jersey, there was absolutely nothing in the official record. Either she'd gone straight, and her apparent connection to the Tucson Ripper was just coincidence, or else she'd gotten a lot better at covering her tracks. Or *something.*

So they had some data, even some really interesting data, but nothing to actually support a specific, genuine suspicion. At this point. And neither of them really believed in coincidences.

****

Chuck leaned back in his chair. "Potential targets, my ass. Having checked out the first three, I can say that this list" – he tapped the paper with his finger – "is hardly worth the effort, and I'll give odds that the Ripper's next targets aren't on it. One of mine is having an affair, but in a little crackerbox that doesn't have the sort of street access out the back door and away from the back yard that the Ripper appears to use every time. Another seems to be screwing his secretary in his office and nowhere else, and the third is actually just a total workaholic who never leaves the office and probably never even *thinks* of his dick unless he has to go take a leak."

Reesa was nodding. "I've got one out of four that might be a possible. I like the house, and he was definitely having an affair. The problem is that 'was' seems to be the operative term. He doesn't seem to have been doing anything since his wife filed for divorce last month. *Shit!*"

Chuck stretched in his chair until his joints cracked. "So just what do you think of your CI's info now?"

Reesa sighed. "No change there. Honestly, there was never any promise that the Ripper would be targeting any of these people. It was just that this information had gone out and was available to the Ripper, so we got it, too. Not our fault if the Ripper didn't find anything worthwhile in it, and not my CI's fault, either. Just the breaks of the game, I suppose."

"Would it help if I made contact with your CI?"

Reesa laughed. "Chuck, not only would it not help, it wouldn't get you anywhere. It's a personal thing, not something you can tap into."

"Oh, I don't know. I'll just bat my eyelashes" – he demonstrated – "and be my usual charming boyish self. That ought to do it." That brought a smile from Reesa.

"Seriously, even I can't go back to this particular well for anything more. It's dried up. Just a fluke I could get this much."

****

"This is Lynne Fox, KOPN 12 News, first on the scene, up close and personal, with another special report for our viewers in our series on the homicides of couples that have been committed recently around the Old Pueblo. For those of you who missed our on-the-scene live report, we had still another couple murdered in Tucson this past week. Let me recap the previous murders for you before we get into the gruesome details of this latest one."

Reesa ground her teeth together. *I don't know which is worse. The frustration these cases are causing me or having to watch this bitch flick our noses and the Sheriff's Department's noses, every frickin' one of us, because we can't find the sick bastard, or bitch, who's committing all of these goddam murders. And who, at least so far, hasn't shown any signs of running out of ideas about how to do each pair of the victims in differently!*

I wonder how long it's going to take Schuler to set up a pool on the next method the Ripper is going to use? Oh, wait, he was talking about doing that two days ago, wasn't he? And those goddam emails! Why does she get them? Why not me? And dammit, I want to get the originals off her computer! Damn the First Amendment! I need a break. Of some kind.

Chapter 18

Jeff watched through his binoculars from a safe distance as Rachel Lindstrom pulled into Bob Trujillo's driveway and parked. She got out of the car, reached into the back seat, and pulled out a large plastic bucket filled with cleaning supplies. *Just camouflage*, Jeff thought. *I can still see the wrappers on a couple of those items, so they've clearly never been used. Any more than they'd been used last week. Do either of them really think that the neighbors care? Or that they'd be so easily fooled if they do? Of course, people see what they want to see.*

He continued to watch, taking the occasional picture, as she punched a code into the outside garage door control to open the door. The garage door closed behind her as he drove off slowly. He needed to find a place to park where he could get to a vantage point behind the house since, as he'd found out last week, this one was all windows on that side, and while there were plenty of windows facing the street, they didn't seem to show any room where the pair was actually doing anything.

He finally located a spot well behind the house where he could kneel between two close-together palo verdes, like thick scrubby undergrown trees with vicious thorns as much as an inch or longer on their green-barked limbs, so far away from the house that he had to use nearly every bit of magnification he could squeeze out of his bag of photo tricks. A deep lens shade would not only keep the lens from flaring, it would also keep any telltale reflections from giving his position away. The distance would help keep him unseen, too, but by the time he was completely satisfied, he had his longest lens in place with the tele-extender on and hardly any magnification to spare. That setup wasn't the best, but at least it did let him get some very clear shots. Then the heat rising from the desert began to shimmer, breaking up what he could see through the lens, and the wind picked up as it so often does of a desert afternoon, adding that much more movement in his field of view. *Shit!*

Of course, the shimmer and movement would only have mattered if he had been able to see anything going on inside the house. He did catch the glimpse of some occasional slight movement inside, but every time he tried to focus on it, it was gone. *Damn!* But he'd stay in place, trying. Maybe he'd be lucky. Or maybe not, but notes on what he could see were better than nothing. He took a deep breath and worked at calming down. Using the camera, he began looking over the entire area behind the house.

Noticing a black plastic garbage bag sitting on the table outside the patio door from the house, he took a shot of it to include the doorway and nearest window. *Reference*, he told himself. *What the hell, it's just digital. Maybe the shimmer will break up for a moment, the wind'll die down, and it's not like I'm wasting film. I've got memory space to burn.* Then he settled down to wait as patiently as he was able.

When the door opened, he was ready. Well, prepared, at least. When the figure came through the door dressed in painter's whites, he was utterly nonplused, but took a couple of pictures anyway. Then, when the figure began stripping off blue nitrile gloves, he realized what he was seeing and began shooting in earnest. Only when the figure turned towards him and let him get at least an impression of the face through the lens during a fraction of a second's break in the shimmer did his jaw drop the rest of the way.

One last series of shots, hoping desperately for another break in the movement, but he knew that the heat from the patio and the intervening desert would almost certainly make any pictures so fuzzy that he wouldn't be able to enlarge the picture digitally without losing the sharpness he needed to confirm the identity he now strongly suspected, and there was just no way to make certain that the person he'd seen would be identifiable in the pictures he could get.

Then he crouched even lower and slowly squirmed his way backwards into the plant behind him, heedless of the stabs of the thorns digging into his back but taking as much care as he could not to make the branches shake any more than the wind was doing already. Only when the figure was long gone, carrying the garbage bag and walking off through the desert towards a road that Jeff had, luckily for him, passed on as a place to park, did he finally begin to move out a bit from his concealment.

Even then he didn't leave the spot he was in between the palo verdes for a good fifteen minutes more. Without clearer pictures, he couldn't prove the killer was the person he now was personally certain was the actual killer, but he needed to be sure. That meant heading for his computer without delay.

Chapter 19

Jeff tried every trick he knew on the computer to bring up workable images, without any success at all. Even Amy couldn't improve on the surreal images Jeff had gotten, to their mutual frustration. Finally Jeff reached two decisions. First and foremost, he needed to warn Reesa, because if he was right about the killer's identity, she could be in serious danger by being left in the dark.

Second, at the same time, he'd have to do whatever he could to track the killer. Whether he could stop the next murders was an open question, but he had to at least try. It definitely wouldn't be possible to convince anyone else to do it on nothing more than some shimmery pictures that could have shown any of a thousand people plus his own gut feeling. But he could do it himself.

The phone was picked up on the second ring. "Homicide, Esquivel." The voice was gruff, and Jeff couldn't remember if he'd met the man or not.

"Detective Esquivel, this is Jeff Escarton. I'm trying to reach Detective Malloy. Her cellphone goes right to voicemail, and it's important that I speak with her."

"She's not available. Escarton, you said? You're the fellow she's been seeing, aren't you?"

"Yes, sir, I am. And it's vital that I speak with her as soon as possible."

"'Fraid it's not going to happen. She's off for the week at some course. Don't know what or where. I just know that she waltzed out of here Friday saying that she was going to turn her phone off when she got home and leave it off until she was ready to come back to work, and she'd be back here bright and early on the first."

Jeff felt his guts twist into a knot, but he worked hard to keep his voice level. "I guess that's what she meant when she said we wouldn't be able to do lunch this week. Is there any way to reach her before then?"

"Not to my knowledge, no. She said she needed the time off and since she wasn't even going to be in town, she was taking full advantage of it and going incommunicado for several days. Sorry, Mr. Escarton. Wish I could have been more of a help."

"Is Detective Palmer there?"

"Nope, sorry. Chuck's out at the moment, too, and may not be back in until tomorrow. Like I said, I wish I could have been more help."

Jeff thanked him and set the handset gently back into the cradle, his mind racing. Now what? Well, if Reesa was going to be back at her desk on the first, then she'd probably be back in town sometime during the day on Halloween. Did she have a landline? Jeff didn't remember seeing a phone in her house outside of the cellphone that had been on her credenza.

What did it matter? If she did have one, he didn't have the number anyway. And if she were out of town, that phone could ring until the cows came home and she'd never answer it. There was also no way he was about to put his information on a recording. Too much speculation, too much basis in his unprovable belief rather than facts. Too much explanation needed to go with it. He knew, in his gut, but that wouldn't be good enough for a message. No, he had to speak with her directly. There was just no other option out there.

He and Amy kept several pre-paid cellphones just for this purpose. Sometimes it was just, 'Sorry, wrong number.' Other times, especially if a subject might recognize the voice, nobody said anything. The computer attached to the phone only needed moments to download the software that would give Jeff a tap on everything that happened around the phone on the other end and continue to do so for ten days before disappearing without a trace. Not legal, but both Jeff and Amy were careful to use it as sparingly as possible, only when they had no alternatives. Getting up from his chair, he headed for Amy's office. He was definitely going to need her help with this one.

Chapter 20

Jeff stuck the earbud into his left ear. With any luck, the next time the killer struck, he'd have enough forewarning, and enough information about the location, to be able to call someone in TPD Homicide or the Sheriff's Department, whichever was appropriate, about the killing while there was still time to catch the killer either in the act or at least before departing the scene. Of course, if he was stuck up in the foothills then, the way he was at the moment, about all he could do outside of that was listen in, and he figured it was likely to be a lot worse than the explosion in the Petrovik house had been. Although he could certainly be sorry about Ritchie; he liked dogs.

He had set up his tripod and was just getting his camera aimed at the proper window when he started to hear things over his earbud. Putting his left index finger on it to make sure it stayed put, he stopped worrying about his photography momentarily and just listened. When he was satisfied that all he was hearing was the killer's usual daytime work routine and that nothing worth paying special attention to was happening at the moment, he returned his concentration to the camera and to the job at hand. This promised to be a fairly easy case, as the attorney had specified that he didn't want, or at least need, any more right now than some good shots of the 'other woman' arriving at his client's house while she was out of town. Simply some additional leverage to help get a good settlement. Jeff had managed to develop a schedule for the trysts, and now here he was, all set up and prepared. If his schedule was good, she should be driving up right about … now.

And right on time, the tan Audi made the last turn in the road before the driveway. Jeff caught a good shot of the mailbox with the house number and the woman in question just before her car obscured the box. Several more as she drove down the driveway, parked in front of the garage, got out of her car, and headed for the front door. The last was as the door opened and the client's husband greeted her rather demonstrably. As the door closed behind them, Jeff began disassembling his camera equipment and packing it away for the hike back to his car.

****

After two days of listening in on the killer's day-to-day life on the earbud, Jeff was getting both sick and tired of listening to it and frustrated as hell. When was something worthwhile going to happen? He only had about another week before the software that gave him a tap on the killer's cellphone self-destructed, and calling the killer again to say, "Sorry, wrong number," or simply letting the killer hear a dead line while the attached computer downloaded the parasitic software into the phone again was quite low on the list of things he wanted to do. Of course, tonight was Halloween. Who knew what might happen? He'd tried calling Reesa half a dozen times today already, only to find that her phone still went straight to voicemail. Was she back in town yet? Jeff didn't know, but he'd be calling her first thing in the morning. That was a certainty – assuming she didn't answer during one of the several more calls he was probably going to try making this evening. Hopefully she wouldn't think he was stalking her.

Then, following a period of extended silence, or at least without voices, he abruptly heard something that made him drop everything he was doing, which was setting up for another set of photographs at another residence, and sit up straight.

A man's voice. "Who are you? What are you doing here?"

A woman's voice. "Don't I know you? I know I've seen you somewhere before."

A metallic *clack-clack* that sounded to Jeff like a pump-action shotgun being racked. *This is not going to turn out well*, Jeff thought. He had no idea where the killer was, so there was no way he could have sent anybody out to try to apprehend the killer before the deed was long done and the killer long gone from the scene. Besides, if that really had been a shotgun action, then this was going to go down in minutes anyway. Badly.

"You will burn in Hell! Repent! You are going to hellfire and damnation! God will punish you! Make your peace with Him! You are going to die a horrible death!"

Oh, shit, Jeff thought. *Henry, give it a rest. In fact, shut up. This spiel of yours isn't going to do anyone any good. Nor is it going to accomplish anything. And it's not like you believe any of that anyway.*

Then the woman's voice again. "There's a detective after you, you know. I've seen her on the TV. What's her name? Malloy? Yeah, that's it. She's gonna stop you."

The killer's voice. "Detective Malloy won't be stopping anybody. She's going to be next." Jeff felt a definite chill run down his spine. Suddenly he didn't give much of a damn where the killer was right now. Reesa was in danger, either because she was back in town and he couldn't warn her, or because she wasn't back yet but she'd be walking straight into a trap the killer would have set, and he still couldn't warn her. In fact, he was stuck in the far reaches of the Tanque Verde valley, in a residential area way the hell and gone to the northeast of the city – just about as far from Reesa's house as he could possibly get without actually leaving Tucson.

Screw this job. He started undoing all of the preparation he had already done and jammed his equipment back into his bag any which way. Some of it didn't want to go, but he forced it and pulled the straps as tight as he could in closing the bag. He grabbed the tripod as he stood up, and after trying to trot with it still extended, settled for walking for the time it took him to collapse it. Then he resumed his trot. His car was at least a mile away and over some rough terrain. He kept listening.

A blast from the shotgun stopped all conversation. *Yeah, that's no surprise.* The woman screamed – or was that the man? Another blast and Jeff realized that there was no doubt, that had definitely been the man screaming before. The woman could reach some truly astonishing high notes. They continued to scream and cry for several minutes. Only as their volume began to diminish, almost as though someone had been enjoying watching them die, did two more blasts finally silence them, one by one. Jeff could only imagine what the killer was doing now. He was within sight of his car by then, and broke into a full-out run.

Bad idea, he thought as he picked himself up from the ground. The camera bag seemed undamaged; it had landed almost as hard as he had, but at least he hadn't fallen on it and it was padded, not that he really cared all that much at the moment. Camera gear only meant money and could readily be replaced. That was the easy part. He'd develop an interesting bruise or two from the tripod, which he had fallen on. But he was in the car in seconds and barely took time to fasten his seatbelt with one hand while starting the car with the other. Once the car was running, he tried Reesa's number again. Still voicemail.

****

Jeff had no idea if he could get to Reesa's home before the killer did. If the murders he had just eavesdropped on had been out in Vail or Rita Ranch, say, way on the southeast side of greater Tucson, there'd be no problem. He'd be waiting at her house when the killer arrived. On the other hand, it could just as easily have been in north Tucson or Marana and the killer could be pulling into her driveway right this minute, while he had at least a half-hour's drive into the setting sun to go. He could go faster, but getting pulled over by some attentive Pima County deputy on Sunrise or Orange Grove might mean Reesa's death just through the delay, and that he just wouldn't, *couldn't*, risk. Nor, for that matter, could he totally ignore the possibility of some trick-or-treating kids who might be out early crossing the street. So he kept it just a couple of miles per hour over the speed limit. Just a couple. When he wanted desperately to floor it. *Needed* to floor it. Once again, he tried her number. Once again, he got her voicemail.

****

Halloween was an evening Reesa thoroughly enjoyed, and she was delighted to have been able to be back in town for it. Sometimes she got a couple of dozen children, sometimes only a few, always shepherded carefully by their parents. The parents knew she lived alone, but as far as she could tell, now that she worked in plainclothes, few if any in the neighborhood were aware that she was a cop. The Gorhams next door knew, of

326

course, but their children were too old by now to do the trick-or-treat routine. Well, maybe not the youngest, he was just barely old enough to drive and might have another year or two in him if he had enough of a sweet tooth. But the rest, for sure. She always made certain that she had a bowl of candy ready by the front door and her outside light on. It was almost dark when she had the first ring of the doorbell and heard a small voice through the door piping, "Trick or treat!"

As Reesa approached the door, she glanced at the peephole viewer she'd bought, still in its packaging and lying on the table near the door, waiting to be installed. *This is one night I won't need it*, she thought. With a small smile, she grabbed a couple of pieces of candy with her left hand before opening the door.

Just as she unlatched it, though, it was thrown open abruptly, slamming into her forehead, nose, arm, and shoulder with unexpected force. As she staggered backwards into the room, momentarily disoriented from the sudden pain and the force of the impact, the killer stepped through the door and closed it from the inside. The killer's pistol was pointed squarely at Reesa's face.

Reesa didn't know what it was, beyond its not being a Glock like she carried. Or maybe it was; this wasn't a viewpoint she had a lot of familiarity with. Exactly what it was wasn't all that high on her priority list at that moment, either. Any nearer and she might have tried to take it away, but she was too far away for that sort of close-in grappling.

Unnoticed, the candy in her hand had gone flying when she was hit by the door. Instinctively she backed up another step, and the killer reached behind, locked the door, and groped around on the wall before finding the switch and turning off the outside light. "Ah, yes. Detective Malloy. You're next. I hope you've said your prayers." Reesa considered her options, none of them good. Both her pistols were in the dining room, cleared and lying on the credenza as always. She wasn't going to need them on Halloween, after all, and hadn't really wanted to leave them where neighborhood kids coming to her door might see them.

The relatively bare living room didn't offer much in the way of potential weapons, and since the killer already had the drop on her, the options left open to her were few indeed. The pistols in the coffee table were not only locked in it but unloaded to boot and there was no ammunition for them in there. She didn't waste a moment's thought even considering them.

Reesa had come to terms with her own mortality years before. As a rookie, she had run down one perp who, surprised at how quickly she was gaining on him, had suddenly swerved into traffic and right into the path of an oncoming car. Reesa was actually straddling his body, cuffs in hand, when the spreading red pool from under his head strongly suggested to her that he probably wasn't going anywhere except in a body bag, and that had made her begin to think about how close she herself had come to being hit by a vehicle.

Then, of course, her field training officer, the more experienced partner she'd been teamed with to learn the ropes, had had to pound that point home afterwards. Repeatedly.

This, though, was rather more immediate than she had ever really expected to face, in addition to its being a *major* violation of her own sanctum. That latter, of course, wasn't all that much of an issue at the moment compared to the very immediate danger she knew she faced. Now, standing in her own living room, she worked hard to project a calm she didn't begin to feel. "Do I need to have said my prayers? Am I supposed to have done something wrong?"

"Oh, you know what you've done. You and Mister Jeffrey Escarton. And of course, I can't have you interrupting my own project here, either, which you're getting ready to do. So you're going to die. It's customary to say your prayers first."

"Jeff? We've had some meals together, but that's all. We don't exactly have a relationship going here, other than maybe a casual friendship. Is that what you're really upset about?"

"Oh, that's a good one. And after the two of you have been going to the meetings of the Avowed together, I know for a fact that it's total bullshit. But you know, at this point, it really doesn't matter. You're both going to die, and that's all there is to it."

Both of us? Oh, brother. Reesa decided to try to change the subject a bit. Keep the conversation going. Time might not be a help, but it couldn't possibly hurt her. She'd buy as much of it as she could. "So where do the Avowed fit into this?"

The killer simply laughed. "The Avowed? They're a bunch of sheep, led by a man who's not even qualified to be a sheepdog. Well, wasn't qualified. He's not exactly in any position to do much of anything, now."

Reesa's eyebrows went up. "What do you mean?"

"When I met him, Henry Blodden was a sot. Nothing more than a street drunk. A falling down wreck in the gutter. He tried to beg the price of a drink from me and told me he'd been a preacher until his wife ran off with another man. It sounded like there might be a tale there, something worth hearing. So I told him I wouldn't buy him a drink, but I'd get him some coffee to help him sober up.

He stank so bad we couldn't even go inside the coffee shop, but we sat at an outside table for a couple of hours while he drank coffee on my dime and unloaded his life story on me. Very interesting indeed, once you sorted through the bullshit. By the time he left, he was just about sober, and because of my suggestions, he began the Avowed. Did quite well at it, too, until he forgot to practice what he preaches. He was really only a con man at heart, but he had a good line and a good ride. Unfortunately for him, he had to amuse himself with his dick along the way."

"So I take it that you've killed him?"

The killer smiled. Reesa thought a wolf facing dying prey might not smile quite so triumphantly. "Oh, yes. He and his bimbo are another in the line of executions. Just another pair of entries in the ledger, as it were."

If only she could keep the killer talking until some opportunity presented itself. Time might be on her side, she thought again. Might be? Definitely was, if only because there wasn't any alternative she could see. "So just how big is this ledger?"

The killer's smile didn't shrink. "You won't care. You'll just be one more line in it. No more than that."

"And Jeff?"

"He'll be the line right below yours. Never fear, he'll get his. Just as soon as I'm done with you." Did Jeff know who the killer was? Might he be tailing the killer? He was really her only chance, and a slim chance it was

indeed. She hadn't even told him she was going out of
town, hadn't told him she was shutting off her phone. For
all she knew, he'd been trying to call her for days. Or
maybe he was going to be just as surprised as she had been.

If that was the case, then they were probably both
dead. She'd hope he was coming, if only because she had
no choice. Right now, she didn't see any other halfway
decent way out of this. The killer's gun never wavered, and
with Reesa's two in the dining room, they might as well
have been in another state.

If she dashed for them, track star that she was, she
was still almost certain to be shot. She knew that the
stopping power of pistol bullets was popularly overrated,
but that was a small chance to depend on since she could
possibly take two or even three bullets before she could
reach her own gun, and her body armor was, as usual,
draped over one of the dining room chairs and had been for
the last week.

Then, after taking whatever shots she could survive,
she'd still have to slam the magazine home and rack the
slide, if she could, if she were still able to … plan to head
for the kitchen and dive into the far corner on her back after
snatching up the gun and magazine on the way past. That
might possibly buy her the time she needed and leave her in
a position to shoot back, if she wasn't wounded too badly at
that point. Not the best plan, merely the only one she
seemed to have left.

Bottom line, though, she was almost certainly a
goner unless some angel intervened. Some angel named
Jeff, since nobody else even knew where she lived, much
less could have any idea what was going on. Perhaps she
could buy some time, enough time for something, *anything*,

331

to happen. If nothing else, she was calm within herself. Or so she thought.

A tremor started, faintly, in her right leg. The killer seemed utterly at ease. Reesa felt a bit annoyed with her own body at this, but she had to admit to herself that since she was the one on the hot seat, there was a certain logic to it, inconvenient as it might be. She shifted her weight subtly to make it stop. "So tell me, if you would. What do you get out of these killings? Is it something sexual?"

The killer's smile got even broader, if that was possible. "Oh, you can't *begin* to imagine the sexual rush of a killing like the ones I've done face to face. To *watch* your victims, to look them in the eyes, as they realize they're going to die, caught in their own infidelities! And to die in terror! To *watch* them die! It's just ... it's beyond description. It's just the greatest thing ..."

"So why'd you tape Tennenholz and Hocksley's eyes?"

The killer's smile disappeared. "That ... was a bit of a mistake. I used the tape to throw them off, to give me a moment to bind them up together. I hadn't considered how disappointing it would be when I couldn't watch their eyes, but once the process was underway, I didn't want to stop enjoying the process to take the tape off." The smile reappeared, only slightly diminished. "Even with the tape, though, I could still see them turn all shades of red and purple and then watch them as they died. It was ... almost good enough."

"So it *is* a sexual impulse that drives you."

"Oh, *no*. That's just a side benefit. What *drives* me is cleansing society of these people who lie about their vows. People who promise to be with one person exclusively and then ignore that promise when it suits them. People like Henry used to condemn. People like Henry turned out to *be*. They don't *deserve* to live. So I remove them. It's that simple."

This is crazy, Reesa thought. *Infidelity as a reason to kill people? Stop analyzing, dammit! You've got a major problem here to deal with!* "You cut off Nathan Bridgton's genitals."

"Of course I did. Didn't he deserve it? You bet he did. He was a lousy lover, too, even besides his affairs. That's the sort of thing that I just won't tolerate."

"And you shot Ron Harris in his genitals."

The killer shrugged. "Another lousy lay. What can I say?"

"But according to his wife, Freddy Gardner was expected to, ah, spread himself around. She wasn't surprised by it at all. In fact, she said she was pretty much all right with it."

The killer reddened a bit. "That doesn't matter! He promised her when they were married. If it turned out that he couldn't keep his zipper up, and his wife finally decided to accept it because she couldn't change it, he still broke that promise! And he paid for it, just like he should."

"That one was … a stroke of genius. The snakes, I mean. Made it kind of interesting for those of us who had to go into the house afterwards."

The killer smiled again. "You liked that? I worked hard on that one. It wasn't easy even to find all the snakes, but eventually I did. Had to keep three of them for almost a month before I had enough of them to do the job."

"Well, if it's any consolation, I think the ME had nightmares for a couple of weeks afterwards."

333

"And is *he* being good?"

Oh, shit, Reesa thought, *this conversation isn't going the way I'd hoped. Not if we're picking out possible future targets from whatever I might say.* "Oh, yes. He's quite devoted to his wife. Boringly so, I could say. And what about me? And Jeff, for that matter? Neither of us is being unfaithful to anyone. We haven't broken any vows here."

"Well, you haven't, no. He's ... a bit of a different issue." The killer's voice was getting harder.

Reesa's eyebrows went up a fraction of an inch at that response. The hardening of the voice, though, suggested that this might not be the best time to pursue that angle.

The killer's expression changed – Reesa's impression was that it became thoughtful, although characterizing what it looked like wasn't really all that high on her list of priorities, either. Not compared to finding a way out of this predicament. If there was one. "So aren't you going to beg? Plead with me to spare your life?"

Fat fucking chance, Reesa thought. *Like it'd do me any good, either. But damn it, I'll die on my* feet *before I die on my knees, and if there's one thing I'm sure of, it's that dying is the only reasonable likelihood here. I'm probably not going to get out of this one. Not by myself, anyway. Dammit, I'm a sworn police officer and I do not beg.* "No."

The killer began to step sideways, away from the door. The new position made it that much harder for Reesa to see her way clear to get to the dining room for her own gun, but since she'd given up on that except as a last chance desperate attempt, it didn't really matter all that much. Was that a crunch on the driveway gravel she heard? It was just a faint sound, so faint she could have imagined it. Or maybe not.

Her iron control kept any reaction, as well as any faint hope arising from it, out of her expression. Once again Reesa considered her options. Rushing the killer wasn't a great idea where she already had a gun trained on her. If nothing else, it didn't exactly require much skill with a pistol to hit a target coming at you dead-on, and remembering the Harris crime scene, the killer seemed to be reasonably skilled with a pistol anyway. A dash for the dining room looked like the best of a very poor – and very *short* – list of options. Reesa again plotted her course over the seat and arm of the Eames chair – just a broad hurdle – and into the dining room mentally as the killer talked about regretting Reesa's refusal to beg for her life.

I'm sorry, Uncle Frank. I don't have a weapon to surrender, and I remember what you taught me. I wouldn't ever have done that. I also haven't surrendered what control I have over the situation. It's just that I've got so damn *little of that at the moment. Maybe in a few minutes you can tell me how I did. I know you're watching, and I'm going to keep trying as long as I can, but honestly, that just may not be enough. If there's any way you can help me right now, I could sure use it.*

"It's really too bad that you're being this way. Begging is *so* nice. It's a real turn-on, in fact. And you never know, I might take pity on you. Not that I still wouldn't kill you, you understand, but I could do it fast and painlessly. It's not like you're running around on anyone, after all. *You're* not breaking any promises. There's no real reason why you should suffer here. But you'd have to beg.

I'm not going to give you the easy way out just because. You've got to give *me* something here."

Already on edge, understandably, Reesa's patience was just about at an end, and that last statement was just too much for her frayed nerves. "Give *you* something? You come to my home, stick a gun in my face, tell me you're going to kill me, and you expect *me* to give *you* something? That takes the cake! I'll give you something, all right! I'll hold off from describing your ancestry and breeding habits! I'll even give you a head start. Turn around, go out the door, and I'll let you get to your car before I call it in. How about that?" She could feel her face growing hot.

The killer's mouth was open to respond when there was a loud crash as the front door opened violently and slammed against its stop, the jamb splintering around the lock and spraying fragments of wood into the room.

Chapter 21

Jeff parked at the outer end of the driveway, barely off the road, just in case the crunch of his tires on gravel might alert the killer. He moved carefully, quietly, to the front step and paused at the door, listening intently. Yes, the voices were still going. Thank God! As best he could tell, though, Reesa was just about out of ways to drag the conversation out, and whatever she was saying, she sounded like she was getting a bit angry. That definitely wouldn't help matters any.

Drawing himself back, Jeff hoped the door frame wasn't going to be too solid. Or the door. Banging into the door without bursting it open and getting into the room definitely wasn't going to help matters either. He took a deep breath, let it out. He drew his pistol with his right hand, braced himself as best he could, and drove his left foot into the door right at the deadbolt. The door cracked around the lock, the doorframe splintered and the door slammed open against its stop. Jeff stumbled into the room.

The killer turned her head momentarily to see what the noise was, but her own pistol never left Reesa. Jeff was recovering his balance, but his gun was trained directly on her. "Drop it, Lynne." Reesa stood stock still, apparently utterly surprised by Jeff's entrance.

"Oh, I don't think so. Especially not now that I've got both of you together. Trust me, Jeff, I was coming for you next. You see, you may think that you called it off between us, but it was always *my* choice whether you left or not, and I never really agreed to let you go. I've just given you some free rein to see where you'd go with it, and you … failed the test. I know you think you've found this bitch, but you're both going to pay the price. She's going to be first, but you'll be right behind.'"

Jeff barked an unfelt laugh that belied, or at least camouflaged, the sinking feeling in his gut. This was a rotten situation by any standard. Could he divert her focus to him? More importantly, away from Reesa? Worth a try. *Anything* was worth a try by now. "This is a bit more 'up close and personal' than your usual, isn't it? For Chrissake, Lynne, you're talking like a frickin' *schoolgirl* here. I mean, c'mon! We're all supposed to be mature adults, aren't we? Well, two of us are, anyway."

Her face now a mask of fury, Lynne Fox turned her full attention back towards Reesa and straightened her arm. As her finger began to tighten on the trigger, suddenly Reesa tensed for a dive to her right as Jeff's pistol barked and red blossomed bright on Lynne's white shirt, just on the side of her breast. Her expression was puzzled as she turned her head back to him. Jeff fought the recoil, brought his pistol back on target and shot her again, this impact not an inch from the first. As her gun started to sag, Reesa moved as Lynne finally managed to pull the trigger. A heartbeat later, Jeff fired his third shot.

Lynne's bullet barely missed the ulnar nerve on the underside of Reesa's left arm, although the shock of its passage would be enough to disrupt impulses along the nerve for weeks, if she lived that long. In tearing its way through the muscles of her arm, though, it also took a significant piece out of the wall of the brachial artery. Blood flowed freely from the vessel, pumped by a heart already racing as Reesa, stunned by the impact, fell to the floor.

Jeff put a fourth shot into Lynne, then a fifth and kept on shooting. After the eighth shot, when the slide of his pistol locked back on an empty magazine, she finally fell. He dropped his now-useless pistol and saw Reesa on the floor, more than a trickle of blood already making its way across the floor from underneath her. Leaping over Lynne's body, he knelt beside the fallen detective. "Reesa!" Groping blindly under her left arm, around her armpit, he finally found the entrance wound and applied pressure. The bleeding slowed. Fumbling with his left hand, unwilling to risk taking his right off her wound even for a second, he pulled out his cellphone. Clumsily he dialed 911. When the operator answered, he all but screamed, "Officer down! I need an ambulance fast!"

"Sir, please calm down. I need to take down your information."

"Dammit, I've got a TPD officer seriously wounded here. The shooter is down, too, and probably dead, but this detective is in major trouble. I need an ambulance and I need it fast. 2925 Tierra Incognita, in north Tucson."

"Sir, I'm putting in the request now. Do you need me to stay on the line?"

Jeff's voice was somewhat calmer now. Just knowing that he'd managed to make the call for help while there was still time to save Reesa took the edge off. "I really don't care. I'm applying pressure to the wound, but I've got no idea what damage has been done inside. She's bleeding badly. All I can do right now is try to control the bleeding and hope she makes it." He let out a shuddering sigh.

"Do you have the officer's identification?"

"It's Detective Reesa Malloy, from TPD Homicide."

"I'm passing that information along." In the distance, Jeff began to hear a siren, gradually growing louder.

Two uniformed Pima County deputies, guns drawn, were first through the door, with a paramedic close behind. One of the deputies, noticing the bowl of candy, muttered, "Trick or treat." Jeff ignored him.

The paramedic came and knelt by Jeff as the deputies began to clear the house. "There's nobody else here," Jeff called after them. They ignored him in return, although one of them crouched briefly to check Lynne's body for a pulse below the corner of her jaw without actually looking at her. Neither one had really looked at the face, so they didn't know who she was yet. There was a crash from down the hallway as they forced the door to Reesa's private room. When they were satisfied that there was nobody else lurking in the house, they returned. "Please stand up, sir." They didn't sound as polite as their words did.

The paramedic looked at Jeff. "You may as well, sir. I've got her from here. You've probably saved her from bleeding out, but I've got her now. I'll take her from here. Go with the deputies. Please."

Too wrung out to stand immediately, Jeff just remained on his knees for close to a minute, his head bowed. The deputies waited impatiently. When he finally did stand up, one of them took his arm and, somewhat roughly, pulled him outside. Chuck Palmer was just pulling into the driveway, his car crowding it all but to overflowing. As he stepped out of the car, flashing his badge, he called to them. "Hey, let me take him from here, okay? She's my partner, and I know him." The deputies were reluctant, to say the least.

Chuck stepped closer to them. "Look, he's not the problem. He'd have taken the bullets for her if he could have. I'll get the whole story out of him and send you whatever you need, okay? Just let me take him from here." Chuck was displaying an unusual (for him) command of the situation, and it was clear that the deputies had a serious jurisdictional issue with turning Jeff over to him, but Chuck persisted and they finally let Jeff go in his care. Maybe they were just trying to be rid of both of them. Chuck put his arm around Jeff's shoulders. "Are you all right, Jeff?"

"Oh, I'm absolutely fucking *dandy*," Jeff replied with a snarl. "I just shot and killed Lynne Fox, she shot Reesa in the process, and I've got no fucking idea how she's doing. Reesa, I mean. I'm pretty sure Lynne's dead. Just how do you *think* I feel?"

Chuck's jaw gaped. "Lynne Fox? The reporter?" Jeff nodded. "What was *she* doing here? And why'd you shoot her? I mean ..."

Jeff was swaying, almost too emotionally drained to remain on his feet, but there was nowhere to sit. He stumbled towards the ambulance with Chuck trailing close behind, ready to offer whatever assistance Jeff might need as well as to get Jeff's answers. Jeff half-sat, half-collapsed onto the rear bumper of the ambulance. "Lynne was the Tucson Ripper. All of her on-scene reporting, all of her special reports, her statements, the emails ... she was taunting all of you with them. TPD and PCSD, I mean. She knew the cases were all related because she was committing the murders herself.

341

"She came here tonight to kill Reesa and then she was going to find me and kill me, because I dumped her a year or so ago. Lynne decided that Reesa was my new girlfriend and she didn't like that. Felt she hadn't really let me go, back when, and that the decision was hers to make, not mine. Totally screwball.

"She had her gun on Reesa when I broke in the door and she wouldn't put it down. I tried to get her to focus on me, but she wouldn't be diverted from Reesa, even though I already had my gun on her. When she went to shoot Reesa, I shot her. And kept shooting her." His voice broke. "And then she shot Reesa anyway!" It wasn't quite a cry, not quite a wail, but close. The anguish, the agony was so evident in his voice that it was almost overwhelming.

Chuck tried again to comfort him. Just then the paramedics rolled a gurney out of the door. Showing more agility and energy than would have been expected a moment before, Jeff leapt to see how Reesa was doing. Her eyes remained closed, but the oxygen mask fogged regularly with her breath. He touched her cheek just behind the mask with his fingertips, lightly. Chuck said nothing, though, just watching; he was pretty sure Jeff and Reesa hadn't actually gotten to the point of being lovers. Not yet, although he recognized that if Reesa felt even close to the way Jeff did, it probably wouldn't be too much longer, if she made it. No matter, Jeff would probably be good for her, in Chuck's opinion. He seemed to make her happy.

And if they had by now, then so much the better. Not that it was any of his business, he reminded himself. He was a happily married man, after all, and he was well aware that she wouldn't get involved with anyone in the department anyway. Not that way. Of course, Reesa was his partner, and he cared. Hell, she'd never see it for herself, but every one of the other detectives in Homicide cared about her. Even Schuler, when he wasn't being a total pain in the ass. But she was *his* partner.

Her hand moved, groped blindly for Jeff's. Her eyes flickered open momentarily, then the paramedics lifted the gurney into the ambulance. As it drove off, siren wailing, Chuck gradually led Jeff back to the detective's own car.

"Come on, Jeff. She's in good hands, she's on her way to the hospital, and there's nothing more you can do for her now. But you and I need to go downtown. I need to ask you some questions and get the straight story on all of this. You know the drill. If nothing else, I have to do it because the Sheriff's Department is going to need the account." Jeff looked back towards the house.

The ME was shepherding another gurney, this one with a body bag, out the door. Other Pima County deputies were unrolling the yellow crime scene tape around the house while a crime scene tech carrying his case headed into the house. With a sound that might have been a stifled sob, Jeff turned towards Chuck's car and climbed in.

Once inside one of the TPD homicide interrogation rooms, Jeff, now in more control of his faculties, regarded Chuck. "Before you get into the questions, I think I'd like to have a lawyer here. Not that I believe I've got any real problem with this, and I'm certainly willing to give you the whole story, but I'd feel a lot better having a lawyer with me."

Chuck nodded. "Use your cell."

"Let's hope there's no irony there." Jeff's voice was dry as he dialed Amy's number. "Amy, Jeff. Is Alec by any chance available? I need him."

Amy sounded puzzled. "He's not here, but I can call him. What's up?"

"There's been … I just shot Lynne Fox. Killed her, as she shot Reesa. Reesa's in the hospital and I'm down at the station, TPD, in Homicide. They want to ask me some questions."

"Oh, shit! He'll be there as soon as I can shake him free, and that won't take long, trust me. Just hang tight and don't tell them anything." As she hung up, Jeff punched the button to hang up his end of the call.

"He'll be here as soon as he can make it. He's out at his home on the west side, I expect. Got a cold drink for me in the meantime?"

Alec was there in just under a half-hour, still wearing jeans and a t-shirt. Jeff and Chuck were by now sitting easily in one of the interrogation rooms with the door open, talking about utter inconsequentials, when he arrived. Alec asked for a few minutes alone with his client. When Alec called Chuck back in, Jeff began. "I was conducting some surveillance on Rachel Lindstrom, just before her death. As a result of that, I was outside of the Trujillo house, in back. Well in back, actually, looking for a better vantage point, when I saw a black plastic garbage bag on a back patio table. I finally saw a person dressed in painter's whites exit the rear door of the house, and I continued to photograph from a hidden location. When the person had finished removing all of her covering clothing, she turned and faced me. Due to the heat shimmer and wind, I couldn't get a usable photograph, but I was fairly certain that it was Lynne Fox. I tried to reach Detective Malloy, but her phone was turned off and remained that way through tonight. I decided to put Lynne under surveillance myself, primarily in the hopes of catching her in the act of setting up for or committing another pair of murders.

"I followed Lynne electronically for several days, and before today, all I heard was her usual daytime routine. Then today, with no warning, I heard her interrupt and then kill Henry Blodden and whoever he was having his current affair with. As she was preparing to kill them, she spoke of her intention to go kill Detective Malloy next, so I quit the surveillance I had been working on and headed for Reesa's house, too."

He took a deep breath and hesitated for a moment before continuing. "Upon arriving at her residence, through the door, I heard Lynne inside, talking to Reesa and using threatening language. She was asking Reesa to beg for her life, and Reesa was refusing. Silently I tried the latch but found that the door was locked. I then broke in the door and found that she, Lynne, had a gun trained on Reesa.

"She made threats against me as well, promising to kill me as soon as she had killed Reesa. I tried to distract her, to divert her focus from Reesa to me, but that didn't work."

He paused and took a breath, shuddering just slightly, before resuming. "When I saw her straighten her arm and begin to tighten her finger on the trigger, as she was going to shoot Reesa, I began shooting. She had taken a couple of my shots, two or three, I think, before she fired the only shot she got off, and I continued shooting her until she finally went down. I emptied my gun into her." The pain he was feeling was more than evident in his face. "You know the rest."

Chuck thought for a minute. "How did you know she was going to Reesa's to threaten her? She might just have been going to interview her." Jeff sat mute. Chuck leaned forward to ask the question again, and Alec broke in.

"Detective, if you continue to ask, I'll instruct my client to remain silent. As things stand, it really isn't a relevant or germane question. My client was clearly acting in defense of another, specifically Detective Malloy, when he shot Ms. Fox. You've got the gun with Fox's prints that was by her hand when she was found, there'll be GSR on her hand, and the lab will confirm that bullets from that gun will match the bullet in Detective Malloy. Or that went through her. They may also match bullets from one of your earlier crime scenes. On top of that, I find it just a bit difficult to consider a pistol a normal part of an interview, especially in the absence of a camera or microphone anywhere. I suggest we leave it as it is."

Jeff looked up. "You can ask Reesa. She knows what I do."

Chuck thought about that, then nodded sharply. Just then Benny Benavidez opened the door and stuck his head in. "She's going to be all right. Just got the word." He looked at Jeff. "Thanks, Jeff. We're all glad you were there for her." He stepped into the room and shook Jeff's hand before leaving again.

Chuck seemed to sag slightly as the tension left his body. Jeff just looked completely relieved. Standing up, Chuck motioned Jeff and Alec ahead of him out of the room. Ruben Esquivel was standing outside of the interrogation room, waiting to shake Jeff's hand and murmur his own thanks. Chuck, too, shook Jeff's hand and simply said, "Thank you, Jeff. From the bottom of my heart. I mean that. I'll … I'll take care of the rest of this. I'm glad you're her friend. She needed someone tonight, and I'm thrilled that you came through for her. She'd almost certainly be dead now if not for you."

Jeff stood where he was for a moment. "I've got one favor to ask. When this goes to the media, can you guys leave me out of it? Give Reesa the credit, both for figuring out that Fox was the Ripper and for shooting her. I don't need the attention, and it'll only make my work harder. Can you do that?"

Chuck considered it for a moment. "I can't make any promises, but I'll pass it along. If we can, we will. Okay?"

Epilogue

Jeff turned off Speedway. "Just to try to keep from having any surprises, you should know that Becky Swan, Amy's cousin and best friend, lives up there with Amy and Alec. I expect she'll be there tonight, too. Beyond that, Betsy is the little girl, and Bruno is the older dog. The puppy is Callie."

Reesa was silent for a moment, then said, "Huh. Okay, well, they're the ones doing dinner, so I guess however many people are going to be there is their concern, not mine."

Jeff chuckled. "Well, trust me, when Amy wants things done a certain way, they get done that way. I can tell you up front that Amy and Becky have been best friends all of their lives, and off the record, Amy's kind of ... controlling. Well, no, that's not really fair. She's very nice, but she's also *very* strong-willed. The rest should really wait for them to tell you. They can be awfully private people."

Reesa just shrugged. *Strong-willed and senior investigator my ass*, she thought once again. *Well, strong-willed, sure. But she's really your boss and the Family CEO. I know that, and she knows about me, too. Of course, you don't know that I'm Family, just like you and Amy. You're the only one still in the dark about everything.*

"Oh, and Betsy is Amy's daughter. She's going on three, I think, and precocious as all hell, but you need to know that Bruno is Betsy's guardian angel. He's protection trained, among other things, he sticks to her like glue when any outsiders are around, and it's probably more than my life is worth to make any moves that he thinks are a threat to her. He likes me, I believe, but I've never tried to push it around Betsy. Callie is simply sweet, although she's still just a puppy."

"And you said something about their all being together in that little place where you're living now? Talk about crowded."

Jeff shook his head. "I can only imagine. No, actually, I can't. But yeah, they were all together there for about two years before they moved out here. Not Betsy, she hadn't been born. But the three adults were all living there."

The introductions went very smoothly. Reesa put her detective face on and made sure to keep her emotions well-hidden, although she noted that both Amy and Becky did a fair job of putting on poker faces themselves. Amy she understood very well by now, and when she found out that Becky was a psychologist, her demeanor became understandable as well. Amy's guarded reactions were really no surprise to Reesa at all, under the circumstances.

After the obligatory, if abbreviated, house tour, Reesa found herself out on the patio (a heated patio, no less!) that would overlook the desert parks to the west of the mountains were it not dark already, with all of the adults, a cold scotch on the table by her. A *very* nice scotch, far better than anything she bought for herself and even noticeably better than the nice scotch Jeff had given her at his place. Her left arm was resting in the sling that she no longer had to completely rely on but still found helpful much of the time, Betsy was playing off to one side under Bruno's watchful gaze, while Callie chewed on a toy by Amy's feet.

Amy, Alec and Becky had related some of how they wound up living together, but Reesa was still a bit puzzled. She turned to Becky. "Do you mind if I ask a question or two?" Becky gestured for her to go ahead. "I can certainly sympathize with your problems after Amy got you out from under the murder charge, but living here with them" – she waved her hand to encompass Amy and Alec – "seems like an odd way to take care of it."

Becky smiled. "Well, yes, to an outsider, I suppose it does seem that way. In my profession, we're taught the value of talking out problems. How to lead the patient through the issues, expose and defuse the emotions, that sort of thing. Personally, being a very private sort of person myself, I have a great fondness for journaling, writing down what you might say instead of saying it out loud, but sometimes you just have to have someone on the other side to respond to you. One problem I had then was that there was hardly anybody in town I could possibly have gone to see, because I already knew almost all of them.

"Another was that, honestly, I'm so private that I find it difficult to open up to others. It probably sounds funny, when I'm in the business of listening to them open up to me, but that's the way I am. Amy, on the other hand, after the way she grew up, with an author for a father and having lost her mother when she was a pre-teen, tends to think more in terms of family – fold in and embrace, hold tight, support and just love until the problems go away or at least become manageable. And as close as she and I have been over the years, it was a natural reaction for her when I was in such need. Our habit, hers and mine, from way back when we were very young, was always to cling to each other when upset, to the point that we'd even sleep together. Nothing sexual, just the contact comfort of someone you're very close to."

Now that was interesting, Reesa thought. Out of the corner of her eye, she'd seen Jeff's head suddenly swivel towards her while Becky had been speaking. *Oh, yes, when she mentioned Amy's father, the author. Well, the fiction had it that the author was his* boss's *father and Amy was merely senior to him in the office. Becky probably didn't know about that. Shit, what a tangled web we're weaving, trying to dance all around the Family without Jeff revealing anything to me or any of the three letting slip anything about me or the Family when everybody already knows. He just doesn't know about me. Well, he doesn't yet, although they're all probably just letting me decide whether to tell him. And big surprise, I'll just* bet *that Amy's reaction is to think in terms of family. Or is that Family?*

Amy broke in. "What you need to understand, Reesa, is that she's the mind-bender."

Becky, with a smile, responded, "Snoop."

Amy grinned. "Better watch out, dear. The snoops outnumber the mind-benders tonight, three to one."

Alec waved an arm. "I'm calling a foul on that one. Amy, you can't count guests on your side."

"Oh, pooh. Anyway, Jeff isn't a guest, he's an employee."

Alec stood his ground. "Still won't fly, Amy. This is after hours, this isn't work, and you're not in the office." Conceding the point, Amy gestured her agreement.

Reesa cocked her head towards him. "Alec, are you always the referee between these two?"

351

Now he laughed. "Between the two of them, sure. But the way it works around here, most disagreements, whether they're good natured like this one or more serious, are between two of us. Any two. And by now, the third is really expected to, and normally does, take the referee role.

"We'll call fouls on things like that, or on personal attacks – those are rare, thank God – but generally whoever's refereeing just tries to keep things calm and let the problems get resolved quietly. It works for us. And the one time that we all got into it, Amy suddenly announced, quite loudly, that she was going home to her father while Becky hollered that she was going home to her mother. Since those two're married to each other now, I asked these two if they were going to be sleeping in Colin and Lori's guest bedroom together, and at that point they looked at each other in shock and finally we all started laughing. No more problem."

What an interesting family dynamic, she thought. *Of course, it's an interesting sort of family arrangement to start with, under any circumstances. A married couple living with a female friend? In the same house, even one as big as this? Go figure. I wonder where Becky ... no, not my business. And speaking of family, switch gears. Amy knows about me. Since she knows, Becky and Alec almost certainly know, too – but they really don't concern me here. Of course, since Becky is Amy's cousin, she may well be Family herself. The only question is whether I tell Jeff, since it looks like Amy still hasn't. If I do, I'm kind of committing to going further with him, aren't I? Not necessarily right now, but in the future. Near future. Or ... shit. Right now, really. Should I? Do I want to keep the relationship at this level? Or let it move further? This is*

what he said he wanted to be around for, isn't it?
Remember, he did charge a killer holding a loaded gun for
me and saved my life after I was shot. And he's done a
bang-up job of taking care of me ever since. Oh, hell. I
should just do it. Somehow.

After several minutes of silence while Reesa's mind
was going around in those circles, Amy looked at her
directly. "So, Reesa, a penny for your thoughts."

Reesa simply continued to look around the patio
and, at least in her mind's eye, off toward the desert to the
west for a few more moments. Then, deciding that this
might be the best opportunity she'd ever have, she took
another sip of her drink before speaking. "Actually, I was
thinking that this house really is the sort of place I'd have
expected to find the head of the Family living in. Certainly
more than that little place on Helen Street that Jeff's in
now."

Jeff's jaw dropped. Looking at Reesa in some
shock, he said, "Oh, my *God!* You're Family?" She
nodded, her attention still focused on Amy.

Amy simply smiled. "I figured you'd probably get
around to telling him some day. But one question for the
great detective. Have you figured out what 'A.M.' stands
for yet?"

Now Reesa smiled. "That was a bit harder than
figuring out who you were in the first place, since none of
the official records gave me 'Alannah Meav,' but I
managed to luck into it."

Alec snorted. "That marriage certificate, I'll bet.
You had to send her to our bathroom, remember, and it's
hanging right there on the bedroom wall. It's got your

353

entire maiden name on it. Probably the only time in decades that you've used it."

Amy glanced at Alec. "It wasn't *my* doing that put the powder room out of order. But you're right about how long it's been since I've used that name."

Nodding, Reesa said, "Yes, that was it. Personally, I think Alannah Meav is a pretty name. I don't know why you don't use it."

Amy frowned. "Your privilege. I've *never* liked it, even though my grandmother was named Alannah, and I dearly loved her. I've been Amy ever since before kindergarten, because I refused to respond when my parents called me Alannah. Mom had to call me 'kiddo,' and Daddy usually called me 'squirt.' Then Mom got me a backpack for school with my initials embroidered on it and I jumped at the opportunity. Told her Amy was my name from then on, and eventually she and Daddy gave in. You should understand such things ... Merissa."

Reesa colored some and she ducked her head momentarily. Did Amy know her other secret, too? Hopefully she wouldn't speak of it if she did, and God willing, she didn't even know. *But how in the hell had she even found out about Merissa? Probably from when my mother registered me with the Family when I was born. That's the only way I can think of, at least at the moment.* "Touché. But you do know that it was changed."

Amy, silent, simply nodded.

Jeff, regaining some of his composure, asked, "Merissa?"

Reesa whirled on him. "Jeff, if you call me that again, I will *hurt* you." He held up his hands to ward off her sudden flash of anger. Heatedly she went on, "I *hate* it.

·

354

Anyway, it's not my name any more. Just call me Reesa. That *is* my name. Do that and everything will be fine. Understand?"

Jeff looked a little hurt. "You didn't respond to *her* like that."

Reesa's expression softened. "I'm sorry, Jeff. That didn't come out right, and you certainly didn't deserve it. I genuinely am sorry for the reaction, but I do *really* hate that name. I don't *ever* want to hear it again." She nodded towards Amy. "*She*'s the Family CEO. She could probably have me shot at sunrise."

Amy chuckled. "Not here, and I wouldn't do it at sunrise anyway. I *like* sunrise. Now if we were in Golondrino, at high noon, as I told you before, it would be a different matter. But I try to avoid doing that. It's tacky and bound to get me talked about."

Jeff looked back at Amy. "She's Family, and you never told me? You knew, didn't you?"

Amy nodded. "Yes, I did. I checked her out after Daddy told me about her calling him and I … stumbled on to her being Family. I mean, I couldn't think of any other reason why she would even have been concerned, much less gone to the trouble of checking on me. Then when I found out she'd called the business office, I knew she was Family. Had to be, since without a Family ID number, they wouldn't even talk to her. Then of course, even if I hadn't already known by then, her mother called to thank me for sending in the specialists to consult on her case after she was shot."

Now it was Reesa's turn to goggle. "Mother called you?"

Amy looked at her. "Yes, when they were here in town. We wound up having your parents out here for drinks and dinner. It was a most enjoyable evening, but I asked them not to tell you about it at the time." She turned back to Jeff. "Reesa's your twelfth cousin, once removed, Jeff. She's a tenth cousin to Becky and me. Neither one is exactly close. But there was no reason to tell you, and frankly, it wasn't my place to do so. I knew she'd realize that you were, soon enough. I mean, with a last name of Escarton, and working for 'A.M. Youngston,' it's kind of a dead giveaway to anyone in the Family right there. If she wanted you to know, I figured she'd tell you. She could, of course, since she knew about you. Or she might choose not to, in which case I certainly had no business letting you know."

She turned to Reesa again. "The thing about the certificate is that you're really unusual. Other people who come here either already know who I am or in a few cases, they aren't Family in the first place, so the name means nothing to them. I knew that you knew who I was already, after our meeting, but I asked you at the time not to spread it around and I presume you did as you said you would. Then after you were shot, your mother called the office and addressed me by name. When I tried to tell her I was just Amy Trevethen, she asked me not to insult her daughter's intelligence and investigative skills, that you had already confirmed who I was." Amy grinned. "Obviously you'd told her before our meeting. Right?" Reesa nodded. "Checking the certificate was the easy part after that."

Reesa shrugged. "Being Family really hasn't meant all that much to me. Sure, I got my education paid for, and I probably took more courses and in a better college than I would have if I'd had to pay for them myself. Other than that, though, I've used the extra income for some things that made my life more pleasant and otherwise pretty much ignored it. And yes, I knew about Jeff as soon as he showed me his business card."

Becky laughed. "That pretty much describes both Amy and me to a 'T,' at least up until Amy was tapped to be the CEO. I suspect it applies to most Family members. But one other thing I can say about your earlier question, now that you're out of the closet, so to speak. It took me several years to put together in my own mind, but this is significant and it might matter to you, at least some day. You need to understand that as private and guarded as Family members normally are, my profession is very unusual in the Family. Amy tells me I'm the only psychologist, and I only know of two psychiatrists, including Jon." Her eyes glistened momentarily. "It's been a matter of serious interest to me, but I've not had anyone else to talk to about it professionally.

"One of the things I have felt all my life, well, since I learned about the Family, and because of it, is a feeling of belonging, at some deep level. For me, at least, it was a significant source of my personal strength. Even if you have nothing in particular to do with the Family growing up, that feeling is there, at least judging from the people I've spoken with, both here and in Golondrino, among other places. Insofar as I can judge from my patients and some others, people who aren't Family tend not to have a similar feeling unless they've come from a really good extended family background, because that's really what the Family is – the ultimate extended family.

"Anyway, when I was in jail, I lost that. I knew, thanks to Alec, that conviction of a crime of violence is grounds for terminating Family membership, and while I figured that Amy probably wouldn't let it stand for me, the fact is that that *is* the rule, and she'd have had to break the rules in order to override my expulsion, if she did. The only thing I had to keep me going during that time was these two" – she gestured to Alec and Amy – "and really, nothing else whatsoever. Believe me, when you lose that feeling of belonging to the Family after having had it for years, you're at rock bottom. I was, at any rate. I desperately needed a family, some family, *any* family to cling to. I needed my *friend* to cling to. If Amy had still been single, there's no question but that the two of us would have been sleeping together afterwards, probably for a long, long time. Since she now came with Alec, and he was also a dear friend, I sought out one and got both. Without them, without the sort of familial support they freely gave me, I would likely have taken my own life out of sheer desperation. I owe them my life, and all I can repay them with, all I *have* to repay them with, is my love. Does that make it clearer?"

Reesa took several seconds before responding, uncomfortable with the discussion of feelings but seeing no way to avoid it politely. She'd make sure to change the subject as soon as she could. "I think so. In fact, as I consider it, definitely it does. Definitely. But I never knew you can be removed from the Family. I always figured that if you were Family, you were Family for life."

Amy spoke up. "Actually, under the by-laws, you can be terminated for – Alec, check me on this – conviction of a crime of violence, moral turpitude, or fundamental dishonesty." Alec was nodding. "Your only appeal, and it's automatic, is to me. And I have no idea whatsoever how I'd have gone on Becky's case if it had come to that. But to change subjects, there is one other thing you should know. Well, maybe you should, maybe not, but it's my choice, so I'll tell you anyway. You were one of the people on Ray Fields' initial list to be considered for the new CEO. According to his notes, you were on the young end of the age range he was considering at the time, he didn't think he had enough of a record on you then, and there are some ... issues with trying to tap a public employee to be CEO. But your name was definitely included in his first search results."

Reesa just shook her head. "Thank *God* he didn't ask me. It's not a job I'd want, ever. Even with all of the ... perks" – she gestured around – "that come with it. I mean, I don't gamble, not at all. Jeff and I went to dinner at the steak house at Desert Diamond Casino a week or so ago. I wouldn't play so much as the penny slots, not even with his money. There's just no way in hell I could ever make investments like you do."

Amy chuckled. "It's not really gambling, you realize. But there is a definite similarity, you're right about that."

Over the meal, Becky brought up something new. "Reesa, we'd like to invite you and Jeff to Christmas dinner next week."

Amy looked at her sharply. "Becky–"

Becky looked back calmly. "It's my turn to cook the turkey this year, and that makes it my privilege to invite, doesn't it?"

"We're not doing turkey this year, remember? Daddy and your mom are coming and I got the wine cellar at Anthony's for Christmas Eve. We decided to do that instead of cooking."

"Well, there's room enough, so I think we could manage it anyway. Do I need to kick in something?"

Amy laughed. "You know better, love. If you'd prefer, we could all go to brunch at Dove Mountain Christmas day instead."

Becky shuddered. "My God, no, Amy! The last time we went there, I couldn't move for two days afterwards!"

Amy smiled and jerked her head towards their husband. "And Wonder Boy ate more than you did. Seemed to be moving just fine afterwards, too."

Alec looked at both women calmly. "I've got a lot of demands to meet. Need to keep my strength up. I burn it off. But I vote for Anthony's." Becky was nodding in agreement.

Amy chuckled. "Okay, I'll call Anthony and tell him we'll have two more coming. But what the hell, it's only money, right?" Becky smiled. Inwardly, Reesa goggled a bit involuntarily. Knowing how pricey Anthony's was, from the times Jeff had taken her there, she understood what Becky had just committed Amy to. Of course, as the CEO, Amy had to have plenty, but still …. Then another thought struck her.

She clapped her hands. "Your father? Would he autograph the rest of my books?" The hopeful smile on her face appeared almost childlike in utter contrast to her usual solemn expressions.

Amy laughed again. "That, I can promise. Bring
them along. Or, if you'd like, I think I can get him to bring
you a whole new set. That might be even better. All
suitably autographed, of course."

****

When Jeff and Reesa were driving off, Jeff broke
the silence in the car. "I really would like to know about the
name thing. I understand you don't want to be called …
that name. But I'm curious. I suppose, if I'd thought about
it, that I'd have presumed that Reesa was short for Teresa
or something like that. Obviously it's not."

Reesa hesitated. Amy had found out about the
name, but even she didn't know the depth of Reesa's
violent gut reaction to it, and Reesa figured that Amy
probably had Family resources Jeff couldn't tap into.
Actually, she'd said she did. Back to Jeff. Could she trust
him? Would telling him come back to bite her on the ass
sometime, somehow? Well, he was Family. He understood
about keeping secrets. And rationally (hard as it was to
separate reason from emotion where her birth name was
concerned), it was difficult to figure out just what sort of
ammunition it might represent to anyone who wanted to
hurt her. "Jeff, I'll tell you on one condition. That you
never repeat it, not to anyone, even me. It's just as much a
secret as the Family is. More. Understand?"

"Nobody, not now, not ever. That I can promise. Is
it that bad?"

She sighed. "No, not really. It's just that I really do
hate it that badly. When I was born, my parents named me
Merissa Miranda Malloy. It didn't bother me too much at
first, or so I guess. I mean, I was a little kid, what did I
know? But after I began reading, I found a character in

some book that had that same sort of triple alliteration of names, and because I was always trying to be more grown up, more mature than I was, it upset me to be named like a character in a little kid's book. Then it began to eat on me, and by the time I got to first grade, I hated my name with an absolute passion. I even plotted all sorts of revenge against my parents, just because of that name. Silly, isn't it? But one of the kids in my class pronounced it 'M'reesa,' and I kind of liked that. So I decided that I'd start the next year at school as Reesa – not knowing anything about what the name meant, but because I liked it, everybody could pronounce it, and initially at least, I could justify it well enough as a nickname for Merissa.

For my Christmas present, senior year of college, my parents gave me a name change. Dad did it, I mean, and it was Mother's first official action after being named to the Court of Common Pleas. That's the equivalent of Superior Court here. The court officially changed my name to Reesa Malloy, no middle name, and in time for me to get it that way on my diploma. I've never used my birth name or hardly even thought of it since, until tonight." *And God willing, I won't again*, she thought.

Jeff's voice was soft. "So what does Reesa mean?"

"'One who laughs.'"

"Probably don't do a lot of that in your job."

"Outside of the pitiful humor we engage in, you got that right. Now, that's all I want to hear. No more about the Family, no more about the names. One is just the way things are for both of us, and the other is ancient history. Understand?"

Jeff took his time responding, but finally said, "Yes, I hear you. Won't say I completely understand why, but I certainly understand what you expect, and that I can do. Well, not discuss it, anyway. Sometimes I may need to mention the Family, even if it's just in connection with Amy. I hope that's not going to be a problem. Are your parents good with the name?"

"Oh, yeah, *now*. I mean, they kind of had to be to do the name change. Originally they resisted, and it took me several years, but I eventually taught them that I expected to be called Reesa, I *would* be called Reesa, I wouldn't answer them unless *they* called me Reesa, and that was that. Now they're fine with it."

Jeff glanced at her. "You don't have to keep up the tough lady act with me, you know."

Reesa snorted again, louder this time. "I have to keep it up with *everyone*. All day, every day. All the time. That's the only way I know how to do it, and that's the way I *will* do it."

Reesa could see Jeff's shrug in the dim light inside the car. Rationally, she knew she probably could let her hair down with him, especially after he'd saved her life the way he had. Emotionally, she didn't dare. Did she? Not because she couldn't trust him. She was coming to realize that of all of the people in her life, *him* she probably could, but she still didn't. Not that completely, anyway, because at least right now, she couldn't trust *herself* to compartmentalize her life like that. To have, to *accept* that she had, some place safe enough, some*one* safe enough, outside of her home when she was alone, to let her defenses completely down with and allow herself to be vulnerable.

Although perhaps with him … she reached out, laid her hand on his leg and then pulled it back sharply as she realized what she was doing. Jeff said nothing, but she saw his eyes flick in her direction. Just once.

When they got to her house, Jeff turned off the engine and came around to open Reesa's door. Something inside of her reached a decision at that moment. "Jeff, come on inside, would you? There's something I want to show you." Puzzled, Jeff walked alongside her up to her door and waited while she unlocked it and disarmed her alarm. He opened it for her and she led the way inside.

Shutting the door behind them, she came into his arms. "I want to show you my bedroom." Awkward, to say the least, but it would have to serve. *Maybe one of these days I can get into the subject of sex with him without talking like a goddam teenager*, she thought. He opened his mouth as she laid a finger across his lips. "Don't say a word. I'm afraid I'll lose my nerve." A long, deep kiss, and then she took his hand.

The next thing she knew, a gentle touch on her shoulder accompanied Jeff's voice. "Reesa, you're home." Her eyes snapped open. Clearly she'd dreamed that last. Good. She opened the car door before turning back to give Jeff a brief kiss goodbye. Lips closed.

Before she got out, though, she stopped for a moment. "Wait here, Jeff. Please?" She dashed inside, grabbed some fresh underwear and her toothbrush, stuffed them into her purse and headed back to his car. "Let's go to your place. Don't say a word. Just drive." *That's better. At least you don't sound like a kid with that one.*

On Monday, the Honorable J. Franklin Malloy's cellphone vibrated, buzzing its way across the desktop. Sitting at her desk, more than ready to take a break from the brief she'd been studying, she read the text message that had just come in. "Yes, Mother, I have, I'm going to again, and you're right. I AM happier this way." One of her law clerks looked up as she closed her phone. She simply shook her head and went back to the brief. Smiling.

The End

About The Author:

Insurance sales, collections, and even the practice of law get old after a while. A.J. Kohler did all of those, but is mostly a retired attorney who practiced law in Denver before heading south for a warmer climate. Winter sports were never an interest, and shoveling a driveway, not to mention careening around town on ice- and snow-covered roads got real old, real fast, so the desert beckoned and a love affair blossomed (with the desert; the partner was already a commitment).

If there is one thing that A.J. would say about Tucson and the desert to those who aren't familiar with it, it's this: Out here, gardening is a blood sport. Cactus is hardly ever friendly to work with, but the results are worth it (after you've healed up).

A.J. lives on the outskirts of Tucson with a partner of the opposite sex and two long-coat Akitas, also of opposite sexes.

Acknowledgments:

First and foremost, my thanks go to Solstice Publishing, my editor, Brian Cavit, and everybody else involved with this book, for all of the work to finally bring it to publication.

I also have to thank those long-suffering friends who read various versions of this book and provided feedback that made it better, made the forensics more accurate, the characters more believable and more real, found typos that everyone before them had missed, or even just gave me the encouragement to keep on going. In no particular order, Joi

Pettigrove, John Stevenson, Jan McGonagle, Sean Gerritson, Cathleen Moore, Jerry Dixon and Keith Moyer — thank you, one and all. If I've overlooked anyone, my deepest apologies — and my thanks to you, too.

My thanks, too, to the (by request) unnamed TPD officer who was kind enough to pose for the cover shot that I think gives this book a bit more immediacy and authenticity than my others.

Finally, there is a special place of honor for my partner, Cynthia Ochs, who not only gave me the encouragement and impetus to start *No Third Choice* in the first place, much less *No Other Choice* and now *Ripped in Two*, but who also suffered through not only version after version, question after question, conversation after conversation, but has also listened to me tell innumerable other people about the same things she's heard over and over. Your patience has been incredible and invaluable. I couldn't have done it without you.

<u>Social Media Links:</u>

Website: www.ajkohler.net

Facebook: https://www.facebook.com/aj.kohler.39

No Third Choice on Facebook:
https://www.facebook.com/NoThirdChoice

No Third Choice

Amy Youngston is Family. It hasn't done much for her until one day, when Raymond Escarton Fields, the head of the Family, hires her to find out who's trying to kill him.

The Family has many doctors, lawyers and other professionals, but in all of those thousands of cousins, there's only one private investigator, and that's Amy.

She takes the case, but when some party or parties unknown start by bugging her office that very night, it's clear that she can't handle this alone. The only person she can turn to is the one close friend she has (of two) who isn't Family, and, because it is secret, he doesn't even know about it. Until now, because Amy has to tell him. She's not supposed to tell outsiders, but he has to understand what's going on, doesn't he? She could tell him if she married him, and they're certainly close enough, but . . . let's not go there. Amy's got some serious problems with intimate relationships, especially with Alec. Problems she'd rather not think about (but they still keep coming back).

When Amy finds that there's as much of a target on her back as Fields had told her was on his, she begins to wonder. Did he hire her because she was the only choice he had – or because he had it in for her? Without some handle on the bad guys, there was no way she could find the answer to this question except to carry on with her investigation.

The most frustrating part for Amy is that there doesn't seem to be any reason for someone to want to kill the head of the Family. Of course, the same can't be said for whoever it is that's sending her repeated messages that she's in their crosshairs as well. Especially when they ambush her and Alec, tie them up and proceed to torture them in her own kitchen. As they say, expecting to be killed in the immediate future tends to get one's attention. They've definitely got hers.

No Other Choice

Becky is in jail. The charge? Murder. There's also a very deep and dark place inside her own head that she's found, crawled into and pulled in after her. That's going to be even harder to get her out of than jail, which will be plenty difficult by itself.

Amy is doing everything she possibly can to clear Becky. She has identified the actual killer and is working hard at getting the goods on her. Amy knows exactly what she needs to clear Becky, if she can only get the crucial evidence in time. It would be hard enough to do for any client, but when it's someone Amy has internalized to the degree she has Becky, her cousin and best friend, she can't even defend herself against the pain and agony she goes through when she fears she won't be able to do it in time.

When she ends up hauling the killer into court, she's lucky enough that the victim's widow screams out in open court that she'll kill Amy just like she did her no-good cheating husband!

That works. It gets Becky out of jail.

Getting her out of that pit in her own mind is going to be lots harder.

Especially when Becky confesses to Amy that she has become so introverted, so fearful of making new intimate connections with people, that the only man she could possibly have a relationship with now, the only man she wants, is Amy's husband. It's ripping her up inside, because she can't do that to Amy. Or Alec either, for that matter.

How much does Amy love Becky?

Really?

Amy sees one way out, but that means trouble.

www.ingramcontent.com/pod-product-compliance
Lightning Source LLC
Chambersburg PA
CBHW072308020726
47501CB00002B/433